"I love you, Daddy."

"I love you, too, darlin'," Matt replied.

He galloped Sarah into her bedroom, tucked her against the feather tick, sat on a stool by her bed and opened the book of Mother Goose stories. He could see the picture of Cinderella with her blonde curls and blue eyes.

Sarah rolled to her side. "I think she looks like Miss Pearl."

So did Matt. "A little."

"A lot." Sarah folded her hands across her chest. Then she did something Matt had never seen her do. She closed her eyes and mouthed words he couldn't hear.

"What are you doing?" he asked.

"I'm praying."

Matt had no such inclination. A long time ago he'd prayed prayers, but not anymore. That boy had turned into a man who had to live with his mistakes. He couldn't change the past, but he could stop others from making the same mistakes. That's why he'd do anything to protect the innocent…anything except put Sarah at risk.

"Daddy?"

"Yes, darlin'?"

"I'm praying for a mama."

Victoria Bylin
and
Sherri Shackelford

Wyoming Lawman
&
Winning the
Widow's Heart

LOVE INSPIRED
INSPIRATIONAL ROMANCE

LOVE INSPIRED®
INSPIRATIONAL ROMANCE

Recycling programs for this product may not exist in your area.

ISBN-13: 978-1-335-45471-3

Wyoming Lawman & Winning the Widow's Heart

Copyright © 2020 by Harlequin Books S.A.

Wyoming Lawman
First published in 2010. This edition published in 2020.
Copyright © 2010 by Vicki Scheibel

Winning the Widow's Heart
First published in 2012. This edition published in 2020.
Copyright © 2012 by Sherri Shackelford

This edition published by arrangement with Harlequin Books S.A.

For questions and comments about the quality of this book, please contact us at CustomerService@Harlequin.com.

Love Inspired
22 Adelaide St. West, 40th Floor
Toronto, Ontario M5H 4E3, Canada
www.Harlequin.com

Printed in U.S.A.

CONTENTS

Victoria Bylin fell in love with God and her husband at the same time. It started with a ride on a big red motorcycle and a date to see a Star Trek movie. A recent graduate of UC Berkeley, Victoria had been seeking that elusive "something more" when Michael rode into her life. Neither knew it, but they were both reading the Bible.

Five months later they got married and the blessings began. They have two sons and have lived in California and Virginia. Michael's career allowed Victoria to be both a stay-at-home mom and a writer. She's living a dream that started when she read her first book and thought, "I want to tell stories." For that gift, she will be forever grateful.

Feel free to drop Victoria an email at VictoriaBylin@aol.com or visit her website at victoriabylin.com.

Books by Victoria Bylin

Love Inspired Historical

The Bounty Hunter's Bride
The Maverick Preacher
Kansas Courtship
Wyoming Lawman
The Outlaw's Return
Marrying the Major
Brides of the West

Visit the Author Profile page
at Harlequin.com for more titles.

WYOMING LAWMAN

Victoria Bylin

Unless the Lord builds the house, its builders labor in vain. Unless the Lord watches over the city, the watchmen stand guard in vain. In vain you rise early and stay up late, toiling for food to eat— for he grants sleep to those he loves.
—*Psalms* 127:1–2

To my husband, Michael,
for his patience, support and sense of humor.
Thank you, Bears, for helping with the bad guys.
Only a true good guy would have your wisdom.
Love you!

Chapter One

*Cheyenne, Wyoming
October 1875*

Pearl Oliver stepped out of the carriage in front of Dryer's Hotel and glanced down the boardwalk in search of her cousin. Instead of spotting Carrie, she saw a little girl with hair as pale as her own. Pulled loose from two braids and wisping around the child's face, it glinted white in the sun. Pearl's mother had told her daughter that a woman's hair was her crowning glory. Pearl knew from experience it could also be a curse.

She turned back to the carriage intending to lift her son from her father's arms. Before he could hand the baby to her, she heard an excited cry.

"Mama!"

Expecting to see another mother, she looked back at the little girl. What she saw stopped her heart. The child, with her pinafore flapping and a rag doll hooked in her elbow, was charging across the street. Behind her, Pearl saw a freight wagon about to make the turn. The girl hadn't looked before stepping off the boardwalk, and the driver wouldn't see her until he rounded the corner.

"Stop!" Pearl cried.

The girl ran faster. "Mama, wait!"

Unaware of the child, the freight driver shouted at the team of six mules to pick up their pace. As the beasts surged forward, Pearl hiked up her skirt and ran down the boardwalk. "Stay there!" she cried. "I'm coming for you."

Instead of stopping, the child ran faster. The mules gained momentum and the wagon swayed. Pearl cried for the driver to stop, but he couldn't hear her over the rattle of the wheels. The child, now halfway across the street, saw only the woman she believed to be her mother.

Praying she wouldn't slip in the mud, Pearl dashed in front of the mules, each one snorting and chuffing with the weight of the load. The driver cursed and hauled back on the reins, but the wagon kept coming.

So did the child.

So did Pearl.

She could smell the mules. Puddles, mirroring the clouds, shook as the animals lumbered forward. With more speed than she rightly possessed, she dashed in front of the beasts, hooked her arm around the child and pulled her back from the wagon. Together they fell in a tangle of skirts and pinafores with Pearl on her belly. Her knees stung from hitting the dirt and she'd muddied her dress.

She didn't give a whit about her knees, but the dress mattered. She planned to wear it to her interview at Miss Marlowe's School for Girls. A woman in her position had to always look her best. One wrong impression and she'd be worse off than she'd been in Denver.

With her heart pounding, she raised her head and looked at the child. She saw eyes as blue as her own and hair that could have grown on her own head. The girl looked to be five years old, but there was nothing child-like about her expression as she clutched her doll to her chest. Like Pearl, she had the look of someone who'd learned not to hope…at least not too much.

Her voice squeaked. "Mama?"

"No, sweetie," Pearl said. "I just look like her."

The child's mouth drooped. "You do."

Pearl rocked back to her knees. Reaching down, she cupped the girl's chin. "Are you hurt?"

"No."

"What's your name?"

"Sarah with an *H*."

Pearl couldn't help but smile. "You must be learning your letters."

"I am. I go to school."

Pearl wondered if she attended Miss Marlowe's School, but other questions were more pressing. She pushed to her feet and offered Sarah her hand. "Who takes care of you?"

"My daddy."

"Let's find him," Pearl replied.

Sarah looked at the ground. "He's gonna be mad at me."

Pearl had an angry thought of her own. What kind of father left a five-year-old alone on a busy street? The more she thought about the circumstances, the more irritated she became. Sarah could have been killed or maimed for life. Pearl's problems paled in comparison, but she'd just ruined her best dress. Pale blue with white cuffs and silver buttons, it now had mud stains. She had another dress she could wear to the interview, but she'd stitched this one with her friends in Denver. The love behind it gave her confidence.

As she looked around for Sarah's father, she saw the start of a crowd on the boardwalk. The driver, a stocky man with a bird's nest of a beard, came striding down the street. When he reached her side, he swept off his black derby to reveal a bald head. "Are you okay, ma'am? Your little girl—I didn't see her."

She's not mine. But Pearl saw no point in explaining. "We're fine, sir. I saw what happened. You weren't at fault."

"Even so—"

"You can be on your way."

He looked at Sarah as if she were a baby chick, then directed his gaze back to Pearl. "Pardon me, ma'am. But you should watch her better."

Pearl's throat tightened with a familiar frustration. She'd been in Cheyenne for twenty minutes and already she was being falsely accused. Memories of Denver assailed her…the whispers when her pregnancy started to show, the haughty looks before she'd taken refuge at a boarding house called Swan's Nest. She'd gotten justice in the end, but she longed for a fresh start. When her cousin wrote about a teaching job in Cheyenne, Pearl had jumped at the chance for an interview.

Winning the position wouldn't be easy. As an unwed mother, she had some explaining to do. Not even her cousin knew she had a baby, not because Pearl wanted to keep her son a secret, but because she couldn't capture her thoughts in a letter. The two women didn't know each other well, but their mothers had been sisters. Carrie Hart was Pearl's age, single, a respected teacher and the daughter of one of Cheyenne's founders. If Carrie spurned her, Pearl would be adrift in a hostile city. Even so, she refused to pretend to be a widow. More than anything, she wanted to be respectable. If she lied about her son, how could she respect herself? And if she couldn't respect herself, how could anyone else? She had a simple plan. She'd tell the truth and trust God to make her path straight.

She had also planned to arrive in Cheyenne quietly. To her horror, a crowd had gathered and people were staring. She'd be lucky to avoid the front page of the *Cheyenne Leader.* Her father broke through the throng with her son in his arms. Even before she'd stepped out of the carriage, the baby had been hungry and wet. Any minute he'd start to cry.

"Pearl!" Tobias Oliver hurried to his daughter's side. A retired minister, he'd once been her enemy. Now he lived for the grandson sharing his name. "Are you all right?"

"I'm fine, Papa." She touched her son's head. "Take Toby to the room, okay?"

"But you need help."

She shook her head. "I have to find Sarah's father."

As he looked at the child clutching her doll, his eyes filled with memories, maybe regret. Pearl had once shared Sarah's innocence but not anymore. She'd been raped by a man named Franklin Dean, a banker and a church elder. Her father blamed himself for not protecting her.

"Go on, Papa," she said. "I don't want all this attention."

When Tobias met her gaze, she saw the guilt he lived with every day. He nodded and headed for the hotel.

Squeezing Sarah's hand, Pearl turned to the opposite side of the street where she saw twice as many people as before, almost all of them men. She couldn't stand the thought of shouldering her way through the crowd. Most of the onlookers were gawking.

"Please," she said. "Let us pass."

A businessman removed his hat and bowed. A cowboy tried to step back, but the crowd behind him pressed forward. A third man whistled his appreciation and another howled like a coyote. She turned to go in the other direction, but another crowd had gathered. She heard more catcalls, another whistle.

Sarah buried her face against Pearl's muddy skirt and clutched the folds. The child didn't like being the object of so much attention especially after falling in the dirt. Neither did Pearl. She patted the girl's head and mumbled assurances she didn't feel. Her own breath caught in her throat. She had nowhere to go, nowhere to hide. She was back in Franklin Dean's buggy, fighting him off.... She whirled back to the first side of the street, the place where she expected to find Sarah's father.

"Get back!" she shouted at the mob.

The crowd parted but not because of her. Every head had turned to a man shouting orders as he shoved men out of his way. As he shouldered past the cowboy who'd whistled, Pearl saw a broad-brimmed hat pulled low to hide his eyes, a clean-shaven jaw and a badge on a leather vest. She judged him to be six feet tall, lanky in build but muscular enough to command respect. He also had a pistol on his hip, a sure sign of authority. The city of Cheyenne, fighting both outlaws and vigilantes, had enacted a law prohibiting men from wearing guns inside the city limits. Foolishly Pearl had taken it as a sign of civility. Now she knew otherwise.

When the deputy reached the street, his eyes went straight to Pearl. They flared wide as if he recognized her, but only for an instant. Pearl thought of Sarah calling her "mama" and realized she looked even more like the girl's mother than she'd thought. The man's gaze narrowed to a scowl and she knew this man and his wife had parted with ugly words. Loathing snarled in his pale irises, but Pearl didn't take his knee-jerk reaction personally. She often reacted to new situations the same way...to crowds and stuffy rooms, black carriages and the smell of a certain male cologne.

The deputy's gaze slid to Sarah and he strode forward. When he reached the child's side, he dropped to one knee, muddying his trousers as he touched the back of her head. "Sarah, honey," he said softly. "Look at me, darlin'."

Pearl heard Texas in his voice…and love.

The child peeked from the folds of her skirt. "I'm sorry, Daddy. I was bad."

"Are you hurt?"

She shook her head, but her father wasn't convinced. He ran his hand down the child's back, looked at her muddy knees and inspected her elbows. Apart from the scare, Sarah and her doll were both fine. Pearl watched as he blew out a breath, then wiped the girl's tears with his thumb. When Sarah turned to him, he cupped her chin. "You shouldn't have left the store."

He'd put iron in his voice, but Pearl knew bravado when she heard it. He'd been scared to death.

Sarah hid her face in Pearl's skirt. "I know, Daddy. But I saw a puppy."

The man frowned. "Sarah—"

"Then I saw *her*." She raised her chin and stared at Pearl.

Instinctively Pearl cupped the back of Sarah's head. She'd been close to grown when her own mother died, but she missed her every day, even more since Toby's birth. If she'd ever caught a glimpse of Virginia Oliver in a crowd, she'd have acted just like Sarah.

The deputy pushed to his full height, giving her a closer look at his clean-shaven jaw. Most men in Cheyenne wore facial hair, but the deputy didn't even sport a mustache. He had a straight nose, brown hair streaked with the sun and the greenest eyes she'd ever seen. If her life had been simpler, she'd have smiled at him, even flirted a bit. Instead she pulled her lips into an icy line. Until she secured the job at Miss Marlowe's School, she didn't want to speak with anyone.

He took off his hat, a sign of respect that made her belly quake because she longed to feel worthy of it. The intensity in his eyes had the same effect but for different reasons. He frightened her.

"I can't thank you enough, miss." His drawl rolled like a river, slow and unstoppable. "I was in the store. I had an eye on her, and then…" He sealed his lips. "The next thing I knew, someone said a child was down in the street."

Pearl knew how he felt. Toby had suffered a bout of croup once, and she'd been worried to death. Her heart swelled with compassion, but she blocked it. "As you can see, your daughter's fine. If you'll excuse me—"

"But I owe you."

"No, you don't." She tried to step back, but Sarah tightened her grip.

The man skimmed her dress the way he'd inspected his daughter for injuries. "Your dress is ruined. I'll buy you a new one."

"No!" She could only imagine what kind of talk that would cause.

Instead of backing off, the lawman thrust out his hand. "Forgive my lack of manners. I'm Matt Wiley, Deputy Sheriff."

If she accepted the handshake, she'd have to give her name. She'd be trapped in a conversation she couldn't have until she spoke with Carrie and the school board. The less she said to this man, the safer she'd be. She indicated her muddy glove. "I don't want to dirty your hand.

I have to go now." Before he could argue, she pivoted and headed for the hotel.

"Wait!"

The cry came from Sarah. Every instinct told Pearl to hug the child goodbye, but she couldn't risk a conversation with the girl's father. Walking faster, she skirted a puddle and stepped on to the boardwalk. Thinking of Toby, her father and the new life she wanted for them all, she hurried to the hotel.

No way would Matt let Miss No Name walk away from him. He owed her for the dress and he always paid his debts. He scooped Sarah into his arms and settled her on his right hip. His left one sported a Colt Peacemaker in a cross-draw holster he'd worn for ten years. It had been a gift from Howard Cain, the confederate captain who'd welcomed a weary soldier into the ranks of the Texas Rangers. Matt had stopped being a Ranger, but he still liked the chase.

"Hold up," he called as he followed the woman.

Miss No Name ignored him.

Fine, he thought, she didn't want to talk to him. He didn't want to speak with her, either. She looked enough like his wife—his former wife, he reminded himself—to be her sister, except Bettina had abandoned her daughter and Miss No Name had ruined her dress to save her. At the very least, he intended to pay for the gown. She could have it laundered or buy a new one, whichever she preferred.

First, though, he had to catch her. He tightened his grip on Sarah. "Hold on, darlin'. We're playing horsey."

She giggled and nestled against his neck. "Go fast, Daddy!"

Matt broke into a jog that brought him within three

feet of Miss No Name. Just to hear Sarah's laugh, a treasure he'd almost lost, he made a neighing sound. As she squealed with delight, the woman turned her head and gaped at him. He hadn't seen a colder stare since Bettina left. Either she didn't like horses or she didn't like men. Matt didn't care. He didn't like blondes, so they were even except for the dress.

He reached her side in three steps. "Sorry to startle you."

"What do you want?" she said coldly.

"Like I said, I owe you for the dress, either a new one or a good cleaning."

"That's not necessary."

"I say it is."

Matt didn't like owing favors. In this town, a man's debts came back to haunt him. He'd learned that lesson his first week on the job when he'd let Jasper Kling give him a deal on a pair of boots. Never again. The merchant had expected special treatment for a measly six-bits off the already-inflated price.

Her eyes darted over his shoulder and down the street. Earlier he'd attributed her unease to the crowd of rowdy men. Now he wondered if trouble had followed her to Cheyenne. Matt didn't give a hoot about a person's past. Everyone in Cheyenne had a story, including him. But he cared very much about the here and now. He'd have to keep an eye on this woman.

Still tense, she looked back at his face. "If you must, you can pay for the laundering."

"Fine."

He set Sarah on the boardwalk, dug in his pocket and extracted a handful of coins. Before he could sort through the silver, Sarah grabbed the woman's skirt and looked up. "Would you braid my hair?"

His daughter had caused enough trouble for one day. Matt gritted his teeth. "Sarah, don't pester—"

"Pleeese," she whined to the woman. "My daddy can't do it."

That was a fact. He could splice rope, shoot straight and smell trouble a mile away, but he couldn't braid his little girl's hair. The white strands slipped through his fingers just as Bettina had done a year ago. For Sarah's sake, he wished he'd held on tighter. Instead of chasing Indians and outlaws with Captain Cain, and then dealing with the corruption of the Texas State Police, he should have stayed home and raised cattle. Maybe his wife wouldn't have cheated on him, and they'd still be a family.

He didn't miss Bettina at all, but Sarah did. His daughter needed a mother, someone who could make proper braids and teach her about life. A better man would have married to meet that need, but Matt couldn't stand the thought of repeating the mistakes he'd made with Bettina. Neither did he think a sham of a marriage would benefit his daughter. They were doing just fine, and he intended to keep things as they were…except his daughter was clinging to this woman's skirt and she looked so hungry for female attention that it made his chest hurt.

Pushing back old regrets, he touched Sarah's shoulder. At the same instant, Miss No Name dropped to a crouch and clasped Sarah's arms. Face to face, they looked like mother and daughter, mirror images separated only by time. Matt thought of Sarah's book of fairy tales and wondered if a child's dreams really could come true.

The woman spoke in a voice just for Sarah. "I wish I could do it, but we don't have a brush."

Sarah's lower lip trembled.

Matt didn't want to owe this woman another favor, but he'd swallow fire for his little girl. He also had a comb in his pocket, a tortoiseshell trinket shipped to Cheyenne from Boston. He'd learned to neaten up before doing business with busybodies like Jasper Kling. He took out the comb and held it in front of the woman's nose. "Here."

Looking both pleased and mistrustful, she plucked it from his fingers, straightened and clasped Sarah's hand. "Let's go in the hotel," she said to his daughter. "We can sit in the corner of the lobby."

Where people won't see us.

She didn't say the words, but Matt heard them. He glanced down the street, saw nothing suspicious and stepped in front of the females to open the heavy door to the hotel. As the woman guided Sarah inside, she skirted the desk and went to a group of chairs behind a pedestal holding a vase of dried flowers. Matt couldn't stop his eyes from admiring the sway of her dress. The front of it was a mess, but the back looked brand-new. He didn't know beans about fashion, but the bow at the small of her back made him think of tying knots…and untying them. Being a gentleman, he blocked the thought by silently whistling "Dixie," especially the part about looking away.

Miss No Name sat on a brocade chair, set the comb in her lap and removed her gloves. "Now," she said to Sarah. "Stand right in front of me."

Looking solemn, Sarah squared her shoulders.

Matt stayed by the pedestal, watching as the woman freed the disheveled braids from their ribbons and went to work with the comb. He couldn't stop himself from watching her hands. Maybe he'd learn something about braiding hair…at least that's the lie he told himself. In truth, he found Miss No Name attractive in a way he'd sworn to forget. He'd never marry again. Not even for his daughter's sake.

With a deft stroke, the woman parted Sarah's hair

down the middle, wrapped one half around her hand
and pulled it tight. Matt made a mental note of her firm
touch. He worried so much about hurting Sarah that he
didn't pull hard at all.

Miss No Name looked up and frowned. No one liked
being watched, but she had an air of worry that went beyond natural reserve. She looked scared and angry. As a
deputy, he had an obligation to find out why. As a man,
he had instincts that went beyond duty. Unless he'd lost
his ability to read people, this woman had a weight on
her shoulders, one she couldn't put down.

To put her at ease, he sat in the chair across from her
and set his hat on the table. He indicated the growing
braid. "You're good at that."

"I've had a lot of practice."

Sarah tilted her face upward. "Do you have a little girl?"

"No," the woman replied. "But I know about braids."

As calm as she sounded, she'd blushed at the mention
of having a child. Matt searched her hand for a wedding
band, the cheap kind a woman bought for herself to hide
an indiscretion. He saw nothing on her slender fingers,
not even a hint of white where she might have worn a
ring. The more he watched her with Sarah, the more
curious he became. He wanted to ask her name, but he
didn't want to make her uncomfortable. Sarah, though,
had no such qualms. She was chattering about her doll,
hair ribbons, last night's fairy tale and what they'd had
for breakfast. Whatever crossed her mind came out of her
mouth, including the question Matt had wanted to ask.

"What's your name?" the child asked.

The woman took a breath. "I'm a teacher. You can
call me Miss Pearl."

She sounded natural, but Matt figured she'd omitted
her last name for a reason. Whatever secret she had, it

concerned a lack of a husband. He draped a boot over one knee. "Is that your given name or your last?"

She paused to stare at him. "It's how I wish to be addressed."

He raised an eyebrow. "Even by strangers?"

She shrugged as if she didn't care, but her cheeks turned even pinker. Looking back at Sarah's hair, she braided the last inch, wrapped the end with a ribbon and jerked it tight. Matt counted it as both a lesson in hair braiding and a glimpse of Miss Pearl's character. She could be tough or tender. He liked that in a woman.

Fool!

He'd never marry again, not after the misery he'd known with Bettina. In Matt's experience, there was no middle ground between companionship and craziness. Looking at Miss Pearl, he felt sure of it. When she smiled at Sarah, he felt soft inside. When she looked at him with her troubled eyes, he tensed with the instinct to protect her.

The woman handed the comb to Sarah. "You're all set."

"Thank you, Miss Pearl."

As the females hugged, Matt stood. He still owed her for the dress, so he reached in his pocket and held out the silver coins. "For the laundering."

"Use it for Sarah." She touched his daughter's silken head. "Buy her something pretty."

In that instant, Matt forgot all about paying debts and surrendered to his curiosity. Who gave Pearl pretty things? Who made her smile when times got hard? He didn't know, but a thought stuck in his mind and wouldn't budge. He'd express his gratitude for saving Sarah's life, but not with a visit to the laundry. Instead of paying for the dress, he'd buy Pearl something pretty.

Chapter Two

Pearl unlocked the door to the suite, shut it behind her and leaned against the wood. She'd never forget the way Matt Wiley had looked at her when he'd thanked her for saving Sarah. She'd felt honorable, whole. If she were honest, she'd felt something even more powerful. She refused to give voice to secret hopes, but she blushed with an undeniable truth. Matt Wiley made her feel pretty again.

"Pearl?"

"I'm here, Papa."

Tobias came out of the back bedroom with Toby in his arms. At the sound of her voice, the hungry baby let out a wail, kicked and tried to get to his mama. Pearl reached for him. "He needs to nurse."

Tobias handed her the squirming infant. "I gave him water, but he's not happy. Is everything all right with the little girl?"

"Just fine." She jiggled Toby to calm him. "Her father's a deputy. He found us."

"Good."

"She misses her mother," Pearl added. "Apparently I look like her."

With Toby in her arms, she thought of Sarah's hopeful eyes. Under different circumstances, she'd have given Matt Wiley her full name. She'd have offered to braid Sarah's hair again. If he'd asked her to supper, she'd have said yes and worn her prettiest dress. Toby kicked again, reminding her such dreams were foolish. What man would want her now? She was damaged goods and had a baby to prove it.

"I better feed him," she said to her father.

Tobias motioned to the second bedroom. "Your trunk's in there."

"Thank you, Papa."

"We have plenty of time," he added. "Carrie left a message at the desk. She's expecting us at six o'clock for supper."

Pearl had mixed feelings about meeting her cousin. Four months ago, when the trouble in Denver had reached a peak, Tobias had written to Carrie and asked for information about Cheyenne. She'd written back and invited them to visit her. They'd accepted, and Carrie had generously made arrangements for Pearl to interview at Miss Marlowe's School for Girls.

Tonight Pearl would tell Carrie about Toby and the circumstances of his conception. She'd either keep her cousin's respect or she'd lose it. If she lost it, she wouldn't have a chance of being hired as a teacher and would have to find another way to earn a living. Tobias had a small pension from his years as a minister at Colfax Avenue Church, but it wasn't enough to support all three of them. Neither did Pearl want him looking for work. Twice in the last month he'd had bouts of chest pain.

Sighing, she glanced at the clock on the mantel. If she moved quickly, she'd have time to feed Toby, wash the train grit from her face and take a nap. Determined to be at her best, she closed the bedroom door and did all three.

An hour later, a rap on the door to the suite pulled her out of a troubled slumber. In her dreams she'd seen the wagon bearing down on Sarah. The picture had shifted and she'd been braiding the child's hair. It had turned to shining gold, and Matt Wiley had been watching her hands.

The knock sounded again.

Had Carrie come to meet them? Pearl bolted upright and inspected herself in the mirror. She'd put on her oldest day dress and her hair looked a fright. The knocking turned hammer-like. Not Carrie, she decided as she turned from the mirror.

In the sitting room she saw her father, pale and stiff, coming out of the other bedroom. He motioned her aside, but she couldn't bear the sight of him trying to hurry. Ignoring his gesture, she opened the door and saw a delivery boy holding a small package wrapped in brown paper.

"Are you Miss Pearl?"

"Yes, I am."

"This is for you." He held out the package and Pearl took it. Perhaps Carrie had sent a welcome gift, though the gesture seemed too formal for cousins.

As the boy waited expectantly for a coin for his trouble, Pearl looked at her father. Tobias reached in his pocket, extracted a few pennies and handed them to the boy. As he shut the door, Pearl fingered the package in an attempt to guess its contents. It felt soft, like fabric of some kind. Perhaps a pretty handkerchief. That seemed like the kind of gift Carrie might send. Pearl lifted the card bearing her name and turned it over. Instead of her cousin's prim cursive, she saw bold strokes in a man's hand. As she read the message, her cheeks flushed pink.

"Who's it from?" Tobias asked.

"Deputy Wiley."

Her father hummed a question. "What does it say?"

"'To Miss Pearl with our deepest gratitude. You are a woman of uncommon courage.'" She looked up at her father. "It's signed 'From Deputy Matt and Sarah.'"

His gray eyes misted. "I like this man."

"Papa, don't—"

"Don't what?" He scowled at her. "Don't hope for happiness for *my* little girl? Don't believe God for a second chance?"

Pearl wanted the same things, but she couldn't go down the same road, not one lined with mysterious gifts and the curious shine in Matt Wiley's green eyes. She set the card on the table, then looked at the package. The brown paper spoke of ordinary things, but someone had tied it shut with a lace ribbon instead of twine. Pearl didn't know how to cope with a man's interest, not anymore.

Her father nudged the package with his index finger. "Open it."

She felt as if it held snakes, but she tugged on the ribbon. The bow came loose and the paper unfolded in her hand. Instead of snakes, she found hair ribbons in a dozen shades of blue. The colors matched the sky in all seasons, all times of day. Some of them matched the dress she'd ruined saving Sarah. Others were the pale blue of her eyes.

Pearl would have known what to do with a snake. She'd have cut off its head with a shovel and flung it away. The hair ribbons struck her as both treacherous and lovely…but mostly lovely. Startled by the thought, she caught her breath.

Her father touched her shoulder. "What's wrong?"

"I think you know."

Tobias indicated the divan. "Sit with me, Pearl."

"I should check Toby."

He gave her a look she knew well. For ten years he'd pastored the biggest church in Denver. He'd learned when to bend and when to fight. Right now, he looked ready for a fight. Pearl gave up and sat next to him. "There's nothing to say."

"Yes, there is."

Looking older than his fifty-eight years, he lifted a cobalt ribbon from the pile of silk and lace. "Look at it, Pearl. What do you see?"

She saw a pretty snake. It declared a man's interest and tempted her with hope. To hide her feelings, she shrugged. "I see a ribbon."

Her father held the silk within her grasp. "Touch it."

"No."

"Why not?"

Because hope would sink its fangs into her flesh. Her mind would spin tales of princes and husbands, and she'd see Matt Wiley in her dreams. What woman wouldn't be charmed by the deputy? He loved his daughter and did honorable work. His brown hair framed a lean face and his eyes were the color of new grass. They had a subtle sharpness, a sign of a fine mind, but they also looked steady and true.

Her father turned his wrist, causing the ribbon to shimmer and twist. Her fingers itched to touch it. Knowing Tobias wouldn't budge until she surrendered, she lifted the ribbon from his hand. As the silk slid across her palm, she thought of braiding Sarah's hair and telling the deputy to buy his daughter something pretty. Had he bought ribbons for Sarah, too? She hoped so.

Tobias gripped her hand. "We came to Cheyenne for a fresh start. If a man's interested in you—"

"Papa!"

"I'm serious, Pearl." He pushed to his feet, crossed to a mirror etched with leaves and faced her. "If your mother were alive, she'd know what to say. I'm not much good at woman talk, but I know one thing for certain." He paused, daring her to ask and forcing her to listen.

"What's that?" she finally said.

"A man sends a gift to a woman for just one reason."

"He *had* one." She nudged the card with her finger. "He's saying thank-you."

Her father harrumphed.

Pearl wanted to fire back a retort, but she couldn't look her father in the eye. Deep down, she wanted to believe him. How would it feel to be properly courted? Blinking, she flashed back to Denver. Two days ago she'd caught the bouquet at her best friend's wedding. She'd imagined—just for an instant—wearing a fancy dress and saying "I do" to a faceless man. That man wasn't faceless now. He had green eyes.

Pearl placed the cobalt ribbon on top of the others. "I'm a daydreaming fool."

"No, you're not," her father insisted.

Could he be right? Did she have a chance at love? Looking at the ribbons, she thought of all the things the gift could mean. Hair ribbons could be casual or personal, practical or romantic. She thought of the card and how he'd signed it. "Deputy Matt" echoed "Miss Pearl," a sign that he'd understood her need for discretion and accepted it. She thought of the purpose in his eyes as he'd said goodbye. Were the ribbons more than a thank-you? Was he asking the first sweet question between a man and woman?

What if...

She didn't know, but she wanted to find out. Never mind the fear chilling her feet. Never mind the threat of humiliation. Matt Wiley had called her a woman of uncommon courage. Like her father said, she'd come to Cheyenne to start a new life for her son. Most important of all, she had faith in the God of second chances. She touched the card with her fingertip, then looked up at her father. "I suppose I *should* send a thank-you note."

"That would be very fitting."

"It's just..." She shrugged.

"Just what?" her father said gently.

"It's hard to start over."

He lowered his chin as if she were Sarah's age. "That's true, but we worship a God who loves his children. I can't explain what happened to you, Pearl. It was hurtful and ugly and I'll never forgive myself—"

"Don't say that." She didn't blame her father for the violence she'd suffered. She blamed Franklin Dean for being evil.

He held up one hand. "Let me finish."

She obeyed but only out of habit.

"God has a plan for your life," he said. "It's good, but you need the courage to walk that path. You can do it, Pearl. You're brave and smart and as beautiful as your mother. Any man in Cheyenne would be blessed to have you for a wife."

She wanted to believe him, but her father saw her through rose-colored lenses. When he kissed her good-night, he still called her "princess." Even so, she smiled at him. "Thank you, Papa."

"Now go write that note."

Her stomach twisted. "I don't know—"

"I do." Tobias aimed his thumb at the secretary in the

corner. "Get busy. We'll ask the clerk to deliver it when
we leave to see Carrie."

"If you're sure…"

"I'm positive." He gave her a look he'd often used in
the pulpit. "It's about time you showed a little faith—both
in God and in people."

Pearl had no assurance Matt Wiley wouldn't laugh at
her note, but she had walked with the Lord as long as she
could remember. "All right. I'll do it."

"Good." Tobias glanced at the wall clock. "I'm going
to finish that nap."

As he left the sitting room, Pearl went to the secretary,
opened the drawer and removed stationery, an inkwell
and an elegant pen. She positioned the paper on the blot-
ter, filled the well and wrote the note. Both formal and
friendly, the wording struck her as just right and she blew
the ink dry. On a whim, she added a P.S., then sealed the
note and checked on Toby. Satisfied he'd stay asleep, she
took the note to the front desk before she could change
her mind about asking a "what if" of her own.

The instant Matt set foot in the sheriff's office, his
friend and partner, Dan Cobb, held up two envelopes
and grinned. "Here you go, Romeo."

Scowling, Matt snagged the letters. They were both
written on ivory stationery and sealed with white wax.
One displayed his name in a script he recognized as be-
longing to Sarah's teacher. Miss Carrie Hart taught the
youngest girls at Miss Marlowe's School, and she fre-
quently sent home glowing notes about his daughter.
They often chatted when he met Sarah after school, and
they'd become casual friends.

The other letter displayed pretty writing that said, "To

Deputy Matt and Sarah." Pearl must have gotten the hair ribbons.

Fighting a smile, he dropped down on his chair and started to open the letter from Pearl. As the seal popped, Dan's chair squeaked. Matt looked up, caught his friend staring and scowled. "What are *you* looking at?"

Dan grinned. "Looks to me like a couple of pretty ladies have their eyes on you."

Matt had no interest in ladies, pretty or otherwise. He held up the first envelope. "This one's from Carrie Hart. She's Sarah's teacher."

"I know Carrie." Dan sounded wistful. "I see her at church."

Matt saw a chance to take a friendly jab. "Judging by that hangdog look, you're sweet on her."

"What if I am?"

Matt huffed. "Beware, my friend. Marriage isn't what it's cracked up to be."

"That's your opinion."

"It's the voice of experience." He'd never forget quarreling with Bettina, how she'd cried when he'd left to go with the Rangers. He'd felt guilty for leaving and even worse the times he'd stayed.

Dan wagged his finger at the second envelope. "Who sent that one?"

"None of your business."

"Sure it is," Dan replied. "We're partners."

Matt considered the deputy his best friend, but he didn't want an audience when he read the notes. He gave Dan a pointed stare. "Don't you have some outlaws to catch?"

"No, but I hear you had a run-in with Jasper."

"Unfortunately, yes."

The quarrel especially rankled because he hadn't

been on duty when Jasper summoned him. Matt wore his badge and gun all the time, but he'd taken the morning off to be with Sarah. Last night she'd fussed about his long hours, so he'd promised to spend the morning with her. To his chagrin, she'd wanted to play dolls. Matt wasn't much on dolls, so he'd suggested a tea party with real cake at Madame Fontaine's bakery. Halfway to the shop, Jasper had waylaid him and Sarah had run off.

Matt told Dan everything except the part about Sarah's braids. Neither did he mention his trip to the dress shop. After choosing the ribbons—all the blue ones he could see—he'd arranged for a delivery to Pearl, then left Sarah eating cookies with Madame Fontaine while he patched up things with Jasper. It hadn't gone well.

"Jasper's a nuisance," Dan complained. "What did he want this time?"

"Same thing as before."

"The Peters kid?"

"You guessed it." Matt propped his boots on the desk. He didn't usually sit that way, but something about Jasper inspired bad manners. "Teddy Peters swiped some candy off the counter. My gut tells me Jasper put it out to tempt him. The kid bolted, and now Jasper wants him tossed in jail."

Dan shook his head. "Seems like a talk with his folks would be enough."

"That's what I did. Teddy's mother made him pay, and he's doing extra chores."

"Sounds reasonable."

"Jasper didn't think so." Matt could hardly believe what he was about to say. "He threatened to have my badge."

"He *what?*"

"He thinks I'm too soft for the job."

"That fool!"

"Don't waste your breath." Matt swung his boots off the desk. "Jasper's a thorn, but I've dealt with worse."

Dan stayed silent a moment too long. "Don't underestimate him, Wiley. The man's got a dark side."

Matt's brow furrowed. "What are you talking about?"

"Secrets," Dan answered. "Jasper's got one, and I'm willing to bet he'd do anything to keep it."

Matt knew about secrets. He had one of his own. "Tell me."

"You know the hog ranch north of town?"

Dan wasn't talking about farm animals. *Hog ranch* was slang for the lowest form of prostitution. Women in that regrettable line of work had often taken a downhill slide from fancy brothels to run-down saloons. As they lost their looks and their health, they slid further and ended up at wretched establishments located on the outskirts of town. Such places were called hog ranches, and they attracted men and women who couldn't sink much lower. As a Ranger, Matt had walked into such places in search of wanted men. "Are you saying Jasper—"

"Yep."

Not a week passed that Jasper didn't send a high-and-mighty letter to the newspaper about prostitution. Being caught at a hog ranch would shame him more than anything. Matt had to hold back a snort. "The man's a flaming hypocrite. How'd you hear about it?"

"Ben Hawks told me before he left."

A fellow deputy, Ben had left town shortly after Matt arrived. An aunt in St. Louis had died and left him a small fortune. Matt hadn't questioned the timing, but he did now. Had Jasper bought the man's silence?

Dan steepled his fingers. "After Ben left, Jasper

started up with those letters. Just before that, the other trouble started."

Matt's brow furrowed. "You mean Jed Jones."

"And the fire at the livery."

A month ago Matt had found Jones, a suspected horse thief, hanging from a tree in Grass Valley. A few days later the livery had been torched. Some folks thought the owner had bought stolen horses. Last week the Silver Slipper Dance Hall had been the target. Riders wearing masks and black derbies had shot out the windows while chanting "Go! Go! Go!"

Matt recognized the work of vigilantes, but who were they? And why were they striking now? Both questions had possible answers. Horse thieves had raided Troy Martin's place three times since August. Another rancher, Howard Moreland, had lost a prize stallion. The men were friends and active in the Golden Order. Matt didn't care for the civic organization at all. The group tended to make unreasonable demands like the one Jasper had made about Teddy. Chester Gates, a banker, served as president. Jasper belonged to the G.O., too. He'd been a founding member.

The news about Jasper's secret made Matt wonder about the trouble at the Silver Slipper. What better way for the shopkeeper to hide his visit to the hog ranch than by attacking another place of prostitution? Chester Gates also had a beef related to the dance hall. The owner, Scottie Fife, had outbid him for some prime land. Whoever owned the property would make a fortune if the railroad expanded its headquarters.

Matt had taken "Go! Go! Go!" to be a command, but perhaps it had been a calling card. Everyone in Cheyenne knew G.O. stood for "Golden Order." If these men had gone bad—a strong possibility, Matt had seen cor-

ruption in Texas—they had to be stopped before innocent people suffered.

Matt knew the cost of such violence and not as a victim. As long as he lived, he'd be ashamed of what he'd
done in Virginia. Until that night, he'd been a man who
prayed. Not anymore. He looked at Dan. "We need to
keep an eye on the Golden Order."

"I agree." The deputy gave a sad shake of his head.
"Jed Jones was a liar and a thief, but he didn't deserve
a necktie party."

A lynching... Matt's blood turned to ice. With every
nerve in his body, he wished someone had stopped him
and his men the night they'd tossed a rope over the branch
of a tree. He couldn't change what had happened to Amos
McGuckin, but he could stop it from happening again.
"We'll stop these men. The only question is *how*."

"Any ideas?"

"Not yet, but I'll figure it out."

Dan went to fetch his hat. "We won't catch anyone sitting in the office. I'm going to take a walk."

"Watch your step," Matt replied.

As Dan passed Matt's desk, he noticed the letters and
put his hand over his heart. "Romeo... Romeo..."

"Shut up," Matt joked.

Dan put on his hat. "You ought to take one of those
ladies to see *Romeo and Juliet* at the Manhattan."

The new theater offered fine plays and bad acting. The
performance of *Romeo and Juliet* was said to be particularly awful. "Forget it," Matt answered.

Chuckling, Dan walked out of the office, leaving Matt
alone with the notes. He knew what the one from Carrie
would say. Yesterday she'd invited him to bring Sarah to
have supper with some cousins of hers, a minister and his
daughter arriving from Denver. He figured the daughter

was a little girl who liked to play with dolls. The note would be a reminder to come at six o'clock. The thought of an evening with a minister set Matt's teeth on edge, but he could tolerate anything for a couple of hours. Except church, he reminded himself. He hadn't set foot in a house of God for ten years, and he didn't plan to change his habits.

He ignored Carrie's letter and lifted the one from Pearl. He liked how she'd called him Deputy Matt, echoing the way he'd signed the card with the ribbons. Pleased, he peeled off the wax and read.

> Dear Deputy Matt and Sarah,
> Thank you for the beautiful ribbons. I've never seen lovelier shades of blue and will enjoy them very much. You've made a newcomer to Cheyenne feel welcome indeed.
> Regards, Miss Pearl

Below the curly writing, she'd added a P.S. in block printing. It read, "Sarah, if you'd like me to braid your hair again, I'd be happy to do it."

His daughter couldn't read the words, but she'd know the letters.

Matt read the letter again, grinning like a fool because he'd charmed Miss Pearl out of her shell. Why he cared, he didn't know. Not only did she have blond hair, he'd been straight with Dan when he said marriage wasn't for him.

He opened the note from Carrie and saw exactly what he expected. Her cousins had arrived and were coming for supper. Good, he thought. Sarah needed a friend.

Matt glanced at the clock. He had a couple of hours before he had to be at Carrie's house, so he opened the office ledger and recorded his conversation with Jasper. If vigilantes were at work in Cheyenne, they had to be stopped. And if Jasper and Gates were behind it, they had to be brought to justice. Matt wished someone had stopped *him* that night. He wished for a lot of things he couldn't have...a mother for Sarah, a good night's sleep. Maybe someday he'd be able to forget. Until then, he had a job to do.

Chapter Three

As the hired carriage neared her cousin's house, Pearl considered the neighborhood. Cheyenne still had the ragged feel of a frontier town, but railroad executives and entrepreneurs had brought their families with the hope of bringing a touch of civility. Carrie's father had been among the Union Pacific leaders. An engineer by trade, Carlton Hart had built a fine house for his wife and daughter. Tragically, he'd died two years ago in a blasting accident. A few months later, his wife had succumbed to influenza.

Rather than go back east, Carrie had taken a position at Miss Marlowe's School for Girls. Pearl hoped to carve out a similar place for herself, but she had no illusions about her chances. Toby, swaddled in blue and snug in her arms, called her character into question. Some people would gossip about her out-of-wedlock child. Others would shun her. She knew from her experience in Denver that only a few would be kind. Without Carrie's support, Pearl didn't have a chance of being hired as a teacher.

As the carriage rolled to a halt, her father touched her arm. "You can still change your mind about explaining to Carrie. I'll talk to her first."

"No, Papa."

She hadn't come to Cheyenne to be a coward. If she couldn't face her cousin, how could she manage an interview with the trustees of Mrs. Marlowe's School? Meeting Carrie would be good practice. That's why she'd worn her second-best dress, a blue-gray silk with a lace jabot. For added courage, she'd tied three of Deputy Matt's ribbons into a fancy bow and pinned them to her hat. Not only did they complement her dress, they also matched Toby's baby blanket.

Tobias climbed out of the carriage, paid the driver and offered his hand. "Are you ready, princess?"

She wished he'd stop using the nickname. It made her feel small when she needed to be adult. She'd have spoken up, but her father looked as nervous as she felt. Being careful not to jostle Toby, she took her father's hand and climbed out of the carriage. The door to the house opened and she saw a young woman with a heart-shaped face and brown hair arranged in a neat chignon.

"Pearl! Uncle Tobias!" Beaming with pleasure, Carrie hurried down the path. "I'm so glad you're—" She stopped in midstep, staring at the bundle in Pearl's arms. "You have a baby."

"I do."

Her brows knit in confusion. "I didn't know you were married."

"I'm not." Pearl took a breath. "I wanted to tell you in person. A letter just didn't... I couldn't..." She bit her lip to keep from rambling.

As Carrie stared in shock, Pearl fought to stay calm. First reactions, even bad ones, meant nothing. She had them all the time, especially to men who reminded her of Franklin Dean. A person's second response was what mattered.

Carrie's gaze dipped to the baby, lingered, then went back to Pearl. She didn't speak, but her eyes held questions.

Pearl didn't want to explain herself in the street. She wanted the privacy of four walls, the dignity she'd been denied by the man who'd taken her virtue. Thinking of the ribbons on her hat, a declaration of her courage, she squared her shoulders. "I'll explain everything, but could we go inside?"

Carrie touched her arm. "It'll be all right, cousin."

Pearl's throat tightened.

"Whatever happened, we're family."

"You don't even know—"

"I know *you*," Carrie insisted. "We've been writing for months now. Besides, our mothers were sisters."

Tears pushed into Pearl's eyes. No matter what happened, she had a friend.

"Don't cry," Carrie said. "You'll get all puffy."

As if being puffy were the worst of her problems… Pearl laughed out loud. She tried to speak but hiccupped instead. As she covered her mouth, Carrie pulled her into a hug. The gesture shot Pearl back to Swan's Nest where Adie Clarke, now Adie Blue, had opened her home and her heart. Mary, another boarder, had taught Pearl to be bold. Bessie and Caroline had delivered her baby and proved that a faithful woman could survive any heartache.

Courage, from her friends and from the ribbons, gave her the strength to spell out the facts for Carrie. "I was attacked by a man I trusted. I refuse to call him Toby's father."

Carrie hugged her as hard as she could. "You poor dear!"

Eager to get past the ugliness, Pearl blurted the facts.

She'd gone for a buggy ride with Franklin Dean, the man she'd expected to marry. A wolf in sheep's clothing, he forced himself on her and left her with child. He'd demanded marriage, but Pearl had refused. Instead she'd taken refuge at Swan's Nest, a boarding house for women in trouble.

By the time she finished the story, Carrie had guided her up the steps and into the foyer. Her father had followed at a distance, giving them time to talk. As he approached, Pearl gave him a watery smile. "We're going to be all right."

"More than all right," Carrie insisted.

Relief brightened Tobias's silvery eyes, but the creases edging his mouth had deepened. "We're grateful to you, Carrie."

The brunette waved off the praise. "We'll talk about the school over supper. I've invited a friend. I hope that's all right."

"Of course." Pearl loved the women at Swan's Nest. She hoped to make good friends in Cheyenne.

Her cousin's eyes sparkled. "His name is Matt Wiley."

Pearl gasped.

"Don't worry." Carrie reached for her hand. "I know you're in a delicate situation, but Matt's not one to judge. He might even help us. His little girl goes to Miss Marlowe's."

Tobias touched Pearl's back. "We've met Deputy Wiley."

"You have?" Carrie's brows arched.

As Tobias told the story about the freight wagon, Pearl's cheeks burned with embarrassment, not with humility at his praise, but because of the note she'd sent. The ribbons had been a thank-you, nothing more. Even worse, she'd flirted with a man her cousin seemed to like.

Deputy Matt—Deputy Wiley, she reminded herself—would be here any minute. The ribbons had to come off her hat *now*.

She turned to Carrie. "I need to check Toby. Is there a place—"

Three knocks rattled the door.

"That's Matt." Forgetting Pearl, Carrie flung the door wide. Light fanned across her full cheeks, revealing faint freckles and the smitten glow of a woman in love. Pearl wondered if she'd ever feel a similar pleasure in a man's presence. Envy at Carrie's innocence ripped through her, but she shoved it away.

With a blush on her cheeks, Carrie stepped back to make room for the deputy and his daughter. "Come in," she said. "I want you to meet my cousins."

In a feeble attempt to hide her hat, Pearl moved closer to the coat rack. Maybe Matt Wiley wouldn't notice the ribbons. Maybe the clerk had been slow to deliver the note and she could get it back.

Sarah came through the door first. Carrie crouched to hug her, but the little girl stopped short. Unruffled, Carrie touched the doll in Sarah's arms. "You brought Annie. She looks pretty today."

Sarah scowled. "She's *mine*."

"Of course, she is," Carrie said gently.

Pearl ached for them both. Her cousin plainly cared for the man and his daughter. Sarah, though, probably saw her as a rival. Pearl knew how she felt. When a child lost a mother, life became fragile. When Carrie straightened, Sarah spotted Pearl, cried out with delight and ran to hug her knees. Pearl shot Carrie a look of apology. When her cousin forced a smile, Pearl knew they'd be as close as sisters. They thought alike. They loved alike.

Pearl smoothed Sarah's hair. Smiling, she made her voice bright. "Did you know Miss Carrie's my cousin?"

"What's that?" Sarah asked.

"It means we're family, and I like her very much. She likes you, too."

Pearl glanced at Carrie for approval. Her cousin mouthed "Thank you," then crouched next to Sarah. "I like Annie, but I know she's yours."

Sarah stayed by Pearl, but she held up the doll for Carrie to see. "Her dress got dirty, but I changed it."

"You did a good job, darlin'."

That Texas drawl could only belong to one man. Knowing she'd be looking into Matt Wiley's green eyes, Pearl dragged her gaze upward. Just as she feared, he was staring at the bow she'd made from the ribbons. She forced a nonchalant smile. "Good evening, Deputy."

He took off his hat with a gallant sweep of his arm. His hair, a bit shaggy, touched the collar of a green shirt topped with a dark vest. "Good evening. It's a pleasure… again."

The scent of bay rum tickled her nose. So did the lingering smell of lye soap. Did he have a housekeeper, or did he send his clothes to the laundry? The thought twisted in her mind until it formed a hard knot of truth. She had no business wondering about Matt Wiley's laundry.

He stepped deeper into the entry hall and reached back to close the door. As he turned, the vest pulled across his broad chest. With six people in the small space, including Toby in her arms, she had nowhere to hide. Deputy Wiley's gaze landed on her son, lingering while he grappled with his thoughts on her marital status. Gurgling, Toby scooted up her chest like an inchworm. She loved it when he moved against her, and she smiled in spite of the awkward moment. As she shifted the baby's weight, the deputy watched her son with a father's knowing smile. She wondered if he'd held Sarah the same way.

Carrie straightened. "You've met, but I should finish introductions. Matt, this is my cousin Pearl and her father, Reverend Tobias Oliver."

Tobias held out his hand. "Good evening, Deputy."

As the men shook hands, Pearl tried to signal Carrie for a place to remove her hat. Her cousin didn't notice. She had eyes only for Sarah and was already leading the little girl into the parlor.

When Matt broke his grip, Tobias offered his arm to Pearl. "Shall we join Carrie?"

Before she could reply, Deputy Wiley spoke in a low tone to her father. "If you don't mind, sir. I'd like a word with your daughter."

Tobias wrinkled his brow. "I don't think—"

Pearl interrupted. "It's all right, Papa." She wanted a word with him, too. If he'd received her note, she needed to make her position clear. She'd been completely unaware of his interest in Carrie and her cousin's claim on him. She'd still braid Sarah's hair, but she'd invite Carrie to join them.

As Tobias stepped into the parlor, Deputy Wiley glanced again at her hat. "I see you got the ribbons."

"Yes. They're lovely."

Using a quiet tone, one meant for Pearl alone, he said, "I got your note."

He'd spoken as if they had a secret, a thought that shamed her because of Carrie. She had to make her loyalty clear. "My *thank-you* note," she said.

"Exactly." He looked relieved. "Since I sent the ribbons to *thank* you, and you sent the note to *thank* me, I'd say we understand each other."

Pearl sagged with relief. "Yes. Of course. We certainly do. Thank you…again."

Why was she babbling? And why were his eyes twinkling with pleasure? She didn't know, but she sensed goodness in this man. If it weren't for Carrie, she wouldn't have regretted the note at all. She'd have mustered her courage and gone after Deputy Matt Wiley with her best smile. But that could never be. Not only did Carrie have a claim on him, Pearl was damaged goods and she knew it.

Pearl's discomfort hit Matt with surprising force. He didn't know why he felt compelled to protect her dignity, but he knew the impulse went beyond gratitude. He liked her. Unless he'd lost his instincts concerning women, she'd needed courage to add the P.S. to the thank-you note. Like a lot of the folks in Cheyenne, she'd probably come to Wyoming for a fresh start. Looking at the baby, he thought he knew why but wanted to be sure.

The blue blanket clued him to the child's gender. "Is that your son?"

"Yes."

"He's a cute little fellow. What's his name?"

"Toby." She raised her chin, daring him to ask the obvious question.

He spoke gently. "And your husband?"

"I don't have one."

So the preacher's daughter had skipped "I do" and gone straight to "I will." Matt didn't hold it against her. His own slate had enough marks to cover a barn.

With a baby in her arms and no husband, she had a good reason to be reserved. People would judge her to be lacking in moral character. The ribbons on her hat told him she had even more courage than he'd guessed. He felt bad about discouraging a friendship, but it had to be done. That's why he'd asked for a private word. She deserved to know he'd been flattered by her interest, but she wouldn't be braiding Sarah's hair.

The baby in her arms made a funny squeak. The sound reminded him of Sarah as an infant and he grinned. "He's lively, isn't he?"

"Very."

With her blue eyes and tilted chin, she reminded him of the picture of Cinderella in Sarah's book of fairy tales. He blinked and imagined a white coach and glass slippers, a prince chasing after her and mice turning into dashing white horses. His mind went down a long, strange road before he pulled himself back to the entry hall.

Pearl jiggled the baby. "We should join the others."

As he motioned for her to lead the way, Carrie came back from the parlor. She smiled at Matt, then focused on Pearl. "There's a guest room behind the stairwell. You can tend the baby there."

As Pearl went down the hall, Matt watched the ripple of her silver-blue dress, thought again of Cinderella and scowled. He had no business thinking about glass slippers and Pearl in the same breath. He'd been a lousy husband to Bettina, and he'd doubtlessly make the same mistakes if he ever lost his mind and remarried. As much as Sarah wanted a mother, she'd have to make do with Mrs. Holcombe, the widow who lived across the street from them. Mrs. Holcombe loved Sarah and treated her like a granddaughter.

"Matt?"

He turned back to Carrie and saw a sweet smile. He truly appreciated the interest she'd taken in Sarah. The preacher's daughter hadn't been a little girl like he'd expected, but Sarah would enjoy a fancy dinner with feminine touches. He could see why Dan liked Carrie. She had a good heart and generous nature. And his friend had no reservations about marriage.

Pleased for Dan, he felt good as Carrie led him into the parlor. She sat on the divan, so he took the armchair next to Reverend Oliver. Sarah sat at his feet with her doll in her lap, talking to Annie as if she were a real girl. Her loneliness punched Matt in the gut. So did Pearl's arrival in the parlor. Instead of the hat and ribbons, he saw a braid wrapped so tight he wondered if her scalp hurt.

Holding Toby, she scanned the room for a place to sit. Carrie patted the divan. "Sit with me. I want to hold the baby."

Pearl sat and handed over her son. Cuddling him, Carrie looked at Matt and smiled. He liked babies, so he smiled back. He wanted Pearl to know he didn't hold her indiscretion against her, so he studied Toby a long time, then said, "He looks like you."

When she beamed a mother's smile, Matt recalled the joy of being a family. For a short time, life with Bettina had been good. Pearl made him long for things he couldn't have, things he didn't want because he'd be a bad husband. At the same time, he enjoyed pulling her out of her shell. Wise or not, he wanted to know more about her. As the four of them chatted about the train ride from Denver, Matt gauged her expression. When she looked relaxed, he ventured a question.

"What brings you to Cheyenne?" He'd addressed the question to both Pearl and her father, but his gaze stayed on Pearl.

When she stiffened, Carrie answered for her. "Pearl's going to teach at Miss Marlowe's School."

"That sounds rewarding."

"I hope so." She knotted her hands in her lap. "I don't have the job *yet*. I'll be interviewed first."

"You'll do fine." Carrie patted Toby's back. "The interview with the school board is next Tuesday. That'll give us time to meet with Miss Marlowe. She's going to love you."

"You'll do great," Matt added.

He tugged on Sarah's braid, a reminder to Pearl that she'd risked her life for a child. At the same moment, Toby fussed. The cry brought another truth to light. A single woman with an out-of-wedlock baby would have some explaining to do. He didn't know if the people of Cheyenne would look past her indiscretion. Matt wanted to help her and he had the means. If he wrote a letter describing how she'd saved Sarah, surely the board would see her true character and forgive her past mistakes.

When Pearl cooed to soothe him, the baby wiggled and reached for her. Carrie scooted toward Pearl and handed him back. "I think he wants his mama."

Pearl propped Toby against her shoulder. In spite of the difficulty the baby posed, her smile turned radiant. Matt's belly clenched again. Pearl loved her son far more than Bettina had loved Sarah.

Carrie stood. "If you'll excuse me, I'll check with the cook about supper."

"Can I help?" Pearl asked

"No, but Sarah can." Carrie smiled at his daughter, still glued to his leg. "Would you and Annie like to see what's for dessert?"

Sarah needed all the female attention she could get, so he patted her back. "Go on, sweetheart."

"Don't tell your daddy." Carrie feigned a whisper. "But I baked cookies. I don't think tasting just one will spoil your supper."

Ah, temptation! The war waged on Sarah's face until the cookie won. She pushed to her feet. "I like cookies."

With Annie in tow, she crossed the parlor. Carrie guided her out the door, leaving Matt to consider how different this day could have been. If Sarah had been hit by the freight wagon, he'd have been burying her instead of waiting for a good meal. He'd thanked Pearl with the ribbons, but he still owed her a favor. The interview at Miss Marlowe's School gave him an opportunity and he decided to take it.

"I don't know how much it will help," he said. "But I'd be glad to write a letter to the trustees about what happened today. We haven't been acquainted long, but what you did proves you'll be a good teacher."

She bristled. "Thank you, Deputy. But no."

"Why not?"

"My situation is…complicated."

He'd figured that out already. "So?"

Tobias cleared his throat. "Why would you offer? You barely know my daughter."

"I know her better than you think." Matt spoke to the reverend but kept his eyes on Pearl. "Not many people would do what she did today. I owe her." He'd told the truth, but there was more to his reasoning. Guilt for what he'd done in the war never left him. Every time he helped someone, his conscience eased a bit. By helping Pearl, he'd sleep tonight instead of tossing like he usually did.

She looked at him with hope and hesitation. "I appreciate the offer. It's just that…" She shook her head.

"You want your privacy," he finished for her.

"Yes."

"I understand about private matters." He flashed a grin he hoped would be roguish. "If you don't ask questions, neither will I."

If Pearl knew he didn't hold her son against her, maybe she'd accept his help. If she accepted his help, he could feel good about paying her back. He didn't know who had fathered her baby, or why the man hadn't married her, but he knew how it felt to live with a bad decision. Hoping to persuade her, he gentled his voice. "I'm not the most influential man in Cheyenne. The letter might not change any minds, but it won't hurt, either."

Pearl looked at her father.

He gave a crisp nod. "Say yes, princess."

Matt smiled at the nickname. He didn't like ministers, but he was impressed by Reverend Oliver. The man clearly loved his daughter in spite of her mistake. Pearl, though, looked mildly irked at the childish moniker.

She turned to Matt. "Thank you, Deputy. I accept."

"My pleasure."

She smiled, then blushed and looked away as if she'd committed a crime. Matt had no idea what she was thinking, but he liked knowing he could make her grin...and blush. The thought gave him pause. He had no business flirting with Pearl Oliver, except he liked her and she'd worn his ribbons. Not only did she make him want to whistle "Dixie," he admired her integrity. Matt didn't know what to make of his wayward thoughts, but he couldn't deny a simple truth. He liked Pearl Oliver far more than was wise.

Chapter Four

"Carrie!" Pearl cried. "It's lovely."

The women were in the parlor ready to leave for the meeting with Miss Marlowe. In the middle of the room sat a baby carriage. Pearl had never seen such a fine buggy. Narrow spokes graced the large metal wheels, and powder blue satin lined the wicker basket. Earlier, when Carrie announced she had a gift for Toby, Pearl hadn't known what to expect.

"Do you like it?" Carrie asked.

"I *love* it." Pearl pulled her cousin into a hug. "You've been so kind. I can't thank you enough for what you've done."

Not only had Carrie arranged a private meeting with Miss Marlowe, but she'd also invited Pearl and her father to move out of the hotel and live with her. Pearl now had the pleasure of Carrie's company and the benefit of a housekeeper and nanny. Martha Dinwiddie, a widow, came daily to cook and clean. When she'd set eyes on Toby, she'd vowed to spoil him like a grandson. With Martha's help, Pearl and Carrie had aired out the rooms on the second floor. While beating rugs and laundering bed linens, they'd become as close as sisters.

Carrie touched the wooden handle of the carriage. "I know you planned to leave Toby with Martha, but I think we should take him."

Pearl's nerves prickled. "Are you sure?"

"Miss Marlowe loves babies."

"But this is an interview."

"Not exactly," Carrie replied. "We're going to her house, not the school. Toby can sleep in the carriage. If he gets fussy, I'll hold him."

Pearl had mixed feelings about going out in public with her son. She wanted the world to know she had a beautiful baby boy, but his lack of a father raised questions she didn't want to answer. Today, though, she had to answer them for Miss Marlowe. Having Carrie at her side made the decision easier. She refused to be ashamed of her child. "We'll do it."

Her cousin beamed a smile. "Get Toby. I'll meet you outside."

Pearl hurried up the stairs. By the time she returned with the baby, Carrie had the carriage pointed down the street. Pearl set her son on the cushion and tucked a blanket around him. She'd nursed him earlier and hoped he'd be content. Keeping him fed and happy while she taught was a big concern, but she had a plan. Carrie's house was a short walk from the school. She could hurry home during lunch. In a pinch, he'd be satisfied with goat's milk she'd keep in the ice box.

Carrie looped her arm around Pearl's elbow. "Are you ready?"

"I have to be."

Steeling herself for curious neighbors, Pearl pushed the carriage down the street. As they bumped along, Toby opened his little mouth and found a new sound. He sounded like a tiny locomotive. Laughing, Pearl touched his cheek.

Carrie turned wistful. "He's wonderful, Pearl. I can't wait to have a baby of my own."

Toby had come at a cost, but Pearl loved him without shame. "It's the best feeling in the world."

"I want a *huge* family," Carrie declared.

A long time ago, Pearl had felt the same way. "Three boys and three girls?"

"Maybe." She sighed. "First I need a husband, and Matt Wiley doesn't know I'm alive."

Pearl had to agree with her cousin's assessment. While preparing the bedrooms, they'd spoken at length about Matt. Carrie had met him in September, the first day of school when he'd brought Sarah. They often chatted, but he hadn't done more than express appreciation for her interest in his daughter. Thanks to watching Adie and Josh at Swan's Nest, Pearl knew what love looked like. Matt had been friendly to Carrie, but he didn't look smitten.

At least not when he looked at Carrie. To Pearl's chagrin, she'd seen a spark in his eyes when he'd noticed the ribbons, and again at dinner when she'd passed the potatoes. Not that his mild interest in her mattered. As far as Pearl was concerned, Matt belonged to Carrie.

A gust of wind tugged at their skirts. Carrie tightened the shawl around her shoulders. "I wish I knew what to do. Matt said more at supper than he's ever said before."

"Really?"

"You impressed him. I'm glad he's writing a letter."

Pearl had told her cousin about Matt's offer after he left. Carrie had sung his praises, and the women had talked about the evening for hours. True to his word, Matt hadn't asked a single nosy question. Instead they'd all shared stories about children and growing up. Sarah had glowed with the attention, and Pearl had been happy to show off Toby. They'd all agreed he was exceptionally bright and destined to be president of the United States. Sarah had announced she wanted to be a teacher at Miss Marlowe's School.

Pearl hadn't been that relaxed in a year. "Matt definitely enjoyed the meal."

"I guess that's a start."

"I hope so." She meant it. More than anything, Pearl wanted Carrie to be happy.

Her cousin twisted the ends of the shawl. "It's just that Matt doesn't *see* me. I'm nothing but Sarah's teacher."

"Maybe he's been hurt," Pearl said. "Do you know what happened to Sarah's mother?"

Carrie's mouth formed a grim line. "They're divorced. She left him. She left Sarah, too."

"I can't imagine—"

"Neither can I." Carrie leaned into the wind. "He told me so I wouldn't say something awkward to Sarah."

Pearl couldn't imagine a woman abandoning her child, though for a short time during her pregnancy, she'd considered giving up Toby for adoption. In those dark days, she'd feared Franklin Dean and she'd had no way to support herself. Her friends at Swan's Nest had come to her rescue and she'd be forever grateful.

Carrie broke into her thoughts. "Matt's wife broke his heart when she left. You can see it in his eyes."

Pearl understood too well. She'd seen that look when they'd first met. "How long ago was it?"

"A year or so." As they turned toward the school, Carrie squinted against the sun. "I know Matt likes me. He's just scared. He needs to know I'd never hurt him."

"Of course, you wouldn't."

Carrie bit her lip, then released it. "He needs convincing, that's all."

Pearl didn't doubt her cousin's sincerity, only her reasoning. Matt hadn't shown even a spark of interest. "I don't know."

"I do," Carrie insisted. "Matt needs a push."

Pearl loved her cousin, but she had strong feelings about *pushing* anyone. Even before the attack, she'd been pressured by Franklin Dean and she'd resented it. She considered sharing her doubts with Carrie, but what did she know about men and courtship? Her perspective was skewed and always would be. Carrie's instincts had to be better than her own. "What do you have in mind?" she asked.

"I don't know. Any ideas?"

"Not a one."

Carrie's eyes twinkled. "How about a supper party? I could invite a few people over."

Pearl couldn't bear the thought. Carrie would invite single men. They'd tease and flirt with her.

"It's perfect!" Carrie declared. "You're new in town. The party will be in your honor."

"No, Carrie. I'm not ready for something like that."

"Please?" She made a winsome face.

How could Pearl say no? She owed Carrie for the food on her table, the roof over her head. She wanted to say yes, but she croaked with panic. "I'll think about it."

"It'll be great," Carrie insisted. "It's just what Matt needs. And you, too!"

Right now, Pearl needed to collect her thoughts. They'd reached the school. Behind the main building she saw a cottage. She tightened her grip on the handle of the carriage. "Is that Miss Marlowe's house?"

"It is," Carrie answered. "Isn't it charming?"

Pearl loved the little house. Ivy climbed the porch railing, and the gabled roof boasted a turret. As they walked up the path with the baby carriage, Miss Marlowe herself came out the door. Pearl saw a woman in her forties with chestnut hair and ivory skin. Petite and wearing a pea-green dress, she looked more like a leprechaun than the founder of a prestigious girls' academy. Pearl relaxed, but only until the carriage hit a rut and Toby started to fuss.

"Oh dear," she murmured. If he didn't settle, she'd have to pick him up. Meeting Miss Marlowe with her son tucked in the carriage would have been challenging. Meeting her with a crying infant in her arms made Pearl shake.

Miss Marlowe greeted them with a wave. "Hello, ladies!"

"Be brave." Carrie touched her hand. "She's going to love you."

"And if she doesn't?"

Carrie shot her a look of confidence. "I'll still love you, and so will Toby. Don't be afraid. We're in this together."

Pearl squeezed her hand. "Thank you, cousin."

Carrie waved a greeting to Miss Marlowe. "This is my cousin, Pearl Oliver. We have someone very special for you to meet."

Thinking of the hair ribbons—a gift to a woman of uncommon courage—Pearl lifted her squawking baby out of the carriage. Mercifully he found his fist and started to suck. As Carrie moved the carriage into a shady spot, Pearl climbed the stairs alone and faced Miss Marlowe.

"This is my son," she said quietly. "I'll tell the story now, but I won't repeat it. A year ago I was attacked by a man I trusted. I was—"

"Oh, child."

Miss Marlowe's pale eyes asked questions—*the* question—and Pearl answered with a nod. The woman touched her cheek, then lowered her hand, leaving a warm spot that felt empty. Pearl's heart turned to stone. Sympathy didn't mean Miss Marlowe would approve of her desire to teach.

Carrie joined them on the porch. "We wanted you to know Pearl's circumstances before the board meeting."

"Of course." Miss Marlowe indicated the door. "Come inside, girls. We'll talk over tea and scones. I made them myself."

Carrie gave Pearl an encouraging smile. "Miss Marlowe is known for her scones."

The older woman indicated a cane rocker. "Have a seat, dear. New mothers need their rest. Carrie and I will bring the cups."

"Thank you," Pearl managed.

She sat and put the rocker into motion. The rhythm delighted Toby and he kicked for the fun of it. Arching back, he gave her his first-ever smile. Happy tears pushed into Pearl's eyes. She longed to share the moment with a husband, but her friends would have to do. She'd tell Carrie on the way home, and tonight she'd write to everyone at Swan's Nest.

Miss Marlowe arrived with the tea service and placed it on a low table. Carrie added a plate of scones and a pot of raspberry jam. After serving the refreshments, Miss Marlowe sat tall on a chair that resembled a throne. She studied Pearl for several seconds. "Let me be frank, dear."

"Of course."

"I've reviewed your application and am satisfied with your qualifications. Carrie has provided a wonderful reference for you. As for your son, I have no doubt you've been victimized. In fact, I greatly admire your forthright handling of the situation. A lesser woman would lie to save face. You chose an honorable path. Not the easy one, mind you. But the right one."

Pearl's belly started to unknot. "I did, and I have no regrets." Toby burrowed his head against her neck. She loved the tickle of his hair.

Carrie cradled the teacup in both hands. "We understand Pearl's situation will raise eyebrows."

Miss Marlowe's eyes twinkled. "I'm quite accustomed to raising eyebrows."

Carrie grinned. "I think you enjoy it."

"I do," the woman declared. "So let's do some politicking. There are five board members including myself. We need three votes. I should be able to twist my nephew's arm, but the third vote will be a problem."

Pearl's heart soared and crashed in the same breath. She'd earned Miss Marlowe's support, but she had a fight ahead of her. As Carrie and Miss Marlowe debated the options, Pearl heard references to Chester Gates and Lady Eugenia. Both women thought Lady Eugenia could be persuaded, but that Mr. Gates would be difficult. Carrie named the fifth board member. "What about Jasper Kling?"

Miss Marlowe grimaced. "The man annoys me."

"Who is he?" Pearl asked.

Carrie set down her cup. "He owns a shop on Dryer Street. I'm not ready to write him off."

Miss Marlowe wrinkled her brows. "I must admit, I don't know Jasper well. Why do you think he'll bend in our direction?"

"He went to church with my parents."

"I see." Miss Marlowe sipped her tea. "You're hoping he'll respect Pearl's refusal to lie."

"Yes."

"He might." She set down the cup. "Jasper's quite determined to build moral character among our girls. Just last week he championed the purchase of McGuffey Readers for the entire school."

Pearl had fond memories of the textbook. The primer was full of Bible stories, moral tales and lessons for life. If Jasper Kling believed in the principles of truth and honesty, he just might support her. "There's always hope," she said to Miss Marlowe. "I'll have to persuade him at the interview."

Toby kicked and the women chuckled. Pearl saw envy in Carrie's eyes and something deeper in Miss Marlowe's. Maybe regret. The older woman offered the scones. "I'll speak to the trustees myself. You won't have to tell your story, but you might have to answer questions."

"Of course."

After Pearl took a scone, Miss Marlowe set down the plate. "You have two letters of reference. One from Carrie and one from Reverend Joshua Blue. Do you know anyone in Cheyenne?"

Before Pearl could answer, Carrie told the story of Sarah's rescue from the freight wagon and Matt's offer to write a letter.

"Excellent," Miss Marlowe replied. "A letter from a parent will carry weight. He's new to Cheyenne, but he's respected.

Carrie looked at Pearl. "It's going to work out, cousin. You'll see."

Pearl hoped so, but she felt like Sarah alone in the middle of the street staring at a team of mules. Needing to be brave, she thought of the ribbons. Matt belonged to Carrie, but Pearl valued his friendship. Hopefully, his letter would tip the scales in her favor.

* * *

Matt didn't like cooking supper, but he did it for Sarah.
He liked washing dishes even less, but it had to be done.
As he dumped the scrub basin out the back door, he
thought of his little girl tucked in bed, wrapped in the
pink quilt she'd clutched all the way from Texas. The
blanket no longer reached her toes, but the fabric still
held the softness of a mother's touch.

As he shook the basin dry, he thought of his last chore
for the evening. This morning he'd bought stationery
and a bottle of ink. All day he'd composed the letter for
Pearl in his head, but nothing sounded right. With her
interview just two days away, he had to deliver the letter tomorrow. He didn't regret his offer. He just wished
he knew what to say.

He looked at the sunset and thought of her cheeks,
flushed pink as she weighed his offer to write the letter.
He stared up at the sky, a medium blue that melted into
dusk. He thought of the ribbons and felt good that he'd
brightened her day. Inspired, he went back into the house,
stowed the basin under the counter and fetched the stationery and ink from the shelf where he'd put them out
of Sarah's reach. He sat at the table, smoothed a sheet
of paper, uncorked the bottle and lifted the pen. In bold
strokes he wrote the date, then added, "To Whom It May
Concern."

He wrinkled his brow.

He scratched his neck.

He'd have been more comfortable throwing a drunk in
jail, but he'd made a promise and he'd keep it. He inked
the pen and wrote, "It's my pleasure to provide a letter
of reference for Miss Pearl Oliver."

So far, so good. He dipped the pen again, wiped the
excess and described how she'd run in front of the wagon

to save Sarah. As the nib scratched against the paper, he relived the rattle of the wagon. He imagined his little girl lying in the mud and Pearl protecting her with her own body.

He owed this woman far more than a letter. Not only had she saved Sarah, she'd restored a sliver of his faith in human beings, even in women with blond hair. Bettina had thrown Sarah to the wolves. Pearl would have died to save her. The thought spurred his hand and he told the story with ease. By the time he finished, he couldn't imagine anyone not hiring her. In closing, he described her as loyal, honest, dedicated and kind. After the way she'd handled the awkwardness of the ribbons, he believed every word.

He blew the ink dry, then closed his eyes. As he rubbed the kink in his neck, his mind drifted to Jed Jones hanging from a cottonwood tree. Matt had seen men hanged, but he'd never cut one down after three days. He'd lost his breakfast and done his job, but he'd paid a price. The nightmares from Virginia had come back with a new intensity. He hadn't slept well since then, and he doubted the dreams would settle until he figured out who was behind the recent violence.

His mind wandered until he felt a tug on his sleeve. As he looked down, Sarah leaned her head against his arm. The warmth of her temple passed through the cotton and went straight to his heart. Earlier he'd laced her hair into a single braid. Long and smooth, it gleamed in the lamplight. Thanks to Pearl, he'd gotten the hang of fixing hair. The trick was to pull with a firm hand. Before he'd seen how she did it, he'd worried too much about hurting Sarah's head.

Dressed in a store-bought nightie, she looked up at him with her big blue eyes. "Daddy, I can't sleep anymore."

He draped his arm around her shoulders. With her tiny bones, she reminded him of a baby chick. "You will if you try."

"I want to hear *Cinderella* again."

The week they'd arrived in Cheyenne, he'd bought a storybook with colored pictures for Sarah's birthday. He'd found it at the fanciest shop in town, and a clerk had told him the story behind it. A Frenchman named Charles Perrault had collected fairy tales in a book called *Tales of Mother Goose.* Someone else had translated the stories into English, and someone else had drawn pictures that sent Sarah into raptures of delight. She didn't like the gruesome parts, but she enjoyed the rest. Matt had read *Cinderella* so many times that he had passages memorized.

"We already had a story," he said. "It's bedtime."

"Pleeeease."

Whining couldn't be tolerated. It reminded him of Bettina. "No, Sarah. It's time to sleep."

She tried to climb on his lap. Matt picked her up by her underarms and plopped her down on his knee. Rather than march her to bed, he'd play one last game of Horsey, then tuck her in with a kiss on the nose. She liked that.

As he scooted the chair back, Sarah saw the stationery. "What's that?"

"A letter."

"Who's it to?"

"It's for Miss Pearl." He wanted Sarah to show respect, so he'd used the "Miss." "We're helping her get a job as a teacher."

"*My* teacher?" She wiggled with excitement.

"Maybe."

Twisting in his lap, she put her hands on his shoulders.

The lashes fringing her eyes fluttered upward. "Maybe she could be my mama, too."

The question didn't surprise him. Sarah had been talking about mamas since the day she'd seen Pearl. At supper she'd asked him why she didn't have one anymore. Matt had given the only answer he could manage. *Something happened, sweetheart. She had to leave.*

What else could he say? *I let your mother down and she ran off. She found another man...a better man.*

A five-year-old couldn't fathom such things, but someday Sarah would want to hear the truth. What could he say? That he'd been a rotten husband? The thought turned his stomach. Sarah needed a mother, but there was no reason to think he'd become a better man. Never mind Pearl's pretty hair and easy manner. Matt had no business noticing her.

"Come on," he said to Sarah, lifting her as he stood. "You talked me into one more story."

She wrapped her arms around his neck. "I love you, Daddy."

"I love you, too, darlin'."

He galloped her into the bedroom, tucked her against the feather tick, sat on the stool by her bed and opened *Mother Goose.* If he angled the book toward the door, enough light came from the hall that he could make out the words. He could also see the picture of Cinderella with her blond curls and blue eyes.

Sarah rolled on her side. "I think she looks like Miss Pearl."

So did Matt. "A little."

"A lot." Sarah folded her hands across her chest. Then she did something Matt had never seen her do. She closed her eyes and mouthed words he couldn't hear.

"What are you doing?" he asked.

"I'm praying."

Matt had no such inclination, not anymore. A long time ago he'd prayed the prayers and he'd felt relieved of his misdeeds, but not anymore. That boy had turned into a man who had to live with his mistakes. All that remained of his faith were the pangs of guilt that had driven him to work harder than any lawman in Texas. The effort had cost him Bettina, who hadn't liked playing second fiddle to his badge.

Matt couldn't change the past, but he could stop others from making the same mistakes. That's why he'd do anything to protect the innocent…anything except put Sarah at risk.

"Daddy?"

He stumbled back to Sarah's land of fairy tales. "Yes, darlin'?"

"I'm praying for a mama."

Matt didn't expect God to answer Sarah's prayer, but neither could he burst the bubble of a child's faith. He brushed a strand of hair from her cheek. "Go ahead and pray, sweetheart. There's no harm in it."

"Mrs. Holcombe says it's good to pray. She says God listens."

"Uh-huh."

"She reads me Bible stories."

"That's nice."

"I like fairy tales better," Sarah said with authority.

So did Matt, though he didn't believe in either one. "Close your eyes now."

As she breathed out a sigh, he started to read about the poor girl enslaved by a wicked stepmother. By the time he reached the second page, Sarah's eyes had drifted shut and her breathing had settled into the rhythm of sleep. He closed the book without making a sound, then went to the kitchen where he reread the letter for Pearl. Satisfied, he folded it into thirds and sealed it.

As he put the stopper in the ink, he wished he could bottle his feelings as easily. His insides were churning and not only because of Pearl. Tonight he'd dream about Jed Jones and bullets flying at the Silver Slipper. Neither could he forget Jasper Kling and his strong reaction to the Peters kid. No one got away with anything in front of Jasper, not even a crude joke. Matt knew all about men who lived two lives. They did things in the dark they'd never do during the day.

Jasper had that tendency. So did the other members of the Golden Order. Matt knew how easily a good organization could go bad. Politics had turned the Texas Rangers into the Texas State Police, and not everyone had been honorable. Rather than become part of it, he'd come north with Sarah. They'd done well together, and he hadn't had nightmares until Jed Jones's lynching. Since that day, he hadn't slept more than a few hours at a time. He doubted he'd sleep tonight, but catnaps were better than nothing. Hoping the dreams wouldn't come, he blew out the lamp and went to bed.

Chapter Five

Matt woke up tired but not because of the usual nightmares. Instead of dreaming about Jed Jones or that night in Virginia, he'd been visited by Cinderella. Blue ribbons had graced her hair, and Sarah had called her "mama." He didn't know which dreams he found more disturbing. He knew how to deal with shame and darkness. Cinderella's smile filled him with false hope. As much as Sarah needed a mama, Matt had no desire for a wife.

Yawning, he threw his legs over the side of the bed, rubbed his jaw and decided not to shave. After splashing water on his face and chest, he got dressed and went to the kitchen to fix Sarah a bowl of mush. As he lit the stove, a cantankerous thing he wanted to shoot dead, he thought of mornings back in Texas, the good days before he'd gotten short-tempered with Bettina. He had his doubts about marriage, but he'd have welcomed bacon and eggs in place of the fare more suited to life on the trail. When he'd ridden with the Rangers, he'd lived on jerky and had been fine. Sarah had taken to calling their morning meal "gruel." Today he had to agree with her. It looked awful.

As he filled a chipped bowl, she walked into the

kitchen. She'd dressed herself for school, but her hair was a tangle. She chattered mindlessly while she ate, then she fetched her hairbrush and Matt did the best job ever of fixing her braid. Just as Pearl had done, he pulled the hair tight and tied it off fast.

With Sarah helping, he washed the dishes and put an apple, cheese and good bread from Mrs. Holcombe in her lunch bucket. Sarah picked it up and headed for the door. Matt put Pearl's letter in his pocket and together they walked to Miss Marlowe's School. Knowing she had the interview tomorrow, he wanted to hand it to Miss Marlowe himself.

Still tense from his dreams, Matt enjoyed Sarah's chatter as they walked. When they arrived at the school, he saw Carrie waiting for her students and waved at her.

Smiling broadly, she waved back. Matt considered asking her to deliver the letter, but he wanted to do it himself. As he handed over Sarah, he spoke quietly to Carrie. "Is Miss Marlowe around?"

"Not yet." Carrie beamed at him. "She'll be in around noon. Can I help you with something?"

"No, that's all right."

"Are you sure?" Her eyes clouded with worry. "If it's about Sarah—"

"It's not." He wanted to keep the letter to Pearl as private as possible. "I'll catch her later."

Carrie's expression dimmed. "Sure."

Matt glanced around for Sarah. She'd joined a group of girls and looked happy today. The move to Cheyenne could have been far worse than it had been. He owed Carrie a great deal for making the move easier. He looked at her now and saw a good woman.

"Thank you, Carrie," he said in a quiet tone. "You've made things easier for Sarah and I'm grateful."

Her eyes sparkled, an indication of how much she loved children. "Thank you, Matt. She's a wonderful little girl. If there's anything more I can do, I'd be glad to help. I could take her to buy clothes or teach her to sew. I'd love to…" She kept rambling, but Matt stopped listening. He'd never understand why women talked so much.

When Carrie paused to catch her breath, he excused himself with a tip of his hat and headed for the sheriff's office. He pushed through the door and saw Dan looking cantankerous. Matt didn't bother to sit. His gut told him there had been trouble and he'd be making calls this morning. "What happened?"

The deputy made a show of rolling his eyes, then he clapped his hand over his heart in a display worthy of the actor playing Romeo. "It was terrible, Mr. Deputy. Just *terrrrible!*"

Matt grimaced. "This has to involve Jasper."

"Yep."

"The Peters kid again?"

"Nope."

Matt propped his hips on his desk. "Spit it out."

"You're not going to believe it."

"Try me."

"One of Scottie's girls did some shopping in Jasper's store yesterday. Only she didn't buy anything. She just looked." Dan threw up his hands in mock horror. "She *touched* a hairbrush. Jasper says he can't sell it because it's tainted."

"That's silly."

"It gets sillier." Dan rocked forward in his chair. "I know this girl. Her name's Katy. She cleans the saloon because it's the only work she can get. Her husband died, and she wants to go back to Indiana. She's saving for train fare."

A ticket to Indiana wasn't cheap, but Matt knew the stationmaster. Maybe he could get the girl a bargain. He went to the potbelly stove in the corner and poured himself coffee from an enamel pot. "What does Jasper want?"

"For us to arrest her."

"On what charge?"

"He didn't say, and I didn't ask." Dan shook his head. "I figured you'd have better luck with him."

"Thanks," Matt said drily.

His friend flashed a grin. "That's what you get for being new around here."

"It's been two months."

"I've got seniority. That means *I* don't have to deal with Jasper and *you* do."

Matt swallowed the dregs of the coffee, then put down the cup. "As my mama used to say, there's no time like the present."

As he headed for the door, Dan called after him. "Good luck. You'll need it."

With the sun in his eyes, Matt walked the four blocks to Jasper's store. Merchants opened their doors and bid him good morning. Wagons rattled by and drivers nodded in greeting. In the time he'd been in Cheyenne, he'd made a point of getting to know people. They talked to him. They trusted him. To stop the rash of violence, he'd need those eyes and ears on every corner.

As he approached Jasper's shop, Matt passed the display window where he saw wares from back east. Jasper changed the merchandise often, and today Matt saw women's hats, lace gloves and hankies. No wonder Katy had stopped to browse. Matt went inside and sauntered down the aisle, taking in the assortment of whatnot. The clutter irritated him, but Sarah would have been enchanted by the pretty things.

"Good morning, Deputy."

Matt turned to the counter where he saw Jasper. What the shopkeeper lacked in height, he made up for in fancy clothing. Today he was wearing a green-and-yellow plaid vest, a starched shirt and a fancy tie. A mustache hid his upper lip, and wire spectacles sat on his pointy nose. With his hair slicked behind his too-small ears, he reminded Matt of a rat. "Good morning, Jasper."

"It's about time you got here."

"You're my first call of the day." Matt spoke amiably, but the sniping annoyed him. The clock had just struck nine. Jasper's store had been open for three minutes. Annoyed or not, Matt resolved to be polite. "I hear you've got a complaint."

"I do."

"Tell me about it."

"One of Fife's girls came in here and touched things. She left *marks* on them."

Matt kept his face blank. "What kind of marks?"

"Smudges."

If the girl had done real damage, he could have asked her to pay for it—or paid for it for her—and been done with the entire mess. Instead he had to reason with Jasper about smudges. "Could you wipe them off?"

The man reared back. "I don't think you understand."

Matt hid a grimace. "Maybe not."

"She besmirched my property!"

Matt had arrested a lot of people for a lot of crimes, but *besmirching* wasn't on that list. Did he explain to Jasper that nothing had been damaged? Did he fib and tell him he'd speak with Katy? What Matt wanted to do—call Jasper a two-faced hypocrite—wouldn't solve the problem. The man had a lot of nerve to accuse a cleaning girl of "besmirching" when he himself had visited prostitutes and possibly bribed Ben Hawks to cover it up. If Matt's hunch was correct, Jasper had done other things, too. He'd been one of the riders who busted out the windows at the Silver Slipper.

Annoyed, Matt tapped the counter. "Let me see the brush set."

"Of course."

Jasper stepped into the back office and returned with a box holding a silver-plated brush and comb. Sure enough, Matt saw a fingerprint on the handle. He also thought of blue ribbons and Pearl braiding Sarah's hair.

He looked at Jasper. "How much is this?"

The shopkeeper named a high but manageable price.

"Tell you what," Matt said. "Sarah likes pretty things, and she's too young to know about…besmirching."

"Of course."

"I'll give you half price for it."

"Half?" Jasper's nostrils flared.

"You said yourself it's damaged goods."

"Well, yes. But—" He clamped his lips. If he kept talking, he'd trip over his own greed.

Matt ran his palm over the bristles. They tickled. "That's fine quality."

"The very best."

"What's a fair price?" If Jasper believed the brush had been rendered worthless, he had no call to charge full price. On the other hand, he liked money.

The shopkeeper drummed his fingers on the counter. "I'll take off ten percent."

"Make it twenty."

"Fine," Jasper answered.

Matt slid a silver dollar across the counter. As Jasper put it in the cash drawer, he looked over the top of his spectacles. Matt saw questions in his eyes and prepared himself for another inquisition. Jasper never asked a direct question. His thoughts twisted like a lariat, going round and round until he tossed the loop.

The shopkeeper made a show of pushing up his spectacles. "I hear your daughter had a near miss with a freight wagon."

"That she did."

"I also heard a new woman in town came to her rescue."

Matt didn't care for Jasper talking about Pearl behind her back. Gossip ran fast and furious, and Jasper served on the school board. She didn't need word to leak that she had a baby out of wedlock. "That's right," he answered evenly.

"I hear she's pretty."

Matt thought so, but he shrugged.

Jasper tugged on his cuffs. "I'm looking forward to meeting her."

He wouldn't be so pleased when he learned about her son. Matt had no intention of spilling Pearl's secret. She deserved to handle the situation as she saw fit. "I'm in the woman's debt," he said simply.

"Do you recall her name?"

The shopkeeper sounded far too eager. Why the interest in Pearl? Matt had an idea and it turned his stomach. He didn't dare let the irritation show. The less Jasper knew before the school board meeting, the better off Pearl would be.

Matt worked to sound bored. "Her name is Pearl Oliver."

"Ah!" Jasper said. "Carrie Hart's cousin."

"Yes."

"A preacher's daughter."

"That's her."

Jasper's nose twitched as if he smelled cheese. "We need a new church, a disciplined one. Her father might just be the man to lead it."

Matt thought Cheyenne had enough churches. He felt no call to worship a God who let men do what he'd done in Virginia, or who gave sweet girls like Sarah to women like Bettina. Matt didn't know which he loathed more— his own failure as a man, or God's failure to protect the innocent. He snatched up the comb and brush. "I've got work to do."

"One more thing, Deputy."

Matt met Jasper's stare. "What is it?"

"The Golden Order meets next week. I'll be mentioning today's vandalism. You should be there to explain what you're doing about it."

Matt would have rather punched a beehive, but Jasper's invitation served another purpose. If he attended the meeting, he could watch and listen. He'd see who had the biggest axes to grind. He wouldn't leave early, either. In his experience, the real business took place after the meeting when men shared cigars.

"I'll be there," he said.

As he left the shop, Matt thought of the letter in his pocket. He wanted to be at the school at twelve sharp. With a man like Jasper on the board, Pearl would need all the help she could get. The shopkeeper, he felt certain, would judge her as unfit because of her son. Matt had no such prejudice. People made mistakes. He'd made a bad one when he'd married Bettina, and a worse one during the war. No way could he judge Pearl for giving in to the oldest of temptations.

But Jasper would. A man who'd be offended by a smudge on a hairbrush would see an illegitimate child as the blackest mark a woman could have. The thought made Matt furious. A woman like Pearl deserved under-standing, not judgment. She also needed protection from the likes of Jasper Kling. Matt hoped his letter would be enough to give her a fresh start. If it wasn't, maybe he could help her find a job. Or maybe…his mind went down a road that led to a nice supper at the hotel and that horrible performance of *Romeo and Juliet*.

"Don't be a fool," he muttered. If he wasn't careful, he'd do something stupid like ask Pearl to supper. He had no business courting her. None at all. Keeping that thought firmly in mind, he whistled "Dixie" all the way to the sheriff's office.

Someone knocked on Pearl's bedroom door. Before she could say "Come in," Carrie cracked it open. "Hi!"

Pearl wished her cousin would wait for permission to enter. Toby had nursed and fallen sleep, giving her a moment of quiet. With the interview tomorrow morning, she'd been fighting an upset stomach all day. She'd been about to lie down when she'd heard the knock.

"Come in," she said belatedly.

Turning, she saw Carrie displaying the dress she'd ruined helping Sarah. To Pearl's amazement, the gown looked brand-new. Gone were the mud stains at the knees and bosom. It had been laundered and pressed into im-maculate folds.

"You worked a miracle!" Pearl declared.

"Mrs. Dinwiddie helped." Carrie hung the gown in the wardrobe, then sat on the edge of the bed with a grin. "Guess what?"

Pearl sat at the vanity. "You bought a new hat at the dress shop?"

"Even better!"

"What could be better than a new hat?" Pearl teased.

Carrie's cheeks turned as pink as a June rose. "How about a *real* conversation with Matt?"

Envy raced through Pearl with a fierceness she'd never known. What would it be like to enjoy a man's attention…and Matt's attention in particular? She didn't know, but thoughts of him filled her mind with poignant regret. She pushed the images back because of Carrie, but she still felt ashamed of herself. She forced a smile. "That's wonderful."

"I saw him before school." Carrie put her hand over her heart. "He thanked me again for helping Sarah, but this time he really saw me. For an instant, I thought he'd ask me to supper. He didn't, but he wanted to. I could *feel* it."

Pearl knew all about feelings. They couldn't be trusted. "Are you sure?" she asked gently.

"I'm positive," Carrie insisted. "This is a start, a real one. I'm more excited than ever about that supper party."

Pearl's heart dropped to her toes. Carrie hadn't mentioned the gathering since they'd visited Miss Marlowe, and Pearl hadn't brought it up. Considering her own wayward feelings for Matt, the ones that came suddenly and unbidden, the idea of a dinner party had less appeal than ever. To hide her upset, she faced the mirror and pulled a pin out of her hair. "I don't know, Carrie. I'm still…" she shrugged.

Carrie stood behind her and removed another pin. "You're just like Matt. You need a push."

"I need time," Pearl said gently.

"You need courage." Carrie put her hands on Pearl's shoulders. "I'll invite Matt, of course. And Dan Cobb. He works with Matt. You'll like him."

"Carrie, no."

She didn't seem to hear. "Meg Gates will come. So

will Amy Hinn. And the Hudson brothers. They work for the railroad."

Pearl couldn't bear the thought of a supper party. Men would flirt and women would ask questions. Every nerve in her body quivered, but her heart ached for Carrie. Her cousin loved Matt and needed Pearl's help. If Pearl agreed to the party, she could return a measure of the love she'd received.

"All right." She smiled at Carrie's reflection. "We'll do it."

Pearl decided to look at the bright side. She'd come to Cheyenne for a fresh start. At the party she'd make friends with Amy and Meg. As for the Hudson brothers, she'd be friendly without being forward. She'd wear her plainest dress and braid her hair tight. She'd be fine… really she would.

Carrie started to unravel Pearl's braid, but Pearl stopped her with a touch of her hand. "I'll do it."

"Let me," Carrie insisted.

"No." Pearl had to speak her mind. She didn't like anyone touching her hair, not even Carrie. "I'll do it later."

"Sure." Carrie sat back on the bed. "We have plans to make."

Together they planned the menu and set a date for the Saturday after next. With each minute, Pearl grew more anxious. Her only peace came from Carrie's excitement and the hope that tomorrow she'd be hired as a teacher.

Chapter Six

"Good morning, Miss Oliver."

Pearl looked up from the bench in the foyer of Miss Marlowe's School and saw Miss Marlowe herself. Her formal tone fit the mood of the day. So did the woman's attire. She stood before Pearl in the full regalia of a navy dress loaded with trim. Pearl stood and offered her hand. "Good morning, Miss Marlowe."

"Are you ready?"

"Yes, I am." She put iron in her voice, but her palms were damp inside her gloves.

Miss Marlowe indicated a corridor. "Follow me."

With their heels clicking in unison, they walked toward a fan of light indicating an open door. As voices filtered from the room, Pearl recalled the past hour. She'd been nervous and hadn't eaten breakfast. Toby had spat up twice. When she couldn't manage her hair, Carrie had stepped in and fixed it. Mercifully she hadn't argued about winding the braid in a tight coronet. Last, she'd helped Pearl into the blue dress and given her a hug.

Bolstered by the gown and Carrie's kindness, Pearl entered the conference room with a smile. The men stood and greeted her with solemn nods. The woman she sur-

mised to be Lady Eugenia looked bored. When Miss
Marlowe took a seat, Pearl did the same. No one would
help her with her chair at a business meeting. As she sat,
so did the men.

"Introductions are in order." Miss Marlowe indicated
the man on her right. "This is my nephew, Nigel Briggs."

He nodded but said nothing.

Miss Marlowe turned to the woman. "This is Lady
Eugenia, wife of Lord Calvin Anderson."

According to Carrie, Mrs. Anderson was married to
the fourth son of an English nobleman. Carrie and Miss
Marlowe hoped to earn her support, but her expression
filled Pearl with doubt. Her brows were either perma-
nently arched, or she didn't like what she'd heard from
Miss Marlowe.

"Next we have Mr. Gates."

The banker, Pearl recalled. He served as chairman.
In the event of a tie, he'd break it. Carrie described him
as cold-hearted. Pearl hoped she wouldn't need his vote.

"And last," Mrs. Marlowe said. "May I present Mr.
Kling."

Pearl recalled Carrie's hope that he'd respect her honesty. When he nodded at her, she smiled back.

Mustering her courage, she surveyed the faces around
the table. "Good morning. I appreciate the opportunity
to meet with you."

"It's our pleasure," Miss Marlowe answered. "Now,
Miss Oliver, please tell us about your teaching experience."

Pearl folded her hands in her lap. "I taught Sunday
School for four years. I love children and believe they
learn best with kindness *and* discipline."

Lady Eugenia spoke next. "What of your education?"

"I earned a teaching certificate before leaving Denver."

"Yes, we know." Mr. Gates riffled through some papers. "We have your file."

Lady Eugenia looked unimpressed. "I was inquiring of your *formal* education, Miss Oliver. Have you attended normal school? Perhaps you've studied French and mathematics?"

"No, I haven't." Pearl doubted Miss Eugenia would support her. Regardless of Toby, she disapproved of Pearl's credentials. Even so, Pearl did her best to present her skills. "I attended a private school in Denver where I graduated with honors."

Mr. Briggs pursed his lips. "My aunt tells me you'll be teaching our youngest girls." He shot an annoyed look at Lady Eugenia. "I don't imagine they'll be learning French."

Pearl hoped she'd found a friend. She made eye contact with Mr. Briggs, but he looked annoyed by the entire proceeding. Instead of giving her a supportive nod, he scowled as if she'd ruined his day.

Mr. Gates gave Mr. Briggs a sour look, then turned to Pearl. "As you know, Miss Oliver, our teachers must have impeccable reputations."

She raised her chin. "Of course."

"You've provided three letters of reference. They speak well of you."

She said nothing.

"You're not married. Is that correct?"

"Yes."

"Yet you have a son." Mr. Gates raised his brows. "That implies poor judgment at best."

Pearl nearly shot to her feet and walked out. They'd been told of the circumstances surrounding Toby's conception. How dare he act as if she were a tart! She'd fought Franklin Dean, but he'd been stronger and cruel. Why couldn't Mr. Gates see how vulnerable she'd been? Why did people doubt her integrity?

Lady Eugenia cleared her throat. "How old is your *son?*"

She said "son" as if Toby were a mongrel. She wanted to shout with indignation, but a show of temper would sabotage her dreams. Fighting to stay calm, she answered the question. "Toby is three months old."

Lady Eugenia sniffed. "I presume he's nursing. How do you expect to care for him?"

"The school has a lunch hour," she said carefully. "I'll make a quick trip home. We have a wonderful house-keeper, and my father lives with us."

The woman looked down her nose. "I see."

Pearl doubted it. Lady Eugenia had money and ser-vants, not to mention a husband. She didn't have to worry about feeding her children or keeping them warm, but Pearl worried all the time. She desperately needed an in-come. She had to make this wealthy woman understand. "May I be blunt, Lady Eugenia?"

"I suppose."

"If my son gets sick, he'll need a doctor and medi-cine. Medicine costs money. So does food and clothing. I'm his sole support. Not only would teaching allow me to meet that obligation with honor, it's a worthy occupa-tion." She took a breath. "I'm hardworking and respon-sible. You won't regret hiring me."

Nigel Briggs grimaced. "Your situation is…compli-cated."

"*And* dubious," Lady Eugenia added.

Pearl saw the position slipping through her fingers. No way would she surrender without a fight. With her head high, she addressed Mr. Gates. "May I speak frankly, sir?"

"Of course."

She scanned the faces around the table, gauging the expressions without guile. "It's true my son was born out of wedlock. As you know, I was attacked and a child resulted. I love my son very much. I also believe in the Ten Commandments. Among them is 'Thou shalt not bear false witness.' I could have pretended to be a widow. No one in this room would have known any better. But I will *not*...willingly...break God's commands."

Lady Eugenia frowned.

Miss Marlowe beamed a smile.

Mr. Briggs scratched notes with a pencil. Did she have his support or not? Pearl couldn't tell.

Mr. Gates, an experienced negotiator, blanked his expression. She wondered how many desperate men he'd turned down for loans.

Last she observed Mr. Kling. Behind his spectacles she saw a sheen of admiration. He'd squared his shoulders and looked approving of her stand for the truth. He held her gaze until she blinked, then he looked at Mr. Gates. "May I address the trustees?"

"Of course."

Mr. Kling folded his hands on top of the table. "Miss Oliver's circumstances are indeed troublesome. Above all, we must protect our girls from moral turpitude. Even the appearance of improper behavior can't be tolerated. Young minds are impressionable."

Pearl's heart turned to stone.

"Yet," he continued. "We must recognize a sad truth. We live in a sinful world. Miss Oliver is a victim of the vileness we hope to end by raising principled young ladies, who in turn will raise principled sons and daughters. I appreciate her truthfulness today. No matter how we vote, Miss Oliver deserves our respect."

Pearl's heart swelled with gratitude. Carrie had been right. He shared her values.

Miss Marlowe broke the silence. "Your candor is admirable, Miss Oliver. I want to express my support for giving you the position."

"Thank you."

Lady Eugenia stifled a yawn, a sure sign of disregard. Mr. Briggs said nothing, but his aunt had influence over him. Counting Miss Marlowe, Mr. Briggs and Mr. Kling, Pearl had three votes. Hope welled in her chest.

Mr. Gates cleared his throat. "You're excused, Miss Oliver. We'll discuss your application and take a vote."

She stood. "When might I hear?"

"We'll vote now," he said. "Wait in the foyer."

Pearl left the room, closed the door and returned to the bench she'd occupied before the interview. With her hands in her lap, she stared at the painting on the opposite wall. It was a landscape depicting mountains and a herd of sheep. *The Lord is my shepherd. I shall not want.* Her heart took comfort in the familiar psalm, but her mind relived the past ten minutes. Mr. Gates had told her to stay for the answer. Was that good or bad? A long wait meant intense discussion among the board members, maybe a split decision. A short one would signal—

"Miss Oliver?"

She saw Miss Marlowe and stood. "Yes?"

The woman gripped her hands. "I'm so sorry, dear."

Pearl went numb.

"The vote was two to three. I can't tell you how the others voted, but you know how I feel."

"Thank you," she murmured.

"The decision is positively foolish..." Miss Marlowe

rambled on, but Pearl didn't hear the words. How would she support her son? She couldn't impose on Carrie forever. Her cousin had championed her. Would the board hold it against her? Hot tears filled her eyes. "I have to go," she mumbled.

Hoisting her skirts, she ran out the door and down a dirt path. As the chill of autumn slapped her face, the sun beat on her back. The tears in her eyes acted like a veil, blurring her surroundings into a white haze. Almost running, she cut across a field of dry grass. Carrie's house was two blocks away, but Pearl couldn't go home until she composed herself. If her father saw her, he'd be upset. With her neck bent, she turned down an unfamiliar street and paced down the boardwalk.

She didn't see the man approaching from the opposite direction. She didn't see his boots or his badge. She didn't see anything at all until she plowed into a broad chest and looked into a pair of familiar green eyes.

Chapter Seven

Matt clasped Pearl's arms to steady her. As his fingers tightened on her sleeves, a trembling shot to his elbows. She dipped her chin to hide her face, but he'd already seen the sheen of tears. If she'd been Sarah, he'd have pulled her against his chest, held her and rocked her. The thought rocked *him*. He had no business comforting this woman, but neither could he bring himself to step back. "Are you all right?"

"I'm fine."

"You don't sound fine."

"I am," she insisted with a wave of her hand. "Everything's fine. Really, it is."

Except her voice had a wobble, and she'd lowered her chin another notch. The angle gave him a view of the top of her hat, the same one she'd worn to Carrie's house. No ribbons graced the brim. He couldn't see her blue eyes, but damp trails marked her cheeks.

Like most men, he found a woman's tears unnerving. He knew how to deal with anger, even violence. As a lawman, he handled fights every day. As a husband, he'd dealt with Bettina. When he'd left the Rangers, she'd pouted. When pouting didn't make him stay, she'd shouted at him. *You care more about the Rangers than you do about me!* Matt wasn't proud of himself, but he'd shouted back. The woman with him now wasn't pouting or yelling. Her tears came from a deeper place. As a lawman, he had a duty to protect her. All business, he lifted his hands from her shoulders. "What happened?"

She shook her head. "I need to get home."

"To the hotel?"

"No, to Carrie's house." Her voice cracked.

"I'll walk with you."

"No!" Her chin jerked up, revealing the stubborn set of her mouth. "I appreciate the offer, but I'm fine."

He wanted to respect her feelings, but she was heading toward Ferguson Street. Soon she'd attract attention she didn't want. He knew that for a fact, because she looked lovely in the blue dress that no longer had mud stains at the knees. If he didn't mind his manners, he'd be whistling "Dixie" again. He decided on a compromise. "I'll walk you as far as Dryer Street."

"It's not necessary—"

"It is," he insisted. "You're headed for a bad part of town."

"Please," she murmured. "Just go."

Matt put tenderness in his voice…and strength. "You know I can't do that. How about I buy you coffee?"

She pressed her hand to her mouth, but a sob escaped between her fingers. What had he done to make her cry? Confused, he searched the street behind her. His gaze shifted to the path that led to Miss Marlowe's School. The pieces of the puzzle slammed together. "You had the interview today."

She took a hankie from her pocket and dabbed at her eyes. "Obviously I didn't get the job."

Matt saw red. "Those fools—"

"It's over." She lowered the square of linen. "There's no use crying about it."

He admired her fortitude. Bettina would have moped for weeks. "I guess my letter didn't do much good."

"Oh, it did!" Her gaze rose to his face. "At the very least, it made me feel better."

"I'm glad. Now let me walk you home."

She grimaced. "I don't want my father to see me like this."

"We'll walk slow." He had no business sounding pleased, but he didn't mind escorting Pearl in the least. Aside from adding another good deed to his account, he enjoyed her company.

Worry whipped across her face, but then her eyes brightened as if she'd had a pleasing thought. Maybe walking with him wasn't so bad. Matt let his eyes twinkle. "How about it?"

"That would be nice," she answered. "If we walk slow, Carrie will be home for lunch. I'm sure she'd fix you something."

Matt didn't see what Carrie had to do with anything, but he liked the idea of walking slow with Pearl. He motioned for her to pass, then fell into step at her side. He preferred silence to chatter, but he sensed she needed to talk. If he'd misread her, fine. She could tell him to hush. "What was the vote?"

"Two to three."

He considered the five trustees. "I figure Miss Marlowe voted yes. Who else?"

"The vote was secret, but I think it was Mr. Kling."

"Jasper?"

"Yes." She looked up at him. "You're surprised."

"I know Jasper. You're mistaken."

"I'm sure of it." Her voice held authority. "Other than Miss Marlowe, he was the only trustee to speak kindly."

Matt couldn't believe his ears. Jasper had wanted a girl arrested for besmirching a hairbrush. He'd never give an unwed mother a chance to teach little girls. No matter what Jasper had said, Matt felt certain he'd voted against her. As he'd learned from Dan, Jasper Kling did one thing in public and another in private. The thought of Pearl trusting him put Matt on full alert. He wasn't in a position to enlighten her about Jasper's bad habits, but neither could he leave her thinking the man was her friend. He also wanted to know what Jasper had said during the interview. Considering the G.O.'s possible turn to violence, any comments by Jasper could be revealing.

They were across the street from Madame Fontaine's bakery. Instead of going to Carrie's house, Matt steered Pearl in to the brightly decorated café. "I'm buying you a piece of pie."

"But—"

"We have to talk," he said. "It's business."

She hesitated but allowed him to guide her into the café. Knowing she didn't want attention, and not wanting it himself, he led her to a table in the back. As he pulled out her chair, she arranged her skirt and sat. Matt dropped down across from her, then wished he'd taken a table by the window. The corner felt dark and intimate. It was too isolated for the two of them, yet he needed privacy for what he had to say.

She raised her chin. "What's this about?"

"Jasper Kling."

Her mouth tensed. "I don't gossip."

She had doubtlessly been the victim of wagging tongues in Denver. He could imagine the speculation. *The preacher's daughter! Can you imagine? Who do you*

think is the father? Matt had no time for gossiping fools
who judged others but didn't see themselves. In his line
of work, people shamed themselves every day, just as
he'd shamed himself in Virginia. Regardless of his personal failings or maybe because of them, he had to cau-
tion Pearl.

Madame Fontaine came to take their order. "Good
morning, Deputy." She smiled at Pearl. "And to you, *ma-
demoiselle.*"

As Matt looked up, Madame Fontaine winked at him.
"I see you've brought another darling girl this morning.
Where is your Sarah?"

"In school."

"Ah…" She raised a brow. "So you and the *mademoi-
selle* have this lovely day to yourselves."

Pearl blushed to the roots of her hair. Matt didn't like
Madame Fontaine's easy words, but it was the way of
the French. Rather than correct her wrong impression,
he asked Pearl if she'd like cherry pie. Still blushing, she
answered primly. "Yes, please."

"Two slices," he said to Madame Fontaine. "Coffee
for me and milk for the lady."

As the bakery owner left, Matt turned to Pearl. Even
in the dim corner, her hair had a shine beneath the hat
that matched her dress. He had to remember why he'd
brought her here, and it wasn't to look at her hair. "I'd
like to hear more about the interview."

"Why?"

"I'm concerned." He had to quiz her without revealing
his suspicions about Jasper and the G.O., so he weighed
his words carefully. "Jasper asked me about you."

"He did?"

"He heard about Sarah's accident." He told her how
Jasper had asked her name and learned of her father's

profession. "He seemed interested, if you know what I mean."

Her brows shot up.

"I just thought you should know." Leaning forward, he kept his voice low. "It's none of my business, but you're new in town. You're not aware of certain things." *Like Jasper's letters to the editor and his rantings at the Golden Order.*

"That's true," she said quietly. "But I know what I saw today."

"What did you see?"

Pride burned in her eyes. "He gave me respect. No one else even tried to understand. Except Miss Marlowe, of course."

Matt couldn't figure it out. Why had Jasper been kind to a fallen woman? "You must have impressed him."

"I told the truth," she said quietly.

He still couldn't make the pieces fit. Jasper never forgave anyone for anything. Matt didn't believe for a minute he'd supported Pearl. He might have *appeared* to support her for his own reasons—reasons Matt found repulsive—but he doubted he had voted for her. When it came to impropriety, Jasper had no tolerance for anyone.

A waitress brought the coffee, milk and pie. They ate in silence until Pearl set down her fork. "I don't understand. Why don't you like Mr. Kling?"

Because he keeps secrets. He's a hypocrite and liar. Matt wanted to enlighten her, but he had no business talking about Jasper. He shrugged. "I just don't."

Pearl sliced a bite of pie. "I do. He was kind to me today."

The more Matt said against Jasper, the more she'd defend him. He considered telling her about the besmirched hairbrush, but he didn't want to mention hair. Neither did he want to talk about hypocrites and hog ranches with a preacher's daughter. Annoyed, he stabbed at the pie. "I still think he voted against you."

"Why?"

Matt didn't want to go down that road, but she'd insisted. "They know about your son, right?"

"Of course."

If she could shoot straight, so could he. "Jasper's not one to overlook a person's mistakes."

Her brows hitched together. "What *mistake?*"

She hadn't gotten with child by herself. Did he have to spell it out for her? "You know what I mean."

She gasped in shock, then shot to her feet and raced to the door.

Matt didn't understand. Until now, she'd been candid about her situation. He hadn't said anything she hadn't acknowledged herself. He couldn't let her leave in a snit, so he slapped some coins on the table and went after her. Before he could catch up, she pushed through the door. It swung shut behind her, nearly slapping his face. By the time he'd gone through it, she gained half a block.

"Hold up," he called.

She hoisted her skirts and ran faster. He broke into a run. Chasing Pearl was getting to be a habit. When he reached her side, he jumped in front of her to block her path. She stopped short and glared at him through her tears. "Go away!"

He clasped her arms. "Pearl, I'm sorry."

"Leave me alone!"

"Whatever I said, I didn't mean to offend you."

"You said I made a mistake!" Fury blazed in her eyes. "I didn't! I didn't want—I pushed him—*I said no!*"

She broke into sobs and hunched forward as if she'd been socked in the belly. If he hadn't been holding her arms, she'd have crumpled to her knees in the middle of the street, a heap of helpless skirts and tears and that's when he understood… She'd been raped.

His heart caught fire. He wanted to kill the man who'd touched her. A noose and a tall tree…. A bullet to the man's brain. The violence carried him to Virginia in a haze of rage. He'd never take the law into his own hands again, but sometimes he thought about it. If anyone harmed Sarah—he clenched his jaw. If someone hurt his daughter, blood would run thick.

Right now, he needed to help Pearl. She'd straightened her back, but her eyes were still gleaming. "I'm tired of defending myself! I'm tired of being blamed and accused! I won't stand for it."

"Good."

She glared at him. "I don't want pity, either."

"I don't give it." Everyone in this world had a story to tell, including him. Most of those stories had lousy endings. "I don't feel sorry for you, Pearl. Not a whit."

"You don't?" She sounded steadier.

"No, I don't. But I'd like to kill the brute who hurt you."

"He's dead."

"Good." Matt wouldn't have to go to Denver and arrest someone. "You're alive. You survived."

"Yes." She seemed to breathe the word. "I did."

"I can see that." He saw everything about her and he liked what he saw. She was brave, smart and pretty to boot. "I jumped to a very wrong conclusion, and I'm sorry. I'd be grateful if you'd accept my apology."

"Of course."

Matt let his eyes twinkle. "You're a force when you're angry, Miss Oliver. I'm glad that fury's not directed at me right now."

In spite of his teasing, she looked bleak. "I'm not mad anymore. Just disappointed."

"So am I," he said quietly. "You'd be a wonderful teacher."

"Do you think so?"

"Sure." He smiled.

Pearl's eyes clouded. "Sometimes I wonder if the trouble will go away."

"I don't know," he said truthfully. "Something like that stays with a person, but it doesn't have to stop you from living. You're a good woman, Pearl. And a good mother. Some man is going to be honored to have you for a wife."

A whimper escaped from between her lips. She covered her mouth with her fingers, a gesture that made him wonder if she'd ever been kissed with true tenderness...if she wanted a husband...if she felt damaged or whole. He had no business thinking such thoughts, no call to hurt for what she'd endured. But he did. He wiped her tears with his thumb. "Feel better?"

"I do."

"Good."

Her eyes clouded again, this time with resignation, and he thought of the ribbons he shouldn't have sent, the ribbons he wouldn't take back for anything.

She lifted her chin and smiled. "I'm glad you and Carrie are friends."

So was Matt. Carrie had brought him closer to Pearl. He indicated the way to Carrie's house. "I'll walk you home."

"Thank you, Deputy Wiley."

The formality annoyed him. He'd called her Miss Oliver to show respect, not to put up a wall. "Call me Matt. We're friends now."

"All right, Matt."

She smiled shyly, then started down the boardwalk. After ten steps, she commented on the weather. Matt commented back. It was indeed a lovely day, but not as lovely as the woman at his side. It wasn't a matter of whistling "Dixie," either. She had his heart tied in knots. Not that it mattered.... No way would he court a blond-haired preacher's daughter. Not when he'd failed so badly as a husband. And not when he didn't respect her faith.

With that thought squarely in mind, he commented on the clouds. Pearl talked about the wind. And that was that.

Pearl hoped Carrie had already arrived for lunch. Asking Matt to share a meal with them was a small way to repay her cousin's kindness, though she'd had to swallow a surge of envy. She liked Matt far more than she wanted to admit. His apology had touched her deeply. So had the flash of anger when he'd understood the circumstances of Toby's conception. In that moment, Pearl had felt both safe and understood.

What if... But the question had no bearing. Matt belonged to Carrie and Pearl intended to help her cousin in every way she could.

To her pleasure, Carrie hurried down the front steps. When she saw Pearl with Matt, she hesitated, but only for a moment. "I haven't heard a thing! What happened?"

Pearl took a breath. "I didn't get the job."

"Oh no."

Carrie tried to hug her, but Pearl pulled back. Kindness would make her cry, and she wanted to keep the dignity she'd regained. She indicated Matt. "I invited Deputy Wiley for lunch."

With a winsome smile, Carrie faced him. "We'd love to have you."

"No, thanks," he answered. "I've got work to do."

"You still have to eat," Carrie insisted.

Matt smiled his appreciation. "I'll be fine, Carrie. Don't worry about me at all." He turned to Pearl. "Take care now."

"I will."

His eyes lingered a bit too long and her throat tightened. She couldn't let his friendship matter to her. She couldn't care about this man or want his attention. She had to help Carrie. "Are you sure about lunch? Martha's a good cook."

He looked pleased. "I wish I could, but Dan's waiting for me."

"Of course."

He gave Carrie a nod, looked at Pearl a last time, then walked away. Pearl wished he'd been friendlier to Carrie than he'd been to her. The circumstances were all wrong. She turned to her cousin. "I was upset after the interview. I ran into Matt—"

"You don't have to explain."

"But—"

Carrie looped her arm around Pearl's elbow. "Matt takes care of people. I'm glad he helped you."

He'd done more than *help*. He'd looked at her as if she were whole and pretty, as if he were interested in her. Pearl stomped the thought like a bug. "I thought you'd be home. That's why I asked him to lunch."

As they climbed the steps, Carrie sighed. Pearl felt both guilty for liking Matt and sad for Carrie because he hadn't been happy to see her. Hoping to make things right, she touched her cousin's arm. "Maybe the dinner party will open his eyes."

"I hope so."

So did Pearl, though she still dreaded questions and looks. As they entered the house, she smelled the soup but had no appetite. More than anything, she wanted to hold Toby and grieve in private. "I'm exhausted," she said to Carrie. "Would you mind if I skipped lunch?"

"Not at all," she answered kindly.

After a quick hug, Pearl went upstairs. She told her father the bad news, pleaded a headache and went to her room. There she changed into an old dress, picked up Toby and moved the rocker to the window. With the sun warming her face, she rocked with her son in her arms, praying for the strength to endure the rest of her life.

"Why, Lord?" she whispered.

She hadn't asked that question in a long time. After the rape, her feelings had run amok. At first she'd been numb. She'd stopped praying and hadn't confided in a soul. When her monthly hadn't started, she'd begged God to let the cup pass from her lips. Instead he'd given her the grace to bear the hardship.

In those dark days she'd clung to God instead of questioning him. She'd accepted the situation the way she accepted bad weather. She didn't know why blizzards struck, but they did and somehow the snow, sometimes deep and treacherous, nourished the earth. God hadn't abandoned her. He'd given her good friends and a beautiful son. He'd also exacted justice on her behalf, both in Denver and on Calvary.

She hadn't been angry with God at all…until now. Why had He given her feelings for a man she couldn't have? Not only did Matt belong to Carrie, but Pearl had a deep fear of being a wife. Rocking steadily, she thought of her mother's favorite psalm. *I lift my eyes unto the hills from whence cometh my help?* Never before had the Lord let her down, but today she felt bereft as she thought of the next verse. *My help cometh from the Lord.*

Yes, but where was He?

Through the window she saw a puffy cloud. It reminded her of cauliflower, her least favorite food in the world, and surprisingly she found comfort. God knew her likes and dislikes, her needs and wants. He'd made *her*. He'd made Toby. In spite of the circumstances, she'd rejoiced at the child being knit in her womb. She'd rejoice now, too.

The rocker kept time as she spoke out loud. "Father in Heaven, I know you love me, and I know you'll provide. I need a job. Please open the right door."

Closing her eyes, she prayed for Toby and her father, then Carrie. Unbidden, Matt's face appeared in her mind and she recalled his expression when he'd turned down their lunch invitation. If he had any interest in Carrie at all, Pearl couldn't see it. Yet she'd seen something in his eyes. Loneliness? Yearning? She didn't know, but she'd sensed a deep-rooted longing. Bowing her head, she whispered, "Lord, Matt needs you, too. Draw him back into your arms. And Carrie.... She needs a husband. Bless them, Lord. Amen."

The prayer hurt, but she meant every word.

Chapter Eight

Two days after the interview, Pearl put Toby in the carriage and asked her father to accompany her on a hunt for "Help Wanted" signs. She needed a job and she intended to find one. Surely a decent shop would need a clerk. Her father had agreed to accompany her, and now they were on Dryer Street, the block filled with fashionable shops that included Kling's Emporium.

After discussing the interview with Carrie, Pearl still thought Mr. Kling had voted for her. Carrie thought Mr. Briggs had cast the other "yes" vote, but she hadn't seen the way he'd glared at Pearl across the table, as if she'd insulted him by wasting his time. Pearl had also considered Matt's comments about Mr. Kling's interest in her. Not likely, she'd decided. Like anyone, he'd been curious and had asked questions. A natural reaction, nothing more. As they neared his shop, Pearl glanced at her father.

"Let's visit Mr. Kling," she said. "I want to thank him for speaking up at the interview."

"Good idea," Tobias answered.

When they reached the shop, Pearl saw a collection of womanly whatnot in the window. "Such lovely things!"

Her father smiled. "You sound like your mother."

"I miss her."

"So do I, princess. She'd be proud of you *and* her grandson."

Bolstered by the memory, she lifted Toby out of the carriage. Her father held the door and together they stepped into a world of china and silk, silver trinkets and expensive clothing. As they approached the counter, Mr. Kling stepped out of his office.

His brows shot up. "Miss Oliver! This is a surprise. A nice one, I might add."

His enthusiasm reminded her of Matt's warning. Suddenly nervous, she forced a smile. "This is my father, Reverend Tobias Oliver."

The shop owner came around the counter and the men shook hands. "Good morning, Reverend."

"Good morning, Mr. Kling."

The man's gaze went to Toby, then rose to Pearl's face. "This must be your son."

"Yes."

"*And* my grandson," her father added.

Toby didn't have a father, but he had a good man in his life. Pearl and her father traded an affectionate look. Fortified, she turned to Mr. Kling. "I want to thank you for your support at the meeting."

"You're welcome." He made an awkward bow, then faced Tobias. "You raised a fine young woman, sir. I admire her integrity."

"Thank you," Tobias replied.

Behind his spectacles, Jasper's eyes looked huge. "I've been thinking about you, Miss Oliver. I understand your need for employment and happen to have an opening for a clerk. Would you be interested?"

Could her prayers be answered so easily? She wanted to take the job on the spot, but any position she accepted had to allow her to go home at lunch to nurse Toby. She'd also learned to ask questions before jumping into new ventures. "It's an appealing offer. What would I be doing?"

He laced his hands behind his back. "My clientele expects a high standard of service. You'd be assisting customers, arranging merchandise and making sure the shelves are *always* free of dust.

"And the hours?"

"The store opens at nine o'clock and closes at four. You'll have Sundays and Mondays off. Would that be acceptable?"

If Mr. Kling allowed her to go home at lunch, she wouldn't be away from Toby for more than three hours at a time. She'd have to hurry, but her father and Martha would help.

"If I can go home for lunch, the hours would be fine."

"I expect you to take exactly one hour."

She'd have plenty of time to feed Toby, but she had one more question. "And the salary?"

"Two dollars a week."

The amount was fair. Not generous, but adequate as long as they stayed with Carrie. Relief swept through her until she saw her father's tight expression. "Papa? What do you think?"

"I have a question for Mr. Kling."

"Of course," he replied.

As always, Tobias spoke with authority. "The trustees found my daughter's situation questionable. I have to believe you agreed with the vote."

"I did."

Pearl's heart plummeted. Matt had been right.

Tobias's frown deepened. "If you don't think my

daughter is fit to teach, why are you offering her a position in your shop?"

"She's honest."

Tobias looked dissatisfied. "She also loves children. She'd be a fine teacher."

"You're a minister, sir." Mr. Kling's voice had a hint of condescension. "I'm sure you understand the implications. Her situation raises questions for impressionable schoolgirls. Appearances matter."

And they could be deceptive. Franklin Dean had been a wolf in sheep's clothing. Jasper didn't strike Pearl as a wolf, but neither was he a pillar of honesty. In the meeting he'd said one thing and done another. The man couldn't be trusted. Her gut told her to walk out of the store, but her next thought was more practical. He'd offered her good hours and a reasonable salary. She needed the job.

"I'd like to accept the position," she said to both men.

Her father hesitated, then nodded his agreement. Jasper acknowledged her with an awkward bow from the waist. "I'll see you tomorrow at nine o'clock."

"I'll be here."

Her father extended his hand. "Thank you, Mr. Kling."

As the men shook, the shopkeeper bobbed his head. "Please, call me Jasper."

"Then I'm Tobias."

Pearl sagged with relief. A job.... She had a job!

As she silently celebrated, the men made small talk. Her father and Mr. Kling discovered they both enjoyed chess, and they shared a deep concern for the moral climate of Cheyenne. Before they left the store, Mr. Kling invited her father to a meeting of something called the Golden Order and he accepted. Pearl welcomed her father's involvement. His heart condition limited his ability to work, but he needed a purpose. Joining the Golden Order would give him a chance to make friends in Cheyenne.

When they left the shop, she put Toby back in his carriage and hugged her father hard. "We're going to be fine, Papa. I know it."

"So do I, princess."

Today the nickname didn't bother her at all.

Matt didn't usually work Saturday nights. He claimed the privilege as a family man and left Saturdays to men without children. Tonight he'd enjoyed a quiet evening with Sarah. They'd played checkers—he let her win—then he'd read her a story and put her to bed. Knowing he wouldn't sleep, he sat staring into the fire, pondering his suspicions about the Golden Order.

If they'd crossed the line as he suspected, they had to be stopped. *How* was the problem. If he asked too many questions, the vigilantes would lay low. The problem would go away for a while, but they'd strike again without warning. Matt needed to set a trap. A trap needed bait, but he hadn't been in Cheyenne long enough to have the connections for an effective ruse. He needed a break but didn't see one coming.

Yawning, he banked the coals of the dying fire. As he headed down the hall, someone pounded on his door. He opened it and saw Dan. "What happened?"

"Someone beat Scottie Fife to a pulp."

Matt strapped on his gun belt. "Where did it happen?"

"Behind the Silver Slipper." Dan described how Scottie had been tricked into the alley. Instead of the customer he'd expected, he'd encountered five masked men in black derbies. "Doc says he'll live, but he's lost an eye."

"I want to talk to him." Matt punched into his coat. "Any witnesses?"

"Maybe. The girls are waiting for us."

Matt went to Sarah's room where he scooped her into his arms. Blanket and all, he carried her across the street to Mrs. Holcombe's house. The widow would understand. He'd woken her up before. Tomorrow she'd remind him that Sarah needed a mother, as if he didn't already know it. As Dan knocked on her door, Matt called her name so she wouldn't be alarmed. She opened the door and he carried Sarah to the sofa, kissed her forehead and tucked the blanket around her shoulders. Bless her heart, she didn't wake up. He thanked Mrs. Holcombe profusely, then left with Dan.

As they neared Ferguson Street, the night turned rowdy with noise from a dozen saloons. A tinny piano played a rambunctious tune, and Matt heard female laughter from an upstairs window. Forced and empty, the sound depressed him. So did the plink of bottles as he and Dan passed one saloon after another, each with a name more tempting than the last.

When they reached the Silver Slipper, the noise died to silence. With Dan behind him, Matt pushed through the batwing doors into a room blazing with light. The customers had moved down the street, leaving behind the smell of whiskey and an abandoned Faro game. The six women who worked as dancing girls were huddled around a table.

Matt tipped his hat. "Good evening, ladies."

"Good evening," they murmured.

He'd have wagered a month's salary that not a single woman in the room had chosen this life. They'd fallen into it because of hunger and shame and only God knew what else. The rouge on their cheeks did nothing to hide the pallor of fear. Katy the cleaning girl sat on the fringe of the group. With her clean-scrubbed face, she looked more ashen than the others and twice as scared.

Matt surveyed the women. "Did anyone see anything?"

After a pause, a brunette named Lizzy raised her hand.

"Speak freely," he said.

"I saw their horses as they galloped off."

"I did, too," said another girl.

The dam broke and the women all started talking at once. Matt raised his hands. "One at a time, ladies."

After a couple minutes, he discerned there had been five attackers. In addition to wearing masks, the riders had chosen horses with no discernable markings. Sometime during the beating, one of the men had scrawled "God is not mocked" on the back door with white chalk.

"I'd like to speak to Scottie," he said to the group.

Katy pushed to her feet. "I'll take you."

Leaving Dan to continue with Scottie's girls, Matt followed Katy up two flights of stairs to a third story as ornate as a New Orleans hotel. Katy tapped on the door. When someone called for her to come in, she led Matt into a bedroom furnished from top to bottom with fancy things.

Matt made eye contact with the doctor. "May I speak to Scottie?"

"Only if you're quick," he answered. "I just dosed him with laudanum."

As Matt approached the bed, he saw the damage to the man's face. As Dan had said, he'd lost an eye. The remaining one was swollen shut, and bruises covered every inch of his face.

"Hello, Scottie," Matt said quietly. "What can you tell me?"

"Not much."

"Did you recognize anyone?"

"They got me down too fast."

"How about voices?"

Scottie swallowed painfully. "They're sly, Wiley. They didn't say a word.

Matt had to admire the group's discipline. They had a secret and intended to keep it.

When Scottie motioned for a glass of water, Katy stepped forward and lifted it to his lips. The gesture held tenderness, but Matt didn't think there was anything improper between the two of them. Katy had cared for her ailing husband before his death and had the demeanor of a nurse. When Scottie groaned, the doctor motioned for Matt to leave. As he headed for the stairs, he heard footsteps, turned and saw Katy following him.

"It's the men who shot out the windows, isn't it?" she asked.

"I think so."

Tears welled in her eyes. "I know Scottie's business is wrong. So do the other girls. We don't want to be here. It's just…" She shook her head.

"Sometimes there's not much of a choice," he said for her. He'd seen it too many times. A woman lost her way and couldn't make ends meet. Prostitution was a downhill slide that ended at places like the one Jasper Kling had been visiting. Matt had to wonder what would happen if the businessmen leading the Golden Order offered decent jobs to these woman? What if someone gave them a second chance?

Katy bit her lip. "I have enough money saved for train fare home. I'm leaving next week."

"That's good."

"I wish I could take Lizzy and everyone with me."

So did Matt. He couldn't make that happen, but he

could stop the vigilantes. "Did you see anything else tonight?"

"I only remember the hats."

The black derbies claimed authority and made the group known. Eventually they'd make a mistake, but how many people would suffer before they stumbled? Matt had to take action *now*. As he and Katy arrived in the main dance hall, he made eye contact with Dan. The deputy shook his head, a signal he hadn't gleaned any useful information. The two men bid good-night to the women and paced out the door.

As the bright light of the dance hall faded to black, Matt saw the answer to the problem with startling clarity. He and Dan had been *inside* the saloon. Now they were *outside* in the dark. They were also outside of the G.O. If they could somehow get *inside,* they'd have the information they needed to make arrests during the next attack.

"We need a spy," he said to Dan.

"A what?"

"Someone who can get inside the G.O." Matt picked up his pace. "They're not going to stop, and they're smart. We need to find a man they'll trust but who sees them for what they are. It's the only way."

Dan's brows lifted. "Who do you have in mind?"

Matt scanned faces in his mind, disregarding one after the other. If he approached someone favorable to the vigilante activity, he'd tip his hand to the Golden Order. On the other hand, the G.O. knew where everyone in Cheyenne stood on the issues of crime and Ferguson Street. "We need a newcomer to town. Someone they don't know."

"A wild card," Dan added.

"Exactly." Only one man fit that bill. Matt didn't care

for ministers, but he liked Pearl's father. "What do you know about Tobias Oliver?"

"Carrie's uncle?"

"That's right."

"I haven't met him, but I expect I'll see him at church tomorrow."

"Good." Matt saw the pieces coming together. "See if you can get a feel for what he thinks of what's happening."

With their boots tapping on the wood, Dan chuckled. "I have a better idea. Come with me. You can talk to him yourself."

Matt answered with a laugh of his own. "Not a chance." He hadn't prayed since Virginia and he wasn't going to start now.

The men parted at the corner. Dan left whistling a nameless tune. Matt walked alone in the dark with only his thoughts for company. As he neared the edge of town, coyotes joined in a song that would haunt his dreams. Would he ever sleep well again? Maybe, if he could stop the Golden Order. With the wind pushing him, he hoped he'd found the answer in Tobias Oliver. A minister.... The irony nearly choked him. Matt had no faith in God and even less in men who claimed to know Him, but what else could he do? The G.O. had to be stopped, and Tobias Oliver offered his only hope. With a little luck, the man would be on their side, and soon Matt would sleep without dreams.

Pearl woke up in the middle of the night to the call of howling coyotes. As the endless wind stirred the cottonwood outside her window, she felt the restlessness in her gut. She'd been working for Jasper—that's how she thought of him now—for two days and she'd grown weary of his persnickety ways. Neither did she care for how he treated people. Wealthy patrons received the utmost respect. Customers of lesser means were made to feel uncomfortable until they left. Pearl would have quit, but she needed the money.

Unable to get back to sleep, she padded downstairs for a glass of water. To her surprise, she found Carrie sitting at a desk in the parlor with a pen in hand.

"You're up late," Pearl remarked.

Carrie smiled. "I'm writing the invitations to the dinner party."

Pearl's belly lurched, but she'd made up her mind to go through with the party for her cousin's sake. "Do you need any help?"

"I'm almost finished." She signed a note and set it aside. "That's the last one. I'll deliver them at church, or early in the week for anyone who's not there."

In spite of her good intentions, Pearl sighed.

Carrie looked up from the pot of sealing wax, saw Pearl's expression and spoke in a tone as gentle as cotton. "What's wrong, cousin?"

"Everything," Pearl admitted. "I don't like Jasper, and I hate being away from Toby so much. Teaching would have taken me away from him, too. But it's a noble occupation. In Jasper's shop, I'm dusting trinkets and kowtowing to people like Lady Eugenia. It feels all wrong."

"You could quit," Carrie said. "We don't need the money."

"*I* need it," Pearl insisted.

"That's pride talking." Carrie came to sit on the divan. "I've got more than enough for our needs. We're family, Pearl. Please don't feel beholden."

"But I do."

"You shouldn't." Carrie sounded brusque but in a good

way. "Do you know how lonely I'd be without you and Toby? Do you have any idea how wonderful it is to have Uncle Tobias telling stories at supper?"

Pearl said nothing, but she knew what Carrie meant. Meals were a joy. The three of them traded stories and they all loved Toby. Pearl missed her friends at Swan's Nest, but she'd found a connection just as true with Carrie. "We *do* get along, don't we?"

Carrie gripped her hand. "We're sisters now. Don't ever forget it."

"I won't."

With a gleam in her eye, Carrie tightened her grip. "Since we're sisters, I'm going to say something you probably don't want to hear."

Pearl hesitated. "What is it?"

"There's more than one way for you to solve your money problem. I know you've been hurt, but a husband—"

"Carrie, no."

"Why not?" she said gently.

Pearl didn't know what to say. How could she explain the helplessness of being attacked, the fear that shook her bones? It was like describing a toothache to someone who'd never had one. Knowing Carrie couldn't understand—and being glad for that innocence—Pearl skipped over the most primal reason for her doubts and focused on a lesser one. "I have an illegitimate son. What man would want us?"

"A good one," Carrie insisted.

"I don't know."

"I do." Her cousin's face lit up. "I can't wait for you to meet Dan Cobb. He's funny and sweet, and he loves children. He'll—"

"Carrie, no."

"Why not?"

"I'm not ready." Except her mind had conjured up a picture of Matt. She'd tasted cherry pie and remembered his hands on her arms, steadying her as he gazed into her eyes. If it hadn't been for Carrie, she'd have worn the blue ribbons every day. Matt made her feel brave, but thoughts of other men sent tremors down her spine. She had to stop Carrie from getting ideas. "I want you to promise me something."

"What is it?"

"No matchmaking."

Carrie laughed. "I won't push, I promise. But that's not going to stop Dan and the Hudson brothers from noticing you."

Pearl went pale. "I hope they don't."

"Look at yourself!" Carrie chided. "You're *much* prettier than I am."

"That's not true."

"I'm being honest." She lifted her chin. "I'm pretty enough, but you're like sunshine. Any man would be glad to marry you."

Pearl didn't want *any* man. She wanted—*Stop it.* She had to stop thinking about Matt. For Carrie's sake, she'd be friendly at the dinner party, but she wouldn't wear her best dress. She'd braid her hair tight and she'd get to know Amy and Meg. As for Dan and the Hudson brothers, she hoped they'd sense her reluctance and leave her alone.

She managed a small smile for Carrie. "I'm not interested in a husband, but *you* are. If Matt has a lick of sense, he'll see that you're pretty and smart and just plain good."

Carrie blushed. "Thank you."

Eager to change the focus, Pearl grinned. "Now we have a party to plan."

Together they planned the menu, including the desserts they'd make themselves. Carrie decided to buy a new gown. Pearl would wear navy blue and no ribbons in her hair. With a little luck, Matt would notice Carrie at last and Pearl could be happy for them both. Never mind her own rebellious thoughts. They belonged with the ribbons in the back of a drawer, destined to be forgotten with all of her impossible dreams.

Chapter Nine

"Daddy, this is for you," Sarah said as she came down the steps from Miss Marlowe's School. "It's from my teacher."

"Thank you, darlin'." Matt tucked the small envelope in his shirt pocket, then swung Sarah into his arms. He figured the note was about his daughter's schoolwork, or maybe she'd been talking too much. He'd read it tonight in private, then remind her not to chatter like a magpie.

Sarah had other ideas about the note. She tugged the envelope out of his pocket and shoved it under his nose. "The paper's pretty. Open it now."

"Nope," he said.

"Yes!" She wiggled against him. "Miss Carrie asked me to give it to you special."

"She did?"

Sarah nodded. "It's an invitation." She stretched the unfamiliar word into a serious matter indeed.

Perhaps Carrie had planned a class event. The sooner he knew if he had to rustle up cookies, the better off he'd be. He set Sarah down and reached for the letter. "In that case, we better see what it says."

Matt popped the wax seal, read the invitation to a supper party on Saturday evening and grinned. Dan had received the same invitation yesterday at church, and he'd nearly busted his buttons at the prospect of socializing with Carrie. Matt's buttons were busting, too. He hadn't seen Pearl since the day of the interview. The party would give him a chance to see how she was doing. It would also give him a chance to chat with Tobias Oliver. On Sunday Dan had been impressed with the man. Not only did he have a level head, he'd already attended a meeting of the Golden Order. They'd agreed Matt would chat with the minister at the next opportunity, drop a hint about their suspicions and possibly ask for his help.

Pleased with the turn of events, especially the prospect of an evening with Pearl, Matt swung Sarah back into his arms. Giggling, she hugged him hard. He was about to set her down when he noticed Carrie watching them from the top of the steps.

"Hi, there," he called with a stupid grin on his face. "I got the invitation."

Carrie's eyes went wide, then she hurried toward them. The exercise must have been a bit much, because her cheeks were blazing pink. He almost asked if she was feeling all right but decided to keep his concern to himself. She'd probably had a hard day with a dozen girls as lively as Sarah.

She looked at his daughter and smiled. "You did a good job delivering the invitation. Thank you."

Sarah hugged his neck. He squeezed her tight, set her down, then looked at Carrie. "Thanks for including me. I'll be there."

"Oh good!"

"Dan's looking forward to it." He hoped she'd take the hint about his partner. Dan would like nothing better than sitting next to Carrie during supper. With a little luck, Matt would end up next to Pearl.

When Carrie got tongue-tied, Matt hoped it was because of the mention of Dan. Stammering, she told him the other folks who'd be attending. He knew and liked them all.

"I best be going," he said. "See you Saturday."

"Wait!" Carrie called after him.

She'd sounded urgent. "What is it?"

"I was wondering…" She bit her lip. "Did you know Pearl's working for Jasper Kling?"

"She's *what?*"

"She's clerking at his shop. I was about to visit her. Would you and Sarah like to go with me?"

Sarah tugged on his hand. "Can we go, Daddy? Please?"

"Sure, darlin'."

He sounded at ease, but his gut had done a somersault. He couldn't stand the thought of Pearl working for Jasper. Yesterday he'd had another run-in with the two-faced hypocrite. It must have been Pearl's day off, because he hadn't seen her when Jasper summoned him to deal with three of Scottie's girls. The problem had started when Katy visited the shop. Predictably, he'd called her a Jezebel and ordered her to leave. When she'd run back to the dance hall in tears, Lizzy and two other women had shown up in skimpy dresses.

Jasper wanted the women arrested for trespassing. Matt had told them to leave, but he'd refused to toss them in jail. Instead he'd given them a warning, and the women had left with a wink and an offer he'd definitely refuse. Jasper had been less obliging. He'd called Matt a milksop and said he'd take care of the problem himself. How, he didn't say, but Matt had his suspicions. If men in black derbies attacked Scottie or the dance hall again in the next few days, he'd have another sign of Jasper's involvement, which in turn pointed to the Golden Order.

Having Pearl in Jasper's store made Matt's hackles rise. He swung Sarah up to his hip so he could move faster. "Let's go."

Carrie moved to his side and the three of them walked the five blocks to Jasper's shop. Carrie chattered as much as Sarah, but Matt barely heard a word. His mind was on Pearl and Jasper's nosy questions about her. He'd tried to warn her about the man, but she'd been too trusting for her own good.

When they reached the front of the shop, Matt saw new items in the display window. Yesterday it had held womanly whatnot. Today he saw men's neckwear, a walking stick and a black derby…the same hat worn by the men who'd beaten up Scottie Fife. A hat in the window… Matt couldn't think of a better way to summon the elite of the Golden Order. Men could come idly to the store, exchange information and go on their way.

His nerves burned like fire at the implication for Pearl. She'd see who visited the shop. She'd learn their names. She'd have knowledge that would make her a valuable witness and put her at risk. Matt couldn't stand the thought of Pearl being in harm's way.

He held the door for Carrie, vaguely aware of her passing but keenly aware of Pearl balanced on a ladder in the middle aisle. Unaware of them, she flicked a feather duster along the top of a cabinet while humming "Three Blind Mice."

Sarah wiggled out of his arms. "Miss Pearl!"

Startled, she turned too quickly. She grabbed for the cabinet to steady herself, but the glass front offered no purchase. She swayed to the right, then the left. Her knees buckled, and she toppled off the ladder.

Matt charged forward to catch her. So did Carrie. Being taller and faster, he beat her by three steps. As he gripped Pearl's waist, she twisted and grabbed his shoulders. He lifted her off the riser and guided her to the floor, setting her down with a gentle bounce. Their eyes tangled the way they had after the failed interview. If they'd been alone, he'd have risked a teasing smile. When Pearl blushed, he wondered if she'd had the same thought.

She broke the spell by mumbling "Thank you" and stepping back. Before he could reply, she turned to Carrie. "Matt just saved me from an embarrassing fall. I'm glad you stopped by."

"Me, too," Carrie said brightly.

Sarah plastered herself against Pearl's skirt. "I'm sorry, Miss Pearl. I made you fall."

Matt's heart clenched at his daughter's woeful tone. Sarah had the misguided notion that bad things were her fault. She thought she had to be good to make people love her. That if she never acted up, she'd never be hurt again. He attributed the notion to Bettina's departure, which he blamed on both himself and God. How could the Almighty fail a little girl the way he'd failed Sarah?

Matt opened his mouth to correct his daughter, but Pearl had already dropped to a crouch. "You didn't make me fall, Sarah. You were happy to see me, and I'm happy to see you."

"Really?"

"You bet." She smiled so brightly Matt felt sunshine.

As she straightened, Sarah's head bobbed up. Her braids, more than passable in his estimation, flicked against her shoulders. "Are you *really* happy to see me?"

"Oh yes!" Pearl patted the child's head. "Your braids look pretty today."

"My daddy bought me a special brush." Sarah leaned

closer to Pearl as if to share a secret. "He knows how to fix braids now."

Pearl smiled. "I can see that."

Matt's eyes flicked to another blond braid, the one circling Pearl's head like a crown. No ribbons today. Not a single comb or a fancy curl. Even without adornment, her hair was beautiful. Instead of pushing the awareness aside, he let it unfold into a simple fact. If it weren't for his flaws and their differences, he'd already be courting her. For a cynic like himself, such feelings for a godly woman weren't wise.

Smiling too brightly, Pearl looked at Carrie. "What can I do for you two?"

Two? Matt didn't like the implication. If Pearl thought he had feelings for Carrie, he'd have to set her straight.

"Table linens," Carrie answered. "I want new ones for the party. Matt's agreed to come. Isn't that nice?"

Pearl smiled at him. "I'm glad."

So was he. When he smiled back, her cheeks turned pink and she turned away. "The linens are over here." Pearl led the way to another aisle.

Matt had no interest in napkins but he wanted a closer look at the men's hats. "Where's Jasper?"

"At the bank," she answered.

He ambled to the corner displaying men's attire. Matt didn't care for fancy clothing. He owned a suit for funerals and a pile of store-bought shirts. As for hats, he wouldn't get caught dead in a derby. Thinking of the hat in the window, he looked for others on the shelf but didn't see them. Why would Jasper advertise an item and not put it out? He took it as another sign that the derby was a signal, not an advertisement. He wanted to share the information with Dan before the man left the office, so he crossed the store. "Ladies?"

They both turned.

"I just remembered something." He kept his voice even. "Would you mind keeping Sarah for me?"

"Of course," they said in unison.

Pearl sealed her lips.

Carrie grinned. "I'll take her home with me. You can stay for supper."

Supper would give him a chance to speak with Reverend Oliver. He'd also be able to quiz Pearl about Jasper. Matt wanted to say yes, but he had a bad feeling about the black hat. If something happened tonight on Ferguson Street, he needed to be ready. "Thanks, but no to dinner. I'll get Sarah in an hour."

Sarah scampered to him for a hug goodbye. Matt lifted her, kissed her nose and told her to be good. As he set her down, Jasper came through the door. His small eyes went to Pearl, lingered, then skittered to Matt. He blanked his expression but not before Matt caught the ogle he'd given Pearl.

The shopkeeper stared at him. "Good afternoon, Deputy."

"Jasper."

The man turned to Carrie. "Miss Hart, it's a pleasure. I suppose you've come to visit Pearl."

Since when did Jasper get to use Pearl's first name? It made sense since she worked for him, but Matt didn't like it.

Carrie smiled. "I came to buy table linens."

"They're from Boston," Jasper said with pride. "Pearl can help you. She's learning quickly."

Pearl thanked him for the compliment, but she sounded tense. Matt wondered if Jasper had been overly friendly with her. She'd hate that kind of attention, and he hated the thought of it on her behalf. Looking at Jasper, he

made a silent vow. Every day he'd drop by Jasper's store
to keep an eye on Pearl. The black derby, too. Matt excused himself and left the store. He'd be back, though.
And he'd be watching.

To Pearl's relief, Jasper retreated to his office and
closed the door. She wrapped Carrie's napkins in brown
paper and gave Sarah a piece of candy. After they left,
she put a penny in the till to pay for it. She didn't want
to be accused of stealing or being careless. Her duties
included dusting the store twice a day, so she picked up
the duster and went back to work.

Her nerves felt as twitchy as the ostrich plumes flick-
ing the invisible dust. She'd never been good at hiding her
feelings, and she feared Carrie could see her reaction to
Matt. When he'd caught her from falling, he'd lifted her
up and floated her to the floor. She'd felt weightless in
his arms. His muscles had bunched beneath her fingers
and she'd felt safe. Not frightened. Not panicky…until
she'd remembered Carrie.

Pearl didn't know what to make of the unexpected
visit. She figured they'd met after school, but who had
suggested a visit to Jasper's store? Pearl would find out
tonight, but in her heart she already knew. Matt hadn't
come to the shop for Carrie's sake. He'd come to see *her*.
Catching her had been an act of duty, but his hand had
stayed on her waist after she'd landed. His eyes had lingered on her face and she'd seen a question in his eyes.

What if…

"Stop it," she said out loud. What if pigs could fly?
What if she could kiss a man without fear pressing into
her throat? She flicked the duster over a shelf holding
women's shoes. To distract herself, she admired a pair
of ivory kid boots. She touched the buttery leather and

wished she could afford to buy them. She yearned for all sorts of things, all beyond her reach.

"Pearl?"

She turned and saw Jasper. He'd left his office and closed the door behind him. Maybe he'd leave for the day. She lowered the duster. "Yes, Mr. Kling?"

"Call me Jasper," he said as he approached her. "I insist."

"It's a habit."

They'd had this conversation before. As an employee she didn't mind being addressed as Pearl, but she didn't have to surrender the polite distance of a man's surname. He'd approached her for a reason, so she asked, "What can I do for you?"

His lips pulled back in what might have been a smile. "I'd like to invite you to have supper with me."

Blood drained from her face. She needed to make a polite excuse, but she couldn't think of one. She opened her mouth, closed it, then managed to say, "Hmm."

Jasper's eyes gleamed behind his spectacles. "With your father, of course. We'd need a chaperone."

If she'd had any doubts about his intentions, the mention of a chaperone would have laid them to rest. She had no interest in being courted by this man. Her reaction had little to do with his small eyes and pointed chin. His demeanor put her off. So did the way he treated people. She had to nip his interest in the bud. "Thank you, but I can't accept."

"You're shy," he said kindly.

She said nothing, but her cheeks flushed. Not from embarrassment but anger, though Jasper wouldn't know the cause. She hoped he'd take the hint and leave. Instead he shifted nervously on his feet. "I want you to know, Pearl. I admire how you conduct yourself."

She said nothing.

"Your father, too." He pushed up his spectacles. "He spoke eloquently at the Golden Order meeting. We're glad to have him."

Pearl had to blank her surprise. Her father had come home from the meeting shaking his head. He agreed with the group in principle, but he'd been put off by the vitriol. He didn't plan to go back, and he'd been particularly critical of Jasper's ranting about Ferguson Street. Tobias hated sin as much as the next man, but he knew the folly of a superior tone and refused to throw stones at anyone.

Jasper had no such humility. Pearl had to discourage him, or else she'd be fending off his advances every day. Still holding the duster, she searched her mind for something true that would send him on his way. She settled on the obvious. "I very much appreciate having employment, sir. But you need to know, I'm not interested in… personal attention. I've made a decision to serve the Lord as a single woman."

Jasper gripped her free hand. "God bless you, Pearl. You're as faithful as Paul, the greatest of the Apostles."

She pulled back instantly. Jasper let go, but his eyes stayed on her face. Clutching the feather duster, a poor weapon at best, she stood like a deer sensing danger. Had she overreacted? She didn't think so, but she couldn't be sure. Jasper had an odd manner, but he'd simply complimented her dedication to God.

She had to respond or else she'd rouse his curiosity. "Thank you for understanding," she finally said.

With an awkward bow, he went to the display window. Pearl resumed her dusting, but she couldn't stop trembling. She didn't trust her first reaction, but her second one to Jasper echoed the same uneasiness. She glanced at his back. He'd put out the men's accessories just yes-

terday. Now he appeared to be removing them. The effort
struck her as odd, but she had no desire to question him.

To her relief he finished arranging the new display—
fine china and silver goblets—then went back to his office and closed the door. Pearl continued her dusting,
but she couldn't shake off her nervousness. She read the
Cheyenne Leader every day, so she knew about Scottie
Fife's beating. The riders had worn black derbies like the
one in the window.

She considered mentioning the coincidence to Matt,
but she didn't want to visit him at the sheriff's office.
She didn't want to think about him at all. He belonged
to Carrie. Even if he'd been free, Pearl had no real hope
for a courtship.

She tried to pray for Matt and Carrie, but her temper
flared. Today she'd felt the sweet awareness of Matt protecting her from harm. She'd touched Sarah's braids and
thought of the ribbons stashed in her drawer. How much
more disappointment could she stand? And now she had
Jasper to worry about.

Where are you, Lord?

She didn't know. The Lord had made Heaven and
earth, but it seemed He'd forgotten a frightened woman
in Cheyenne.

Chapter Ten

An hour before the supper party, Matt dragged the straight razor over his jaw, cut himself and grimaced. Fatigue made him clumsy, and the week had been brutal. Since he'd seen the derby in Jasper's window, he'd split working nights with Dan and the other deputies. When he slept during the day or in the wee hours of the morning, his dreams were vivid and intense. He could cope with the smoky images from the war. The shame fit like a pair of old boots. What he couldn't abide were the dreams that followed. Last night he'd seen Sarah and Pearl with matching hair ribbons and he'd jolted awake.

Dabbing at the cut, he thought about his visits to Jasper's shop. He stopped by twice a day now. Jasper assumed Matt was after "besmirchers." In truth he was watching over Pearl. Sometimes he'd bring Sarah, and he'd listen as the two of them jabbered about everything from braids to books to dolls. He could get used to having a woman around. So could Sarah, and that presented a problem. No matter how he felt about her, he was the same man who'd failed Bettina.

He looked at his reflection in the shaving mirror. "Be smart, pal. Don't go hurting anyone."

Someone tapped on the bedroom door. "Daddy?"

"What is it, Sarah?"

"Who are you talking to?"

"No one."

"But I heard you!"

"Hold on, darlin'." He put on his shirt. "Come in."

She opened the door, then looked around the room. "I heard you talking to someone. I *know* I did."

"I know. Pretend you didn't."

"If I had a mommy, you could talk to *her.*"

"Sarah—"

She huffed with an air of a full-grown woman. Did all five-year-olds do that or only his daughter? Since getting to know Pearl, Sarah talked constantly about mothers and babies. Yesterday she'd told him she wanted a baby brother as cute as Toby. Matt understood Sarah's needs, but there was only so much a single father could do.

He finished with his tie, put on his coat and lifted her to his hip. "Want to play horsey?"

"Yes!"

He galloped her into the kitchen where Mrs. Holcombe was dishing up supper. She liked being an adopted grandma, and he couldn't have managed without her. He kissed Sarah goodbye, put on his hat and left through the front door. He'd left his horse tied to a hitching post, so he climbed into the saddle. He usually boarded the gelding at the livery, but tonight he wanted to be ready to ride. If the Golden Order struck, he'd be there quick.

He rode two blocks to Dan's house and dismounted. Before he knocked, Dan opened the door. Bay rum wafted in a cloud. Matt fanned it from his nose. "You smell like a girl."

Dan grinned. "So do you."

It was true, almost. Matt had splashed something minty on his jaw, but he hadn't bathed in it. "You ready?"

Dan put on his hat and closed the door. "Dinner with Miss Carrie Hart? You bet I'm ready."

Matt felt the same way about Pearl but wished he didn't. Tonight he'd be wise to focus on the other business at hand, which meant carving out a private talk with Tobias. From his conversations with Pearl, he'd learned the minister had attended a G.O. meeting and found the gathering troublesome. When Matt had mentioned the vigilante attacks at the Silver Slipper to Pearl, she'd reacted with outrage and said her father felt the same way. Matt was fairly certain he could trust Tobias. Whether the man would volunteer for a risky mission remained to be seen.

Dan mounted his roan and they rode to Carrie's house. Instead of thinking about how to approach Tobias, Matt found himself wondering if Pearl would wear his ribbons. Soon he'd see for himself. The thought shouldn't have pleased him, but it did.

As she considered what to wear to the party, Pearl was tempted to use Toby as an excuse to stay upstairs. He had the sniffles and had fussed when she'd put him down, but he'd fallen asleep and was breathing evenly in his bed. She'd made arrangements with Mrs. Dinwiddie and Hattie, the serving girl they'd hired for the night, to keep a close eye on him, but she planned to sneak upstairs herself for a few peeks.

Considering Matt would be at the dinner party, she'd need those respites. She couldn't bear the thought of an evening in his presence. Every time he visited her at Jasper's store, she liked him more. Her feelings for the man were in a jumble.

She liked him.

She feared what she felt.

Most of all, she felt guilty for coveting her cousin's beau…except he didn't belong to Carrie. The more Pearl spoke with Matt, the more clearly she saw his feelings. He liked Carrie, but she'd never be more than Sarah's teacher. Pearl didn't dare think about what he felt for *her*. She only knew she had to put Carrie's feelings before her own. That meant putting on a brave smile for tonight's party and hoping her cousin wouldn't be hurt.

What it *didn't* mean was flirting with Dan or the Hudson brothers. Instead she'd get to know Meg and Amy, and she'd be friendly to Mrs. Griffin, the widow Carrie had asked to serve as chaperone with Tobias. If her plan failed, she'd retreat to the kitchen with Mrs. Dinwiddie and the serving girl. With that duty in mind, she lifted a navy blue gown with narrow sleeves from the wardrobe. As she checked the dress for wrinkles, Carrie pushed through the bedroom door.

"You can't wear that!" she declared.

"Why not?"

"It's depressing!"

Carrie usually spoke more gently. Pearl attributed her shrill tone to nerves. "It's fine." Although she had to admit, the color *was* a bit gloomy. The last time she'd worn the gown had been to a funeral.

Carrie shoved the dress back in the wardrobe. As Pearl reached to take it back, Carrie pushed through her dresses, a mix of grays, blues and drab browns and pulled out the gown Pearl had worn to Josh and Adie's wedding. As she held it out, her face lit up. "This is perfect!"

"Carrie, I can't."

"Why not?"

Because Matt will notice me instead of you. Because

I'll feel pretty and alive and I'll want things I can't have.
"I just can't."

"But it's beautiful!" Carrie held the dress to her chin. Powder blue with an overskirt and white ribbon trim, the gown reminded Pearl of her friends at Swan's Nest, especially Mary who had ordered her to hold her head high. What would it be like to slip into the shimmering folds? To slip her arms into the sleeves that puffed and narrowed at her wrists? She ached to feel pretty, but not with Matt at the supper table. She'd want to smile at him, maybe flirt. She couldn't. Not when he belonged to Carrie. Not when she feared men and marriage.

Carrie shoved the dress into her arms. "You've *got* to wear this one."

She didn't understand. "But why?"

Her cousin looked close to tears. "If you wear that dreary navy blue, I'll look like a strumpet."

She had a point. A week ago they'd gone shopping. Carrie had selected a pink taffeta gown with oodles of ruffles. Pearl thought the dress was overdone and she'd said so. Carrie had loved it. Pearl hadn't pressed the point because she'd doubted herself. What did she know about fashion these days? She hadn't cared about looking nice for a long time. But she cared tonight…. She cared because of Matt.

The admission left her deeply disturbed. If she said yes to her cousin's request and wore the dress, she'd be risking Matt's attention. If she said no, Carrie would look silly in the rose-colored ruffles. As Pearl weighed the choice, she touched the sleeve of the silky dress. It warmed with her touch and she knew. She wanted to look pretty tonight. Not for Matt or Carrie, but for herself. "You're right," she said. "The silk is prettier."

With Carrie's help, Pearl put on three petticoats and

slipped into the shimmering gown. When she looked at herself in the mirror, she saw the woman who'd caught Adie's bridal bouquet and boldly come to Cheyenne for a second chance.

"You look perfect," Carrie said. "Now let's fix your hair."

Her crowning glory...the white mane that had attracted Franklin Dean. Her breath hitched at the memory, and her stomach knotted. Blinking, she flashed back to the buggy ride and the terrible memory of being trapped. She yearned for the safety of the navy blue, but she couldn't explain the reason to Carrie without more upset. Trembling, she sat at the vanity. "Put it in a coronet."

Carrie huffed. "And hide your pretty hair?"

"I like it that way."

She put her hands on Pearl's shoulders and pressed to keep her in place. "I have an idea."

"Don't—"

Carrie had already loosened Pearl's braid. As the white-gold strands brushed her nape, she recalled her mother putting up her hair for the first time. She'd been fourteen and confident. She wanted to be confident again. "All right," she said. "Make it pretty."

"You won't be sorry."

Carrie went to work with a brush and a comb. Ten minutes later Pearl had the loveliest chignon she'd ever worn. The style struck her as the perfect mix of beauty and restraint. She liked it.

"Thank you, cousin." She meant it.

"One more thing."

When Carrie opened the drawer holding Pearl's hair ornaments, Pearl went pale. She didn't want her cousin to notice Matt's ribbons.

Pearl lifted a comb from the drawer. It was made of

mother of pearl and had been a gift from her parents on her fourteenth birthday. She treasured it. "How about this?"

"It's too fancy."

She selected a comb made of bone.

"It's too plain."

Just as Pearl had feared, Carrie dug past her everyday ribbons to the blue ones. She set all of them on the vanity, then selected the palest blue.

"This one's perfect," she said. "It matches your eyes."

Pearl didn't want to wear one of Matt's ribbons not only because of what he'd think, but because of what they meant to her. The ribbons were a memory, an impossible dream. If she wore one tonight, they'd become as ordinary as her others. She wanted to tell Carrie to put them back, but her cousin would fuss and Pearl would have to explain. Resigned, she let Carrie fashion a blue bow above her ear.

Carrie stepped back. "You look beautiful, cousin."

She *felt* beautiful. For the first time in a year, she felt the lift that comes with a pretty dress, the pleasure of silk on her skin. She owed Carrie for this moment, so she stood and smiled. "Now it's your turn."

They went to Carrie's room where they repeated the ritual of petticoats and looking pretty. The pink dress made Carrie look like a blooming rose, a bit overblown but still lovely. Carrie bit her lips to make them pinker. "I hope Matt likes my dress."

"So do I." She meant it, but her wayward mind went to her own blue gown. As she put the finishing touch on her cousin's hair, someone knocked on the door.

"Come in," Carrie called.

The serving girl they'd hired for the night stepped into the room. "Your guests are arriving, Miss Hart. I've seated Mr. Cobb and Mr. Wiley in the parlor like you said."

"Thank you, Hattie."

With a nod, the girl left. Carrie looked at herself in the mirror, pinched her cheeks until they glowed, then bit her lips for the third time. They were beginning to look like overripe plums. Pearl touched her shoulder. "Carrie, stop."

"Stop what?" Carrie's voice quavered.

"Stop biting your lips." Pearl took her hand. "You look beautiful. Matt will see you for the woman you are, or he won't. If he doesn't, he's a fool."

"If he doesn't, I'll die."

"No, you won't," Pearl said gently. "We don't always get what we want, but the Lord gives us what we need."

Carrie's eyes misted. "You sound like my mother."

"Mine, too."

The women hugged, then Carrie took a breath. "I'm ready."

Together they walked down the stairs. As they entered the parlor, Matt and another man stood to greet them. They both looked polished in dark coats and string ties, but the resemblance ended with their clothing. Matt looked weary and had dark crescents under his eyes. The fellow she guessed to be Dan had a cheerful air. Brown eyes twinkled below his straight brows, and he had an easy smile. He looked rested and ready for a good time.

"Good evening," Carrie said to the men. "Matt, you know Pearl, but I don't think Dan does." She hooked her arm around Pearl's waist and nudged her forward. "Dan, this is my cousin, Pearl Oliver. Pearl, this is Deputy Dan Cobb. He's Matt's partner."

Dan held out his hand. "The pleasure's mine, Miss Oliver. Welcome to Cheyenne."

"Thank you, Deputy."

As the four of them sat, someone knocked on the door. The maid answered and the Hudson brothers walked in. As the servant took their coats, Tobias came down the stairs and issued a jolly hello. Amidst the chatter, Mrs. Griffin arrived with Amy Hinn and Meg Gates.

Pearl tensed every time Carrie introduced her, but the knots in her stomach loosened as she settled into small talk with Meg and Mrs. Griffin. On the other side of the room, Carrie angled into a conversation with Matt, Dan and her father. Dan looked charmed, but Matt's brow furrowed. When he shot Pearl a look from across the room, she realized she'd been staring at him. She looked away, but not before his eyes found the ribbon and he smiled.

Just like that, they'd shared a secret. Pearl hated herself for enjoying the moment, but she couldn't help it. For the first time in a year, she hadn't turned into jelly because a man had noticed her. She'd been pleased. But now she felt guilty. If she couldn't keep her eyes to herself, the night would be long and tense.

"Pearl?"

She turned and saw Amy Hinn, another teacher at Miss Marlowe's School. Glad to be distracted, Pearl made room for Amy on the sofa. As they chatted, Garth Hudson brought them each a cup of punch. Judging by the look in his eyes, Amy wouldn't be single for long.

The parlor was buzzing with conversation when Pearl heard a faint whimpering from the top of the stairs. Toby had woken up because of his sniffles. As she pushed to her feet, the whimper turned into the wail of a cranky baby. Pearl hurried in the direction of the stairs, but she didn't have to go up them. Hattie was approaching the parlor with Toby propped on her shoulder.

"I'm so sorry, miss," she said to Pearl. "I tried to calm him, but he won't have nothin' to do with me."

"It's okay, Hattie." Pearl whisked Toby out of the girl's arms and into her own. "He doesn't know you, that's all."

Hattie gave Pearl the towel she'd had over her own shoulder. "Take this, miss. He'll drool on your pretty dress."

Pearl cared more about Toby than the gown, but she appreciated the girl's thoughtfulness. Holding Toby with one arm, she draped the towel over her shoulder. "I've got him. You can go back to helping Mrs. Dinwiddie."

Hattie curtsied and slipped out of the room. Pearl took a step to follow her, but someone gripped her arm. She turned and saw Carrie.

"You can't leave," her cousin whispered with a hiss. "I need you here."

"But—"

"I'll hold him," Carrie said in a voice that carried over the shrieking. "I love babies!"

She'd made the comment for Matt's sake, not to help Pearl or even Toby. Pearl resented it, but only Toby mattered. She had to calm her son. "I need to rock him back to sleep. Go take care of our guests."

Carrie reached for the baby. "Let me try," she said too loudly.

Rather than cause a stir, Pearl let Carrie take her wailing son. If he settled, she'd be relieved. If he didn't, she'd follow her original plan.

Carrie settled the baby in her arms, carried him into the parlor and made a show of rocking him. To Pearl's consternation, her son reared back and screamed even louder. She'd heard enough—more than enough—and followed Carrie with the intention of rescuing Toby. As she approached her cousin, so did Matt. They traded a look, one that linked them as parents, then Matt spoke in the tone of a man accustomed to being obeyed. "This boy needs his mama."

Carrie, suddenly speechless, let him lift the baby without an argument. He propped Toby against his shoulder, patting the boy's back as he carried him to Pearl. To her utter shock, Toby wiggled his bottom against Matt's arm, reared back, stared at him and stopped crying.

"Silence is golden," joked one of the Hudson brothers.

Amy smiled. "Matt's got a special touch."

Pearl thought so, too. Matt turned sidewise so that Toby could see her. Instead of reaching for her, the baby batted at Matt's jaw and grinned. It was the biggest smile she'd ever seen. Matt smiled at her to share the moment, then made a cute face at her son. "Hello, there, Toby."

The boy answered with a grunt.

Matt bounced him on his arm. "I thought you wanted your mama, pal."

Yes, but he also wanted a father. As her son looked at Matt with awe, Pearl could barely breathe. The sight nearly broke her resolve to keep her distance from this man. Toby needed a father, and Matt had a knack. Sarah needed a mother, and Pearl wanted a daughter. They'd make a perfect family...except Pearl couldn't bear the thought of being a wife, and Matt didn't want one.

It all seemed crazy and unfair, even more so when Toby put his head against Matt's neck and popped his thumb in his mouth. Matt hummed a tune he'd probably sung to Sarah at bedtime. A hush settled over the room as everyone watched and waited for Toby to fall asleep. When the baby's breathing deepened to indicate a steady slumber, Matt looked at her and whispered, "Want me to carry him upstairs?"

The thought of going upstairs together, as if they were

a family, sent shivers down her spine. Whether from fear or hope, she couldn't say. She also had to think of appearances and Carrie's reaction. Her cousin would feel left out if Pearl accepted Matt's offer. She was about to decline when her father approached.

"Let's all go," Tobias said with a smile.

As if he were herding sheep, Tobias motioned for her to lead the way. The three of them went up the stairs and turned into Pearl's bedroom, dimly lit by a lamp on her vanity. Matt spotted Toby's cradle in the shadows and went to it. Pearl stepped to his side, neatened the bedding and lifted the coverlet.

As gentle as snow falling, Matt placed Toby on his tummy. Pearl covered him with the blanket, then patted his back until he settled again. As she lifted her hand, she turned and saw Matt watching her with stark admiration.

"You're a wonderful mother," he said in a hush.

But could she be a good wife? She didn't know and she doubted it. Besides, Carrie had feelings for Matt. Pearl would never betray her cousin's trust. Afraid her emotions would show, she mumbled, "Thank you."

Her father must have seen her consternation, because he motioned them both to the door. "Let's go before he wakes up again."

"Good idea," Matt whispered. He smiled again at Pearl, then rested his hand on Toby's back. "Sleep tight, little boy."

The sight of Matt's fingers, strong and masculine, filled Pearl with the longing to be together as a family. With her heart aching, she kissed her fingers and touched her son's head. As she moved, her shoulder brushed Matt's bicep and he didn't move. The moment felt natural and right, but all wrong at the same time.

Turning abruptly, she led the way to the hall and hurried down the stairs. Needing to calm herself, she detoured away from the parlor and headed to the dining room to light the candles.

As she lit the first one, she saw the card with her name and frowned. Someone had switched her seat with Meg's and she knew who'd done it. Yesterday she and Carrie had disagreed about the seating plan. Carrie wanted to be next to Matt and across from Pearl. Pearl wanted to be on the opposite end of the table, next to her father and as far from Matt as she could get. The change put Pearl directly across from him. Annoyed, she lifted the place card. Before she could switch it back with Meg's, Carrie glided into the room with their guests. To avoid a scene, Pearl left the cards alone.

As she looked up, Matt flashed a smile and approached to hold her chair. "May I?"

Why yes, Deputy. Thank you. Instead she schooled her features. "I have to check something in the kitchen." She indicated the seat next to Carrie. "You're across from me."

Matt looked amused...and challenged.

To avoid him, Pearl slipped through the side door. She asked Mrs. Dinwiddie for extra butter, then went back to the dining room. As she'd hoped, Matt was helping Carrie. Dan, seated on her right, held her chair and she sat.

She tried to avoid Matt's gaze, but he seemed just as intent on gaining her attention. When a smile tipped his lips, she turned to her father who was helping Mrs. Griffin with her chair. A widow of two years, she was wearing mauve with silver brocade. She looked vibrant. So did Tobias. Pearl had never seen her father smitten, but he had that look tonight. The realization put a lump in her throat. Everyone at the table, except her, could chat with the opposite sex with ease. Most men frightened her. Matt didn't, but he belonged to Carrie.

When Tobias sat at the head of the table, Pearl cleared her throat. "Father?"

"Yes, princess?"

She hid a cringe. "Would you say grace?"

"Of course."

The Lord already knew Pearl appreciated the food on the table. She needed provision of another kind, so she asked God for peace, good will and the discipline to keep her eyes off Matt Wiley. He provided those mercies right up until dessert.

Chapter Eleven

Matt should have seen the trouble coming, but he'd missed the signs. If he'd been alert, he'd have realized Carrie liked him…a lot. Enough to bump his foot under the table. Enough to brush against his arm every time she passed the potatoes.

Dan must have noticed her interest, because he'd shot daggers at Matt all through the meal. Matt had shot back a few of his own. Twice Dan had made Pearl smile at a stupid joke. When she'd tipped her head with pleasure, jealousy had ripped from one side of Matt's chest to the other. He wanted Pearl to look at *him* that way, but that was crazy. He had no business courting any woman, especially a preacher's daughter. To add to his frustration, Carrie had honed in on his conversation with Tobias. Matt had planned to invite him for a cigar after dessert, but he hadn't gotten the chance. Considering Carrie's persistence, he doubted he would.

The entire evening had been filled with frustration. Instead of leaving tonight with Tobias as a new ally, he'd have to figure out another way to speak with the man. He also had to make his position clear to Carrie without hurting her feelings. As for Pearl, he hadn't been able to take his eyes off her. If he slept at all tonight, he'd be dreaming of Cinderella with ribbons in her hair.

He'd had about all he could take when the maid came through the kitchen door carrying a serving plate in each hand.

"Dessert's here!" Carrie said brightly.

Matt joined the others in admiring the sweets. One plate held a chocolate cake. It looked simple and tasty. The other tray showed off cream puffs dusted with sugar. Tasty or not, they were too complicated for his simple ways. He had his heart set on the cake, but Carrie put a pastry in front of him.

"I made the cream puffs," she said proudly. "It's a family recipe."

Matt tried not to scowl at the pastry. After Pearl and Carrie finished serving the desserts, everyone lifted their forks. He tried to slice a bite of the cream puff, but the filling squished out the sides. He sawed with his knife but got nowhere. When he pushed harder, the pastry shot off the plate and landed in his lap.

Dan laughed out loud.

Pearl pressed her napkin to her mouth, but her eyes were dancing. Matt figured the joke was on him. If it made Pearl smile, he didn't mind. As their eyes met, his lips curved into a smile.

Carrie gasped. "Oh no! They're overbaked!"

Muttering apologies, he wrapped the mess in his napkin and stood to take it to the kitchen. As he turned, the tablecloth came with him and he realized he'd caught it in the napkin. Chocolate cake landed in Carrie's lap, and coffee spilled all over the pink dress. Pearl and Amy jumped up to steady the candles. Everywhere Matt looked, he saw sloshing coffee and crooked plates. He also had custard on his coat.

"Sorry," he muttered.

Dan cackled. "Man, you're a klutz!"

"Thanks, buddy." Matt sounded wry, but he meant it. Someone had to put the levity back into the evening and he couldn't do it. Carrie was close to tears, and Pearl looked nearly as upset as she darted around the table to help Carrie. He almost said he'd pay for all the laundering, but the words shot him back to the day they'd met. A lot had changed since that moment. Blond hair no longer made him crazy, and he felt a tug in his heart he'd never expected to feel again…a tug he didn't want to feel. Not only had he been a terrible husband, he also knew the sting of a woman's betrayal. Except Pearl would never betray anyone. She had a good heart, too good for the likes of him.

The women were all furiously blotting the dress, so he wadded the napkin and carried it to the kitchen. With the meal done, the cook had left. The hired girl was alone with a basin of steaming water and a mountain of dishes.

As the door clicked shut, she looked up and saw the blotch on his coat. "I'll get you a towel, sir."

"Thank you."

She opened a cupboard, saw the empty shelf and excused herself. "I'll be right back."

Matt dumped the cream puff in a garbage pail without regret. He didn't care for cream puffs. He liked chocolate cake, blue ribbons and women who took care of others. Sighing, he found a rag, dabbed at his coat and made an even bigger mess.

The door opened and Pearl entered with the plate of chocolate cake in one hand and the leftover cream puffs in the other. She set the desserts down, then glanced at him with a mix of mirth and worry. The spill didn't bother her at all, but she cared about Carrie and her cousin had been terribly embarrassed. He shook his head. "Sorry about the mess."

"It's all right," she answered. "We can clean it up."

"Maybe."

She tipped her head. "What do you mean?"

"I have a bigger mess than a cream puff." He looked Pearl in the eye. "Tonight meant a lot to Carrie, didn't it?"

She said nothing.

"More than I knew, I'm afraid."

When her eyes widened into moons, Matt knew a simple truth. Not only couldn't Pearl Oliver tell a lie, but she also couldn't keep a secret, either. He hadn't imagined Carrie's flirting. She'd set her cap for him, and she'd set it hard. His stomach churned and not from the meal. Not once had he thought of Carrie as more than Sarah's teacher. It was Pearl who filled his thoughts and made him crazy. The thought of coming between these two good women upset him.

He shook his head. "I didn't know she'd gotten ideas. I thought—"

"Your coat's a mess," Pearl said. "I'll get a damp cloth."

She turned her back, a sign she wouldn't talk about her cousin. Out of respect, he said nothing as she dampened a dish towel at the sink. With her eyes still averted, she handed it to him. "Here."

The awkwardness irked him. They hadn't done anything wrong. He valued Pearl's friendship and didn't want to lose it. Being stubborn, he let the towel dangle between them. When she finally looked at him, he indicated the flap of his coat. "I'll make it worse. Would you mind?"

She hesitated, then came closer. With her eyes on the coat, she put one hand behind the smear and dabbed at it with the towel. When she bent her neck to get a bet-

ter view, he smelled her flowery soap. He told himself
to look away from her ivory skin. He didn't have to see
the ribbon above her ear. He didn't have to touch it. He
could do the right thing and step back, except stepping
back felt all wrong. He cared for Pearl and knew she had
scars. He wanted her to feel pretty again, so he touched
the silky ribbon above her ear.

Startled, she looked up. She didn't pull away, but her
eyes had a wild shine and she looked ready to bolt.

"Sorry." Matt lowered his hand. "I thought I recognized the ribbon."

"You did, but it's just a ribbon." Her voice came out
high and thin, as if she were trying to convince herself
more than him. He thought of Sarah's reaction when she'd
caught him talking to himself. He'd told her to pretend
she hadn't heard, but she had. Matt wanted to pretend he
didn't know Pearl's thoughts, but he did. She liked him
as much as he liked her. She also loved Carrie and felt
loyal to her cousin.

She turned abruptly to the wash basin. "That's the
best I can do."

Matt glanced down. The coat looked new.

Pearl rinsed the towel, then went to work scraping the
plates. Matt wanted to talk some more, but he had no
business being with Pearl until he squared things with
Carrie. He didn't know exactly how he'd do it, but he'd
find a way to protect her dignity.

He headed for the door. "Thanks for your help," he
said to her back. "I better talk to Carrie."

The dishes stopped rattling, but Pearl didn't turn.
"She's upstairs. Everyone went home."

Matt stopped at the door. He and Pearl were alone.
The serving girl would be back, but they could sit in the
dining room. They could share a piece of chocolate cake.

He could talk to her in the candlelight and no one would know, which was why he had to leave. He knew from experience that secrets had dangerous consequences. "Tell Carrie I said thanks for supper."

"Of course."

As he opened the door, she pivoted. "Wait. I have something for Sarah."

She dried her hands, then cut two generous slices of cake and put them on a plate. After wrapping the dessert with a towel, she handed it to him. "There's a piece of you, too."

"Thank you." With the cake in hand, he paused at the door. "Good night, Pearl."

"Good night, Matt."

He shut the door behind him, but he couldn't block the echo of her voice in his mind. He'd be hearing it when he ate that chocolate cake, and he'd be touching that blue ribbon in his dreams. As soon as he could, he'd square things with Carrie, but then what? He couldn't deny his feelings for Pearl, but neither could he court a preacher's daughter. With the cake in hand, Matt left with his stomach in a knot. He had some thinking to do, and he'd doubtlessly be doing it all night long.

Pearl helped the serving girl clean the kitchen, then she climbed the stairs and tapped softly on Carrie's door. The quiet sobbing ceased, but Carrie didn't call for her to come in. Knowing the need for privacy, Pearl extinguished the wall sconce and went to her room. There she lit a lamp, checked on Toby and sat at the vanity.

Her eyes went to the ribbon above her ear, the one Matt had touched. She'd ignored him all through supper, but then the cream puff had skittered and she'd seen the shock on his face. She'd wanted to laugh with him, and that's when she'd admitted a frightening truth. If it weren't for Carrie, she'd be willing to go down a dangerous path.

What if...

She closed her eyes to block the fearful yearning, but she saw Matt's face. She recalled his Texas drawl and the minty scent of his skin. From the day they'd met, she'd fought her feelings. She'd prayed. She'd stifled her thoughts and denied her dreams. She'd done everything she could to fight her fear of men *and* to protect Carrie, but she couldn't stop her heart from leaping when Matt looked into her eyes. She couldn't stop herself from yearning for the things she deeply feared. A husband... affection...a father for Toby.

Pearl wept into her palms. Her friends at Swan's Nest would have understood. Adie had lived with a secret and knew the cost. Mary knew how to fake a smile. Bessie, a nurse, would have made tea and listened to her woes. Caroline, the victim of a forbidden love, would have cried with her.

Lifting her face, she stared at her reflection in the mirror. Tomorrow she'd be a friend to Carrie. But how? What could she say? She'd stopped Matt from talking, but she knew what he'd been about to say. He didn't have feelings for Carrie and never would.

Would her cousin accept the truth? Pearl hoped so, but love couldn't be easily denied. She knew, because she felt the seeds of it growing in her own heart. The seeds had to be plucked out, so she lifted her hand to her hair and loosened the ribbon. She pulled it free, laid it flat on the vanity, then rolled it tight. As the silk warmed with her touch, she placed it in the back of the drawer, far from the ribbons she wore every day.

She'd never forget this night. When he'd touched her

hair, she'd almost swooned and not from panic. The panic had come an instant later. Had it started because of his touch? Or when she thought of Carrie? She didn't know. The way things stood, she'd never find out. It hurt, but a small thought gave her comfort. Because of Matt's touch, the ribbons were special again.

Chapter Twelve

Matt set the cake on the counter and asked Mrs. Holcombe to stay a few more hours. The revelation about Carrie and the private moment with Pearl had left him tense, and he couldn't shake a feeling of dread. If the Golden Order planned to strike, tonight seemed likely. Full of Saturday night revelers, Ferguson Street made an appealing target. When Mrs. Holcombe agreed to stay, he changed clothes and climbed back on his horse.

As he rode across town, the wind sent leaves skittering down the street. The air was rarely still in Cheyenne, and tonight the rush matched his mood. Pearl had him all stirred up. So did the black derby Jasper had removed from the display window. A message had been sent, and Matt was worried. With each attack on the Silver Slipper, the G.O. had become bolder. Broken glass had become broken bones. Neither could he forget Jed Jones. The man's thievery had led to a broken neck.

Brokenness… Matt knew all about it. Shuddering, he thought back to the night his own life had been shattered. Good intentions had gone awry and he'd done the unthinkable on a humid night in Virginia. Riding down the street now, he recalled arriving at Amos McGuckin's farm with his men. He remembered the haze of the smoky torches, the orange glow against an inky sky. He blinked and smelled smoke. He coughed, and his eyes burned. It was too real to be a dream. Fire bells cut through the night and he knew…the Golden Order had gone from breaking bones to burning down buildings.

Six blocks away the sky took on an orange glow. Matt kneed his gelding into a gallop. If he hadn't been at Carrie's party, he'd have been patrolling Ferguson Street when the fire started. He might have seen the riders running off at a gallop.

Nothing struck fear in the citizens of Cheyenne like fire. The wooden buildings stood side by side and were as dry as tinder. As the crowd in the street thickened, he slowed his horse. A block away he saw the Silver Slipper being swallowed alive by flames. Like an animal breathing its last, the building roared as the roof collapsed into flaming rubble. He hoped no one was inside, because there would be no survivors.

As he passed through the crowd, he spotted a cluster of women from Scottie's place. Scottie, still bruised and using a cane, stood apart from them. A black patch covered his damaged eye. Matt rode over to the saloon owner and dismounted. "What happened?"

Scottie stared at the flames. "They killed her."

Matt's belly knotted. "Who?"

"Katy."

An oath spewed from his lips. Where was God when the Golden Order set the fire? Why hadn't he saved the sweet, innocent woman who only wanted to go home?

Scottie pounded the ground with his cane. "She didn't deserve to die."

"I liked her," Matt said simply. "I'm sorry."

"You're *sorry?*" The female voice came out of the dark.

He turned and saw Lizzy sweeping in his direction. Ashes were clinging to her skimpy gown, and soot had painted shadows on her face. Matt didn't blame her for being angry. Being sorry wouldn't bring Katy back to life anymore than Matt could change what had happened in Virginia. He steeled himself for a lambasting, maybe a slap across the jaw.

Lizzy shuddered. "I couldn't find her. I looked *everywhere*. She-she—" The woman burst into tears.

The women crowded around her like a flock of nervous birds. A scrawny blonde glared at him from over her shoulder. "We were already out when we saw her in the window. She must have gone back for Scottie, but I'd helped him downstairs."

Scottie surveyed the pile of smoldering timbers. "I'd like to kill those—"

"Me, too!" Lizzy cried.

Matt felt the same way, but he wouldn't give in to the anger. "I figure this is arson."

Scottie snorted. "Good work, Deputy."

Matt ignored the sarcasm. "Did you see anything?"

"What do you think?" Scottie stared at him with his one good eye.

Matt turned to the women. "Ladies?"

A blonde raised her voice. "I saw them."

"Who?" Matt asked.

"The men in black derbies." She started to weep. "They had torches and were threatening to burn us out. Sparks were flying everywhere. I ran to get the others... and Katy." The girl broke into sobs. Lizzy hugged her tight and glared at Matt.

"What are you going to do to stop them?" she demanded. "Katy was just plain good. She was going home. She—"

Matt cut her off. "I know."

A redhead glared at the remains of the Silver Slipper. "I lost everything. The picture of my baby—" She burst into tears.

"They should hang for this!" Lizzy cried.

Matt tended to agree. Anyone playing with fire on a windy night deserved to swing high and fast. The thought gave him pause. If he wasn't careful, he'd become what he loathed.

His gaze narrowed to the dying embers. An innocent woman had died a horrible death, and it had happened on his watch. With his blood flowing hot and bitter, he got down to business. Tonight that meant linking the men in black derbies to the members of the Golden Order. The masked riders had disappeared into the night, but someone could be observing on their behalf.

Matt surveyed the crowd. Most of the men had joined the bucket brigade, but they were losing the battle with the spreading flames. A second saloon had turned into a flaming skeleton, and the dance hall next to it would soon follow. Matt spotted the fire marshal, Bill "Crawdad" Pine, manning the steam engine. The city had invested a fortune in the fancy equipment, but the wagon had arrived too late to save the Silver Slipper. Judging by the wind, the rest of the block would suffer the same fate. All the businesses were of a tawdry nature, but that didn't ease Matt's conscience. An innocent woman had died tonight. Considering the extent of the blaze, he feared others had died with her.

He studied every face in the crowd. Most of the people were strangers or regulars on Ferguson Street, but a particular man—Chester Gates—didn't belong. The banker lived on the other side of town. Why was he speaking to the fire marshal? Looking at him now, Matt recalled his interest in the prime land purchased by Scottie Fife. If the G.O. forced Scottie to sell the property, Gates would cash in. Sensing trouble, Matt led his horse toward the men and called a greeting.

Crawdad answered in the Louisiana drawl that had earned him his nickname. Matt nodded at Gates but spoke to the fire chief. "I hear this is arson."

"I'd say so," Crawdad remarked.

Gates coughed against the smoke but said nothing.

Matt watched him carefully. "A girl died tonight. Whoever set the fire will stand trial for murder."

"Murder?" Gates had a face of stone, but his voice betrayed his nervousness.

Matt decided to push. "You got here fast, Mr. Gates. Did you see anything? Maybe men in black derbies?"

"Not a thing, Deputy." The banker schooled his features. "I was working late. I heard the fire bells and came to help. You can't have too many men on a bucket brigade."

Liar.

The banker rubbed his chin. "Any idea who did this?"

"Not a one." Actually Matt had five. Their names were Chester Gates, Jasper Kling and three other members of the Golden Order.

"Fires are serious in this city." Gates glanced at Crawdad. "That new steam engine seems to have worked."

"It's a help," the chief replied.

The talk turned to the need for more wells and pipes from the river. The shift away from who had started the fire seemed natural, but Matt's instincts said otherwise. Most people quizzed him unmercifully when it came to crime. Gates didn't want to talk to him, but he'd come to see the Silver Slipper burn. Matt felt certain the G.O. had started the fire, but he couldn't take action without hard evidence. He hoped that would change when he spoke with Tobias. Tomorrow was Sunday. Matt didn't attend church, but Tobias did and so did Dan. If Dan happened to run into the minister, the two of them could talk. It was late, but his friend wouldn't mind being woken up considering the need.

Matt said goodbye to Crawdad and Gates, then rode to Dan's place. He knocked on the door, calling his friend's name so he wouldn't come out shooting.

Bleary-eyed and haphazardly dressed, Dan invited him inside. "You better have a good reason for being here."

"I do." Matt tossed his hat on a chair. "The Silver Slipper just burned to the ground."

Dan came fully alert. "I'd call that a good reason."

"Five other saloons went with it."

He winced. "Any deaths?"

Matt told him about Katy. "I'm tired of waiting for a break. You're going to church tomorrow to talk to Tobias Oliver."

Dan shook his head. "*You're* going."

"No way."

"Come on, Wiley." Dan raked his hand through his hair. "You know the man better than I do. Bite the bullet and sit through a sermon."

Not a week passed that Dan didn't try to prod Matt into taking Sarah to church. It was good-natured jesting and Matt didn't mind, but he'd drawn a line for himself. No way would he sit through a sermon. "You know my answer to *that*."

"I do," Dan replied. "I also see the perfect place to speak with Reverend Oliver."

Dan had a point. Matt hated the thought of hymns and hallelujahs, but he'd do anything to stop the Golden

Order. He also liked the idea of seeing Pearl. He had no right to such a thought, but holding Toby had stirred him up in powerful ways. The boy made him want to be a father again, to have a son who'd maybe someday wear a badge or be a soldier. Even more important, Matt knew how much a boy needed a man to teach him things. Toby had his grandfather, but the old man wouldn't live forever. No one did.

As the thought settled, Matt flashed to the fire and the need to stop the Golden Order. "I'll go to church," he said to Dan. "But just to see Tobias."

Dan grinned. "Don't look so scared. God's not going to fall off his throne at the sight of you in church."

Matt glared at him.

Dan's expression hardened in return. "Talking to Tobias is smart. We agree on *that*."

Matt heard the dangling thought and scowled. "What *don't* we agree on?"

"The way you treated Carrie at supper." Dan's voice lost its sleepy pitch. "You laughed at her, and then you walked out."

Matt stared in disbelief. "The Golden Order is burning down buildings and you're worried about my *manners?*"

"I'm telling you to wise up about Carrie."

"Me?" Matt couldn't believe his ears. "You're the one who likes her."

"But *you're* the one she wants."

Matt saw an answer to both their problems. "So change her mind. Sweep her off her feet."

Dan scowled at him.

"I'm serious." Sweet Carrie and Iowa Dan.... They fit like bread and butter. "Ask her to supper. I bet she'll say yes."

At the sight of his friend's gaping mouth, Matt almost

laughed. He knew the feeling, because he felt that way about Pearl. It was like standing on a bluff looking at rich land that stretched for miles. It could be his, but only if he took a chance. Could he be a husband again? He didn't know, but the thought wouldn't go away.

Dan eyed him thoughtfully. "Do you think she'd say yes?"

"You won't know unless you ask."

"I suppose." Dan wandered to the window. "Just promise me one thing."

"What is it?"

"That you'll be gentle with her." He turned and looked at Matt. Dan had a soft side, and it showed. "After you ran off to the kitchen, I tried to help her. She cares for you, Wiley. Why, I don't know. But she does."

Matt had seen the look, too. "I didn't know—"

"You do now." Dan's voice came out rough. "If you hurt her, we'll be having words."

Matt had hurt enough women already. "I'll speak to her as soon as I can, and I'll be gentle about it." Maybe he'd see her tomorrow at church. Exactly how he'd approach Carrie, Matt didn't know. Did a man tell a woman he wasn't going to say what he hadn't ever said? The thought gave him a headache.

Dan heaved a sigh. When he looked at Matt, his brows hitched together. "This Golden Order mess has me worried."

"Me, too."

"Reverend Oliver will be at risk. If Jasper suspects us, so will Pearl."

"I know."

"What are you going to tell him?"

"Everything." Matt shared Dan's fear. "The man deserves to know what he'd be getting into. If he has any doubts, we'll look elsewhere."

A smile tipped on Dan's lips. "So you're really going to church?"

"I'm going to see Tobias," Matt corrected.

"You'll see Pearl, too."

"So?"

"You like her, don't you?"

"It doesn't matter what I like," Matt countered. "She doesn't belong with a heathen like me."

Dan laughed out loud. "Who says you're a heathen?"

"I do."

His expression turned thoughtful. "For a heathen, you spend a lot of time being mad at God."

"I do not." Except he felt the old fury now. If God was good, why had Katy burned to death? Why hadn't the Almighty stopped Matt and his men from lynching Amos McGuckin? Matt knew what *he'd* do if he were God. He'd erase that night in Virginia. He'd change Pearl's past, too. He'd give her Toby, but she'd have a husband who loved her. And Sarah would have a mother who'd never leave.

He glared at Dan. "I don't want to talk about this stuff."

His friend shrugged. "Suit yourself."

"I will."

If he could stop the Golden Order, maybe he could forgive himself for having once been like them. And if he could forgive himself, maybe he could forgive God. One thought led to another and he imagined sleeping like a baby and waking up with Pearl at his side. A wife…a mother for Sarah…a father for Toby. Tomorrow he'd go to church and he'd see Pearl. He couldn't help but hope she'd be wearing his ribbons.

Chapter Thirteen

Pearl tapped on Carrie's door, waited for her cousin to answer and stepped into the stuffy bedroom. Propped on pillows, Carrie looked as pale as the bed sheets. Pearl sat on the edge of the mattress. "Church starts in an hour," she said gently. "You need to get dressed."

Carrie sniffed. "I can't."

"Tea will help."

"*Nothing* will help." She blew her nose into a hankie. "I didn't sleep a wink. There's no way I can manage a Sunday school class."

Carrie and Amy shared responsibility for teaching the girls. "They need you, cousin."

"I know." She sighed. "Would you fill in for me?"

Pearl loved the idea, but she couldn't let Carrie wallow in self-pity. "You'll feel better if you go to church."

Carrie dabbed at her eyes. "I can't do it. Not today."

Pearl understood the desire to hide. She'd walked around with a pregnant belly and no husband. People, especially children, could be cruel. If Carrie lost her composure at church, people would gossip. She couldn't hide forever, but she didn't have to face her problems today. Tomorrow would be soon enough.

Pearl absently smoothed a wrinkle out of the sheet. "Do you remember when we first met? You told me not to cry because I'd get puffy?"

Carrie nodded.

"You're more than puffy," Pearl said gently. "You're as sodden as Toby gets."

Her cousin sniffed. "I'm a mess."

"Don't worry. I'll help Amy."

"Thank you!" She gripped Pearl's hand. "I don't know what I'd do without you."

"You'd be fine."

"I'd be miserable," she insisted. Biting her lip, she gave Pearl a look full of love. "I don't know what I'd do without you, cousin. I can talk to you about anything."

Pearl felt the same way…almost. She'd never tell Carrie about the ribbons, but she wanted her cousin to know she'd had a private conversation with Matt. "We need to talk about last night."

Carrie groaned.

"I know it's hard," Pearl said. "But someday you'll laugh about it."

"Maybe, but will Matt?"

"I think so." Pearl thought of the ribbons. Would he forget touching her hair? She wouldn't, but she had to try.

Carrie set a wadded hankie on the nightstand. "I tried so hard, but he ignored me all evening. He kept looking across the table at—at—"

Pearl's heart stopped.

"At Dan!"

Blood stained Pearl's cheeks, but she had no reason to be ashamed. She couldn't stop her wayward feelings, but she'd behaved honorably.

Carrie sighed. "Maybe he was worried about something."

"Maybe."

"I just don't know," Carrie said with a moan. "I thought Matt and I had a lot in common, but last night he seemed like a stranger."

Pearl refused to hide her unexpected meeting with Matt. "I talked to him afterward. We were in the kitchen."

"What did he say?"

Pearl wanted to protect her cousin, but she couldn't distort the truth. "I don't think he realized how you felt until last night."

"Really?"

"I'm sure of it." Pearl described the conversation without mentioning the ribbons or the cake. Some things were private. Others had to be said with the hope of sparing her cousin more hurt. "He likes you, Carrie. But he doesn't seem…interested."

Tears welled in her eyes. "I feel like a complete fool."

"You're not."

"Yes, I am." She stared at the ceiling. "I still care for him."

"I'm sorry. I know it hurts."

Carrie's faced stiffened into a mask. She bit her lips, but the pain showed in her eyes. "I need…a moment. Would you leave me alone for a bit?"

"Of course."

Pearl headed for the door. As she turned the knob, Carrie called out to her. "Wait! I didn't ask about you."

"That's all right."

"But I want to know." Carrie put on a brave smile. "Who did you like best? Grant or Dan?"

The truth froze on Pearl's tongue. She liked Matt. "I'm not interested in courting. You know that."

Carrie hugged her knees. "*I* like Dan. After Matt ran out, he made everyone feel at ease. Even me."

"He's nice."

A smile touched Carrie's eyes. "I think he likes you."

"That's funny," Pearl answered. "*I* think he likes *you*."

"*Me?*"

Pearl saw a chance to boost Carrie's spirits. "He had his eyes on you all night. Didn't you notice?"

"I was too busy watching Matt. And Matt was watching…" Carrie's eyes turned into saucers. "Matt wasn't watching Dan! He was watching *you*."

"Oh, Carrie." Pearl could barely breathe. "He's yours. I know that. I'd never— It wouldn't be right. I'd—"

Carrie leaped out of bed and ran to Pearl. For a terrible moment, Pearl thought her cousin would slap her face. She hadn't meant to get in the way of Matt's affections. Truly, she hadn't. "Carrie, I—"

"Oh, Pearl." Just like the day they'd met, Carrie wrapped her arms around Pearl's waist and hugged her. Emotions swamped them both. Upset. Anger. Jealousy… and love. Their feelings collided and mixed until Carrie stepped back.

"Listen to me, Pearl."

"I'm so sorry. I—"

"This isn't your fault."

"But—"

"*It's not your fault,*" Carrie repeated. "I know what you did for me. You didn't want to have the party, but you put up with it for me. When you asked Matt to lunch, you did it for me."

Pearl bit her lip. "That's true."

"Every time you've had the chance, you've pointed him in my direction." Carrie's face clouded with disappointment. "If Matt doesn't have feelings for me, I'd be a fool to want him for a husband."

"But you care for him."

"I do." Tears welled in her eyes. "I care enough to want him to be happy."

"Oh, Carrie."

"I want you to be happy, too. Now go." She sounded unsteady. "This hurts too much right now. I need to be alone."

"But—"

"Please." The word broke into pieces.

Pearl knew how it felt to fall apart. Aching for Carrie, she left the room and closed the door. As soon as she stepped into the hall, pressure built in her throat and chest. She'd expected Carrie to berate her. Instead she'd offered compassion. If Carrie gave her blessing, Pearl could wear Matt's ribbons.

What if...

The thought stopped her cold. She had no business thinking of Matt as more than a friend. Even if Carrie's feelings for him changed, or if she stepped back, Pearl still lived with a profound fear of intimacy.

Shaking inside, she hurried to her room. She had to finish getting ready for church, so she sat at the vanity and looked at herself in the mirror. She'd already put her hair in a braid and wrapped it tight. Today it pulled at her scalp and gave her a headache. Feeling confused, she touched the braid. For the first time in a year, she wanted to be pretty. She didn't dare touch Matt's ribbons, but she had others.

Pleased and nervous, she opened the drawer and selected a strand of yellow satin. Instead of putting it in her hair, she looped it around the crown of her hat, tied a fancy bow and pinned the hat in place. It felt good to feel pretty and even better to feel brave. Satisfied, she changed Toby into a blue baby gown, then carried him downstairs where her father was waiting with the baby carriage.

Tobias smiled at her. "You look lovely, princess."

"Thank you." Today she felt like a princess.

"Where's Carrie?"

"She's not well."

"I see." Tobias didn't need an explanation. He'd witnessed the cream puff fiasco. "I hope she feels better soon."

"Me, too."

She put Toby in the carriage, and they left the house. As she expected, her father set a fast pace. Tobias refused to *ever* be late to church. Pearl was secretly pleased. His face had a healthy glow and he wasn't out of breath. She would never understand the symptoms that made her worry about his health. They came and went like changes in the weather.

Enjoying the moment, she smiled at him. "I'm excited about teaching."

"I would be, too."

Her father loved being a minister and had led Colfax Avenue Church for many years. He'd given it up to accompany her to Cheyenne. "You miss it, don't you?"

"I do, but I'm slowing down."

"Not today, you're not!" Pearl laughed as they raced past a bungalow. They were practically running.

Tobias got a faraway look in his eyes. "I used to charge into church like a man on fire. Now I'm sitting on my laurels. I'm useless."

"Papa! Don't say that."

"It's true, Pearl. What am I good for these days?"

Looking up at him, she spoke in a scolding tone. "For one thing, you're the world's best grandpa. Toby and I need you."

"If you say so."

"I do."

He patted her arm, but she was still worried about him. Tobias couldn't handle rigorous work, but he needed to do more than watch his grandson. As they turned the corner, she saw the church and felt hopeful. People were milling by the stone steps and speaking excitedly. Pearl spotted Amy and her mother. As they approached, Amy waved. "Did you hear? Half of Ferguson Street burned down last night."

Pearl shuddered. "What happened?"

Amy told them about the devastation and the suspicion of arson. When she finished, her voice turned somber. "A cleaning girl died. Her name was Katy. Sometimes she came here to worship."

Pearl had seen Katy looking in the window at Jasper's store. He'd shooed her away, then related a story about a smudge on a hairbrush. He'd told Pearl to turn away anyone from Ferguson Street.

Mrs. Hinn tsked her tongue. "The men who set that fire have to be stopped."

"I quite agree," Tobias replied.

"Miss Pearl!"

She turned and saw Sarah holding her daddy's hand. Pearl waggled her fingers in greeting, then let her eyes drift to Matt. He was dressed for church in the coat she'd wiped clean. She hadn't expected to see him. Would he think of last night and touching the ribbon? It was too soon for such thoughts, but she couldn't help it.

His eyes met hers and he removed his hat. "Good morning, Pearl."

"Good morning, Deputy."

As he greeted Tobias and the Hinns, Sarah tugged on Pearl's dress. "Do you like my hair?"

She saw a perfect braid. "You look lovely."

The child spotted the baby carriage and squealed. "You brought Toby!"

"That's right."

"He's wearing blue," she said with authority. "That means he's a boy."

When Toby made a noise for attention, Pearl picked him up. If people wanted to judge her, so be it. She proudly showed Toby to Sarah, who thought he was even more special than Annie, her doll. Pearl didn't mean to glance at Matt, but her eyes had a will of their own. The pleasure in his gaze stole her breath. So did the lazy smile on his lips. His eyes flicked to her hat. Was he looking for a blue ribbon? She didn't know, but he frowned slightly at the yellow bow on her hat.

Oh, the fun of making a man wonder! Pearl had to suppress a smile. She couldn't remember ever feeling this way.

Mrs. Hinn broke into her thoughts. "Tell us, Deputy. Is it true those men in derby hats set that fire?"

"Yes, ma'am," he answered. "There were witnesses."

Tobias scowled. "Such a tragedy."

Pearl thought about the hat Jasper sometimes put in the window. In the time she'd worked for him, he hadn't sold a single one. Considering his clientele—business-men and railroad executives—the coincidence seemed odd. Was there a connection to the men who burned down the Silver Slipper? It seemed likely. Later she'd mention her worry to Matt.

Amy broke into her thoughts. "The whole city could have gone up in flames. One girl died, but there could have been more."

Mrs. Hinn huffed. "Arson's no way to fight sin!"

Pearl's gaze stayed on Matt. Instead of looking at

Amy, he had his eye on her father. "What do you think, Reverend?"

Tobias stood a bit taller. "I find Ferguson Street as distasteful as any God-fearing man, but burning it to the ground won't solve the problem. As the saying goes, 'Hate the sin, love the sinner.'"

Amy and her mother started talking at the same time. As Tobias answered them, Matt turned to Pearl. "I don't see Carrie."

"She's ill."

"I'm sorry to hear it." Except he didn't sound sorry. He sounded relieved. "I'll see her at school, then."

He held her gaze for a moment too long, a sign he wanted her to understand his intentions. Tomorrow he'd clear the air with Carrie. Before Pearl could ponder what that meant for her, the church bell rang a familiar call to worship. She put Toby in the carriage and told Amy she'd be taking Carrie's place. With Sarah in tow, they left for Sunday school class.

As they walked away, she heard Matt speaking to her father. "We have something in common, sir. Perhaps we could talk after the service?"

"Of course."

Why would Matt want to speak with her father? Pearl had no idea, and she wouldn't ask. Once a minister, always a minister. Tobias wouldn't breathe a word of his conversation with Matt. Unless... She thought of the way Matt had looked at her today. Was the conversation about her? Did he want to court her? At the thought, she could barely breathe.

What if... The question dangled like a ripe apple. Afraid to touch it, she walked with Amy and Sarah to teach Sunday school.

Chapter Fourteen

On Monday afternoon, Matt picked up Sarah from school and took her to Mrs. Holcombe's house. He'd been hoping for a word with Carrie, but she'd left before he could signal her. He intended to tell her, as gently as possible, that he appreciated her friendship but had no romantic inclinations.

Pearl presented a different challenge. The yellow ribbon had irked him. He wanted her to wear *his* ribbons. The yellow bow looked pretty, but the blue ones stood for something between them. Just what, Matt didn't know. He only knew he had to make things right with Carrie before he thought too much about Pearl. Not only did he owe it to Carrie, but he also wanted to spare Pearl the awkwardness of knowing the truth when Carrie didn't.

Eager to get the job done, he decided to visit Carrie at her house. First, though, he wanted to speak with Dan about his conversation with Tobias. Not only had the minister agreed to help, but he also had a fire in his belly for the cause of justice. It matched the one that burned in Matt, causing him to wonder why Tobias felt so strongly. He'd wanted to ask, but questions would lead to more questions. If Matt quizzed Tobias, the man would quiz him back. Matt had no desire to tell anyone in Cheyenne about his mistakes.

When he reached the sheriff's office, he opened the door and instantly smelled trouble. Instead of stale coffee, he smelled sugar and spice. His gaze landed on a plate of baked goods on his desk. Expecting to see Dan, he turned to his friend's desk. He saw Dan all right. And Carrie. They were seated across from each other. Matt had to make himself clear to her, and he had to do it today.

"Good afternoon," he said as he hung up his hat. "I hope Sarah's not in trouble."

Carrie stood and smiled. "Not at all."

She gave Dan a look. The two of them must have done some talking, because Dan headed for the door. "I'll give you two some privacy."

Matt appreciated the gesture, but being alone with Carrie bothered him. What if she started to cry? He hated it when women cried. What if she screeched like Bettina? Thoughts of his former wife reminded him that he'd been a rotten husband. He was doing Carrie a favor by keeping his distance. He'd be wise to do the same favor for Pearl.

As the door closed, Carrie stood. "I need to explain myself, Matt. I hope you don't mind."

"Not at all."

"About last night…" She bit her lip. "I'm afraid I made a fool of myself."

He hadn't expected her candor. Relieved to face the awkwardness, he saw a chance to do right by her. If he struck the right tone, he could save Carrie's pride. He indicated the chair by Dan's desk. "Have a seat. I need to say a few words."

"No, you don't." She stayed on her feet. "I understand."

"You're a good woman, Carrie. It's just—"

"I know." She managed a smile. "I didn't realize until last night, but Pearl's a very lucky woman."

Had he been that transparent? Apparently, although he didn't consider Pearl lucky. He'd ruined Bettina's life. He liked Pearl a lot, but she'd have been wise to run from him.

Carrie raised her chin. "I'm admittedly interfering here, but I want you to know something about her."

Matt refused to talk behind her back. "I don't—"

"She's a wonderful woman," Carrie insisted. "I know she was standoffish at the party, but she has a good reason. If you talk to her, you'll see how sweet she is. She loves children, and…" She bit her lip. "I'm babbling again."

As long as he lived, Matt wouldn't understand women. He'd expected Carrie to throw a tantrum, to blame him for breaking her heart. Instead she'd come to fight for Pearl. The gesture touched him more than anything she could have said or done. It had taken courage and generosity, a generosity of spirit he didn't often see in females. Bettina hadn't possessed it. Carrie had it in abundance and so did Pearl.

A thought came to mind and it wouldn't let go. Maybe he hadn't been such a bad husband after all. Maybe he'd married the wrong woman. He'd have stuck it out forever if Bettina hadn't left, but he'd realized shortly after the wedding they were mismatched. She hadn't been strong enough for marriage to a lawman, and he'd been unable to compromise more than he had. Their marriage had failed, but not because of him.

Carrie managed a dignified smile. "I brought cookies to make up for the cream puff. They're from Pearl and me. You can share with Dan."

Her kindness touched him. "Thank you."

"You're welcome," she said.

"I mean for more than the cookies." With things settled between them, Matt could be generous, too. "You've been a friend to Pearl and a wonderful teacher for Sarah. Today you've been a friend to me, too. I appreciate it."

"It's the right thing to do." She looked close to tears, so he said nothing. Today she'd given everyone their dignity. She deserved to keep hers.

He lifted a cookie off the plate and took a bite. "It's good," he said with a full mouth. "Oatmeal raisin is Dan's favorite."

"He just told me."

Good for Dan. Matt decided to give his friend some help. "He likes cream puffs, too. His mama makes them at Christmas."

"So do I."

Matt took the interest in her eyes as a good sign. As Carrie headed for the door, he went ahead of her and held it wide. As she passed, she gave him a last lingering look. "Goodbye, Matt."

"Goodbye, Carrie."

As she passed through the door, he saw Dan watching them from down the street. Matt had a good mind to shout at him to walk Carrie home. If Dan didn't ask her, he didn't deserve to call himself a man.

Carrie saw Dan, too.

And Dan saw Carrie.

They met in the middle of the boardwalk, exchanged a few words and then walked together in the same direction. Good, Matt thought. They were fine people who deserved happiness. Pleased, he stepped back into the office and wrapped some cookies in a napkin for Sarah. Not only had Carrie given her blessing to Matt's interest in Pearl, but she'd also opened his eyes to the truth about his first marriage. It had failed, but not because of him.

His mind went down a road that ended with a mother for Sarah, a woman with blond hair and blue eyes that sent beams of light into a dark world. That, he realized, was the problem. Pearl's heart brimmed with love for God and goodwill toward people. Matt simmered with bitterness and loathing. Pearl needed a man who shared her faith, not a heathen like himself.

Even so, the longing in his heart couldn't be denied. Could he become the man she deserved? He didn't know, but he saw a ray of hope. If he could stop the Golden Order, maybe he could forgive himself for what he'd done. Maybe he could stop hating the Almighty for allowing good men to go bad. If Matt could sit in church without knotting his fists, he could court Pearl without guilt. Everything depended on his ability to stop the Golden Order, and that mission depended on Tobias Oliver.

Matt saw a certain irony. For a man who didn't care for God or ministers, he was in a peculiar state of need. Whether he liked it or not, he had to depend on Tobias. He could only hope the man was more reliable than his God.

Pearl was arranging women's shoes when her father walked into Jasper's shop. It was Wednesday. He'd visited yesterday, too. Instead of chatting with her, he'd struck up a conversation with Jasper about the fire on Ferguson Street. Today they planned to have lunch together. Pearl found the friendship troubling. Her father needed friends, but he had nothing in common with the shopkeeper. When she'd mentioned his visit to the shop over supper, he'd brushed off her concern and changed the subject.

Tonight she'd speak to him again. In the few weeks

she'd worked for Jasper, she'd lost what little respect she had for the man. Only the paycheck kept her working for him.

Her father offered a smile. "Hello, princess."

"Hello, Papa."

"Is Jasper here?" He patted his belly. "I'm ready for lunch."

Jasper stepped out of his office. "It's good to see you, Reverend." The men shook hands as if they were old friends. "You're right on time. I appreciate punctuality."

"I do, too."

So did Pearl, but she didn't watch the clock like Jasper. The one on the wall read 11:55 a.m. He'd be back at exactly one o'clock.

Jasper indicated the door. "I hope you don't mind. I've invited Chester Gates to join us."

"Not at all," Tobias replied.

Pearl respected Mr. Gates even less than she respected Jasper. He'd visited the store twice. Both times he'd acted as if they'd never met. She could understand that he'd voted his conscience, but ignoring her was rude.

As the men left, she went back to arranging the shoes. She placed the first pair on the shelf and aligned the toes an inch from the edge. Jasper insisted on perfection. Once he'd measured her work with a ruler. As she arranged the next pair, the bell over the door jangled. She turned and saw Matt. As he took off his hat, his eyes darted around the store. "Is Jasper around?"

"He just left with my father."

The tension left his face. "Good. I'd like a word with you."

Her heart sped up. "About what?"

"The cookies."

Pearl felt the warmth of a blush. Last night she'd had

a heart-to-heart with Carrie. Not only had Carrie given Pearl her blessing when it came to courting Matt, but she'd also decided to play Cupid. Without telling Pearl in advance, she'd visited Matt and delivered cookies as a gift from both of them. Pearl had protested that he'd get the wrong idea. Carrie had looked at her as if she'd lost her mind, then she'd told Pearl to be brave. Considering Carrie's graciousness, how could Pearl do otherwise?

Looking at Matt now, she felt a quickening of her pulse. "Carrie baked them."

"I know," he said. "She came to see me."

"She told me."

"Just so you know, things are square between us." His eyes took on a twinkle. "Maybe she'll take a shine to Dan."

"I hope so!" Pearl could easily hope for love for Carrie, but what about herself? Looking at Matt, she felt a quickening in her pulse. Should she encourage him? What did a woman do when a man interested her? Blinking, she thought of her offer to braid Sarah's hair. Matt had mastered the art, but there were other things a little girl needed to know.

With her cheeks warm, she smiled. "How's Sarah?"

"Just fine."

"She's growing up fast." Butterflies swirled in Pearl's belly. "I seem to recall I offered to braid her hair. You've gotten good at it, but maybe I could show her a different way to fix it."

Matt's expression didn't change, but the air in the shop turned thick. Pearl felt foolish. "Never mind. I was just thinking—"

"No." He waved off her objection. "She'd like that. She likes Toby, too. Maybe we could all go for pie after church."

He looked as surprised at the invitation as she was. Were they talking about their children or the possibility of more than friendship? She searched for the answer in Matt's eyes and found confusion and hope, a mix that matched her troubled thoughts. She had feelings for him, but she also had doubts about her ability to be a wife. She felt safe with Matt, but until now he'd belonged to Carrie. The thought of being courted by a man still terrified her, and those feelings came in a rush.

Her throat closed with apprehension. Abruptly she turned back to the shoes. "I can't. Not this Sunday." *Not ever.*

"Maybe during the week," he suggested.

Pearl shook her head.

Silence hung like a sheet, but it did nothing to hide her nervousness. Her pulse started to race, and she landed back in Denver in Franklin Dean's buggy. If she'd never been attacked, she could say yes to Matt. She wouldn't have this fear. She wouldn't be trembling as she arranged shoes in a store owned by a hateful man.

Matt touched her shoulder. "Are you all right?"

"I-I'm fine."

How had she gotten into this mess? She didn't want to discuss her fears with Matt. "If you'll excuse me, I have to get back to work."

As she nudged a shoe into place, Matt touched her shoulder. His touch couldn't have been gentler, but she startled like a deer and bumped into the shelf behind her. She would *not* let Matt see the painful memories, the fearful reaction she had to fight. She turned quickly back to the shoes. She moved one, then another. When Matt didn't budge, she finally looked at him. "Do you need something else?"

She saw knowledge in his eyes and felt transparent,

as if her fears were marbles on display in a fragile glass bowl. Slowly, giving her time to retreat, he raised one hand and touched the braid wrapped tightly around her head, mimicking the touch they'd shared in the kitchen. She told herself to stay still, but her legs stepped back on their own. She forced herself to look at him, but she couldn't find her voice.

Matt stared into her eyes. "I think I understand. You're not over being attacked, right?"

"Yes," she murmured.

"You live with bad memories." The lines around his mouth tightened into crevasses and his drawl thickened. "It's like walking through a field of gopher holes. If you step the wrong way, you fall and you break all over again."

Looking into his eyes, she saw scars as vivid as her own. "You know what it's like."

"I do."

Aching for them both, she raised her chin. "I hope we can still be friends."

"Sure," he said gently. "I'd like that."

She'd told the truth, but it tasted like a lie. She wanted more than friendship from Matt. She wanted to give him everything he needed. She just didn't believe she could. When she took a breath, so did he. He mentioned the Indian summer, and she agreed the weather had been too warm. She asked about Sarah, and he told a funny story. When they'd both relaxed, he said, "I better get going."

Pearl felt a fresh pang of loss. Someday Matt would marry, and Sarah would finally have a mother. Pearl couldn't be that woman, but she could brighten the child's day.

"Wait," she said. "I have something for Sarah."

She went to the storeroom and knelt beside a newly

arrived crate from New York. It held an assortment of chapbooks. She picked out a story about a shepherd boy and took it to Matt. Later she'd put money in the till to pay for it.

She handed him the gift. "This is for Sarah."

"Thank you. She'll enjoy it."

They traded goodbyes and Matt left. Pearl intended to go immediately to the cash box to pay, but two women walked in as Matt was leaving. They needed help with draperies. After they made a purchase, Mrs. Gates came to look at china. Not for a second did Pearl forget the money she owed. Jasper would fire her instantly if he thought she'd stolen from him. As soon as the store emptied, she reached in her pocket for some coins.

As she took a nickel in change, Jasper came through the door. She startled like a rabbit. "Mr. Kling!"

She had no cause to feel guilty, but the circumstances condemned her.

His brows arched. "Hello, Pearl."

"I was making change for myself." She felt foolish. "I bought one of the chapbooks. I gave it to—to a friend. I would have paid right away, but we had customers. I—"

"Don't fret, Pearl." For once, he looked sympathetic. "You're as honest as the day is long. I know that."

"Oh." She felt vindicated but frightened at the same time. Jasper sounded too friendly. Nervous, she resorted to formality. "Thank you, Mr. Kling."

He looked down his nose. "I *do* wish you'd call me Jasper."

If she declined his offer, she'd antagonize him. If she said yes, she'd be compromising her need for distance. She settled on a simple truth. "Thank you, sir. But I'm not comfortable—

"Jasper," he repeated. "Say it."

Blood rushed to her cheeks, turning them red with a mix of anger and fear. She looked him in the eye. "I can't, sir. It wouldn't be proper."

He looked pleased. "I understand."

She doubted it.

"Pearl?"

She put her hands on the drawer. As she closed it, it squeaked. "Yes?"

"I respect your father greatly. I admire you, too." His voice dropped low...or did it? He hadn't twitched a muscle, but she felt trapped behind the counter and had to work to breathe evenly. Silently she prayed he'd disappear into his office. Instead he tipped his head. "You're affected by what I've said."

"I'm fine," she said too quickly. "It's—it's a warm day."

"Stay here."

He brushed by her, went to the back room and returned with a glass of water. She took it and drank, but she felt like a princess being poisoned.

"Better?" he asked.

"Yes, thank you." As she set the glass on the counter, she thought of the things Franklin Dean had taken from her—purity and innocence, confidence in herself and in the goodness of people. He'd been killed in Denver when he'd attempted to murder the man who'd revealed his hypocrisy to the people of Colfax Avenue Church. Was Jasper a danger like Franklin Dean, or was it in her head? Considering the circumstances, it seemed likely the unease was in her head.

Instead of leaving, he stood with her. "Your color's back."

"I'm fine now."

He smiled again. "I'm *very* glad."

Pearl didn't like his tone. Neither did she like her father befriending this man or Carrie putting Pearl's name on cookies. She was mad at Matt, too. Why did he have to be handsome and kind, a man with a Texas drawl and an adorable little girl who needed a mother? Why couldn't she say yes to supper and risk a kiss? It wasn't fair. Pearl wanted to shout at God, too. How much did He think she could endure? She didn't dare break down in front of Jasper. Squaring her shoulders, she went back to shelving shoes. She knew life could be much harder than what she'd just endured, but she didn't think it could feel any more forgotten.

Chapter Fifteen

At nine o'clock on Thursday morning, a time when Jasper Kling was sure to be at his store and Chester Gates would be counting his money, Matt just happened to walk by Madame Fontaine's bakery. He just happened to see Tobias Oliver seated at a table in the back, the same one Matt had shared with Pearl. The man just happened to be eating breakfast, and Matt just happened to stop for a cup of coffee.

The old adage—hide in plain sight—was the option the men had chosen when they happened to meet at church. For the third Sunday in a row, Matt had taken Sarah to the morning service. Each time he and Tobias had exchanged terse bits of information. Matt had gleaned the names of ten suspects, and he'd spoken with all of them. He'd earned some hard looks, but that came with the job. If things went as he hoped, Tobias had been invited for cigars after last night's meeting.

The sooner Tobias earned the trust of these men, the sooner Matt could bring them to justice. And the sooner he stopped the Golden Order, the sooner he could think about Pearl as more than a friend.

Their meeting at the store had stayed with him for

days now. He wanted more than small talk from her, but he had nothing to give in return. To protect her feelings, he'd stopped visiting the store. He still walked by and looked in the window, but he'd asked Dan to go inside to speak with her. His friend didn't mind a bit. Carrie visited Pearl every afternoon, and Dan and Carrie often left together. Yesterday he'd bought seats for *Romeo and Juliet* and he'd planned to ask her Sunday at church.

Matt wished his own problems were so easily solved. He pulled up a chair across from Tobias. "Good morning, Reverend."

"Good morning," Tobias replied.

"Any news?"

His eyes glinted above the scrambled eggs. "I shared a nice cigar with Chester Gates last night."

Matt sipped his coffee. "Anyone else?"

Tobias gave him five names. In addition to Gates and Jasper, he'd met with Troy Martin, Howard Moreland and Gibson Armond. Martin and Moreland both had ties to the crimes committed by the men in derbies. It took Matt a minute to place Gibson Armond, then he remembered. He owned a freighting company. Recently he'd complained about outlaws hijacking his loads. He was also the man who had almost run over Sarah.

Matt took a sip of coffee, then looked at Tobias. "I don't suppose they offered you a derby?"

"Not yet." He spoke in a hush. "But last night was an interview of sorts."

"What did they talk about?"

"Martin and Moreland complained about horse thieves. They both have axes to grind. Mostly, though, Jasper carped about Ferguson Street." Tobias buttered a slice of bread. "If you ask me, the man has an unhealthy hatred of the place. It makes me wonder if he's hiding something."

Matt thought of Jasper's visit to the hog ranch. His secret hadn't leaked, but the man lived with the threat of it. "He wouldn't be the first," Matt said.

"Nor will he be the last."

"What did Jasper say?"

Tobias shook his head. "He said the fire was God's punishment for the lowest of sins. I'm not one to judge, Deputy. But Jasper has some extreme ideas. He seems sensible enough in public, but he's a different man behind closed doors. Frankly, he scares me."

He scared Matt, too. When he'd asked Tobias to gather information, he'd expected there to be some risk. Now he worried he'd asked too much. "Sir, you don't have to do this. You can still get out."

"Why would I do that?"

"Because you're right about Jasper." Matt lowered his voice. "He's got a secret and he'll do anything to keep it. Once you accept that derby, there's no going back. If they think you're double-crossing them, you'll pay."

Tobias gave him a hard look. "Is my daughter in danger, too?"

"Possibly."

"Then I better move quick," he replied matter-of-factly. "These men have to be stopped before someone else dies."

Matt didn't understand his commitment, his willingness to risk his life. And Pearl... If Jasper suspected Tobias, he'd watch her like a hawk. Matt wished he'd never concocted this crazy scheme. "You don't have to be the one. I'll find someone else."

"Over my dead body."

"Sir?"

Tobias glared at him. "My daughter was raped because good men in my church turned a blind eye to hypocrisy. I was one of them. If I don't stop these men, who will?"

Matt understood. He, too, had failed to stop something terrible. "You're making up for what happened to Pearl."

"That's not it." The man's eyes seemed to catch fire. "My slate's clean because of what Christ did on the cross. I don't have to fix my own mistakes."

Matt wished he felt the same way. "Unfortunately some of us do."

"Are you among them, Deputy?"

A flaming arrow hit Matt, and it hit him hard. His eyes glinted. "With all due respect, reverend. That's none of your business."

Tobias chewed the bacon as if he didn't have a care in the world. Matt wanted to be nonchalant, but he felt as if he'd tripped in one of the gopher holes he'd mentioned to Pearl. His temper flared. "You're a nosy old man, aren't you?"

Tobias chuckled.

Matt didn't see the humor. "Everyone in Cheyenne has regrets. So what? A man learns to live with what he's done."

"But it gets old, doesn't it?" Tobias chewed the bacon for a long time. "All that worry, not sleeping. I had a rough time before Pearl and I reconciled. What I'm wondering, Wiley, is this: Are you stupid or gutless?"

Matt's eye narrowed. "Neither."

"It has to be one or the other." Tobias could have been talking about the weather. "You're either afraid to face up to what you did, or you think you can fix it on your own. The first choice is cowardly. The second is naive."

"I'm no coward."

Tobias smiled. "That means you're stupid."

Weren't ministers supposed to be meek and mild? Matt glared at him. "What are you getting at?"

"You asked why I'm willing to risk my life to stop the Golden Order. I'm asking you the same question." Tobias softened his voice. "If I'm going to accept that black derby, I need to know what's got you working so hard. If they can, they'll use it against us both."

The man had a point. Matt wasn't ready to confess, but Tobias deserved an answer. He fortified himself with a slug of coffee, then looked the minister in the eye. "All right. Here it is. During the war I was a captain in Hood's Texas Brigade. We fought Grant in northern Virginia."

"I've heard of Hood's Army." Tobias sounded respectful. "You saved General Lee's life. Lost a lot of men doing it."

"That we did." Matt wished he could feel proud, but the heroism of the day had died on Amos McGuckin's farm. "Something ugly happened after the battle. I was responsible." From across the table, the men locked eyes. Matt had cowed outlaws, thieves and killers, but today he looked away first. "That's all I'm saying."

"It's enough," Tobias said quietly. "I won't ask you again, but I'd like you to do something for me."

"What?"

"Read the psalms."

Matt snorted. "That's poetry." Even when he'd been a believer, he'd preferred stories about vengeance and war. Sometimes he'd laughed at the Book of Proverbs, especially the verses about fools. The psalms had always struck him as whining.

Tobias took a pencil and a slip of paper from his pocket, jotted a few words and handed the scrap to Matt. "Here."

The note read Psalm 127. "What's this?"

"Your homework."

"This isn't Sunday school."

"Maybe not, but I'll be a minister until I die." He put the pencil back in his coat. "That's my requirement for accepting a black derby. You read Psalm 127."

The old man had him over a barrel. "I hope it's short."

Tobias chuckled. "It's five verses."

"I guess I can tolerate it." He pushed up from the chair. The irony of what he had to say wasn't lost on him. "I'll see you in church."

"I'll be there," Tobias replied.

Matt left the bakery and walked three blocks to the sheriff's office. He stepped inside, didn't see Dan and decided to get his "homework" out of the way. His partner kept a Bible in the bottom drawer of his desk. Sometimes Dan read it at night. More than once he'd handed it to a man locked in a cell. Matt took the book from the drawer, thumbed his way to Tobias's psalm and read it. The part about the Lord building a house didn't hold his attention, but the rest of the verse described a man like himself, a night watchman guarding a city. The lawman in the psalm didn't get enough sleep, either. Matt could relate, though unlike the watchman in the psalm, he felt no desire to call on the Lord for help.

The next verses were about children and he liked them. Matt enjoyed being a father. Until recently, he hadn't thought about having sons. Now thoughts of sons made him think of Pearl and Toby. The thought stirred him in a new and good way, but his talk with Tobias had brought old bitterness to the surface. He felt tainted by it, unfit for female company. He'd been crazy to invite her for pie after church. It was a good thing she'd said no. Matt had nothing to give a preacher's daughter.

Feeling dreary, he drummed his fingers on the cover

of the Bible and wished again he could sleep at night. He didn't want to ask Tobias's God for help, but neither did he want to be like the watchman in the Bible, trying in vain to stop evil. Matt hadn't thought a prayer in years, but he thought one now.

I don't deserve mercy, Lord. I don't deserve a family or even a good night's sleep, but I'm asking you to stop the Golden Order.

"Amen," he said out loud. He closed the book and put it back in the drawer. As he slid it shut, Dan strode into the office. The men traded a look but neither spoke. Matt had to give Dan credit for being wise. Some things were personal for a man. Others were downright humbling. Reading psalms counted as humbling.

Dan scratched his neck.

Matt yawned.

Silence stretched until Dan poured coffee for himself. "Nice day, isn't it?"

"Yep."

And that's all they said. It was all Matt *could* say, at least for now.

For the hundredth time, Pearl looked out her bedroom window at the moonlit street. Leaves skittered with the endless wind, but nothing else moved. The nearby houses were dark with sleep and quiet beneath the November sky.

The clock chimed eleven times and she sighed. Her father still wasn't home. He'd gone to a special meeting of the Golden Order, though why he'd become involved with the contentious group, Pearl couldn't fathom. Her father believed in pouring oil on troubled waters. The Golden Order was more inclined to put a match to tinder, yet he'd become a supporter. Why? Tonight she intended to find out.

But first he had to come home.

She was close to marching to the meeting hall herself when a fancy black carriage rolled down the street. Franklin Dean had driven a similar brougham all over Denver, and she'd ridden in it many times. Like the one coming down the street, it had a hard top, square glass windows and ornate lamps on the sides. A driver sat on the high seat, guiding two matched grays as they clopped down the street.

When the carriage halted in front of Carrie's house, the driver jumped down and opened the door. To Pearl's astonishment, a man wearing a black derby climbed out and shook hands with another man she couldn't see. As the carriage departed, he turned up the walkway and she saw her father's face. Pearl knew what the derby meant. He'd become involved in something ugly, but why? Chills erupted on her skin like blisters. They popped and stung until she pressed her hands to her cheeks in horror.

She listened to the creak of the front door, then her father's footsteps as he climbed the stairs. After his bedroom door closed, she raced down the hall, barged into his room and shouted in a whisper, *"Are you out of your mind!"*

He looked at her as if she were a stranger. "I thought you'd be asleep."

"Asleep? How am I supposed to *sleep* when you're running around Cheyenne in the middle of the night!" She started to pace. "The Golden Order! Papa, you said yourself they're a bunch of troublemakers!"

"It's not what you think."

She pointed at the derby he'd set on the bed. All the pieces came together. The vigilantes and the Golden

Order were one and the same. "If it's not what I think, why are you wearing *that?*"

"Calm down, princess."

"NO!"

Between her father's news and Jasper's prissiness, she'd had enough aggravation to last a lifetime. Adding to the upset, Toby had screamed half the evening with colic. Most irritating of all, Matt hadn't visited the store in days. He'd walked by and looked in the window, but he'd sent Dan inside to talk to her. Even Dan had annoyed her. He'd asked her if Carrie liked stage plays. Of course Carrie liked stage plays! So did Pearl. She also liked Matt, who had forgotten about her.

She put her hands on her hips. "I don't understand, Papa. If that hat means what I think, you've lost your mind."

"I most certainly haven't," he replied. "But neither do I have to answer to you."

"But—"

"I'm your father, Pearl. Not a child."

"Papa, I'm worried about you."

He walked to her side and spoke as if sharing a secret. "I know how this looks, Pearl. I'm asking you to trust me."

"I want to, but I'm scared." With good cause, she thought. "What are you doing?"

He shook his head.

She had only begged once in her life. She'd pleaded with Franklin Dean to stop unbuttoning her dress. She begged now because she feared losing her father. "Please, Papa. Tell me what's going on."

The clock ticked a dozen times. She bit her lip, but a cry rose to her throat. She put a hand over her mouth to hold it back, but it escaped in a whimper.

Her father stepped to her side. "Don't cry, Pearl. It's not what you think."

"Then what is it?"

"I'm helping Matt Wiley."

In a hushed tone, he told her about Matt's suspicions regarding the Golden Order. "I agreed to join because I'm in a unique position to help. It's the right thing to do."

Her body went limp. "But Papa, your health isn't good."

"It's good enough."

"But the danger! If they find out you're double-crossing them, they could—" She sealed her lips. The men in masks were accountable to no one but themselves. If her father exposed their crimes, he'd be a Judas and they'd kill him.

Tobias squeezed her hand. "I know the risks, Pearl. I also believe God called me to this task."

"But why?"

"Because I'm in the right place at the right time." He lifted their joined hands in an oath of sorts. "You know the story of Esther. She was made queen 'for a time such as this.' I believe I'm in Cheyenne for this very purpose."

"You're here for Toby and me." She hated the risk, the danger. "If something happens to you—"

"If it does, you'll be fine." His eyes filled with sadness. "I'm an old man, Pearl. I won't be around forever. You need to find a husband."

"How can you say that?" He knew her fears. She felt betrayed.

"It's true."

"Maybe I don't *want* to get married."

His brows arched. "That may be the first lie you've ever told me."

Her cheeks turned rosy. She *had* lied. She almost

wished he'd call her "princess" so she could be a child again instead of a woman with adult problems.

Tobias looked pleased. "Deputy Wiley's a good man. He's troubled, but that comes with the badge."

She'd seen the pain for herself. "I know."

Her father looked into her eyes. "Do you love him?"

Until this moment, she danced around the question without answering it. She *liked* Matt. She *cared* for him. She worried about him and wanted him to be happy. But love? That meant desiring him the way a wife desired a husband. She had those feelings for him, but they terrified her.

"I don't know," she murmured.

"I didn't ask if you were afraid," Tobias said. "I asked if you loved him."

Her insides shook with a potent mix of hope and fear. "I do," she admitted. "I love Sarah, too."

"Be strong, Pearl." He spoke in his preacher's voice, the one that seemed to move mountains. "I don't know what's lurking in Matt's past, but I *do* know the Lord won't leave him twisting in the wind. The Lord won't leave you either."

"I want to believe that." She took a breath. "I *do* believe."

"So do I, daughter.... So do I."

Chapter Sixteen

Meeting Tobias at the bakery had risks, but it could be explained as coincidence. Matt made a point of visiting often. If a member of the Golden Order saw them, the encounter wouldn't be out of the ordinary. At church on Sunday, Tobias had indicated he'd accepted a derby and wanted to meet. The news had made up for the misery of sitting through a sermon, but it hadn't eased his worry about Pearl. She'd been tense and had watched her father like a hawk.

Neither had she been happy to see Matt, though she'd been delighted to see Sarah. As the females compared dresses, the men had arranged today's breakfast meeting.

As Matt pulled out the chair across from Tobias, he recognized Nicholas Hamblin seated by the window. The man owned a sawmill and went to all the G.O. meetings. He didn't say much, but he'd listened. He plainly recognized Tobias.

Matt kept the subject light. "Nice weather, isn't it?"

"Excellent."

He looked for another bland topic. "How's your grandson?"

"Just fine." A beaming grandpa, Tobias told stories

until Hamblin left. Tobias relaxed but only for an instant. "Stay alert, Wiley. The G.O. doesn't like you."

"That's no surprise."

"They're making plans." His voice dropped an octave. "Be careful, son."

"What kind of plans?"

"The kind that could make your daughter an orphan."

The blood drained from Matt's head. He'd faced death a hundred times during the war, but never had he felt the apprehension he felt now. If he died, who'd love his little girl? Who'd read her stories and braid her hair? He didn't dare sip his coffee. With his jittery hands, it would have sloshed down his shirt. "What are they planning?"

"That's still being decided."

"By the five men you mentioned?" Matt wanted to know his enemies by name.

"The same."

While eating his meal, Tobias told Matt about the meeting. Matt had kicked a beehive when he'd questioned members of the G.O., and now they wanted him gone. Troy Martin and Gibson Armond had called him soft. They wanted his badge but not his life. Howard Moreland had suggested a tree and a short rope. Gates had kept his own counsel. Jasper had gone into a tirade about Matt failing to lock up prostitutes, then he'd sided with Moreland.

By the time Tobias finished, Matt felt as if the walls had sprouted eyes and were watching his every move. His nerves had never been stretched so tight.

"Tell me," said the old man. "Did you read that psalm?"

Matt couldn't believe his ears. "The G.O. wants me dead, and you're bringing up poetry?"

"Sure."

"That's crazy."

"It's not crazy to me," Tobias replied.

Matt felt as if someone had blindfolded him, spun him in circles and told him to find his way home. He'd met with Tobias to stop the Golden Order, not to bare his soul. Matt didn't want to dawdle over trivia, so he shrugged. "The psalm was nice. Now let's get down to business."

"That's what I'm doing." Tobias buttered a biscuit. "What struck you as 'nice' about that little piece of poetry?"

"I didn't think much about it." Actually, he'd read it two more times. He'd thought a lot about the verses, particularly the one about the watchman.

"Take a shot," Tobias insisted.

Matt gave up. He wouldn't spill his secret, but he'd crack open the door. "I liked the first verse," he admitted. "About the watchman."

"Me, too." Tobias pushed back his plate. "I've never worn a badge, but I had a church to run. Without God's help, I'd have been sunk ten times over."

Matt saw a chance to steer the conversation. "Do you think we're sunk when it comes to the G.O.?"

"We'll get to that," Tobias said lazily. "I'm more interested in how you're sleeping."

"Fine." He'd lied and felt bad. "Actually, terrible."

"You look it."

"Thanks." Matt sounded droll.

"I have another verse for you." Tobias spoke as if he were reading a bedtime story. "'The sun shall not smite thee by day, nor the moon by night.' I used to wonder why we needed protection from the moon, then Pearl left and I couldn't sleep worth spit. Those nights were rough. My own daughter needed understanding, and I failed to hear her side of the story. I pressured her to marry the man who attacked her." Tobias shook his head. "Can you imagine anything so stupid?"

Matt recalled his own failings. "I'm afraid so."

"Some nights, I thought I'd lose my mind." Tobias paused to let the words sink in. "I think you know what that's like. Next time you can't sleep, try telling God how you feel."

"No way," Matt said. "My problems are my own business."

"You're wrong."

Matt huffed. "Not only are you nosy, you're meddlesome."

"I've walked the road you're on." He raised one brow. "What you feel now, it affects everyone around you, especially Sarah."

He'd voiced Matt's deepest fear. "You don't know that."

"I know about guilt. It's why you're going after the Golden Order so hard. You've got an ax to grind, not with them but with yourself. Am I wrong?"

If they'd been alone, Matt would have spilled his guts because Tobias understood. He felt a bond with the man…a minister of all confounded things.

Tobias heaved a sigh. "Speaking of guilt, I have a burden myself."

"What happened?"

"Pearl saw the derby."

Matt stifled a groan. Ignorance provided protection. A woman couldn't reveal what she didn't know. "What did you tell her?"

"Everything." Tobias raised his hand in a sign of defeat. "I know. I should have kept quiet."

"What did she say?" Matt asked.

"She's not happy, but she knows to keep quiet." Tobias hunkered forward. "I don't mind saying, I'm eager to end this charade."

So was Matt. If he could finish with the Golden Order, maybe he could sleep at night. Maybe he could settle matters with the Almighty and not want to throw punches when he went to church. "It won't be long, sir."

"I hope not."

Matt made a decision. The more pressure he put on the Golden Order, the sooner they'd come after him personally. When they took aim, he'd fire back with both barrels. Dying wasn't an option. He needed to take care of Sarah.

Tobias stood. "We should meet before Sunday."

Matt thought about the coming week. Carrie had invited the girls from her class to a tea party on Thursday afternoon. When he picked up Sarah, he'd be able to speak with Tobias. "I'll see you after that party Carrie's having."

"Sounds good."

Tobias put coins on the table and left the bakery. Matt waited ten minutes, then pulled his hat low and headed for the sheriff's office. As he crossed the street, his neck hairs prickled. Any minute men in derbies could gallop down the street. A bullet could find his head and he'd be gone. As a lawman and a soldier, he'd faced his enemies head-on. The men in the Golden Order were devious. They didn't play by the conventional rules. They made up their own.

Stepping on the boardwalk, he thought about the watchman in the psalm. Matt could take care of himself, but today he'd have welcomed an all-seeing partner, someone smarter. Someone who'd keep Sarah safe, heal Pearl's heart and give Matt a decent night's sleep.

* * *

On Wednesday morning, a week after she'd seen her father in a black derby, Pearl went to work as usual. She'd grown accustomed to Jasper's persnickety ways, but today he'd been especially attentive. He'd struck up four conversations in the past hour, each one as bland as the last. When he'd gone to his office, he'd left the door ajar so he could hear her every step.

He'd also brought her a croissant from the bakery. She'd accepted it but hadn't taken a bite. Every time Jasper came out of his office, he looked at the roll sitting on a plate on the counter. Hoping he'd leave her alone, she'd finally taken a nibble, thanked him and turned back to the ledger.

"Pearl?"

She startled as he stepped out of his office. "Yes?"

"I have an errand to run." He pushed his spectacles higher on his nose. "I'll be back shortly."

"Of course." She still hadn't called him Jasper and she wouldn't. Neither had she called him "sir" or "Mr. Kling" because she knew he'd challenge her.

She averted her eyes until she heard the bell over the door, then she looked up and saw him pass by the display window. Breathing a sigh, she closed the ledger and rubbed her neck. She'd never been good at keeping secrets, and she found her father's deception exhausting. She wanted to go home and cuddle Toby until she forgot everything except his smile. She wanted to see her father, too. She still worried about his health, but she had to admit he looked well these days. He walked every morning at sunrise and sometimes at dusk. He had a spring in his step and a purposeful air about him.

Pearl wished she felt as confident. Not only did she worry about her father's involvement with the G.O., she couldn't stop thinking about Matt. She prayed every night for wisdom, but she felt no peace.

As she refocused on the ledger, the bell jangled above the door. She looked up and saw two women, both fancily dressed in bright colors. She didn't recognize them, but their revealing gowns belonged on Ferguson Street. In spite of their clothing, both women looked sad, even bitter. Pearl wondered if they'd known Katy. Jasper would want her to order them out of the shop, but she couldn't do it. Pearl knew how it felt to be scorned, so she refused to be unkind. If Jasper objected, so be it.

"May I help you?" she said brightly.

A brunette with frizzy hair gave her a snide smile. "We're just browsing." She turned to the shelf holding hand mirrors.

Pearl had admired the mirrors herself. She especially liked a white cloisonné edged with pink roses. The second woman, a redhead thanks to henna dye, smiled with sealed lips. Pearl wondered if she had bad teeth. Pearl smiled at her. "You've picked my favorite one. Aren't the roses pretty?"

"Oh yes!"

The girl's lips parted enough to confirm Pearl's suspicions. Her front teeth were the color of ash. No wonder the woman had sealed her lips. Pearl refused to add to her embarrassment. "A matching brush set just arrived. It's in the back."

The dark-haired woman eyed her with suspicion. "You work here?"

"I do."

The redhead looked at the brunette with a question in her eyes. They hadn't been expecting courtesy. Pearl enjoyed the surprise. "If you'd like, I'll get the brush."

The brunette huffed. "You shouldn't, not if you want to keep your job."

The woman clearly knew Jasper's ways. If he walked in, he'd be furious. Pearl decided to take that chance. "I'll be right back."

As she turned, she saw Jasper passing the display window. As her stomach clenched, the women straightened their spines to the point of arching them. They reminded her of cats lying in wait for a mouse. Jasper's warning had come soon after the incident with Katy and the hairbrush. Belatedly she realized these women hadn't come to look at mirrors. They'd come to retaliate for Katy's death by making Jasper furious.

As he pushed through the door, his eyes went down the brunette's flashy dress, up to the redhead's cleavage, then across to Pearl's face. The mix of loathing and lust in his gaze turned to confusion. The confusion hardened into the arrogance she'd seen in Franklin Dean.

Jasper paced toward them, inspected the shelf, then blocked the aisle so the women couldn't leave.

"Pearl!" he ordered. "Get the sheriff."

"But Mr. Kling," she protested. "They didn't do anything wrong."

His gaze narrowed to her face. "A mirror's missing."

Pearl looked at the shelf. The cloisonné mirror hadn't been replaced. She looked at the redhead. Wide-eyed, the woman turned to her friend, who said nothing.

"It was just here." Pearl had been with the women every minute.

"I'm telling you," he insisted. "The mirror's been stolen." He glared at the women. "Empty your pockets!"

The women stayed smug and silent. The cats had riled the mouse, and the mouse was roaring. Pearl sensed a trap about to be sprung. She opened her mouth to suggest they look for the mirror on other shelves, but Jasper shouted at her.

"Get Deputy Wiley!"

She raced out of the store, turned the corner and crossed the street, dodging a buckboard going in one direction and a rider coming in the other. Hoisting her skirts, she stepped on to the boardwalk and burst into the door of the sheriff's office. She saw Dan at the far desk. At the sight of her, he jumped to his feet. "What's wrong?"

"It's Jasper, he—"

The door opened behind her and Matt strode inside. He must have seen her running down the street, because he looked ready for a fight. "What happened?"

"It's Jasper," she answered, panting for breath. "Two women came into the store. They were friends with Katy. He's furious."

"Stay here." He looked at Dan. "Let's go."

"No!" Pearl cried. "I have to go back. Jasper thinks the women stole a mirror, but they didn't."

"How do you know?" he asked.

"I was with them the whole time." She told him about offering to fetch the comb and brush set. "Just as I turned, Jasper walked in."

Matt frowned. "Sounds like they were waiting for him."

Dan grabbed his hat. "I'm going with you, Wiley."

When Dan opened the door, Pearl walked through it. Matt followed her, but he didn't look pleased. As the three of them crossed the street, he guided her with a hand at her back. Dan brought up the rear. When they reached Jasper's store, Matt turned the knob on the front door. It didn't budge. Jasper had locked the women inside. Pearl knew how it felt to be trapped. To keep from crying out, she bit her lip.

Matt rapped on the door. "Jasper, open up."

Ten seconds passed before the key turned in the lock. Jasper cracked open the door, saw Matt, then opened it wide. "It's about time you got here."

Matt walked in with Pearl and Dan at his back. She looked past him to the two women, standing by the shelf with the mirrors. The brunette wore a smug expression. The redhead fidgeted with a hankie.

Matt removed his hat. "Good afternoon, ladies."

"They aren't *ladies,*" Jasper replied. "They're Jezebels!"

While matching the shopkeeper's stare, Matt set his hat on the shelf. A gentleman removed his hat in the presence of a lady, and that's what he'd done. Jasper glared at the hat, then at Matt.

Ignoring him, Matt turned to Dan. "Would you take the ladies outside? I'd like to speak to Mr. Kling alone."

"Sure thing," Dan answered.

The women moved to follow Dan, but Jasper stretched his arm across the aisle. "They'll stay. So will Miss Oliver." He turned his beady eyes on Pearl. "You witnessed the theft, didn't you?"

If Pearl told the truth, she'd lose her job. If she supported Jasper's lie, she'd lose her self-respect. "No, sir. I did *not.*"

Jasper's eyes narrowed to slits. "I believe you're mistaken, Pearl. These two *prostitutes* were looking at the mirrors. Now one of the mirrors is missing."

"I was with them the entire time."

"But you turned your back," Jasper said, leading her. "When I came through the door, you were looking away."

"Just for an instant."

He glared at her. "I saw the redhead put something in her pocket."

"This should be easy to solve." Matt struck a relaxed pose. "You're Jenna, aren't you?"

"Yes, sir."

"Would you mind showing me what's in your pockets?"

The girl looked to her friend. The brunette gave an imperceptible nod, as if to give the girl permission to speak. She looked at Matt, then indicated the shelf behind her. "I set the mirror here."

Pearl immediately saw the white cloisonné on the second highest shelf, out of sight but not unreasonably so. Matt picked it up and showed it to Jasper. "Is this the missing mirror?"

He grumbled. "Yes."

Matt put it back in its place. "Looks to me like no harm's been done."

Jasper's face flushed red. "That woman *meant* to steal it. If I hadn't come back, the mirror would be gone."

"I doubt it," Matt answered. "I think these ladies came here to make you mad. It's payback for chasing Katy out of your store."

And maybe for the fire, Pearl thought. Did the women suspect Jasper? It seemed possible.

Jasper glared at Matt, then at the women who were smirking. Pearl wished they'd stop mocking Jasper. No way would he tolerate such disrespect. If they pushed him, she felt certain the Golden Order would cause trouble.

Matt picked up his hat. "I have a suggestion for you, Mr. Kling. Call it even and send the women on their way."

Pearl had never spoken up to Jasper, but she had to speak now. "Mr. Kling?"

"What is it?" he snapped.

"What these women did was wrong." She shot them a look meant to scold, then focused back on Jasper. "Even so, the Bible tells us to forgive. If you leave them alone, they'll leave you alone." She looked at the women again. "Isn't that right, ladies? If Mr. Kling forgets today's incident, you will, too."

The women traded a look, then the brunette spoke to Pearl. "I suppose we—"

Jasper cut her off. "There will be *no* compromise. Right is right, and wrong is wrong." When he turned to Pearl, a chill shivered down her spine. "Thank you, *Miss* Oliver, for your opinion. We'll speak when this incident is over."

Pearl had no doubt she'd just lost her job. How would she provide for Toby and her father? She didn't know, but she had an even bigger fear. Would Jasper suspect her father's true motive for joining the G.O.?

Matt spoke in a too-reasonable tone. "I'll talk to the women, Jasper."

"Don't bother."

"It's my job and I'll do it." Matt looked straight at him. "No one's going to get away with anything while I'm wearing this badge. You can count on it."

If she hadn't known Matt's true motives, his tone might have passed for sincere. Instead she heard a threat. He suspected Jasper of wrongdoing, and he'd let the man know. He'd made an enemy today and so had she. Even worse, their enemy had the power to call her father's bluff. Trembling, she prayed for God to help them all.

Matt struck a casual pose. "You know how it is, Jasper. Women like these are trouble."

The shopkeeper's face flushed red.

Matt smirked. "Some men just can't keep their hands

to themselves. A few have been known to head out to the hog ranch. Seems to me that's pretty low. They don't think anyone sees, or that anyone knows. But people see. And they talk." Matt tsked his tongue. "It's a crying shame what some men will do."

Jasper looked close to choking on his own tongue. Matt turned and spoke calmly to the women. "Ladies, you've had your fun. I expect this nonsense to stop." He turned to Jasper. "When a real crime is committed, I'll handle it. Until then, this incident is over."

Dan indicated the door. "Ladies."

They gave Jasper haughty looks, then sauntered down the aisle. Matt followed without giving Pearl a second glance. She watched him leave, hoping he'd turn to her but knowing he wouldn't. The more distant they appeared, the safer she and her father would be. She hated being alone with Jasper, but she worked for him, at least for a few more minutes. Standing tall, she faced him. "I know you're angry, but I had to tell the truth."

"Yes," he said, sounding cold. "You would."

"I don't believe they intended to steal. Deputy Wiley's right. They're provoking you."

"They shouldn't do that." He clipped each word. "Neither should *you*. I trust you've learned a lesson today."

"Sir?"

"You're naive, Pearl." His spectacles magnified his eyes. "I'm not ending your employment, but I *am* disappointed in you."

She wanted to quit, but she had to protect her father. If she antagonized Jasper, she might cast doubt on his loyalty to the G.O. As disgusting as it tasted, she had to eat crow. "Thank you, sir."

He looked down his pointy nose. "Women of that ilk are the doorway to a man's sin."

In front of her eyes, Jasper's countenance changed from mild to murderous. His mouth tightened into a sneer, deepening the corners into black lines. Perspiration gave a shine to his pasty skin, and his small eyes narrowed into black beads. In the most primitive of ways, he reminded her of Franklin Dean. If it weren't for the risk to her father, she'd have walked out of his shop and never returned.

Love for her father made her strong. She didn't dare speak, but she would *not* be cowed. She wouldn't.

Jasper gave her a suspicious look. "Do you understand me, Pearl?"

She stared hard but only for an instant. She couldn't win this battle with impertinence, so she lowered her voice. "Yes, sir."

"Let's get back to work."

She stepped to the counter and opened the ledger. Jasper went to the storeroom, fetched a black derby and put it in the window. Pearl knew what it meant. So would her father. So would Matt. The Golden Order would meet and make plans. Soon they'd make a move. Silently she prayed her father and Matt would stop the violence before it reached someone she loved.

Chapter Seventeen

Once upon a time, a little girl named Sarah brought home a fancy invitation to a tea party. Like all the other little girls, she wanted a pretty new dress to wear. Unlike the other little girls, she didn't have a mama who could make one for her. She had only a daddy. He loved her very much, but he couldn't spin straw into gold or even fix her hair very well. The little girl needed a mama and she needed one now.

"Deputy Wiley?"

Startled out of the daydream, Matt saw Mrs. Gardner, the owner of the dress shop where he'd brought Sarah to be measured. "Yes?"

The woman smiled. "Take a look at your little girl." With a sweep of her hand, Mrs. Gardner indicated Sarah.

Instead of her usual pinafore, she was wearing a cloud of pink ruffles. She looked almost grown up. A lump the size of Texas pushed into Matt's throat, and he wondered if he'd ever swallow it down.

The dress hunt had started when Sarah brought home an invitation for Carrie's annual tea party for her class. Sarah had heard the girls talking about going with their mothers. He couldn't meet that need, but he could buy his daughter something pretty. The tea party served another purpose. After yesterday's trouble at Jasper's store, the black derby had gone up. When he picked up Sarah from the party, Matt could talk to Tobias unnoticed.

Sarah curtsied for him. "Do I look pretty?"

"You're beautiful, darlin'." He winked at her. "You look like a real princess."

When she grinned, he thought about her baby teeth starting to come loose. Someday he'd be in this shop buying a wedding gown. Dazed, he turned to the clerk. "How did this happen? I thought she was just getting measured."

"I made this dress for the Andrews girl. Her mother changed her mind." Mrs. Gardner smiled at Sarah. "It's a perfect fit."

"Can I have it, Daddy?"

"You sure can." He didn't ask the price. He'd have paid a month's salary for the smile on his little girl's face.

As she ran to hug him, the door opened and in walked another princess. He hadn't spoken to Pearl since the trouble at Jasper's store and he wanted to know how she'd been. He stood a little taller. "Hello, Pearl."

"Hello, Matt."

Sarah did a twirl. "Do you like my new dress?"

"It's beautiful!"

Pearl oohed and aahed for a solid minute, making the womanly sounds Sarah missed so much. Looking at her with his daughter, with their matching hair and smiles, Matt had to admit to another failure, one that didn't trouble him as much as it should have. In spite of keeping his distance, he'd fallen for a blond-haired preacher's daughter. He'd do anything for this woman...even go to church.

The thought shook him to the core. He didn't belong in church, not when he had no love for God and even less respect for Him. Whatever feelings he had for Pearl, he had to deny until he could sleep at night. When that would be, Matt didn't know. Everything depended on Tobias and the Golden Order.

As Sarah scampered off to change, Pearl pushed to her feet. "It's nice to see you, Matt."

It was nice to see her, too. More than *nice*. He wanted to put his arms around her. He wanted to save her from the gopher holes and buy ribbons for her hair. He couldn't do either of those things until he put the members of the Golden Order behind bars. Until then, they were both in danger. If he showed his feelings for Pearl, she'd be at a greater risk from Jasper.

"How are things going?" He hoped she'd read between the lines. *How's Jasper treating you?*

"Okay, I think."

He heard what she didn't say. *I'm not sure what's going on. I'm uncomfortable.*

"I haven't seen your father lately." *Has the Golden Order met?*

"He's fine," she answered. "Nothing new."

At least nothing Tobias had shared with Pearl. Unless the old man sought him out, Matt would have to wait until Thursday for news. He didn't like being in the dark, but he couldn't risk drawing attention to Tobias. The G.O. could ride any day. The episode in Jasper's store had lit the fuse. Whether the fuse was long or short, Matt didn't know. Neither did he know where it ended.

Sarah came out of the back room and went to Pearl. "Miss Carrie's having a tea party. All the other girls have mommies. Will you go with me?"

Matt's heart hitched. Carrie had assured him she'd give Sarah extra attention, but it wasn't the same as having a mama of her own. If Pearl accompanied her, Sarah

would be thrilled. The choice would also bring them
closer to being a family. Matt wasn't ready for that closeness, but he couldn't deny his daughter. He gave Pearl a
meaningful look. "If you could, I'd be obliged."

"I'd like to," she answered. "But I have to work."

"Could you leave early?" he asked. The less time she
spent with Jasper, the better.

As Pearl looked down at Sarah, so did Matt. In his
daughter's eyes he saw a familiar look, the one that
pleaded for a mother's love. It broke his heart. It must
have broken Pearl's, because she crouched to put herself
at eye level with Sarah. "I'd *love* to go. I might be a little
late, though. Would that be okay?"

Sarah nodded solemnly. "But just a little late, okay?"

"I'll do my best."

Pearl straightened, then tipped the child's chin. "I
need to speak with your daddy. How about looking at
the dolls?"

"Okay."

Sarah went to a glass cabinet at the front of the store.
Pearl followed the child with her eyes, then turned to
Matt with a nervous look. He wanted to reassure her
with a touch of their hands, but he couldn't. He settled
for a half smile, the one that didn't quite hide his feelings. "Are you all right?" he said in a hush.

"I just wanted to say, I—I miss you."

"I've missed you, too." The words were out before he
could stop them.

As a blush stained her cheeks, she diverted her gaze to
the dolls. Something had scared her and he knew what it
was. What she felt for him terrified her. He understood,
because he had similar doubts. Pearl probably feared the
physical side of marriage. Matt was afraid he'd disappoint
her with his dark moods. They were a mismatched pair,

especially when he thought of church and God and the peace he didn't feel. As much as Sarah needed a mother, he couldn't court Pearl until he settled matters with the Almighty.

"Deputy Wiley?" Mrs. Gardner had set Sarah's dress, wrapped in brown paper, on the counter. "That will be $3.50."

He opened his billfold, paid and slung the dress over his shoulder like a sack of flour. It weighed next to nothing and he felt ridiculous. At the sight of him, Pearl chuckled and Sarah laughed with her. Surrendering to a grin, Matt hiked the dress up on his shoulder as if it weighed a hundred pounds. "Are you ready?" he said to Sarah.

"Yes, Daddy."

"Good." He looked at Pearl. "We'll see you at the party."

"I'll be there."

He gripped Sarah's hand and headed for the door. He didn't know what the future held, but he hoped Sarah would someday have a mother, and he wanted that woman to be Pearl.

Pearl left the dress shop with the lace she'd come to purchase and hurried home. She arrived ten minutes late and met with her father's wrath. "You're late," he scolded as she stepped through the door.

"I had to stop at the dress shop."

"But, Pearl, we agreed. You come straight home *and* on time."

Because of the trouble with Jasper, they'd decided she'd leave the shop at precisely four o'clock. Never would she be alone with him behind a locked door. Considering Jasper's extreme punctuality, leaving on time wasn't a problem. On the other hand, she resented being treated like a child. She set the lace on the table and removed her hat. "I'm sorry I scared you, Papa. It was only a few minutes." She slipped out of her cloak and hung it on a peg. "I saw Matt at the dress shop. He was buying something for Sarah."

Tobias huffed. "He should have walked you home."

"He couldn't."

They both knew why. Matt had to keep his distance, but she couldn't help but wonder how it would feel to share his life. She hadn't meant to say that she missed him, but she didn't regret the confession. He'd taken her hand and she'd felt safe. In that moment, she'd seen love in his eyes. Could she kiss him without panicking? Could she be the loving wife she wanted to be?

She didn't know and was afraid to find out. Neither did she know *how* to go about such a discovery. She couldn't walk up to him and suggest a kiss.

Her father sighed. "I'll be upstairs."

Pearl took the hint. If she wanted to talk about Matt, he'd be waiting. "Thanks, Papa, but I need to check Toby. Is he in his cradle?"

"Carrie has him. They're in the parlor."

Pearl walked into the front room where Carrie was swaying with Toby in her arms and humming a lullaby. Toby looked sleepy, so Pearl greeted Carrie in a hush. "Hi."

"Hi," she whispered. "He's almost asleep."

The women stood in companionable silence until Toby's eyes closed. Satisfied he wouldn't wake up, Carrie laid him in the basket and turned to Pearl. "I'm glad you're home. I've got something to tell you."

"Good or bad?"

"Good, I think." She bit her lip. "Or maybe not. I'm not sure."

"What happened?"

"Dan asked me to the theater."

Pearl spoke to Dan almost every day at Jasper's store. He never failed to ask about Carrie, a sign he had feelings for her. The situation was complicated because of Carrie's affection for Matt. She'd stepped aside for Pearl, but that didn't mean her feelings had died.

"What did you say?" she asked carefully.

"I said yes." Carrie dropped down on the armchair. "But I'm confused. I *thought* I was in love with Matt. I didn't think I'd ever get over it, but Dan's been wonderful. When we talk, I know he's listening. And when he smiles…" Carrie put her hand on her chest. "I didn't know a man could look so shy and purposeful at the same time."

Pearl sat on the divan near Toby and rested her hand on his back. She felt the beat of his heart and silently thanked God for turning loss into gain. For the next several minutes, the women talked about men, babies and courtship. The more they spoke, the more sure Pearl felt that Carrie had found the right man in Dan Cobb.

"Now it's your turn." Carrie's eyes twinkled. "Has Matt come to his senses and visited you at the store?"

"Not lately."

"I don't see why not." Carrie sounded like an irate mother hen. "I know he cares for you. I saw it when I spoke with him. He's being thick-headed."

No, Pearl thought, he was protecting her. Carrie didn't know about Jasper, her father and the Golden Order, and Pearl saw no need to tell her about the plan. Secrets were a burden, not a gift. She didn't want Carrie to worry about guarding her words. "He has his reasons," she finally said. "He and Jasper don't get along."

"That could be it," Carrie agreed.

"I *did* see him today." Pearl couldn't stop her heart from fluttering. "He was buying a dress for Sarah for the tea party. She asked me if I'd go with her."

"I hope you said yes."

"Of course." She couldn't disappoint Sarah. "I love that little girl as if she were my own."

"And Matt?" Carrie said gently. "Do you love him, too?"

Her body tensed at the prospect of admitting her feelings. If she told Carrie how she felt, she might hurt her cousin all over again.

"It's okay." Carrie came to sit next to her. "He wasn't right for me. I know that now. But I do think he's right for you, and you're right for him."

Pearl stroked Toby's back through the blanket. "Marriage scares me."

"Me, too." Carrie shivered but not with dread. "My mother said love made marriage the most special place in the world. I didn't understand, but I do now. When I'm with Dan, I'm starting to feel like we belong together."

Pearl felt the same way with Matt. Could she overcome her fear of the physical part of marriage? A kiss would tell her what she needed to know, but when would it happen? How could she test the waters without embarrassing herself with Matt? She didn't know, but today she had the faith to hope.

Chapter Eighteen

Pearl looked out the window of Jasper's store and saw a smattering of raindrops. She'd asked Jasper for permission to leave early for the tea party and he'd given it, but he'd also asked her to dust the shelves before she left. The coming storm gave her an excuse to put off the tedious chore. Not only did she want to keep her promise to Sarah, she was also tired of Jasper's company. All day she'd felt his eyes on her back. Was he deliberately crowding her, or was she overreacting? Pearl didn't know, but she'd had all she could take of his strange ways.

Eager to leave, she went to his office. Through the open door, she saw him dipping a pen in ink. "Mr. Kling?"

"Pearl!" His arm jerked and the ink spattered. His brow furrowed with annoyance.

"It's starting to rain. May I leave now?"

"Is the dusting finished?"

"No, but I'll come early tomorrow."

The pen hung in his hand, dripping ink on the ledger sheet. She knew he'd heard her. He heard everything. She tried again. "The rain's getting worse."

"Yes, a storm." He set down the pen.

A gust of rain hammered the window. The glass shook but didn't break. Her belly clenched. "I need to get home."

"But you'll catch your death," he said smoothly. "Wait out the storm here. I'll walk you home when it's over."

"No thank you," she managed. "I have a-a commitment." She didn't want to mention her promise to Sarah. "My father's expecting me."

"Tobias and I are friends." His eyes glittered behind his spectacles. "He'd expect me to watch out for you."

No way would she be alone with Jasper in a store closed for business, especially not in a rainstorm. She wanted to walk out, but she couldn't risk antagonizing him. All week she'd worried that Jasper had begun to suspect her father. If she reacted now, she'd be denying her father's seeming trust of him. She had to behave as normally as possible. "I really do have to leave." She tried to sound regretful. "If you'll excuse me—"

"Just one thing."

Ignoring him, she went to the storeroom where she kept her cloak. The size of a bedroom, it held crates and a hodgepodge of unsold items. Two windows let in light, and a third beam came from the doorway. As she reached for her hat, something cut off the light from the door. She turned and saw Jasper with his hands on the doorframe, blocking the way out.

"Stay," he said in a silky tone. "I'll look out for you."

"I can't." She forced a smile. "If you'll excuse me, I have to get home."

He stepped into the room, cornering her by a shelf holding women's shoes. Rain turned into a torrent against the glass, and the light dimmed to a smoky haze. She smelled the starch in his shirt and the thickness of his breath. In his eyes she saw a gleam magnified by his spectacles…the same gleam she'd seen in Franklin

Dean's eyes when he'd purposely taken a wrong turn on that buggy ride. Sweat beaded on her brow and her stomach recoiled. She needed to think, but she'd been reduced to a bundle of reactions. Fight or flee... She didn't know.

Jasper smiled at her.

She wanted to look away, but she feared turning her back. She settled for taking a step to the side. Her foot caught the corner of a crate and she lost her balance. As she reached for a shelf to steady herself, Jasper gripped her elbow.

"I've got you," he said.

Pearl pulled away from him, but he didn't let go of her arm. Darkness pressed from the ceiling and walls. She thought of the leather hood of Franklin Dean's buggy, the way it blocked the sun. Her pulse pounded in her ears, blurring all conscious thought except for one truth. Not even for her father's safety could she risk another minute in Jasper's presence. She jerked out of his grasp and ran out of the storeroom.

"Pearl! Wait."

As she raced to the front of the store, she realized she'd left her cloak and hat in the storeroom. She didn't dare go back for them. Silently she prayed Jasper hadn't already locked the front door. She gripped the knob and it turned. The door opened and she fled into the rain. Wanting to vanish from sight, she sped across the street, ruining her shoes in the puddles and staining her stockings. Rain drenched her hair and face. Mud clung to the hem of her gown, weighting her down.

She wanted to go home, but the house would be full of little girls and their mothers. Neither did she want to see her father until she'd regained her composure. Desperate for a dry place to hide, she slipped down an alley and took cover under a staircase. Shivering, she huddled next to a stack of wood and a barrel that smelled of food scraps. Bowing her head, she sobbed with the freedom given only by privacy.

When he fetched Sarah from the tea party, Matt deliberately arrived late. He wanted a few words with Tobias, and he didn't want to have them in front of ten talkative women and a bevy of little girls. He also needed to see Pearl. Since the day at the dress shop, he'd questioned key members of the G.O. Every one of them had complained about Scottie's girls shopping on Dryer Street. Would Jasper punish Pearl for her kindness to the two prostitutes? It seemed all too possible.

The dreary weather didn't help his mood. Dark clouds had rolled in from the west and turned Cheyenne into boxlike shadows. Expecting a storm, he'd put on an oilcloth poncho that hung to his knees. It protected his clothing and his gun belt, but it didn't shield his gut from constant churning. With his nerves tight, he walked up the steps to Carrie's house.

Before he could ring the bell, she flung open the door. "Oh! You're not Pearl!"

"She's not here?"

"She's late. She missed the party." Carrie clipped the words. "She said she'd be here. She promised Sarah. Something's wrong. I feel it."

So did Matt. No way would Pearl break her word to a child. He had to get to Jasper's store. If the G.O. had discovered the ruse, Pearl would be in danger.

"I'm going after her," he said to Carrie.

"Hurry!"

As Matt turned from the door, Tobias strode into the foyer and lifted his coat. "I'm going with you."

The old man looked ashen. "It's raining, sir. Stay here."

Tobias glowered. "Do you think I care about getting wet?"

"No, but you can't help me."

"But—"

"Sir, with all due respect, you'll be in the way."

The men traded a look, then Tobias accepted the decision with a nod. "Bring her back, Wiley. If something happens to her I'll—"

"I know." If something happened to Sarah, Matt wouldn't be able to stop himself. The wail of a baby—Pearl's baby—cut through the air from a back room. Toby wanted his mama, and Matt wanted to find her. He looked past Carrie to Tobias. The men exchanged a glance only a father would understand, then Matt turned on his heels and went to find Pearl.

To save time, he cut down an alley that led to Jasper's shop. As soon as he rounded the corner, he heard a woman sobbing. The misery of it carried over the splash of the rain and the thud of his boots. As he picked up his pace, he heard a gasp and the crying stopped.

Peering down the alley, he spotted a stairwell that offered cover from the storm. The dusky light had the sheen of pewter, but he could still see colors. Between a wood pile and barrel of scraps, he spotted a tangle of white-gold hair, blue calico, Pearl's pink cheeks and her red lips rounded with fright.

Looking at her now, Matt surrendered to the love he was utterly powerless to stop. It consumed him. It bullied him. Instead of setting him free, the depth of his love enslaved him. He had to protect her, and that meant shielding her from storms of all kinds—the one in his heart, the one raining down on her now. He didn't know what had driven her into the rain without her cloak, but he had his suspicions. If Jasper had harmed her, justice *would* be served.

First, though, he had to get Pearl out of the rain. Her dress was clinging to her legs and her hair was a soggy mess. When he reached the stairwell, the wind gusted. To shield her, he stretched his arms to make a wall of sorts with the slicker. He put one hand on the beam supporting the stairs and the other on a riser, making himself a wall between Pearl and the wind. He felt a hint of warmth and hoped she felt it, too.

"What happened?" he said gently.

She shook her head.

He couldn't tolerate silence. "Did he touch you? Did he—"

"No." The word came out in a choked cry. "He— he—" She pressed her hands to her face. "Go away, Matt. *Please.*"

"Absolutely not."

"I'll—I'll be all right. I just need to—" As a cry escaped from her throat, she buried her face in her hands. Her shoulders shook with tears she couldn't stop.

Matt knew too much about women who'd been assaulted. Some got mad and wanted to murder their attackers. A few fled. Far too many blamed themselves for what a man did. That reaction troubled him, but he understood the logic. No one wanted to admit to being a victim. It stripped a man of his pride and a woman of her peace. He couldn't let Pearl believe that lie.

"Look at me, darlin'."

She shook her head.

He kept his voice low. "You know I won't leave you like this."

A squeak came from her throat.

"That's right," he drawled. "I'm here to keep you safe."

If he touched her, she'd balk. Except for the sound of their breath, he stayed silent. The next move had to be hers and it was.... Her index fingers twitched, then she moved her pinkies and revealed her tear-stained eyes. He'd never seen a woman so vulnerable, so in need of a man's strong arms. He ached to hold her, but he feared the consequences. The shape of her would be sealed in his memory. Even worse, the closeness might frighten her. Whatever Matt did, he wanted it to be best for Pearl. Whatever she needed, he'd give to her.

He used the tone he used with Sarah when she skinned a knee. "I'm right here. Tell me what you need."

Slowly she slid her hands down her cheeks until they cupped her jaw, then she crossed her arms over her heart and squeezed hard. After a deep breath, she lowered her hands to her sides and looked defiantly into his eyes.

Matt saw fear and something deeper, something he recognized as a man. She wanted to be kissed. The slicker made a wall of sorts, a covering. It made the space small and dark…intimate. More than anything, he wanted to kiss her fully. He wanted to hold her in his arms and keep her safe. But at what cost? He couldn't promise her more than this moment. A woman like Pearl deserved everything a man had to give.

He touched her cheek with his thumb, wiping rain and tears from her hot skin. His heart pounded with a love beyond his understanding. "Ah, Pearl," he murmured. "How did this happen?"

"I—I don't know."

"Neither do I," he said. "But it did."

The both knew what *it* was. She wanted to be kissed, and he wanted to kiss her. He swallowed hard, feeling the tightness and the longing, then he touched her cheek. Gently he tucked a strand of damp hair behind her ear.

He opened his mouth to speak, to say *We shouldn't do this*. But her lids fluttered shut and her chin lifted. When he didn't move, she opened her eyes. What he saw tied his heart in knots. She wanted to kiss him, but she feared her reaction. Would she triumph or panic?

One code of honor required him to maintain his distance. He had no business kissing a woman outside the bounds of courtship, especially not a woman as vulnerable as Pearl. Another code—a code of men at war—demanded he help her up and over this hill. Was she ready for this moment? What if kissing her destroyed the fragile progress she'd made? He saw costs to himself, as well. If they kissed, he'd never forget it. He'd remember the silk of her lips, the saltiness of tears mixed with rain. Not even whistling "Dixie" would chase away the wanting.

So be it. Pearl needed his help.

Stepping closer, he touched her cheek with the pad of his thumb. She bit her lips, then relaxed them. A tremble pulsed to his fingers, but her eyes flared with courage. When she swayed ever so slightly in his direction, he brushed her lips with his. Once, twice. When her eyes stayed closed, he lingered over the third kiss without reluctance. A cry came from her throat. Before he could draw back, she wrapped her arms around his neck and pulled him as close as she could. The kiss turned fierce, as if she were fighting memories. Just as suddenly, she relaxed in his arms and he knew she'd won the war.

He kissed her back sweetly, tenderly…long enough to feel her confidence build. He didn't want to stop, but he had to pull back. A sweet saint and a bitter sinner… They had no future. As he broke the connection of their lips, he tucked her head under his chin. "I didn't mean for that to happen."

"I did," she whispered.

With their hearts beating in perfect time, he searched for the right words. She'd crossed a battlefield today. Together they'd fought an enemy and she hadn't panicked. He hoped the kiss was enough, because he had nothing else to give.

"Now you know," he said with authority.

"I do?"

If she needed reassurance, he'd give it to her. "That kiss… You don't need to be afraid anymore. Someday you'll meet a man. He'll—"

She whispered against his jaw. "I've already met him."

He understood but wished he didn't. "Don't say that."

"Why not?"

"I'm not right for you, Pearl. I've done things. I've—"

She pushed back and looked into his eyes. He saw questions in her gaze, but he also saw a bold certainty. This woman didn't believe in cowering before anyone. She'd risk her heart for him.

"Ah, Pearl." He couldn't deny his feelings, but neither could he tell her the truth. If he admitted to loving her, where would they be? In a hole deeper than the one he'd just dug. He needed to explain himself to her, but not here. Not with the rain pelting them and Pearl soaked to the skin. Not next to a heap of garbage in a dirty alley.

He took off his hat and put it on her head, then he hunched out of the slicker and wrapped it around her shivering body. He put his arm around her waist to protect her as much as he could, then he led her away from the stairwell.

"We have to talk," he said. "My house is around the corner."

Chapter Nineteen

When Matt put his hat on her head, the warmth of the headband reached Pearl's skin. She thought of her mother calling a woman's hair her crowning glory and wondered if Virginia Oliver had ever worn her husband's hat in the rain.

She wanted to skip and dance and celebrate her victory. Franklin Dean had left her with scars, but he hadn't maimed her for life. She loved Matt Wiley with her entire being, and she'd tested herself with a kiss. She couldn't think of a more challenging circumstance than being cornered in a dark alley. Matt's slicker had blocked the light. Shiny and black, it could have reminded her of Franklin Dean's buggy, but it hadn't. She'd been aware only of Matt studying her expression, gauging her courage and giving her a choice.

Today's kiss did more than conquer her fears. It had revealed Matt's heart. He wouldn't have kissed her with such care if he didn't have feelings for her, but something—the gophers holes she'd sensed earlier—were holding him back. As much as she wanted to shout with joy, her happiness had to be contained until they sorted their differences.

The wind pushed them up the street with powerful gusts. Hunkering forward, Matt tucked her against his side. As they rounded a corner, he indicated the third bungalow on the left.

"This is it," he said.

"It's homey."

What it lacked in feminine grace, it made up for in masculine effort. Brown gingham curtains, store-bought and an inch too short, hung in the window, and a scraggly juniper grew next to a rickety porch. The needles shimmered in the fading light, a reminder her father would be worried. She hated to upset him, but she had to speak to Matt.

As he held the door, she stepped into a mix of shadows and empty walls. Another window allowed light into a corner kitchen. Near a galvanized sink she saw a shelf stacked with canned goods and another one holding tin plates, glasses and jars.

A match scraped and she turned. As the tip flared, orange light bathed Matt's face and illuminated a stone fireplace. As he touched the tiny flame to the kindling, it caught with a whoosh and lit up the room. Pearl saw a chair, a table, a hurricane lamp and a horsehair divan. Sarah had left her doll, Annie, sitting primly in the chair.

Matt added a split of wood to the fire, then faced her from across the room. Much like the day they'd met, he looked her up and down. "Are you hurt?"

"I'm fine." She took off the slicker and hung it by the door, then she walked to the fire to dry her dress. Matt had gotten wet, too. She considered telling him to change into a dry shirt, but he looked lost in thought as he stared into the blaze. Pearl stepped to his side. Soon the fire would warm them both.

Staring into the flames, he broke the silence. "We have to talk."

Would he start with the reason she'd run into the rain or with the kiss? Pearl cared far more about the kiss, so she tipped up her chin and smiled at him. Feeling bold, she stood on her toes and brushed her lips across his cheek. His whiskers tickled her lips, and she smelled the dampness of the storm on his shirt. When she stepped back, he looked completely undone.

More confident than she'd ever been, she rested her hand on his biceps. "That kiss was the nicest thing that's ever happened to me."

"Don't say that," he answered. "It was a mistake."

When he looked into her eyes, she saw turmoil in the pale green depths. Just as she'd been hurt, so had Matt. She felt certain of the reason. Sarah's mother had broken his heart. Just as Pearl had needed someone to help her bury the past, so did Matt. Full of hope, she took a chance. "I love you."

A groan rumbled in his throat. "Don't love me, Pearl. I can't love you back."

She didn't believe him. "Why not?"

"I just can't."

The fire showed every crease in his face, the dark crescents under his eyes. The log hissed and snapped. The roof echoed with the rain. Pearl had learned from her father to let troubled souls find their own way. She'd wait all night if that's what Matt needed. Still silent, he poked the fire with an iron rod. Sparks shot up the chimney and died. He set down the poker, then indicated the divan. "Sit down."

As she sat, he stayed standing with his back to her. The glow of the blaze turned his body into a black silhouette. "You don't really know me, Pearl. You don't know what I've done."

"It doesn't matter."

He gave a snide laugh. "You don't know what you're saying."

"Then explain it to me."

A gust of wind rattled the door. A draft reached the fire and made it flare. Still silent, he stood with his hands on his hips, his back straight and his feet planted wide as he spoke to the flames. "I'm a murderer, Pearl. It happened in the war, but that doesn't excuse what I did."

She'd been expecting him to say he'd been a bad husband, that he'd driven Bettina away by being cold and obsessed with his work. A murderer? She knew he'd been a Texas Ranger and a soldier, a man likely to have blood on his hands. She'd never expected some of that blood to be innocent. Her entire body recoiled, a first reaction she chose to ignore. She believed in the God who forgave everyone, including lawmen who made mistakes and men like Franklin Dean who deserved punishment more than mercy. She didn't care what Matt had done, but she cared deeply about his soul.

Her heart ached for him. "How did it happen?"

"I didn't start out bad," he said wearily. "I served proudly as a captain in Hood's Texas Brigade." His voice rang with the pride of a soldier. "We were in northern Virginia near Spotsylvania. We stopped two federal corps that day, but it came at a price. Most of my men died."

Pearl knew firsthand that violence begat violence. After being attacked, she'd beat her pillow as if it were Franklin Dean's face. "It must have been terrible."

"It was." His shoulders relaxed, but he kept his back to her. "Only eight of us lived. That night, we were ordered to patrol for spies. To this day, I don't recall approaching Amos McGuckin's farm. One minute we were in the thick of the forest. The next we'd ridden into a clearing with a big house and a barn. It was late, almost midnight. The old man came out carrying a lantern as if he'd been expecting someone."

Matt blew out a breath. "One of my men—Hardin was his name—accused him of being a spy for the Blues. Why I believed him, I'll never know."

Pearl sprang to his side. "War makes people crazy. You were—"

"Don't make excuses for me." He clipped his words. "I was in charge. I should have stopped what happened. We had cause to question the man, but we didn't take the time. Three of my men charged up the porch and dragged McGuckin into the yard. The torches burned like the sun that night. I saw every line in the old man's face."

Pearl closed her eyes, but she smelled the kerosene and saw the faces of crazed men. She stood up from the divan. "Matt—"

"I'm poison."

She touched his arm, but he jerked away. "You're human. God forgives."

He turned to her with a look of pure hate. "Maybe *He* can forgive me, but I can't forgive *Him*. He let me murder a harmless old man. Why didn't he break my arm or shoot me in the head? Why not strike me blind? I deserve to die for what I did."

"There's still forgiveness." Her words seemed paltry compared to his guilt, but she had to try.

He shook his head. "We lynched him, Pearl. Hardin tossed a rope over a branch, and the next thing I knew McGuckin was kicking and leaking like a side of beef." His voice dropped even lower. "His daughter saw the whole thing from an upstairs window."

Pearl couldn't bear to picture her father dying such a death. She wanted to comfort Matt, but he'd gone to a place she'd never been. "I can't imagine."

"No, you can't." He stood taller. "Do you know who the old man was waiting for?"

"No," she said quietly.

"He was waiting for his son, a soldier just like me…a Confederate officer. He rode into the yard five minutes too late. Why he didn't shoot me dead, I'll never know."

"What did he do?"

"He went crazy with grief. We rode out before he came to his senses."

She had to bite her lip to keep from crying for him. He didn't need her pity. He needed to know he wasn't the first man to do something unforgivable. "I see," she said. "You're as bad as the man who raped me."

His eyes burned with righteous indignation. "I'd *never* hurt a woman."

"Sin is sin, Matt." When it came to forgiveness, Pearl knew the need to give it and the need to receive it. God's love filled the gap in between. "Everyone falls short. Some mistakes are worse than others, but they're all fish from the same barrel. If we leave them to rot, they stink."

She'd earned his attention, so she took a chance and tugged on his arm. "Sit with me."

They stepped to the divan and sat. As she angled her knees toward his, he met her gaze. "I want to ask you something."

"What is it?"

"Have you forgiven the man who raped you?"

A hard question demanded an honest answer. "Not completely, but I've tried. It helps that he's dead."

He sat back as if she'd slapped her. "I should be dead, too."

Belatedly she saw the meaning behind his question. He'd been seeking forgiveness for himself and hadn't found it. She had to explain before he lost hope. "I'm glad he's dead because he can't threaten me anymore." She thought of the harrowing days at Swan's Nest and winced. "If he'd *asked* for forgiveness, I'd have given it. He never did."

Matt held up his hand, taking hers with it in a kind of pledge. "I'd give my life to change what I did."

"Does the man's family know that?"

"I don't know."

"Why not?" Out of respect, she made her voice firm. He needed a man's reckoning, not a woman's pity.

"I wrote a letter," he admitted. "If the son received it, he never wrote back."

Pearl held his hand tighter. "You might not be able to make amends to the McGuckin family, but you don't have to carry the burden. Jesus paid the price for what you did."

As he stared at the fire, she saw their future teetering on the scale of "what if...." If Matt found forgiveness, they could be together. If he clung to his bitterness, he'd be pulling in one direction and she'd be pulling in the other. They'd always be at odds. If she pursued him, she'd be going against both God's ways and her desire for a husband who shared her faith. Even worse, she'd be standing between God and Matt. If he rejected God's grace, she'd have to let him go. Even more than he needed a wife, he needed a day of reckoning for what he'd done.

Abruptly he released her fingers and shot to his feet. He strode to a dark corner, then faced her with his hands on his hips. "That's enough about my stupidity. What happened with Jasper?"

Please, God. Touch Matt's troubled heart. She wasn't

ready to give up on him. "I can see why you're mad at
God. I was mad at Him after what happened to me. Sometimes I still am, but that's part of being human."

His mouth pulled into a sneer. "I hear that kind of talk
from Dan all the time. When some fool gets himself shot,
he tells him about Jesus and those pearly gates." Sarcasm
turned his drawl to syrup. "I've had about all I can stand,
Pearl. Don't pester me."

"You're being stubborn," she said quietly.

"I'm being honest."

"So am I. God's merciful. He loves us."

Matt's lips hooked into a sneer. "How do you know
that? Are you going to tell me Toby's a *blessing* to you?
Are you going to say God's good because you were raped
but not murdered?"

"Of course not!"

He glared at her. "God's either cruel or He doesn't
care. Either way, I'm not interested."

His words were meant to build a wall between them.
She couldn't go through it or around it, nor could she
scale the height of it. All she could do was speak to him
from the other side. "I may not understand everything
that happens, but I know there's more to this life than
being miserable. There's love, Matt. There's family and
hope and helping each other. I believe in Heaven with
my whole heart. When we get there, we'll reap rewards."

With the wall at his back, he chortled. "If God *rewards*
me, I'll be frying in Hell."

"That's right."

Matt eyed her thoughtfully. "I wasn't expecting that
answer."

"You murdered a man." She spoke with calm certainty.
"Someone has to pay for that crime, and someone has.
Jesus died for all our mistakes—every lie, every mur-

der and yes, every rape. That includes what you did to that poor old man."

Matt stayed by the window, a shadow backed into a corner. She prayed he'd find peace. *Please, Lord. Soften his heart.*

She looked for a softening of his features. Instead a hateful gleam burned in his eyes. "Forget it, Pearl. I'm asking you again. What happened with Jasper?"

Pearl gave up. If Matt didn't want to make peace with God, she couldn't force the issue. Until that day came, she had no choice but to love him from afar. With a deep breath, she hid the kiss in her heart, tucking it away just as she'd tucked away the ribbons.

Looking at Pearl, aglow with the fire in the hearth, Matt wished things could be different. A long time ago he'd had the faith of a child. But then he'd gone to war and his eyes had been opened. The past hour had opened them even wider. When he'd kissed Pearl, he'd expected to pay with his heart. Instead he'd paid with something far more costly. He'd told her his secret.

Between the fire's warmth and her sweetness, he'd lost his ability to hold the shame inside. He could have stopped the lynching, but he hadn't. Matt knew men like Jasper in his marrow because he'd been one of them. If he could stop the Golden Order now, perhaps he could forgive himself for murdering Amos McGuckin.

Until he crossed that line, he had no business kissing a preacher's daughter. When she'd kissed his cheek, he'd almost kissed her back. But then she'd told him she loved him and he'd come to his senses. He had to get her home and out of reach, but first he had to know about Jasper. Something had sent Pearl running into the rain without her cloak. "Tell me," he repeated. "Why were you in the alley?"

She stared at him for five seconds, then sighed. "I asked Jasper if I could leave early because of the rain."

She told him how Jasper had followed her into the storeroom and trapped her. With each detail, Matt clenched his jaw tighter. Whether Jasper meant to scare Pearl or harm her, he couldn't say and it didn't matter. The shopkeeper had meant to frighten her.

She raised her chin. "I didn't panic until afterward. That's when you found me. I have to thank you. That kiss—"

"Pearl, don't."

"Don't what?" She said, scolding him. "Don't thank you for finding me in the rain? For being good to me?"

"I'm not good." Hadn't she been listening? Talking about God and Amos McGuckin in the same breath had Matt all churned up. Even if he stopped the Golden Order, he'd never forgive himself for what he'd done. He'd never forgive God, either. With that hate burning in his belly, he'd never be the right man for Pearl. She deserved to hear the decision from him.

"About that kiss," he said. "Don't read too much into it. It was nice. That's all."

She looked at the fire, then spoke in a voice he could barely hear. "It was more than nice."

He tried to sound bored. "I don't mean to be harsh, but you don't know about such things."

Confusion clouded her wide eyes. "The kiss was special. I felt—"

"Forget it, Pearl. It's over."

He'd told the truth and lied in the same breath. The kiss was over but not the memory of it. He wanted to kiss her again. He'd make that one *nice,* too. Nice and long.

Nice and slow. So full of *nice* she'd feel loved and cherished until death did them part. As much as he wanted to tell the truth, he couldn't. Unless he could be a husband to her in heart, soul and deed, he had no business courting her. He'd been half-hearted with Bettina. He wouldn't repeat that mistake with Pearl.

He crossed the room and added a log to the fire. Sarah's doll caught his eye and his belly lurched. His little girl still needed a mother, and they both loved Pearl. Toby needed a father, and Matt wanted to be that man. With the flames bright, he looked at Pearl. The misery on her face nearly broke him, but he had to protect her from false hope. "I enjoyed kissing you, but it *was* just a kiss."

"I see."

"You didn't panic. That's what counts." He felt like a two-faced liar. What mattered was that they loved each other.

She looked at him with a fresh glint in her eyes. "You're making excuses."

"It's the truth."

"I don't believe you."

How could he escape this mess without lying? "Forget it happened. No matter what's going on between us, I'm not the right man for you."

She jumped to her feet. "But you are. I love you."

Her hope rubbed salt in his wounds. "I can't love you, Pearl. Not like you deserve. What happened just now— It's not what you think. It's not love."

"Then what is it?"

"Just…stuff."

"Stuff?"

"Yeah." He latched on to the one thing he knew for sure. "Life isn't a fairy tale, darlin'. You're not Cinderella and I'm not Prince Charming."

"I know that!"

"Do you?"

"Yes." She looked him in the eye. "I also know a lie when I hear one."

He put grit in his voice. He had to stop this before he found himself on his knees begging for her hand in marriage. "Let me make this clear. The kiss meant nothing. If you had more experience, you'd know that."

She turned abruptly to the fire to hide her face. He imagined tears streaming down her cheeks, mimicking the rain that had coursed down them in the alley. He'd never felt lower in his life. He couldn't leave her hurt and confused, so he stepped closer. As he raised his hand to touch her hair, someone pounded on the door.

Pearl shot to her feet. "Who could that be?"

"I don't know." He went to the window and peeked through the curtain. He saw two men. One he welcomed. The other scared him to death.

Chapter Twenty

Pearl desperately needed a moment to collect her thoughts, but Matt had already opened the door. Dan strode into the room with rain dripping off his slicker and the brim of his hat. Behind him she saw her father. A heavy coat protected him from the rain, but his face had lost its color. She hurried to his side and hugged him. "Papa, I'm fine."

He squeezed her tight, then looked at her from head to toe, taking in everything from her wet hair to the muddy hem of her gown. His cheeks changed from pale to ruddy. "What happened?"

"I'm not hurt, but Jasper—"

"What did he do?"

A bluish vein bulged on his temple. She thought of his weak heart and wished they'd never come to Cheyenne. She wished she'd never set eyes on Jasper Kling or Matt Wiley. They'd both hurt her today, Jasper with the threat of violence and Matt with his bitterness. Pearl didn't want to believe the kiss had been "just stuff" to him, but his arrogance about it shook her confidence. Had he meant it? Or was she protecting her from the man he believed himself to be? Pearl didn't see a murderer when she looked at Matt. She saw the man she loved.

"What happened?" her father said again.

She told the story with complete calm, but his expression turned murderous. When she finished, Dan explained how Tobias had come to the sheriff's office and together they'd gone to Jasper's store.

"We saw him leave in the rain," Dan explained. "He went to the bank. Troy Martin, Howard Moreland and Gibson Armond walked in right after him."

"Everyone but me," Tobias said quietly. "We all know what that means."

"They no longer trust you," Matt answered.

Tobias's brow furrowed. "I was told to be at Martin's place Saturday afternoon at three o'clock."

Far from town…far from witnesses. Pearl shuddered at the implication.

Tobias looked at Matt. "I'm afraid I'm not cut out for this kind of work."

"You did fine, sir."

He looked chagrined. "I have to admit, I spoke my mind at the last G.O. meeting. The way Jasper was talking about those women from the Silver Slipper had to be stopped. He took offense."

"I didn't help," Pearl added. "I let them in his store. Today he'd treated me like one of them."

"Don't blame yourselves." Dan crossed his arms. "Wiley and I have been questioning members of the G.O. for days now. We expected trouble, just not this soon."

Matt looked at her with a fury she hadn't seen in him before now. "You're both targets." He turned to Dan. "What time does the train leave for Denver?"

"Denver!" Pearl gaped at him.

"That's right." He put his hands on his hips. "You and Toby and your father are getting on a train *tonight*."

"You can't send us away," she protested. "You don't have that right."

"Oh yes, I do."

No, he didn't. Not if he didn't love her...not if he thought the kiss was "just stuff." She opened her mouth to argue, but her father cut her off.

"Pardon me, Deputy. But I have a say—"

"Not anymore." Matt tapped his own chest so hard she heard bone hitting bone. "This is *my* fight."

"I won't go," she argued.

"Yes, you will," Tobias insisted.

"But Papa—"

"You'll do it for Toby."

If she returned to Denver, she might never see Matt again. How did a woman choose between her child and the man she loved? Even as the question formed, she knew the answer. A mother protected her child. She ran in front of freight wagons, and she got on trains for Denver even if it meant leaving her heart behind. She turned to Matt. "My father's right. When's the next train?"

Dan answered. "Tomorrow at nine."

"We'll go then," Tobias replied.

With her heart breaking, she focused on the tasks at hand. She needed to pack and say goodbye to Carrie. Sarah, too.

Matt let out a breath as if he'd been holding it. "The G.O. knows where you live. A night at a hotel would be wise."

Tobias's brow furrowed. "If we act out of the ordinary, they'll know you're on to them. *We* might be safer, but you'll be in more trouble."

Dan looked at Matt. "He's right."

"We'll stay at Carrie's," Tobias said firmly.

Matt turned to the window. "I don't like it. Things have a way of getting out of control."

"It's the best choice," Tobias argued. "We'll stick to the plan and trust God for protection."

Matt looked back at Tobias with a sneer. "Trust whoever you want, Reverend. *I'm* trusting my instincts. I'll stand guard tonight."

Tobias nodded. "Fair enough."

Pearl saw a problem. "What about Sarah?"

"She can stay with Mrs. Holcombe."

"I need to say goodbye," she said softly. "If I just disappear, she'll be hurt." Sarah would recall her mother leaving the same way. Tonight would leave another mark on her tender heart.

Matt looked as if he'd been kicked. "You can say goodbye at Carrie's. I'll take her to Mrs. Holcombe's, then come back."

Pearl dreaded saying goodbye to Sarah. She'd do it gently, but how did a woman *gently* break a child's heart? Pearl couldn't change the facts, but she'd try to soften the loss. "I'll be careful with her," she said to Matt. "I promise."

"Thank you." His eyes held gratitude and something more...something sharp and painful. She didn't want to leave him, but the Golden Order had given her no choice.

Her father watched her thoughtfully, then spoke to Dan. "Would you take Pearl to Carrie's? I'd like a word with Matt."

"Sure."

"I'll wait with you," she protested. Her father knew how she felt about Matt. She didn't want him interfering.

Matt indicated the door. "Go on now. Your father and I have business."

When the men traded a look, Pearl knew they had a secret. She didn't like it, but nothing would break her father's will and Matt had the same stubbornness. When she looked at Matt, his eyes were as bitter as ever. Tomorrow she'd be on that train to Denver. There would be no tender goodbyes, only the memory of a kiss and a drawer full of ribbons. With her heart aching, she headed for the door.

As soon as Pearl left with Dan, Matt faced Tobias. For one crazy moment, he'd wondered if the old man was going to give him another Bible lesson. Tobias sincerely believed God would be watching over them, but Matt knew otherwise. *He'd* be watching. *God* would be sleeping like he'd slept that night in Virginia. "What's on your mind?"

"They want you dead, Matt."

"Figures." He'd asked a lot of questions and pushed some high-powered people. Chester Gates and Howard Moreland had been among them. "How do you know?"

"Martin's having second thoughts." Tobias described how he'd run into the rancher and they'd had a chat. Martin didn't mind hanging a horse thief, but he'd balked at taking down a lawman for doing his job. "The man's got blood on his hands and he knows it. Under the right circumstances, I believe he'll turn on the others."

"Would he testify in court?"

"Possibly," Tobias replied. "Moreland's the one who's leading the push to see you dead."

"I talked to him last week." Matt had seen craziness in the rancher's eyes, the kind of rage that fed on violence. "The man's got a mean streak."

"So does Jasper." Tobias grimaced. "He said terrible

things about those women who hassled him about the mirror. Why he turned so hard against you, I don't know."

"He's got a secret." Matt stared at the dying embers. "I know what it is, and I let him know it. What about Gates?"

"He goes along with Jasper."

"And Armond?"

"He got robbed again. He says you should've stopped it."

"I wish I could have." Matt wished a lot of things. He wished Amos McGuckin was still alive, and that Pearl hadn't been attacked. If he were God, she wouldn't be in danger. "I'm sorry for what happened to Pearl today. It's best that she leave. You, too."

"I didn't go into this blind," Tobias replied. "I knew it was dangerous, possibly for both of us. I have no regrets, but I *do* have a question."

"What is it?"

"I just walked in on you and my daughter alone in a dark house. I'm not questioning your honor. I know the need that brought you here. I'm questioning your intentions."

"Pearl and I have no future, sir."

"She loves you, Matt."

"She shouldn't."

"That's not your call."

Matt didn't want to be having this conversation, but he respected Tobias. "I'd never do anything to hurt her, and that's why I'm sending her away. Pearl and I…" He shook his head. "She's too good for me."

"We agree there," Tobias said drily. "My wife deserved better than me, but I'm the man she chose." He looked at Matt for a long time, giving him time to speak. Matt refused. If he opened his mouth, they'd be talking about psalms and night lunacy and men standing watch like he'd do tonight.

Tobias finally broke the tension. "We'll be on the morning train, but I have another request."

The old man had a lot of requirements. "What is it?"

"Be straight with her before we go."

"That's not wise, sir."

"Why not?"

"It just isn't."

"You're being stupid again. Prideful, too."

Matt took the insult. He'd hurt Pearl and had it coming. Eager to be done with the conversation, he crossed the room and lifted his hat. "Let's go."

Tobias frowned. "We shouldn't be seen together."

"There's more risk to you walking around alone," Matt countered. "We're headed to the livery. I have to get my horse."

Side by side, they walked across town. The rain had stopped, but massive puddles mirrored the clouds in a way that made the world seem huge. Matt felt that weight on his shoulders. If he blinked, it would crush him. Tonight he'd stand watch. Tomorrow he'd make sure Pearl got on the train to Denver. Once Jasper and the Golden Order were brought to justice, he'd sleep. If the dreams didn't come, he'd take Sarah and find Pearl. Until then, he'd stand guard. He'd be the watchman, sleepless and alone as he protected the people he loved.

Chapter Twenty-One

As Pearl walked up the porch steps with Dan, Carrie flung open the door. When she saw Pearl's disheveled appearance, her eyes flared and she hurried across the porch. As they met, she gripped Pearl's elbows. "Are you all right?"

"I'm fine." Pearl looked past her to the foyer. "Is everyone gone?"

"Everyone except Sarah. She's in the kitchen with Mrs. Dinwiddie." Carrie turned to Dan with a question in her eyes. The sight of them sharing a meaningful look hit Pearl hard. Tonight Matt had sent her away. He had a good reason, but she yearned for a promise. *I'll find you in Denver.* Did he love her? She'd thought so in the alley, but what did she know about men? Maybe the kiss really had been "just stuff" to him. Her heart told her otherwise, but it had been wrong before. Another first reaction…another mistake.

Damp and chilled, Pearl indicated the door. "Let's go inside."

The women turned and stepped into the foyer. Following them, Dan closed the door tight, then hung up his hat and slicker. Carrie led Pearl to the parlor where they sat on the divan. Dan stood by the window, watching the street with his arms folded across his chest.

Carrie took Pearl's cold hand in her warm one. "I was worried to death. What happened?"

"I'll tell you everything, but where's Toby?"

"Asleep in his crib."

Pearl wanted to hold him, but he needed his rest. Calm and confident, she described the trouble with Jasper and how Matt had found her in the alley. She wanted to tell her about the kiss, but not in front of Dan. She finished by telling Carrie about Tobias's involvement with the Golden Order and the fear that the vigilante group would try to harm him. "That's why we have to go back to Denver. We're leaving on the morning train."

"But you can't," Carrie cried. "I'll miss you too much."

"I'll miss you, too." Pearl loved her friends at Swan's Nest, but she and Carrie were family. "I have to think of Toby. And you, too. As long as we're under your roof, you're in danger."

The color drained from Carrie's face. Instinctively, she turned to Dan. "Do you think they'll come here?"

"Possibly." His brown eyes filled with a protective gleam. "You won't be alone, Carrie. I'll be standing guard with Matt. All night if that's what it takes."

"Thank you, Dan."

Carrie's voice rang with the richness of love. Envy washed through Pearl in a wave. Not only did Carrie have the security of her own home, Pearl sensed that she'd soon have a husband to go with it.

Slightly flushed, Carrie turned back to Pearl. "I know you have to leave, but promise me you'll come back."

"Maybe for a visit." Pearl glanced at Dan and saw him trading another look with Carrie. A second rush of envy sucked the air from Pearl's lungs. She wanted Matt to look at her that way. Instead she had to say goodbye to his daughter. She was about to excuse herself when the silence turned awkward.

Dan spoke to Carrie. "I'm going to look around outside. We want to be sure the doors and windows are locked."

When Carrie bit her lip, Pearl sensed Dan's longing to comfort her. She would have left them alone, but he'd already turned to leave the parlor. Carrie's eyes stayed on his back until he disappeared from view.

Hoping to lighten the grim mood, Pearl teased Carrie with a grin. "I may not come back to Cheyenne to live, but I'll be here for your wedding."

"Wedding!"

"I hope so." Pearl had been hurt tonight, but she wanted Carrie to be happy. "Dan's a good man."

"So is Matt." Carrie looked her square in the eye. "You didn't tell me everything that happened in the alley, did you?"

"No, I didn't."

"You're different," Carrie said quietly. "In spite of what Jasper did, you're calm."

She owed part of that new confidence to Matt. With Jasper she'd relived the attack. By kissing Matt, she'd taken back control of herself. She looked at Carrie with all the confidence she felt. "He kissed me." Such simple words. Such powerful words.

"Was it…nice?"

She knotted her hands in frustration. "*I* thought it was wonderful. *He* said it wasn't anything. I don't know what to think."

"Me neither," Carrie admitted.

Pearl knew her cousin had never been kissed, at least

not more than a peck. The conversation had nowhere to go, so she stood. "I have to say goodbye to Sarah."

Carrie pushed up from the divan and they shared a hug. Pearl went to the kitchen where she saw Mrs. Dinwiddie putting on her cloak. Sarah was seated at the table with a pencil and paper. She looked adorable in her pink dress, and her hair crowned her head in a perfect coronet complete with pink ribbons. If Pearl had done nothing else for this child, she'd taught Matt how to make a decent braid. She also realized she'd broken her promise to be at the tea party. She owed Sarah an explanation for missing the party as well as a goodbye.

A lump pushed into Pearl's throat, but she managed a smile. "Are you practicing your letters?"

The child held up the sheet of paper. Pearl saw a backward *S,* but the *A*'s were flawless and so was the final *H.* She looked pleased. "This spells 'Sarah.'"

"It sure does." Pearl glanced at Mrs. Dinwiddie. "How was the party?"

"Exhausting! I'm looking forward to putting my feet up." She smiled at Pearl. "I'll see you tomorrow."

No, she wouldn't. Pearl needed to say goodbye to the woman who'd been so kind to Toby. "I'll walk out with you."

Mrs. Dinwiddie gave her a curious look. "All right."

Pearl turned to Sarah. "I'll be right back, sweetie. Why don't you write some more letters for me?"

"How do I write your name?"

Pearl took the pencil and wrote her name in upper case letters. As Sarah went to work, Pearl walked with Mrs. Dinwiddie to the porch. In the quiet and the dark, she told the cook that she and her father were leaving on the morning train to Denver. Mrs. Dinwiddie clearly wanted to ask why, but she settled for pulling Pearl into a hug. "I'm going to miss you, especially that boy of yours."

"We'll miss you, too."

Holding Pearl by the arms, Mrs. Dinwiddie stepped back. "Are you sure you have to leave? Denver is just a train ride away, but it's still far."

"I'm sure."

"Whatever's chasing you away, I hope it stops."

So did Pearl. As they hugged goodbye, a man cleared his throat. Expecting Dan, Pearl looked to the bottom of the steps. Instead of the deputy, she saw an adolescent boy holding her cloak and hat. Her stomach filled with nervous butterflies.

"Miss Oliver?"

"Yes?"

"Mr. Kling asked me to deliver these to you." He walked up the steps and handed the clothing to Pearl. "There's a note in the pocket. He told me to tell you."

How much had the boy heard? Did he know she and her father were leaving on the morning train? Would he tell Jasper? She couldn't ask without raising suspicion. And the note… What did it say? She wanted to read it now, but she couldn't see in the dark.

"Thank you," she managed through her tight lips. She wished she had a coin for a tip, but her pockets were empty. Sensing the need, Mrs. Dinwiddie gave him a couple of pennies. He left and the women hugged goodbye again. Pearl watched Mrs. Dinwiddie disappear into the dark, then she went back to the kitchen where Sarah had a death grip on the stubby pencil.

The poor child looked tense and fearful, as if her life depended on spelling out Pearl's name in the unfamiliar letters. Pearl sat at the table next to her, turned the paper and studied the crooked consonants and wobbly vowels.

"That's perfect," she said with a lump in her throat.

"It's for you."

"Thank you, Sarah." She touched the girl's perfect hair. "I'm sorry I missed the party. Something happened and I couldn't come."

"That's okay."

The acceptance cut Pearl to the bone. The disappointment in Sarah's life had made her an accepting child. She took what love she could get and treasured it. Matt had given her that hope. In spite of his troubles, he was a good father.

Pearl dreaded the next words. "I have to tell you something else."

"What is it?"

"It's sad." Pearl cupped Sarah's little hand in both of hers. Her fingers were sticky with cake from the party, and she thought of the birthdays they wouldn't share. "My father and I have to go back to Denver."

"That's like Texas!" Sarah cried. "It's far!"

"I know, sweetie."

Sarah's lips quivered. "Are you taking Toby with you?"

The question stabbed Pearl in the heart. Sarah's mother had left her. Being abandoned colored the child's every thought, her every reaction. Pearl couldn't erase Sarah's scar, but she refused to make it deeper. She held her hand even more securely. "Toby's my son. I will *never* leave him. But sometimes bad things happen. People get sick or hurt, or they make mistakes like your mama did."

The child's lip quivered. "She didn't like me."

"Oh, sweetie."

"That's why she left." Tears ran down Sarah's cheeks. "She didn't like my daddy, either." She looked up hopefully. "Do *you* like my daddy?"

Pearl could hardly breathe. "I like him very much. He's

a good man, Sarah. He will *always* be there for you." Except Pearl knew too well that life was full of uncertainty. What if Matt got sick? What if he died in the line of duty?

Sarah looked at her with too much hope. "I want a mama, too."

"I know, sweetie."

"I want *you* to be my mama."

Love welled in Pearl's heart, but she didn't have the right to express it. *I love you, too, Sarah. I'd be honored to be your mother.* But Matt hadn't chosen her. He'd sent her to Denver without a word of love or even the hope of a letter. Pearl made her voice neutral. "It's up to your daddy to pick a mother for you."

"He won't." She pouted. "He works all the time."

In spite of her disappointment, Pearl ached for Matt. Until he wrestled with his need to forgive and be forgiven, he'd be bitter and Sarah would suffer. The poor child needed a mother as much as Pearl needed to be one, as much as Matt needed a wife. Pearl hurt for them all. "Finding the right mama isn't easy."

"It's not hard, either." Sarah sounded wise beyond her years. "He just has to marry you."

Just.

The word belittled everything it touched. Matt *just* had to open his heart to God. Pearl *just* had to have faith God would provide for her. She didn't want Sarah to see her upset, so she kept her voice low. "Sometimes people have to make hard choices, especially daddies. Just know that he loves you. I care about you, too."

"Then why are you leaving?"

How did she explain vigilantes to a child? "Some bad men are causing trouble. My father has to leave to be safe."

"Will you come back?"

Pearl weighed her words carefully. If Sarah was going to ever trust again, she needed the truth. "I don't know."

The child sat as still as a stone cherub. Like Pearl, she knew the futility of hoping for things she couldn't have. With tears in her eyes, Pearl took a sheet of paper and the pencil Sarah had set down. In block letters she wrote her name and the address for Swan's Nest, then she slid the paper to Sarah. "This is where I'm going to live. I'll ask Miss Carrie to help you send a letter, and I'll send one back."

"Really?"

"You bet." Pearl couldn't fix all of Sarah's problems, but she would always be her friend. Sarah looked at the paper for a long time. "I see an *S* like Sarah!"

"That's right." Pearl pointed to the *W.* "That says 'Swan's Nest.' It's where I'm going to live again."

Sarah said each letter out loud. Before she got to the *T* in 'Nest,'" Carrie tapped on the open door. "Matt's here."

Her cousin looked flushed and out of breath. Pearl wondered why. Later she'd ask, but for now the time had come to say goodbye. Pearl stood and pulled Sarah into a hug. She didn't want to see Matt, but neither would she make the moment harder than necessary for Sarah. She also had to tell Matt about the errand boy and Jasper's note.

She took the letter out of the pocket of her cloak, glanced at the writing and felt a cold certainty that it held a threat. Together she and Sarah went into the foyer, where Matt stood with his hat in hand and a grim expression.

Chapter Twenty-Two

Five minutes ago, Matt had arrived at Carrie's house with Tobias. The old man was on foot, so Matt had walked his horse. They'd exchanged a few words but not many. The danger spoke for itself. As they'd neared Carrie's house, Matt had gotten a pleasant surprise. On the far corner of the porch, he'd seen Dan and Carrie kissing in the shadows. Later he'd joke with his friend about dropping his guard while on duty, but for the moment he couldn't have been more pleased.

Tobias had seen them, too. He'd given Matt a sideways glance, but Matt had ignored him. Until he could be the man Pearl deserved, he had no business thinking about kissing her. To give Dan warning, he had cleared his throat. The couple had broken apart, then they'd all gone into the house together with Carrie looking more flustered than Matt had ever seen her. When she left to fetch Pearl and Sarah, Matt slapped Dan on the back. "Now who's the Romeo?"

Dan glared at him. "No jokes, Wiley. I'm going to marry that woman."

"Did you ask her?" Matt half whispered.

"Not yet, but I will."

Matt wished he could ask Pearl the same question. When she came into the foyer with Sarah and Carrie, he recalled seeing her with his daughter for the first time and being reminded of Bettina. He'd never been more wrong in his life. Pearl was nothing like his first wife. She had a sweetness he loved, a generosity of spirit Sarah needed as much as he did. He didn't want her to go, but he had to keep her safe from the G.O. and from his own dark heart.

She still looked disheveled from the rain, a sign she'd spoken to Sarah rather than make herself more comfortable. She also had a white envelope in her hand and a worried expression. Instead of running to him, Sarah clung to Pearl's other hand and glared at him. Tonight he'd read *Cinderella,* but he doubted the fairy tale could ease his daughter's heart.

Looking tense, Pearl offered him the letter. "It's from Jasper. I haven't read it yet."

As Matt took the envelope, their fingers touched. Hers were still cold. So were his. "Who delivered it?"

"An errand boy." She told him about the boy who'd brought her things and her conversation with Mrs. Dinwiddie. "I don't know how much he overheard, or if he'd go back and tell Jasper."

Matt's brow furrowed. "We have to figure on the worst."

Pearl bit her lip. "That means—"

"Let me read the letter." He opened the envelope, unfolded a single sheet of paper and saw Jasper's penmanship. Every letter was slanted at the same angle. The capitals matched in height, and the lower case letters made a straight and perfect line.

"Read it out loud," Tobias urged.

"Dear Pearl." Matt hated having Jasper's words on his tongue. "We seem to have had a misunderstanding. As you know, I think very highly of you and your father. I trust we'll be able to speak tomorrow when you arrive at the store as usual. With warm regards, Jasper Kling."

He folded the letter and looked at Pearl. "Whatever you do, don't go near that place."

"I won't," she murmured.

Matt turned to Tobias. "Sir, Dan and I will put you, Pearl and Toby on the train first thing in the morning. In the meantime, everyone needs to stay alert."

Carrie spoke up. "You'll need coffee. I'll put some on the stove."

"Thanks," Matt answered. He put the letter in his coat pocket. It might be needed for evidence. "The G.O. could be planning something at nine o'clock tomorrow, or they could be watching the house right now. Either way, Tobias knows too much. Once we catch them in the act, his testimony could seal a conviction."

"I'll do whatever I can," the old man said.

"Me, too," Pearl added.

Matt looked at Pearl and felt a surge of love. Instead of trembling at Jasper's threat, she looked defiant. She'd come a long way from being "Miss No Name" and running from a crowd. In some small way, he'd helped her find that strength. It made him proud, but not proud enough to stop the nightmares.

He turned to Dan. "I'll take Sarah to Mrs. Holcombe's. I'll be back with your horse."

"What about more deputies?" Dan asked.

"Dibbs and Murray are on duty tonight. I'll tell them to keep an eye out."

With their business settled, Dan gave Carrie a nod and went to stand guard on the porch. Tobias excused himself and so did Carrie, leaving Matt alone with Pearl and Sarah. Their eyes met and held, but neither of them

spoke. He couldn't bear the sight of Sarah clinging to
Pearl's skirt, glaring at him as if he were an ogre about
to snatch her away. A man did what had to be done, so he
gave her a stern look. "Come on, darlin'. It's time to go."

"No!"

"Sarah—"

"I don't want to go to Mrs. Holcombe's house! I want
to stay with Miss Pearl." She stuck out her bottom lip.
When Matt saw it tremble, he hated himself with the full
force of all his guilt. Unwillingly, he looked to Pearl for
help and wished he hadn't. Her eyes matched Sarah's
too perfectly. The females belonged together. Matt belonged with them both. If he were a better man, he could
have told Pearl he loved her. He could have given Sarah
a mother and ended this charade of uncaring. He would
never have participated in a lynching and he'd be free
to sit in church without resentment coloring his every
thought.

He wasn't that man, so he stepped forward and lifted
Sarah to his hip. She kicked so hard he'd have a bruise.
"Sarah—"

"Wait," Pearl said gently. "Let me talk to her."

Shamefully grateful for her help, he stood so that Pearl
and Sarah were nose to nose. She cupped the child's head
with her hand, kissed her temple and then rested her forehead against Sarah's smaller one.

"I love you, Sarah," she whispered. "I'm going to write
to you, remember?"

The child sobbed.

"And we're going to be friends forever, right? I won't
ever forget you, and you won't forget me."

Sarah settled a bit, but tears kept spilling down her
cheeks. "I don't want you to go!"

"I know, sweetheart." Pearl pulled back, but she kept

contact by touching Sarah's chin. "How about this… I promise I'll come and visit. I don't know when, but some-day I'll come and see you. Would you like that?"

Slowly, as if her head weighed a hundred pounds, Sarah nodded.

"Good," Pearl said with false enthusiasm. "We'll look forward to it. Now go with your daddy, okay? He's a good man and he loves you very, very much. He'll take good care of you, always. I know it."

If Pearl had looked into his eyes, she'd have seen tears. The feelings embarrassed him, but they didn't humble him enough to tell her he loved her. First he had to set-tle matters with God and the Golden Order. Turning his back, he walked out the door with Sarah in his arms.

"Bye, Miss Pearl," the child said in a shaky voice.

"Goodbye, Sarah."

With the words echoing in his ears, Matt closed the door and headed for his horse. Sarah felt as lifeless as a sack of flour. He'd have preferred a tantrum to the dead-weight. He lifted her into the saddle, climbed up behind her and wrapped his coat around her for warmth. She usually chattered when she rode with him. He'd tease her about taking the reins and they'd think of funny names for horses. Tonight she curled sideways against his mid-dle and clutched his shirt, a sign she'd said goodbye too many times. Either God didn't know, or he didn't care. Matt's blood boiled with a consuming anger. He could understand the Almighty turning His back on a man like himself, but how could He forget Sarah?

When they reached Mrs. Holcombe's house, Matt climbed off his horse and carried Sarah to the porch. Mrs. Holcombe opened the door and greeted them with a smile. "Looks like I'm going to have company tonight."

Sarah usually liked staying with Mrs. Holcombe. To-night she muttered, "I guess."

"What's wrong?" the woman asked.

Sarah shrugged. Matt chose not to enlighten her, either.

Mrs. Holcombe respected his silence, but Matt knew her opinions. More than once she'd told him Sarah needed a mother. Tonight he had to agree. "She's tired," he said. "I'll put her down, then fetch her nightie from the house." He'd get the *Mother Goose* book, too.

As he set Sarah on the divan, Mrs. Holcombe sat close. "How about a story when your daddy gets back? We could read *Cinderella*."

"No, thank you," Sarah replied, sounding overly polite. "It isn't true anyway."

It pained him, but Matt had to agree. When it came to Pearl, he'd failed miserably as Prince Charming. He'd failed Sarah, too. He couldn't pray for himself, but he could pray for his daughter and Pearl.

Help them, Lord. They need more than I can give right now.

He didn't expect God to answer, but a small part of him hoped that someday he'd be able to trust God the way Pearl did. Until then, he'd stand guard like the watchman. It wouldn't be in vain, either. He intended to stop the Golden Order on his own. He'd fight and he'd win. If God wanted to watch, so be it. But Matt wouldn't count on Him.

When Pearl walked into her room, she saw her father in the rocking chair, pushing gently as he hummed a lullaby to his grandson. She'd had a harrowing day and still needed to pack, but she welcomed his company. She'd never have a husband, but she had the best father in the world. She sat across from him on the seat of the vanity. "How are you doing?" she asked.

"I'm fine." He kept rocking. "I just wish things had turned out better."

"You did your best," Pearl said. "I'm proud of you."

"I'm proud of *you,*" Tobias replied. "Here's hoping Matt finishes the job fast. I'd like to come back here."

Pearl had the same hope. "If anyone can stop them, it's Matt."

"He's troubled, Pearl."

"I know."

He looked at her with the love she'd known her entire life. "You know I'll be praying."

"Thank you, Papa."

He indicated Toby with his chin. "This little boy's asleep. I'll put him to bed and go pack. I don't think either of us will get much sleep tonight." Her father carried Toby to his cradle, then kissed Pearl on the cheek and said goodnight. As he lumbered down the hall, she closed the door and slumped against it. The emotion she'd been holding back for Sarah's sake leaked into her eyes. A tear trickled down her cheek, then another one. She wiped them away with her knuckles, then went to the wardrobe and opened the doors. One by one, she removed the dresses from the hooks.

The blue one she'd worn the day she arrived reminded her of her first glimpse of Matt. He'd struck her as handsome and troubled, a good man with a chip on his shoulder. He hadn't changed at all, except now she loved him.

As she lifted the gray dress she'd worn to the interview, she thought of Matt taking her to the bakery. She recalled the tenderness of the moment, then the look in his eyes when he realized she'd been the victim of violence. Was that when she'd started to love him? Or had it been sooner? Pearl didn't know and it didn't matter. Unless Matt had a change of heart, her feelings had to be put aside.

As she lifted the fancy dress she'd worn to Carrie's party, she thought of Adie's wedding and her own hopes for marriage. Those hopes had been dead when she'd arrived in Cheyenne. Matt had brought them to life, but they'd faded again when he said the kiss was "just stuff." Had he been lying? Or did he mean it? Either way, the words hurt.

Last, she removed her everyday dresses, the ones she'd worn in Jasper's store. They held no memories, good or bad. She could wear them in Denver without remembering Jasper and running into the rain.

She packed her petticoats and underthings, then opened the vanity. With her throat tight, she took out the blue ribbons one by one, recalling when she'd worn them. When she lifted the one Matt had touched, it warmed beneath her fingers and she remembered everything…the moment they'd met and Sarah's messy braid. The night in the kitchen and the kiss in the alley. Closing her eyes, she pictured Matt's face as she prayed for peace for his soul.

She whispered "Amen," then looked at herself in the mirror. Slowly she unwound the coronet she'd made with her braid, then she loosened the plaits until her hair hung unbound down her back. Over and over, she brushed the strands until they crackled.

Looking at her reflection, she felt beautiful and strong. Never again would she pull her hair so tight that her scalp hurt. The blond lengths were indeed her crowning glory.

"Be with him, Lord," she said out loud. "Remind him of Your mercy. Remind him that he needs You. Amen."

Pearl needed the Lord, too. She also wanted a husband and a father for Toby. With those prayers on her lips, she

felt a rush of courage. Not once in her life had she regretted being brave, but she'd paid dearly for being timid.
Tomorrow she'd wear her hair down for the first time in
a year. She'd wear Matt's ribbons, too. As he'd believed
in the note that came with the ribbons, she'd become a
woman of uncommon courage.

Chapter Twenty-Three

By sunrise, Matt's bones ached like an old man's gout. The coffee he'd consumed tasted bitter on his tongue, although he was certain Dan felt otherwise. Carrie had been up half the night, making sandwiches for them all and keeping coffee on the stove. Matt couldn't help but hope he'd see Pearl, but she'd stayed upstairs. He knew, because he'd watched the light in her window. Long after midnight, she'd blown out the wick.

Alone in the dark, he'd looked up at the sky. Instead of stars, he'd seen a thousand blind eyes. Bands of clouds had swept over the points of light, hiding them and then revealing them again as if God were blinking. Each time he wondered why he couldn't do the one thing that might have given him peace. He couldn't forgive God, and he couldn't ask for forgiveness for himself.

While standing guard, he'd thought a lot about what Pearl had said about that night in Virginia. She'd been wounded by a crime as heinous as the one Matt had committed, yet she'd gone on with her life. He wanted the same freedom, but how did he get it? He owed a debt for what he'd done in Virginia. Somehow it had to be paid. He'd heard what Pearl had said about Jesus dying for his sins. He'd once believed in that gift and supposed he still did, but somehow believing God could forgive him wasn't enough. He felt dirty inside. And he still thought the Almighty had blinked on that fateful night.

Would his feelings change if he stopped the Golden Order? Matt didn't know, but he wanted to sleep without bad dreams. He couldn't bring Amos McGuckin back to life, but maybe he'd find peace if he could stop the Golden Order.

Even more important, he had to protect Pearl and her father. The Golden Order hadn't struck during the night, but Matt couldn't relax. If the G.O. wanted Matt and Tobias, Pearl was the perfect bait. Matt intended to put her on the train before Jasper opened his shop, but what about the errand boy? If he'd revealed the plan to Jasper, anything could happen.

Yawning, Matt leaned against the railing at the far end of the porch. He'd been up all night along with Dan and two other deputies. He'd sent Jake Murray home an hour ago. Charlie Dibbs was checking the horses, and Dan had gone to the livery to fetch a hack for the ride to the train depot. Until Matt saw the train pull out of the station, he wouldn't take his eyes off Pearl for an instant.

As if he'd called out her name, she stepped through the front door. "Matt?'"

"Over here."

As he pushed off the railing, the sun turned the day into a haze of gold. The light glinted off her hair, and his mouth gaped at what he saw. In place of the braid he'd come to expect, she'd swept half her hair up and let the rest fall down her back. Matching blue ribbons held the waves in place, the ribbons he'd given to her to say thank you…the ribbons that now said so much more.

When she saw him, she smiled. It didn't look the least

bit forced, though she had to be hurting. "Good morning," she said. "I thought you might want breakfast. Dan and the other deputies, too."

"Jake left and Charlie's busy."

"What about Dan?" Her eyes twinkled. "I'm sure Carrie would be glad to see him."

"No doubt." Matt was sincerely happy for his friend. "He's getting a hack from the livery."

She paused. "What about you? Are you hungry?"

"I'll pass." A single meal wouldn't satisfy him.

Dressed for the trip in a paisley skirt and a royal blue jacket, she looked both gracious and bold. Only the shadows below her eyes hinted at yesterday's trouble. Matt thought of Tobias urging him to tell Pearl how he felt. He hadn't done it last night, and he wouldn't do it now. He had to stick to the business of protecting her. "Are you packed?"

"Yes."

"And your father?"

"He's having breakfast with Carrie." She spoke as if nothing were wrong. "She leaves for school in a few minutes."

"Good." He wanted today to be like any other day, although he hoped Carrie would pay extra attention to Sarah. The child hadn't been herself when he'd left her with Mrs. Holcombe.

Pearl glanced down the street. "I guess we didn't have any visitors."

"No one. We'll leave for the station as soon as Dan gets here."

"So this is it," she said mildly.

"I guess so."

She looked at him with a kindness he didn't deserve. "I have to say something."

"Pearl, don't."

"Please," she said quietly. "Give me this moment."

How could he deny her a final request? How could he deny himself? Even dying men got a last meal. "What's on your mind?"

She raised her chin, then tried to smile. Her lips quivered, but her eyes stayed dry. "You, Matt Wiley, will live in my heart forever. You've given me gifts I'll treasure, and you've restored a part of me I thought was gone forever. Thank you."

"Pearl, I—"

"Please." She touched her index finger to his lips. "Don't say anything." Leaning forward, she closed her eyes and kissed him sweetly on the cheek.

Every instinct told Matt to pull her into his arms. She deserved to be kissed properly, by a man who loved her and would cherish her. He couldn't be that man, so he settled for taking her hand in both of his. Unable to let her go, he raised her fingers to his lips and kissed her knuckles. He yearned to tell her he loved her. Instead he spoke a painful truth. "I'm sorry, Pearl. I can't say what you deserve to hear."

Her eyes filled with unshed tears, maybe a hint of anger, but she kept her chin up. "Don't be sorry, Matt. I'm not."

"I've hurt you."

"You've helped me. I have no regrets and neither should you."

Just like that, she'd forgiven him.... He'd tied Pearl in knots, yet she stood here loving him without expectation. Saying nothing felt all wrong, but speaking from his heart would confuse them both. Vaguely he thought of Tobias asking him if he was cowardly or stupid. The question fit now, and he didn't have a good answer.

A hack rattled in the distance. Matt looked down the street and saw Dan. At the same moment, Charlie arrived with Matt's horse and his own. Feeling grim, he let go of Pearl's hand. "I'll have Charlie fetch your trunk."

"Thank you."

As she went back in the house, Matt spoke to the deputy. Five minutes later the trunks were loaded and Charlie had climbed on his horse. Everyone else gathered on the porch. With Toby in her arms, Pearl hugged Carrie goodbye. Teary-eyed, Carrie hugged Tobias, then told Matt she'd give Sarah an extra hug when Mrs. Holcombe brought her to school. Dan got a kiss on the cheek. After a last look at them all, she hurried down the steps and headed to Miss Marlowe's School.

Tobias offered his arm to Pearl. "It's time, princess."

Without looking back, she took her father's arm and walked to the carriage. Tobias handed her up, then climbed up and sat next to her. As Dan took the reins, Matt mounted his horse and the little entourage took off for the train depot, with Matt in the lead and Charlie guarding the rear. As they rode down the empty streets, Matt peered between houses and down alleys. He saw nothing out of the ordinary. In the business district—the section well away from Jasper's shop—Cheyenne began to stir and he felt hopeful the G.O. hadn't learned of Tobias's escape. If Matt had been planning a kidnapping, he'd have sprung the trap in a quiet neighborhood, not in a part of town with witnesses.

As they neared the depot, the locomotive sent puffs of steam into the morning sky. Carriages pulled up to the station, leaving passengers and their baggage on the crowded platform. Dan steered to an empty spot, hopped down and went to unload the trunks. Charlie joined him, leaving Matt to hand Pearl and Toby out of the carriage.

Silent, he escorted Pearl and her father to the ticket window. He made the purchase, then handed the tickets to Tobias. "There you go, sir."

The man's brow furrowed. "I expected to pay."

"The city's paying," Matt answered. "You've earned it."

Tobias put the tickets in his coat. "I'll want to know what happens. You'll be in touch, I'm sure."

"We'll need you to testify."

"Of course."

The three of them walked through the crowd to the waiting train. When they reached the passenger car, Pearl stopped at the bottom of the steps. She turned to say a final goodbye, but Matt wasn't about to let her board without seeing who else had gotten on. Brushing by her, he climbed the steps, surveyed the other passengers and saw only strangers. Reassured, he motioned for Pearl and Tobias to come aboard.

Hugging Toby close, she slipped into a window seat. Before sitting, Tobias turned and offered Matt his hand. "Deputy, it's been a privilege to know you."

Matt grunted. "I'd hardly call it that."

"Nonetheless, that's how I feel."

Tobias broke the handshake and sat. Against his better judgment, Matt looked at Pearl. She'd turned to the window, giving him a view of the hair cascading down her back. With her face turned, he could indulge in a long last look and that was what he did, until Toby cooed and reached for him. It would have been the most natural thing in the world to lift the baby and hold him high like he used to do with Sarah, kissing her tummy while she laughed and kicked. Matt imagined holding Toby like that, until the conductor announced the train would leave in five minutes.

"Goodbye, sir," he said to Tobias. "Pearl?"

Turning from the window, she met his gaze with an arched brow. "Goodbye, Matt. Stay safe."

"I will," he murmured. "You, too."

Her chin stayed firm, even defiant. In her own quiet way, she was daring him to speak from his heart. Matt wanted to offer a dare of his own. *Marry me.* But he wouldn't do it. Until he could be the man she deserved, he had no business telling her he loved her. Deliberately stoic, he tipped his hat and left the passenger car.

He had to get off the train, but he'd be watching from the edge of the platform. He wouldn't budge until it vanished from sight. Then he'd go home and sleep…maybe.

"He's gone," Pearl said to her father.

"You'll see him again."

"I suppose." If Dan proposed to Carrie, Pearl would come back for the wedding. Aching inside, she snuggled Toby against her chest. "Today feels so final."

Disheartened, she looked out the window. Hoping for a glimpse of Matt, she scanned the crowd. Instead of the man she loved, she saw a little girl with hair that matched her own.

"Papa!" she cried. "It's Sarah!"

He leaned across her lap and peered out the window. "That poor child! She's crying."

How had Sarah gotten to the train station? Had Mrs. Holcombe brought her? Maybe Carrie? Except Carrie had a class to teach. Pearl didn't see her cousin anywhere. Neither could she see Matt. Pearl jumped to her feet. "I have to help her." She handed Toby to her father, then squeezed past his knees. "I'll be right back."

"Hurry!" he called after her. "The train's about to leave."

She had three minutes, maybe less. Hoisting her skirt, she raced down the aisle of the train car and down to the platform. Waving frantically, she called Sarah's name. The child spotted her and ran sobbing into her arms.

"What are you doing here?" Pearl crooned.

"I runned away from school."

The poor grammar showed the child's distress. Pearl's belly knotted. "We have to find your daddy."

"I don't want my daddy!"

"But Sarah—"

"I want *you!*"

Pearl felt torn in two. Sarah needed her, but the boilers were chuffing and building up steam. The excess spilled into the air, filling it with the smell of water and grit. She pulled Sarah into a hug and lifted her into her arms. Had Matt waited for the train to leave? It seemed likely, so she scanned the platform. She spotted him at the far edge, staring at the window where she'd been seated with a worried frown.

"Matt!" she cried.

At the sight of her with Sarah, his eyes filled with the worry she'd seen the day they'd met, the day Sarah had nearly been run over. Pearl hurried in his direction, but a man with a bushy beard blocked her way.

"Excuse me," she murmured.

When he didn't move, she looked up and saw the man who'd been driving the freight wagon that had nearly run over Sarah.

"Excuse me, missy." He tipped his hat—a black derby.

Pearl's blood turned to ice. She tried to step around him, but he blocked her path. As she turned, a man in a mask ripped Sarah from her arms. A blanket seemed to fall from the sky, suffocating her and blacking out the sun. When she tried to scream, a hand clapped against her mouth.

"Don't do that, Pearl. We have the little girl."

Jasper!

Shouts filled the air and a woman screamed. A man shouted, "Don't shoot! They've got a child!"

Pearl could only imagine the depth of Matt's fear. With Sarah in harm's way, he couldn't fight back. But Pearl could.... She didn't have a chance against her kidnappers, but she kicked and screamed as they manhandled her into a carriage.

Someone, possibly Jasper, tied her hands and feet with a laundry cord. Bound and still covered by the blanket, she felt a man's hand snake through her hair. Forcing her neck to bend, he tugged a black mask over her face, pulled a drawstring and tied a vicious knot. Without a word, he shoved her against the far door of the carriage, maybe the one that had dropped off her father. To both her relief and horror, their kidnappers shoved Sarah on to the seat next to her.

As the carriage lurched forward, the child pressed her face against Pearl's arm. Judging by the lack of a hug, Sarah's arms were bound and her muffled cries meant they'd masked her face. With her own arms tied behind her back, Pearl couldn't embrace the girl like she wanted. She tried to calm Sarah the only way she knew. "Do you know how to pray, sweetie?"

"A little."

"When I'm scared, I pray like this." Pearl moistened her lips. "'The Lord is my shepherd. The Lord is my shepherd.' I say it over and over."

As they spoke the verse together, the carriage lurched forward. Pearl heard shouting and gunshots, then the rhythm of hoofbeats as the driver sped away from the train station. Sarah started to cry. "Who took us?"

"I don't know exactly."

She'd recognized Jasper's voice and had hunches about the others, but Matt and her father had been careful to never mention names. Judging by Jasper's customers, she figured Chester Gates and Troy Martin were among the captors along with the freight driver.

"Where's my daddy?" Sarah whispered.

"He'll come for us."

"How will he find us?"

"I'm not sure," Pearl answered. "But he will." They were bait. The Golden Order wanted Matt and her father to come after them, which meant they wouldn't be hard to find. Pearl heard the fading sounds of Cheyenne and shivered. Wherever they were headed, they'd be at the mercy of the Golden Order. Her captors could harm her body, but they couldn't touch her soul. No matter the cost, she'd fight to keep Sarah safe.

Chapter Twenty-Four

"*Sarah!*"

The cry tore from Matt's lips. Sick with fury, he watched as a black carriage whisked Sarah and Pearl away from Cheyenne. Seconds ago he'd seen his daughter snatched out of Pearl's arms by a man in a mask and a black derby. He'd drawn his pistol, but the men in masks had rendered him helpless by using Sarah as a shield. Dan and Charlie had drawn their weapons, as well, but they couldn't fire without endangering Sarah and Pearl.

The big man who'd blocked Pearl's path had sauntered away as if he were an innocent bystander, but Matt recognized Gibson Armond. Three men in masks had conducted the kidnapping. The tallest one had called out to him, summoning him to the place where the Golden Order had committed its first crime, to the valley where they'd lynched Jed Jones. *Grass Valley, Wiley. Be there. And bring the preacher.*

The Golden Order couldn't have made their intentions more clear. They'd kidnapped Pearl and Sarah to make a trade. Fathers for daughters…the guilty for the innocent.

Vaguely Matt thought of the errand boy. He'd obviously reported back to Jasper, but Matt didn't blame him for today's chaos. He blamed himself. How could he have missed Gibson Armond lurking in the crowd? Why hadn't he noticed the carriage behind the ticket office? The masked men had hidden inside it. He didn't know how Sarah had gotten to the train station, but he'd seen enough to guess that she'd run away from school, and her presence had drawn Pearl off the train.

What happened next confirmed every doubt Matt had about God. The Almighty had blinked, and the Golden Order had kidnapped the two people Matt loved most.

Dan and Charlie jogged up to him. At the same time, Tobias pushed through the crowd with Toby in his arms. If Pearl died today, the baby would be an orphan. Matt couldn't stand the thought. Neither could he bear to think of Sarah.

Tobias looked ready to kill. "I'm going with you, Wiley."

"Me, too," Dan answered.

"We need weapons and a plan." Matt had long guns in the sheriff's office. "Follow me."

Tobias grimaced. "What about Toby?"

"We'll leave him with Mrs. Holcombe."

Matt and Charlie mounted their horses. Dan took Tobias in the hack. They met at the sheriff's office and went inside. Matt considered the Colt on his hip. Six shots wouldn't be enough, so he opened the ammo box and took a handful of bullets. He put them on the desk, then opened the drawer where he kept the Colt Navy he'd carried in the war.

He didn't like the gun at all. The feel of it brought back memories of Virginia, but today it would serve another purpose. He put the weapon in his holster and his regular Peacemaker in his waistband. He took a Derringer out of the top drawer, loaded it and stuck it in his boot. Last he strode to the gun rack and lifted a coach gun. The shotgun had been cut down to eighteen inches and packed a wallop. If he had to use it, the twelve-gauge would knock Jasper Kling and the Golden Order into eternity.

As Dan and Charlie made similar preparations, Tobias stood by the window with Toby. When the baby started to fuss, the old man rocked him as if nothing were wrong. Matt figured they both needed the comfort. So did Matt, but comfort wouldn't come until Sarah and Pearl were safe.

He put on a canvas duster that would hide his weapons, then swept the extra bullets into the pocket. "Here's the plan," he said to the men. "We'll ride out to Grass Valley—"

The door burst open. The men went for their guns, but the intruder turned out to be Carrie. "Matt!" she cried. "It's Sarah. She ran away."

"I figured," he said calmly. "We're going after her now."

Carrie looked confused. "Where is she?"

"She's been kidnapped."

She gasped. "Who would do such a thing?"

Tobias glowered. "The Golden Order. They have Pearl, too."

"What can I do?" she asked.

"Take Toby." He put the baby in her arms.

Her eyes misted. "If something happens to Sarah, I'll never forgive myself. I turned my back for a minute and she ran off. And Pearl—"

"Don't blame yourself." Matt was responsible for Sarah's upset, not Carrie. He'd failed Pearl, too. He should have seen Gibson Armond on the platform. He should have admitted he loved her.

Carrie looked at Dan. "Be careful."

"I will," he answered. "Go on home."

She gave him a hopeful look, then headed for the door. As she turned the knob, she stopped. "Bring them back, okay?"

"We will," Tobias said with confidence.

Matt thought of the watchman. Either the Almighty would be with them, or He'd be napping. Matt prayed He'd be wide awake, but God had failed him before and he had his doubts. As soon as Carrie left, he looked at Charlie. "Fetch Dan's horse from the livery. Get one for Tobias, too."

"Yes, sir."

As the deputy left, Matt explained to Dan and Tobias what he intended to do. "Tobias and I will ride ahead and we'll go alone. We'll meet up with the kidnappers. Dan, you and Charlie follow with more deputies. Don't let them see you. It'll complicate the trade."

"What trade?" Dan asked.

"Fathers for daughters." Matt's life for Sarah's. Tobias for Pearl. "That's what they're after." It was a trade Matt would gladly make. What would happen, he couldn't say. But he didn't intend to die.

Dan furrowed his brow. "Pearl could recognize these men. If she can identify them, she's as much a threat as Tobias. What's to stop the G.O. from hurting her?"

"Their own code of honor," Tobias replied. "Twisted or not, they have *some* scruples, at least that's my hope."

Matt agreed. "They put a mask on her. As long as she can't identify them, she should be safe." He turned to Tobias. "Do you want a weapon, sir?"

"I do today."

Matt took another Colt from the gun safe, checked for bullets and handed the pistol to Tobias.

The minister jammed it in his waistband. "I believe in turning the other cheek, but not when women and children are in danger."

"Same here," Dan said.

"Here's what I expect." Matt spoke more for Tobias's sake than Dan's. His partner knew what to expect. "They'll order us to throw down our weapons. I'll comply, but not completely. They won't expect the coach gun and the second Colt, and they won't know if you're armed. Handle the moment as you see fit."

The men locked eyes. Tobias deepened his voice. "I'll do whatever has to be done."

Matt had had the same thought in Virginia. That night he'd been willing to kill. Today he was willing to die for the people he loved. The difference struck him full force, and he recalled Pearl talking about God's love for him. Matt had thought a lot about dying for a good cause, but until now he hadn't thought about Someone dying for him. Somehow in his angry outbursts at the Almighty, he'd overlooked the fact that Christ had suffered far more than Matt had, more than Amos McGuckin and anyone else. Matt didn't understand why God had made that choice, but today he understood the cost.

It was hard to stay angry with a God who'd make such a sacrifice. Matt couldn't explain the mess in Virginia or why Sarah and Pearl had been taken today, but he knew God wasn't to blame. Human beings had committed those ugly acts.

His anger at God eased, but the guilt remained. He still had to stop the Golden Order. Feeling both the threat of death and a lightness of soul, he led the way out the door. Charlie had arrived with the horses, so the men climbed into the saddles and headed for Grass Valley.

For almost an hour the carriage bumped down a twisting road. Pearl worked feverishly to loosen her hands, but the rope tightened with every effort. Sarah had nestled so far into her side that Pearl's ribs hurt. The little girl had stopped crying, but only after endless assurances that her daddy would be coming for them.

The long ride had given Pearl time to piece the morning together. As she'd feared, the delivery boy had revealed their plans to leave on the morning train. She and her father would have escaped if Sarah hadn't run away from school and shown up at the train station. Pearl didn't know exactly what the G.O. had planned, but they wanted her father and they wanted Matt. She and Sarah were the bait to draw them out. She suspected they had been planning to kidnap Sarah at school but had lucked out when she showed up at the train station.

She'd didn't know how many men were riding with the carriage. She could hear the thud of hooves but no voices. The wheels rattled and spun, changing speeds as they climbed and coasted along the hills.

When the carriage lurched off the road, Sarah cried out, "Where are they taking us?"

"I don't know, sweetie."

As the jostling intensified, she heard the rush of a rain-filled stream. The wind blew against the windows, shaking the carriage as it swayed to a halt. When the driver jumped down, Pearl prepared to be dragged into the open. Instead he walked away, leaving her alone with Sarah in the middle of nowhere. Pearl hadn't tried to remove the mask during the ride. If she saw the faces of her captors, they'd kill her. Now, though, they'd left her alone. If she could see, she could escape.

"Sarah, I'm going to try to get this mask off. That means I have to wiggle around."

"I want mine off, too."

"See if you can drag your head against the seat."

As Pearl rubbed her own head against the leather to

get traction, the cotton scraped her face. The sensation brought horrible memories of Franklin Dean's buggy, but she didn't stop. She twisted until her skin felt raw, then she tried to chew through the fabric. Nothing worked. The drawstring held the mask tight.

"Mine's off!" Sarah cried.

Thank you, Lord.

"What should I do?" the child asked.

"Don't look out the window, sweetheart. We don't want them to know you can see."

"The windows have curtains," Sara said. "It's dark."

"The dark won't hurt us." Pearl had to get her own mask off. If Sarah could reach the drawstring holding it tight, maybe she could bite through it. "Do you see a string on my mask?"

"No."

Pearl turned around. "Look in the back."

"There's a big knot."

"See if you can undo it with your teeth."

Sarah scooted closer and Pearl bent low. The girl gnawed at the string, but the knot only tightened. Pearl gulped stale air. Close to suffocating, she sat back. "We'll try later."

"*Now* what do we do?"

"You stay low and out of sight." Pearl felt nauseous from the lack of air. "Whatever you do, don't open that curtain. I don't want them to see you."

"Okay."

"Let's see if I can untie your hands. We'll sit back-to-back." Pearl did her best to loosen the rope around the child's wrists, but her own fingers were numb from lack of blood.

Sarah moaned. "My fingers hurt."

"I know, sweetheart."

"And I'm scared."

"Me, too." Pearl searched her mind for encouragement. "Your father's coming for us, and so is mine." She blinked and thought of another rider who'd be coming to their rescue, a man on a white horse, a man whose Name was Faithful and True. "Jesus is coming, too. He'll be with us."

Sarah looked quizzical. "Is he like Prince Charming?"

In spite of her fear, Pearl smiled. "In a way, sweetie. But he's more…much more. Now let's work on these ropes."

Chapter Twenty-Five

Matt and Tobias said next to nothing as they rode into Grass Valley. Autumn had turned the grass to gold and the cottonwoods into yellow torches. The sky couldn't have been more blue, nor could the clouds have been any whiter. A handful of evergreens dotted the meadow, rounding out a spectrum of color. It was a beautiful day. A perfect day except for the danger to Sarah and Pearl.

When they rounded a bend, Matt saw the cottonwood where Jed Jones had died at the hands of the Golden Order. As he'd expected, the leaders of the organization had congregated beneath the tall branches. Dressed in dusters, derbies and white masks, they resembled a macabre gathering of the dead. Four of the riders stood in a row. A fifth was holding a bare-backed roan. A rope that ended in a noose hung from a thick branch. They'd come to hold court, and they'd come to sentence Matt and Tobias to death.

To the right of the proceedings and several yards away, he saw a carriage with drawn curtains. He figured it held Pearl and Sarah. He wanted to call out to them, but he couldn't. The less the G.O. thought about the females, the safer they'd be. Matt had fought a lot of battles in his life, but never had so much been at stake. The lives of his daughter and the woman he loved hung on the next five minutes. So did Tobias's next breath…and his own.

Matt would do his best to protect them all, but he couldn't guarantee the outcome of today's encounter. He no longer blamed God for the awful things that sometimes happened, but he hoped that his peace of mind wouldn't be tested with the loss of someone he loved. No matter how he felt, the time had come to trust Tobias's watchman.

"Wait here," he said to the older man.

Loose and tall in the saddle, Matt rode halfway down the hill before the riders noticed him and pointed their guns. "Good morning, gentlemen!" he shouted. "Let the females go and we'll call it a day." He had no illusion they'd agree.

"Deputy Wiley!" The voice belonged to Chester Gates. "We're principled men. We have no intention of harming your daughter *or* Miss Oliver. By the same token, we do *not* tolerate traitors. I'm proposing a trade."

Matt had suspected as much. "What do you want?"

"An eye for an eye," the man replied. "If you and the reverend surrender, we'll let your daughters go."

"Give us a minute to talk," Matt called back.

"Not a chance." Gates's horse shifted under his weight. "The reverend comes down now, or we sacrifice his daughter to the cause of justice."

"You're bluffing," Matt shouted.

"Hardly."

The man next to Gates lifted his chin. Through the eye holes in the mask, the sun reflected off a pair of spectacles. Matt recognized Jasper. Judging by the size and shape of the others, Martin and Moreland were next to him. Gibson Armond had donned a duster and mask and was holding the horse to be used in the hanging.

Matt stalled. "You're asking a man to die. Five minutes is nothing."

"Who said anything about dying?" Gates said in a smooth tone. "We'll have a trial right here. If the reverend's innocent of deception, he'll understand. If he's guilty, he'll hang."

"And me?" Matt asked sarcastically.

"You know too much." Gates smirked. "I'm quite sure you'll trade your life for your daughter's."

Matt wanted to kill this man. He wanted to kill them all, but they had him outnumbered and outgunned. The longer he kept Gates talking, the better his chance of surviving. "How do I know you won't hurt Pearl?"

"You have my word."

"That means nothing."

Gates ignored the insult, but Jasper turned to the man Matt assumed to be Howard Moreland. "Fetch Miss Oliver."

"No!" Tobias shouted.

If the old man hadn't ridden past Matt, Matt would have offered himself in Pearl's place. Wisely Tobias stopped halfway to the hanging tree. "Release our daughters."

"Just one," Gates said to Tobias. "You pick."

"Send out the child."

Matt had never known a deeper gratitude. Tobias loved Pearl beyond measure, yet he'd put Sarah first. Matt would never forget his sacrifice.

One of the riders, probably Moreland, went to the carriage. He opened the door, said something Matt couldn't hear and reached into the interior. Sarah screamed. Matt's fingers itched to pull the trigger, but then where would they be? If he acted on instinct alone, they'd all die. He had no choice but to trust the watchman, so he waited.

To his relief, Moreland pulled Sarah out of the coach and waved her away with his gun. She saw Matt and ran in his direction. "Daddy!"

"No, darlin'! Run away."

Whimpering, she stopped in midstep.

"Go on," he said firmly. "I'll find you."

Please, Lord. Don't let that be a lie. Sarah ran up the hill. If the worst happened, Dan would find her, but then what? If Matt died today, who'd love his little girl? He had to live and so did Pearl. So did Tobias because they were meant to be a family.

Gates called out, "Throw down your weapons, Reverend."

Tobias raised his hands. "I'm armed with the sword of the Lord. It's sharp enough to separate bone from marrow, truth from lies. You men are Pharisees! You're—"

"Get off your horse!" Gates shouted.

Tobias slid out of the saddle. Still quoting Scripture, he walked toward the hanging tree with his hands high. "The Lord is my shepherd! I shall not want! The Lord—"

"Shut up!" Jasper shouted.

"I'm a dead man," Tobias replied. "I've got something to say and you're all going to listen."

He started shouting the Lord's prayer. The familiar words made one of the riders, probably Martin, back pedal his horse. Disgusted, Moreland grabbed Tobias by the collar. "Shut up, old man!"

Gates turned to Moreland. "*You* shut up! *I* give the orders!"

"Then give them!" he shouted. "We're wasting time."

"I promised this man a trial."

"He's guilty," Jasper declared.

With Tobias still shouting, Moreland dragged him to the hanging tree. The man holding the roan shoved him belly down on the horse and attempted to tie his hands. If they got the noose around Tobias's neck, he'd die.

Matt put his hands in the air. "You want me, too. Let the reverend and his daughter go, and I'll come peacefully."

If Gates accepted Matt's surrender, he'd regain the authority he'd lost to Jasper and Moreland. The banker signaled the men by raising his hand. "The deputy wants to do some negotiating."

Tobias went still, and the men stopped wrestling with him. Gates looked at Matt. "Throw down your guns, Deputy."

Matt dragged his left arm down, pinched the Colt Navy from the holster and dropped it to the ground. It landed with a thud, useless and out of reach.

"Throw down the other one," Gates ordered.

Matt slid the Derringer from his boot and dropped it next to the six-shooter. He still had the coach gun under his duster and the Peacemaker in his waistband, but weapons alone wouldn't win this fight.

"Come down here," Gates ordered.

The masked men cocked their pistols and took aim. With his arms in the air, nothing stood between Matt and death except God's grace…the grace he didn't deserve, the grace he'd scorned because of his own arrogance. Without God's mercy, he'd die at the end of a rope. Sarah would be an orphan. Pearl would escape with her life, but she'd be at the mercy of men like Jasper Kling.

In a silent breath, Matt cried out for mercy for them all. With mercy, he knew, came justice. *Forgive me, Lord, for murdering an innocent man. Forgive my pride and my arrogance.*

With his hands up and his eyes on the men in masks, he saw an ironic truth. He was just like these men. He'd taken justice into his own hands, not only in Virginia but in his own life. For the murder of Amos McGuckin, he'd sentenced himself to a life of good deeds. Where had it gotten him? Nowhere… Unless God intervened, today he'd die. Matt had done his best. Now he needed help.

It's up to You, Lord. I'm willing to die, but I'd rather not.

Peace washed him clean. His thoughts cleared and he knew what he had to do. The outcome of this day belonged to the Lord, but Matt had two guns, eight bullets and something to say. With his hands high, he called out to the men who intended to kill him. "Don't do this, gentlemen. You'll regret it. I know, because I've been in your shoes."

"Shut up!" Jasper shouted.

"You need to hear this," Matt declared. "Back in the war, I was part of a lynching. We murdered an innocent man. That's what you're doing now."

Jasper spat on the ground. "We're administering *justice!*"

"No, you're not."

Gates steadied his revolver. "Shut up, Wiley!"

"Not yet," Matt said in a steady voice. "You've hurt a lot of people, both guilty and innocent. You've destroyed property and peace of mind. And for what?" He looked at Howard Moreland, then turned to Martin. "To punish a fool for stealing horses? Jed Jones deserved to go to jail, but it wasn't your call."

Matt turned to Gates. "You love money, don't you? You have a wife and a lovely daughter, but it's not enough. You wanted to destroy Scottie Fife, because he bought land you wanted."

"Shut up, Wiley," Gates ordered.

"Not yet." He looked at Gibson Armond. "I don't know why you're here, Mr. Armond. You've been robbed, I know. But kidnapping a woman and a child? Threatening a minister? You must have lost your mind. Someone's going to know what happened, and you're going to go to jail."

The freighter looked shaken, but he didn't speak.

Last Matt turned to Jasper. "I know why *you're* here. You've got a secret and it's ugly."

"You're lying!" he shouted.

Matt laughed out loud. "Obviously not. You just denied a secret I haven't even told."

Jasper yanked off the mask. "Don't you dare—"

"Dare what?" Matt raised his voice. "Tell your good friends that you're a regular at the hog ranch? That you pay women like the ones you won't let in your store?"

"He's lying!"

Matt spoke to the others in a loud voice. "Kind of hard to imagine, isn't it? Mr. Kling got caught red-handed."

Someone snickered.

Jasper sputtered a protest, but the men knew Matt had told the truth. He'd told the truth on all of them, even himself. The truth had set him free. He was a mere man, a failed man…a man redeemed by love. Before he did what he had to do, he needed to ask one last question, the same question he'd asked himself. He looked each man in the eye. "You're proud men. You're willing to kill for what you believe in."

"That's right," Moreland shouted.

"Killing is easy. It doesn't cost you a thing." Matt looked straight at Jasper. "I want to know what you're willing to die for."

"Nothing!"

"Then you're a coward," Matt shouted.

Goaded by the taunt, Jasper raised his pistol. As he fired, his horse sidestepped and the bullet went over Matt's head. Matt grabbed the coach gun from under his duster and took aim at Jasper. With a prayer for mercy for them all, he shot the man dead.

As if he'd cut the head off a snake, the other four fell back with their hands in the air. Jasper lay dead in the grass, his chest still and his blood soaking into the earth.

With the coach gun in one hand, Matt pulled his colt with the other and aimed it at Gates. "Get that mask off your face."

When Gates did as he ordered, Matt put the coach gun away. "Now hit your knees!"

Gates hit the ground, but his eyes gleamed with the bitterness of a man who regretted his capture but not his acts.

A strange thought ran through Matt's head. He could kill these men and no one would blame him. They'd threatened his daughter and they'd kidnapped Pearl. They'd intended to hang a minister, and they'd have gladly shot a lawman to hide their crimes. They deserved to die, but Matt had no desire for vengeance. The man who'd lynched Amos McGuckin was dead and gone. No more blood would spill today, but he wouldn't let down his guard. He cocked the Colt and aimed it at Troy Martin. "Do you want to die, too?"

"No, sir."

Next he pointed the pistol at Howard Moreland. The man had put his hands in the air, but he hadn't hit his knees. "Get down," Matt ordered.

Moreland raised his chin. "What if I don't?"

Matt cocked the Colt. "I'll have to change your mind for you."

The man must have believed him, because he dropped to the ground one knee at a time.

Matt eyed Gibson Armond next. He'd followed the commands Matt had given to Moreland and hit his knees. He looked truly remorseful. Matt didn't bother to rebuke him. The man's nightmares would be his punishment. Instead he looked back at Moreland.

Tobias had pulled the Colt out of his waistband and was drilling it into the man's temple. "I'm not prone to violence, Mr. Moreland. But if my daughter's been harmed, I *will* hold you accountable."

"No one touched her." The man spat on the ground. "No one wanted to."

Fast and hard, the urge to shoot Moreland filled Matt's trigger finger. Being human, he couldn't stop the hate. Being wise, he ignored the reaction.

He had to get to Pearl. Working fast, he and Tobias tied up the men. As Matt picked up the guns he'd dropped, he heard horses approaching and saw Dan, Charlie and Jake. A fourth deputy came at a slower pace. Matt looked again and saw Sarah tucked behind him. Later he'd hug his little girl. Right now, Pearl needed him. He ordered the deputies to take in the prisoners, then he galloped his horse to the carriage.

From the moment Sarah had been snatched, Pearl had strained to hear what her captors were doing. She'd heard voices, but she couldn't make out the words over the rush of the nearby stream. Out of nowhere, she heard her father shouting the Lord's prayer. Blinded by the mask, she prayed for God to keep them safe. Matt's voice rose above the others and she prayed some more.

A shot rang out and she shrieked.

A second one echoed.

"Matt!" she cried inside the mask. Was he lying dead on the ground? Had her father been lynched? She couldn't bear the thought of losing either of them. And Sarah? What had happened to the child? Pearl struggled again to free her hands. She scraped the mask against the seat, but the drawstring tightened and cut off her air. She strained to hear voices or boot steps, anything that would give her hope, but all she heard was her own labored breath.

"Please, Lord," she murmured. "Let Sarah be safe. Let my father be alive. Dear God in Heaven, save Matt—"

The thunder of hoofbeats jarred her thoughts. As the horse pulled to a stop, a man's boots hit the ground with a thud. She couldn't see a thing. She could only feel the buggy seat, the fabric over her face and the rope binding her hands. No matter who opened the carriage door, she'd be at his mercy. If Jasper touched her, she'd kick and fight. She'd—

"Pearl!"

"Matt!" she cried. As he flung open the door, tears streamed down her cheeks. "You're alive."

"Very much so."

"My father—"

"He's safe. So is Sarah." The seat dipped with his weight. Scooting close, he tried to untie the mask. When the drawstring didn't budge, he cut it with a knife and pulled the black cotton over her head.

Air rushed into her lungs. Breathing deep, she took in the brightness of his eyes. He caressed her cheek, then as he'd done twice before, he looked her up and down for injuries. "Are you hurt?"

"I'm fine."

At the sight of her bound hands, his jaw tightened. "Turn so I can cut the rope."

She shifted to give him access. With a single slice of

the knife, he cut the laundry cord digging into her wrists. Blood rushed to her fingers. It hurt and felt good all at once. Matt bent down and sliced the binding from her feet. She was free, but what about Matt? The ties binding her body could be severed with a sharp blade. His bonds were harder to break.

"What happened?" she asked.

"Jasper's dead." He told her briefly about the gunfight. "Dan's taking the others to jail."

"Thank God." She meant it.

Matt's eyes took on a shine. "I won't argue with you, Pearl. God's mercy alone explains what happened today. I'm grateful for it."

When his lips relaxed into a smile, he looked peaceful. She touched his face. "You're different."

"I feel good."

She wanted more, needed more. "Tell me."

He shrugged. "Let's just say God and I did some talking. He made some good points. I'm not stupid enough to still be angry with Him."

Pearl wanted to cheer. She also wanted to kiss him, a reaction that filled her with joy. She blushed at the thought.

He touched her cheek. "I lied, you know."

"About what?"

"Kissing you…it was a lot more than nice." His eyes burned with their old intensity. "I love you, Pearl. Will you marry me?"

Her breath left in a gasp. *Yes! Yes!* But she couldn't force the words past the lump in her throat.

With one arm around her shoulders and the other cradling her legs, Matt lifted her up and out of the carriage. When she was steady on her feet, he dropped to one knee.

"I can't promise you a perfect life. I'm a hard man with a hard job, but I will live and die for you. I'll—"

"Yes!" she finally cried. "I'll marry you."

He rose to his full height and drew her into his arms. The kiss they shared was joyous and confident, full of love and so nice that her toes curled. Laughing, she stepped back. Matt grinned, then lifted her into his arms and spun her around.

When she landed, she saw her father and Sarah approaching the carriage. Her father's eyes had a knowing shine. Sarah looked hopeful but worried. Hand in hand, Matt and Pearl closed the gap between them. When they reached Sarah, Matt dropped to a crouch. "Hi, there, darlin'. Are you all right?"

She bit her lip. "I was scared."

"Me, too." He smoothed her messy hair. "The bad men are gone now. You were very brave."

"I was."

"I'm proud of you." He touched her cheek. "Do you think you can handle another surprise today?"

She looked uneasy. "Will I like it?"

"I think so." He smiled at her. "Pearl and I are getting married. She's going to be your mama."

Sarah rushed headlong into Pearl's skirts and hugged her. It was just like that first day in Cheyenne, but this time their dreams were coming true.

Tobias smiled. "Looks like I've got a new granddaughter."

"That you do," Matt replied.

The only person missing from the moment was Toby. Still hugging Sarah, Pearl looked at Matt. "My son—"

"*Our* son," he said with a twinkle in his eye.

She smiled. "Where is he?"

Tobias looked pleased. "Carrie has him."

Pearl let out a long breath. She could hardly wait to hold Toby, but mostly she wanted to see Matt cradling their son in his strong arms. "Let's get home. I can't wait to start forever."

Matt made show of rubbing his chin. "That sounds like a good ending for a fairy tale. Do you think we can do some imagining?"

"Like what?" Pearl asked.

He indicated the carriage. "Let's pretend this ugly old coach is white with gold trim, just like Cinderella's."

Sarah giggled. "I want glass slippers."

"Me, too," Pearl echoed.

Matt laughed. "How about fancy dresses?"

"I have one," Sarah declared. "It's pink."

"I have one, too," Pearl said. "It's blue, and I have pretty ribbons that match."

Matt gave her a sly grin. "I seem to recall those ribbons. They look pretty in that blond hair of yours."

When he touched the wave falling down her back, she shivered with happiness. From this day forward, she'd wear his ribbons every day.

Her father cleared his throat. "Matt, you take the girls in the carriage. I'll follow with the horses."

"Sounds good to me, sir."

Sarah tugged on her daddy's sleeve. "I want to ride outside with you."

"Me, too," Pearl said.

Matt agreed. "Let's go, ladies."

Tobias offered Pearl his arm. "Climb up, princess. Your carriage awaits."

And so it did.... Her father led her to the front of the coach and handed her off to Matt. With a debonair smile, he helped her up to the high seat, then he lifted Sarah, so she could sit with them. After a salute to her father, he joined them and took the reins. With the sun bright and the sky a perfect blue, Pearl rode into the future with her very own Prince Charming, the man she'd love forever and ever.

Epilogue

December 1875
Swan's Nest

"It's time to toss the bouquet," Adie Blue announced. "Ladies, get ready!"

From the back of the foyer, Matt watched his new wife climb to the third step of a staircase. Less than an hour ago, Tobias had presided over their wedding vows. Dan and Carrie, newly engaged, had stood with them. Sarah had been a flower girl, and Pearl had held Toby to complete their ready-made family.

Matt would have gotten married anywhere, but he'd been glad when Pearl suggested Swan's Nest. The trip had given him a chance to meet her friends. Adie Blue had spunk, and her husband, Josh, had a wry sense of humor. The sisters, Caroline and Bessie, had cooed over Toby and Sarah.

Matt had especially enjoyed meeting Mary Larue. A former actress, she reminded him of someone he used to know…a man with a chip on his shoulder and an angry past. Pearl had told him a lot about Mary. She'd taken some hard knocks in life. Judging by the way she stood apart from the women waiting for the bouquet toss, she didn't intend to take any more.

With the bouquet in hand, Pearl surveyed her friends. When she spotted Mary against the wall, she waved at her. "Mary! Get over here!"

The blonde shook her head. "Oh no, you don't! I'm *not* getting married. Not ever!"

Matt stifled a grin. He'd once thought the same way.

Adie called to the crowd. "Okay, ladies! Here it comes."

As Pearl turned to throw the bouquet, Matt caught a look in her eye and knew what she'd do.

Adie counted down. "One...two...three!"

Pearl tossed the flowers high and to the left. Sure enough, the bouquet landed smack in Mary's arms. She looked mad enough to throw it back. As she sputtered objections, Matt grinned at his wife. Knowing what he did about love, he had no doubt he and Pearl would someday return to Denver for another Swan's Nest wedding.

* * * * *

Sherri Shackelford is an award-winning author of inspirational books featuring ordinary people discovering extraordinary love. A reformed pessimist, Sherri has a passion for storytelling. Her books are fast paced and heartfelt with a generous dose of humor. She loves to hear from readers at sherri@sherrishackelford.com. Visit her website at sherrishackelford.com.

WINNING THE WIDOW'S HEART

Sherri Shackelford

God setteth the solitary in families:
he bringeth out those which are bound with chains:
but the rebellious dwell in a dry land.
—*Psalms* 68:6

To mothers:

To Rita Rounds Shackelford,
for the beautiful soul I never had a chance to meet,
for all the extraordinary books she never had a
chance to write. Thank you for giving me the
most precious gift of all: my husband, Todd.
Your generous spirit shines through your children.

To Bonnie Preble, for always believing in me,
even when I didn't believe in myself.

Chapter One

Outside Cimarron Springs, Kansas, 1870s

A shrill scream from inside the homestead split the frosty air.

Jack Elder flattened his back against the cabin's rough-hewn logs, his Smith & Wesson drawn. Icy fear twisted in his gut. He couldn't think about the woman inside, couldn't let himself imagine what had ripped that tortured sound from her.

Head cocked to one side, he strained to hear voices over the howling wind. How many men were inside? Was Bud Shaw one of them?

Dense clouds draped the afternoon in an unnatural twilight. Fat, heavy snowflakes sheeted from the sky, pillowing in heaps on the frozen ground. Jack nudged the deepening slush with his boot. No footsteps showed in the fresh covering. No animal prints, either.

The glass-paned windows had been covered with oil-cloth to keep out the cold air and curious eyes. He cautiously edged toward the rear of the house, his shoulders hunched. A sharp gust of wind sucked the breath from his lungs. He stretched one hand around the corner, re-lieved to feel the raised surface of a door latch.

Another harsh shout mingled with the raging blizzard. The desperate cry hardened his resolve. He didn't care how many men were inside—he couldn't let that woman suffer any more.

Mustering his fortitude, he whipped around to face the door and kicked. Hard. Wood splintered. A gust of warm air scented with fresh-baked bread knocked back his hat. He lunged inside, his pistol arm leveled. A wom-an's startled blue eyes met his shocked gaze over the sil-ver barrel of her Colt .45.

Jack froze.

The lady standing before him was young, and nearly as round as she was tall. Her pale hair clung damply to her forehead, and a shapeless gingham dress in drab hues swathed her from head to toe. She kept her body partially obscured behind a tall chair, as if the flimsy wood might somehow repel a lead bullet.

Her hands shaking, the woman wrestled back the gun's hammer. "Take one more step and I'll blow your head off, mister."

Jack thought he'd planned for everything, but staring down the barrel of a quivering Colt .45 was proving him woefully wrong. An armed woman hadn't been on his list of contingencies.

Carefully pointing his own weapon at the ceiling, he cleared his throat. "I'm a Texas Ranger," he called out loud enough to reach anyone who might be hiding. "You're safe now, miss."

Her face screwed up in pain. She tipped forward, clutching her stomach. Her gun weaved a dangerous path in the air. Fearful of a wild shot, Jack extended his arm toward her.

"Don't touch me!"

He searched her panic-ridden features for any sign of injury. "Where are you hurt?"

"Nowhere." She warned him back with a wave of her gun. "So get out."

His instincts flared. She was obviously in pain, not to mention she'd been screaming loud enough to wake a hibernating grizzly moments before, yet she still refused help. Was she trying to warn him? Had the outlaws set a trap?

Jerking his thumb, he indicated a door on the far side of the room. "Is he in there?" he asked, his voice hushed. "Where's Bud Shaw?"

"No one here by that name," she gasped. "Now get out. I don't want any trouble."

Liquid splashed onto the wood plank flooring at her feet. Her face paled, and her eyes grew as large as twin harvest moons. Frigid air swept through the broken door.

The truth hit Jack like a mule kick. She wasn't plump, she was pregnant. Very pregnant. He hadn't stumbled into Bud's hideout—he'd barged into a peaceful homestead. The lady of the house was understandably spooked, and about to give birth at any moment.

He didn't need a sawbones to tell him the woman's bag of waters had just broken. Jack raised his eyes heavenward and offered up a quick prayer for guidance.

"Lady, you got a heap o' trouble," he said at last, "but I ain't part of it."

She staggered to the left, the weapon still clutched in her hand.

With a quick sidestep, he dodged the business end of the barrel. "Ma'am," he spoke, keeping his voice quiet and soothing, "I'm holstering my weapon."

She aimed her gun dead center at his chest.

Anxiety rose like bile in his throat. Nothing was more unpredictable than a frightened civilian with a firearm. Not to mention she was unsteady on her feet and in obvious pain. The sooner he disarmed her, the better.

His decision made, he crept forward, his arms spread wide to display his empty hands. "Where's your husband? Has he gone to fetch help?"

She glanced away, as if considering her answer.

His stomach clenched. "You're alone here, aren't you?"

Her full, rose-colored lips pursed into a thin line. She shook her head in denial.

Annoyed by her refusal to look him in the eye, Jack grunted. He could guess the meaning of those loaded pauses and hesitant answers.

His sharp gaze surveyed the room once more. An enormous cast-iron stove dominated the space to his right. A single pine table and four crude chairs filled the corner behind the woman, a side cupboard and a pie safe flanked the open kitchen area. No masculine boots rested on the rag rug. No overcoat hung on the sturdy hooks beside the door. Ten years as a Texas Ranger had given him a heap of insight into people.

Everybody lied, just not for the same reasons.

He assumed his most charming smile to put her at ease. "I'm Jack Elder, and I'm not going to hurt you. I've been tracking a gang of bank robbers through Kansas. You haven't been robbing any banks, have you?"

She scowled at his joke, then another pain racked her body. She doubled over, pressing her free hand beneath the shelf of her belly.

Taking advantage of the distraction, Jack caught her around the forearm. Her startled gaze flew to his face. Though her wild, frightened eyes pierced his rigid control, he held firm. Careful to keep his touch gentle, he pried the Colt loose from her trembling fingers, swiftly releasing the hammer with a seasoned flick of his thumb.

She narrowed her eyes. "Are you really a Texas Ranger?"

Jack stepped away, hardening his heart against her suffering. Emotions clouded judgment—and poor judgment got people killed.

After hooking his finger into the gun's trigger guard, he flipped back the collar of his jacket to reveal the silver star he'd carved from a Spanish coin. Uncertainty flitted across her face, followed by reluctant acceptance of the tarnished evidence of his profession.

"Ranger or not," she said. "You have no right to be here."

Habits honed from years on the trail had heightened his senses. The woman had a curious lilt to her voice, the barest hint of an accent in the way she spoke. She wasn't from around these parts, but then again, who was?

He let his coat fall back into place. "Ma'am, you need to lie down. That baby is fixing to come."

"No," she cried, stumbling away. "It's not time. I checked the calendar. It's too soon."

"I don't think your baby is on the same schedule."

"But I can't have the baby now. I'm not ready."

Jack heaved an inward sigh. *Marvelous.* She was delusional and in labor. He definitely hadn't planned for this. She appeared oblivious to the telling mess at her feet, to the growing chill in the cabin, to—well—to everything. As if ignoring the situation might somehow make it all go away—make him go away.

He shifted his weight, considering his options. Best not to push her too hard. Mother Nature would deliver the full realization of her circumstances soon enough.

She mumbled something beneath her breath and vigorously shook her head. "No, it's definitely too soon. I have everything planned out for the last week in November."

Another glance at her rounded belly heightened his trepidation. A little nudge in the right direction never hurt. "You look plenty ready to me."

Her expression turned icy. "And what do you mean by that?"

"Well…" he stalled. "You're, you…"

A flush crept up his neck. While there was no polite way to indicate the most obvious symptom of her condition, she was a little too far along in the birthing process for his peace of mind. Wherever her husband had gone, it didn't appear the man would be returning home anytime soon. Without another person to watch over the woman, Jack's options were limited. Unless he took control of the situation and found a reasonable way to extract himself, they were *both* in a mess of trouble.

"Do elaborate," she demanded. "I'm what?"

Suddenly hot, he slid the top button of his wool coat free. He'd just come from Cimarron Springs, and it was forty-five minutes to town for the doctor. Leaving the woman alone that long was out of the question. Grateful for the breeze from the busted door, Jack released the second button. Surely someone was watching out for the woman? Even in this desolate land a person was never truly alone. She must have friends or family in the area.

A teeth-chattering shiver rattled her body, buckling her defensive posture. She wrapped her arms protectively around her distended stomach. "This is my home, and I want you to leave."

"You and me both."

He'd rather face an angry rattler than a fragile woman any day. But the sight of her pale face tugged at his conscience. Of course he'd do the right thing. He always did the right thing, especially when it came to women and children.

That code of honor had been ingrained in him since his youth. "I can't go until I know you're settled."

Conscious of the dropping temperature and her growing discomfort, he backed his way to the broken door, his attention riveted on the woman. Snow swirled around his ankles, dusting the cabin floor with white flakes.

Her gaze skittered to the gun in his holster. "You're trespassing on my property." She tightened her arms over her rounded belly, highlighting the swell. "Return my gun this instant."

He nudged the sagging door closed with his heel. Wind whistled through the cracked hinges. "I can't do that. You might need my help, and I can't have you shooting me."

He rested her Colt on the sturdy worktable before the stove, then covered the weapon with his hat. "I might be a Texas Ranger, but my family owns a cattle ranch. I haven't delivered any babies, but I've brought a passel of calves into this world, and I've got a fair understanding of the process. Once your bag of waters breaks, there's no going back."

She started, as if noticing the wet floor for the first time. "Oh, my goodness. What a mess. I—I need a cloth."

She waddled to the side cupboard, swinging the door wide to rummage through the shelves.

Jack blew out a hard breath, letting her prattle about her chore. He'd seen that same vacant stare plenty of times before. His first year as a Ranger, he'd come upon a homestead after a Comanche raid. The woman of the house was setting the table for supper, her clothing torn and bloodied, while her husband and three young children lay slaughtered on the dirt-packed floor.

His chest constricted at the memory. He'd never forget the mother's dark footprints circling her dead children's bodies. From that moment on, he'd hardened his feelings to the suffering he witnessed in order to preserve his own sanity.

The pregnant woman faced him, her chin set in a stubborn angle, a square of linen clutched to her chest. "The man you're looking for isn't here, so you can leave now, mister."

"What's your name?" he asked, his tone deliberately brusque. Most decent folks responded honestly to a direct question.

"Elizabeth. E-Elizabeth Cole."

He offered her another friendly grin. His questions had the added benefit of keeping her distracted. "See, that wasn't so hard, Elizabeth." He also found people answered to their own name, even when they ignored everything else. "Where's your husband?"

Her eyes welled with tears. Sniffling, she blinked them away. "He's dead."

Jack bowed his head, shielding himself from the agony in her steady gaze. She definitely wasn't lying now. The way her emotions paraded across her expressive face, she'd make a terrible criminal.

"I'm sorry for your loss," he replied.

She was awfully young to be a widow. Jack sometimes felt the good Lord had let evil concentrate west of the Mississippi.

He opened and closed his mouth a few times to speak, finally deciding to give her a moment to collect herself before any more questions. Judging from her condition, the man couldn't have been gone for too long. In this harsh land, it was best not to get attached to anything, or anyone.

When she finally glanced up, he asked, "Do you have any family or friends in the area?"

"The McCoys live just over the rise."

Hope sparked in his chest. "Is there a Mrs. McCoy?"

"There's a Mrs. McCoy, a Mr. McCoy—" she ticked off each name with a finger to the opposite hand "—and five little McCoys."

Relief weakened his knees. Delivering babies was best left to women and doctors—and he didn't qualify as either. "Thank heaven for the McCoys."

He'd find a way to contact the family as soon as Elizabeth was settled. With his immediate worry eased, he stepped forward, motioning with one hand. "Let's get you someplace where you can rest, Mrs. Cole."

She eyed him with obvious distrust.

Flummoxed by her stubbornness, Jack paused. Now what? Give him a raging outlaw or a drunken killer any day. He wasn't equipped for this kind of sensitive situation. Those teary blue eyes were sorely testing his vow to remain detached.

She lurched to one side, clutching the ladder-back chair for support. "Oh, dear," she moaned.

Feeling helpless and out of his element, he cupped her elbow. Her wary gaze swept over his thick wool coat, lingering on his stamped, silver buttons. Her jaw clenched. He had the uneasy sensation she had just sized him up, and found him lacking.

Jolted by her odd reaction, he dropped his hold. "I'm not going to hurt you, Elizabeth."

She pinched shut her eyes against another pain, then fumbled for his hand, threading her fingers through his in a silent plea for comfort. His heart stuttered at the unexpected gesture.

How long since her husband had died? How long had

she been pregnant and alone, solely responsible for the grueling work required to run this homestead?

After a long, tense moment, her delicate features relaxed. The grip on his hand loosened.

"That one wasn't so bad," she said, though her wan smile indicated otherwise.

"Let's get you away from this breeze." He nodded toward the back of the house. "Someone near broke your door in two."

"I hope that same someone repairs the damage before he leaves."

She lowered her head, then yanked her hand free, as if surprised to see their fingers intertwined.

Keeping his gaze averted, he flexed his fist a few times to shake off the lingering warmth of her skin. He didn't want to look at her, didn't want to see the raw edge of fear in her eyes. Didn't she realize he was one of the good guys?

Following the strangely intimate moment, an awkward silence stretched between them. The widow was a curious mix of bold courage and heartbreaking vulnerability. She'd been in labor, isolated and alone, yet she'd met his forceful entrance with rare fortitude. Despite her blustery grit, he sensed her reserve of energy was running lower than a watering hole in July.

She brushed the hair from her forehead with a weary sigh. "Maybe I will have a rest."

"That sounds like the best idea I've heard all day."

She leaned heavily on his arm as he eased her past the cast-iron stove, through the doorway to another room. An enormous four-poster bed dominated the space. A wedding-ring quilt in faded pinks and dull greens covered the mattress. An old porcelain doll with matted chestnut hair rested between two fluffy feather pillows.

Jack scratched his forehead. "That's quite an impressive piece of furniture."

Her cheeks flushed pink. "My husband and I bought the homestead from another family along with the furniture. They made it almost six years before they gave up." Avoiding his curious gaze, Elizabeth shuffled to a sturdy oak dresser. A red kerosene lantern with a floral-etched, fluted cover lit the room. She tugged on the top drawer, sending the flame flickering, then glanced at him askance. "I'm sorry I lied to you earlier. I didn't want you to know I was alone."

"I didn't give you much choice."

She kept her eyes downcast, her discomfort palpable. While he appreciated the awkward impropriety of the situation, his nagging concern for her welfare took precedence over their mutual embarrassment.

They had a more pressing problem to solve. "Is this your first baby?"

She nodded.

"How long have the pains been comin'?"

"About four or five hours."

The knot of anxiety in his chest eased. The birthing processes often took hours, sometimes even days. "If there's one thing I do know, it's that first babies take their good sweet time in coming. I've got three older brothers, and they've blessed me with two nieces and six nephews. Not a one of them took less than twelve hours to be born."

She met his gaze, her pale blue eyes full of hope. "Then you can go to town. Cimarron Springs has a doctor. Two of them."

"Ma'am, there's a snowstorm blowing in. I'll be lucky to make it to the McCoys, let alone town."

Her shoulders slumped and his heart went out to her. Pain and fear had a way of sapping a body's strength.

"This isn't exactly a church social, I know that." He paused, searching for a way to alleviate her fears. "Tell you what. I'll get my horse out of the weather and check on the animals. Won't take me more than a minute. You can change and lay down for a rest. Keep track of the pains, though. They should keep coming closer together. When you're settled, I'll skedaddle over to the McCoy's spread for help. With five children, they should be well versed in delivering babies."

She bobbed her head in a distracted nod, pressing her knuckles into the small of her back with a grimace.

He scooted to her side. "Don't hold your breath through the pains. Just let 'em come."

"Is that what you tell the cows?" she snapped.

"I heard the midwife say that to my sister-in-law. I tell the cows to moo through the pain."

A reluctant smile appeared through her scowl.

"That's better." He'd paced the floor with his brothers through enough births to know Elizabeth was going to need all the humor she could muster. "You've got about six to eight minutes before the next pain. I'll be back lickety-split."

A feather-light touch on his sleeve stilled his retreat. "When you return from the McCoy's, you can bunk down in the barn until the weather clears." She swallowed, glancing away. "But that's all. I expect you to clear out at first light."

Jack tipped his head in agreement. The widow was still a might skittish about his intentions. Considering their less-than-cordial introduction, he couldn't blame her. "Don't worry, Elizabeth. Everything is going to be all right."

"Easy for you to say, mister. You're not the one having a baby."

Jack couldn't help a dry chuckle. There was nothing like a crisis to reveal a man's true character, and he was encouraged by her fortitude. "You'll manage. You faced down an armed intruder, after all."

She cut him a sidelong glance full of wry skepticism before turning her back. Inexplicably annoyed with her cool response, he toyed with the wick on the lantern to cover his confusion. When had his social skills slipped? Usually a few charming words and a friendly smile were enough to put most people at ease.

With a shrug he closed the door to allow her privacy, then crossed through the kitchen. He loped out the splintered rear exit, snatching his hat on the way.

Driving snow pelted his face, stinging his bare cheeks. He tucked his scratchy wool collar beneath his chin as he fought through needle-sharp wind to his disgruntled horse. The gelding snorted a smoky breath, tossing its head. Icicles had already matted in the horse's thick mane and tail.

Jack tugged on the reins. "Sorry, Midnight. I'm just as frustrated by the delay as you are. I should have known that potbellied old sheriff in town couldn't tell a homestead from a hideout."

The gelding nuzzled his shoulder.

"If I'd known the weather was going to change faster than a sinner on Sunday, I never would've risked the journey. Almost makes a fellow believe in divine providence." He tipped his head to the sky. "Mrs. Cole needs us to fetch help, even if she doesn't want to admit it yet. I know as much about the surface of the moon as I do about childbirth, and that ain't saying much."

The quicker he found help for the widow, the quicker he could continue on his journey. The more time passed, the colder the trail out of Cimarron Springs grew. Jack couldn't afford any additional dead ends and delays. If an innocent man was hanged because of his mistake, he'd never forgive himself.

His thoughts dark, he fought through growing snow drifts, sinking to his calves with each step. A flurry of movement caught the corner of his eye. Jack drew his pistol, searching the blowing snow. Wouldn't that just be the bee's knees if the outlaw was squatting right under his nose?

When no one sprang from the shadows, he tucked his gun away. He'd most likely seen one of the farm animals searching for shelter. The sheriff's mistake was troubling him, making him jumpy. He'd take a gander at the horses inside the barn before he returned to the main house. The outlaw he was searching for always rode a distinctive bay mustang. Men around these parts knew horseflesh better than humans, which might explain the sheriff's confusion.

Another thought sent him stumbling. A curtain of snow slid off his hat.

He'd forgotten the Colt sitting on the worktable.

"Well, Midnight," he muttered to the horse, "I hope Mrs. Cole has given up the idea of shooting me."

Jack swung up the bulky T-bar latching the barn door, then heaved the sliding panel to one side. The hayloft hook twirled in the wind above his head, banging forlornly against the loft door. Even before Midnight whinnied, shying to one side, Jack sensed a trap.

Elizabeth pressed the heels of her hands to her eyes, holding back the painful burn of tears. She panted through another sharp pain, her heart still thumping uncomfortably against her ribs.

She'd almost shot a Texas Ranger.

When the oilcloth over the window had flipped up during a wind gust, she'd nearly fainted to see a stranger's dark form lurking outside. She'd grabbed her gun and waited, expecting the worst.

She wasn't expecting a lawman.

With his easy charm and fancy silver buttons, Jack Elder reminded her of her late husband. That charming behavior was bound to wear off, and she hoped he was long gone when it did. Aside from his useless good looks, she didn't need him returning to town with tales destined to send the gossip's tongues wagging.

A familiar sorrow weighed her down. She'd had enough of interfering busybodies as a child, and enough of autocratic lawmen as an adult. If the Ranger wanted to make trouble, there was nothing she could do to stop him. She'd fought the sheriff to stay in her home after Will's death, and she'd fight anyone else who threatened her tenuous security.

Recalling the scene in the kitchen, her blood pounded, and her face grew hot with humiliation. Thank heaven he'd be gone by morning.

Elizabeth cradled her belly, hesitant to offer up another prayer. She'd prayed for a husband, and God had sent her a smooth charmer named Will. She'd prayed for a child, and Will had deserted her rather than care for his growing family. She'd prayed for Will's return, and God had sent her his body to bury.

Hurting and desperate, she'd prayed for help, and God had sent her a lawman. She let out a reluctant sigh. While he wasn't what she'd prayed for, at least he was willing to fetch help.

Elizabeth choked back a desperate laugh. She'd been hoping for a break in the weather, or more time to prepare before the baby arrived—anything but a great bear of a man treating her like a half-wit. *Delivering cows, indeed.* Thank heaven he wouldn't be delivering this baby. After hearing him talk, he'd most likely try to sweet-talk the infant through the process with a rakish grin, or expect her to moo through the contractions.

Overwhelmed by the day's events, she tucked her worn Bible beneath a stack of neatly folded cotton shirtwaists, fearful of praying for anything else lest she inadvertently unleash a plague with her clumsy words.

The only person she could truly count on was herself.

A violent cramp twisted around her middle. Shouting, she slid down the wall, crumpling to the floor. Her vision blurred. A great weight pressed on her stomach, like a full-grown bull sitting on her belly. The torturous spasm kept building stronger and stronger. The urgent need to push overwhelmed her.

"Mr. Elder," Elizabeth called, her faint voice no match for the brutal prairie winds.

That flashy lawman was wrong—this baby was coming. *Now.*

Chapter Two

The pain let up just as quickly as it had begun. Stunned by the intensity of the last contraction, Elizabeth panted. Each time she assumed the agony had peaked, another violent spasm proved her wrong.

A hopeless sob caught in her throat. She wiped the sweat from her brow with the back of her hand, amazed at how quickly her body swung between chilling cold and suffocating heat.

She needed help. She needed to stop blubbering and pull herself off the floor. Mostly though, she needed her mother to be alive, holding her hand and easing this devastating fear.

Elizabeth struggled to form a plan, but her brain refused to function properly. Her thoughts flitted from subject to subject until the torturous pain demanded her undivided attention.

Through the haze of her agitation, the rear door banged open. Surprised Mr. Elder had returned so soon, Elizabeth craned her neck to peer around the corner. She'd seen the panicky look in his eyes at her condition earlier. Once he realized the increasing gravity of the situation, he'd saddle his horse and ride away as if a pack of wolves was nipping at his heels.

She shifted to press her palms against the floor. Her brief marriage had taught her one thing about men—they had a tendency to stay when they should go, and go when they should stay. Her arms collapsed like wet noodles beneath her weight.

Rallying her strength, she stretched to brace her hand against the dresser. This inability to force her body to respond frightened her as much as the pending birth. She had to be stronger. After all, she didn't need a man's dubious help. She'd survived for months without any assistance. She'd survive another day. The eminent desertion of one Texas Ranger was the least of her worries. The weak attempt to comfort herself failed miserably.

"Mrs. Cole," a familiar voice shouted.

Relief swept over Elizabeth like the first warm breeze of spring. "Jo," she called back. Here was the help she had prayed for. "I'm in the bedroom."

The young McCoy daughter burst into the room with her usual boisterous energy. Her frantic gaze swept across the bed. Elizabeth waved a limp hand from her wilted position near the dresser to catch the girl's attention. Jo's eyes widened at the sight of her employer slumped at her feet.

"What happened?" Jo demanded. "Did that man hurt you?" The girl knelt, whipping off her scruffy hat to reveal two long, serviceable braids. "Don't you worry none. I locked him in the barn."

"Oh, dear." Elizabeth struggled to sit up straighter. A band of steel wrapped around her abdomen like a vice. The pressure consumed her, blocking out all thoughts of the trapped Ranger. "It's the baby," she gasped.

"Is that all?" Jo flashed a crooked grin. "Don't you

worry, Mrs. Cole. I told you at least a hundred times that I've helped my ma deliver plenty of babies. You don't understand 'cuz you're from back East, but most folks around these parts don't cotton to no doctor."

Elizabeth bore down on the pain, clenching her jaw against the agony. Jo checked her progress, then squeezed her hand. "The baby's dropped, Mrs. Cole, but I'm pretty sure you still have a ways to go."

"Are you certain?" Elizabeth choked out.

"Pretty sure."

The contraction eased, releasing the aching tightness around Elizabeth's belly. She drew in a shaky breath. "I guess we'll have to muddle through this together for a bit."

"I knew there was something wrong earlier." Jo shot her a black look. "Why didn't you say you were hurting?"

"I didn't know—" Elizabeth stopped herself before she told a lie. Of course she'd realized something was wrong. Knowing Jo would sense her distress, Elizabeth had fought to hide her growing discomfort. The girl was more perceptive than most people twice her age. "I didn't want to worry your mother. You said she wasn't feeling well."

A shadow darkened Jo's bright green eyes. At fourteen, Jo was the oldest of five children, and the only girl. Awash in a sea of males, she'd taken to dressing and acting like a boy herself. She'd been helping Elizabeth with the chores since Will's death six months ago.

Elizabeth trusted the girl's ability to help until they unlocked Mr. Elder and sent him to fetch Jo's mother. "That man you—"

"I couldn't go home, anyway," Jo interrupted, her voice thick with emotion. "Pa shooed me away at the gate. There's influenza in the house. The town's had five deaths already. If Ma dies, I'm all Pa's got to take care of the little ones."

A sound of distress caught in Elizabeth's throat. Concern for the McCoys overshadowed her own worries. "Your family will be fine, Jo. I'm sure. Your mother is a strong woman."

Elizabeth wanted to offer more words of comfort, but another contraction robbed her of speech. An eternity later she gasped, "Oh, my, that hurts."

"I know." Jo patted her hand. "It's going to get worse before it gets better. Mrs. Parker hollered so loud, my ears rang for a week. 'Bout squeezed my hand off, too."

Horrifying images of Mrs. Parker's suffering flooded Elizabeth's thoughts. They were alone. With the storm raging, and the nearest farm quarantined, no help was coming. "Perhaps we could save these stories for another time?"

"Oh, right." Jo flicked her head in a quick nod. "What is it Ma's always saying?" She snapped her fingers. "I remember now. She distracts 'em by talking, and telling 'em to concentrate on that beautiful baby they're bringing into the world."

"That's better."

"Hey, remember all those clothes we sewed this fall?"

Elizabeth rolled her eyes. "You're the worst seamstress in the county. I sewed all those clothes while you complained you were dying from boredom. You'd rather be out shooting game than threading a needle."

"See? You're doing better already." Jo sat back on her heels. "Now deliver this baby so we can decide what to do about that man I locked in the barn."

"I'm a Texas Ranger."

Jo gasped at the intrusion. Hands fisted, she twisted

to block Elizabeth while keeping her defiant gaze fixed on the Ranger.

Slanting a glance upward, Elizabeth found Mr. Elder filling the doorway and looking madder than a wet hen. His coat was torn at the shoulder, and an angry scratch slashed across his cheek.

Gracious. This day just kept going from bad to worse.

"He's a lawman all right," Elizabeth replied, restraining Jo with a limp hand to her forearm.

The girl relaxed her stance. "How'd you get out of the barn?"

"Just you never mind, missy." He plucked a length of straw from his hair. "What's going on in here?"

"Are you touched in the head, Ranger?" Jo flung out a hand. "Can't you see she's having a baby?"

"Imprisoning a lawman can get you the firing squad."

"You don't look imprisoned to me."

Elizabeth shouted as suffocating pressure bore down on her pelvis. The two combatants fell silent, their identical shamefaced expressions almost comical. She panted through the contraction, ignoring the accusatory glares they shot at each other over her head. Silent now, Jack knelt at her side, a concerned frown puckering his brow.

When the pain eased, Elizabeth flashed the younger girl a reassuring smile. "I hope this doesn't take much longer. I was hoping to start another batch of bread later."

Given the girl's pitying smile in return, her joke had fallen on deaf ears. Too exhausted to care, Elizabeth rested her head against the wall to stare at the ceiling.

She'd thought she was capable of delivering a child without collapsing like a fragile greenhorn, but the endless cycles of pain had sapped her strength. Recriminations for her own foolish behavior rattled her composure. Why hadn't she thought to send Jo into town earlier? Instead, she'd dawdled over her chores, thinking she had weeks to prepare. Without Mrs. McCoy or the doctor, she and the younger girl were going to have to deliver this child alone.

Elizabeth turned to Jack. Regrets were a luxury she couldn't afford. "You can go now. We'll be fine."

Jo's head snapped up. "Not on your life. I need a pan of water and linens. As long as we've got ourselves a real, live Texas Ranger, we might as well put him to good use."

Elizabeth held up her hand in protest. Lawmen asked too many questions.

Mr. Elder rose to his feet. "I've got whiskey in my saddle bags for the—"

"Wait." Fear pierced Elizabeth's heart. "You won't bring whiskey into this house."

"Ma says it keeps the baby from getting dysentery," Jo added softly. "I need it to clean my hands."

Elizabeth sensed pity in the girl's eyes, but she brushed aside the feeling. How could Jo know about Will? Elizabeth had confided in no one.

"Can we get Mrs. Cole onto the bed?" the Ranger asked.

"No!" Elizabeth cried.

Every nerve in her body bore down on the pain. Desperate for the agony to end, she didn't want to be jostled or moved. The contractions were coming closer together, giving her less and less time to recover before the next increasingly agonizing spasm.

Her energy waned with each pain. The months following Will's death had been filled with turmoil, leaving her little chance to concentrate on the pending birth. Her shock and grief, her fear, had drowned out all thoughts of the future.

When the nagging backache from this morning had grown worse, she'd refused to heed the signs. As if, with the baby growing in her womb, her dreams were still possible. She'd pictured her future with a loving husband and half a dozen children running underfoot. The hopeful plans for her new life and a growing family had dwindled. She was a widow, alone and vulnerable.

"Mrs. Cole." Jack touched her shoulder, his voice filled with compassion. "Your baby needs you to be strong."

Elizabeth grimaced against another contraction. A salty tear caught on the corner of her mouth. The weakness shamed her, but she was exhausted from maintaining her rigid composure. It was time she faced the harsh reality of her circumstances. Women died in childbirth all the time.

She'd never ducked away from a difficult choice and she wasn't about to start now. "Promise me something, Mr. Elder."

Apprehension widened his eyes.

Elizabeth didn't know anything about the Ranger, didn't know if she could trust him, but she sensed a quiet determination behind his wary gaze. Unlike the local sheriff, he appeared to be bound by a code of ethics. While most men were only interested in their own pleasure, Mr. Elder's job forced him to take the needs of others into consideration.

She clasped his hand, comforted by the hard calluses covering his palm. Will's hands had been soft and smooth. The disparity gave her hope. Perhaps this man was different from her late husband. "Mr. Elder, if something happens to me, you'll see that my baby is raised by a real family. Don't let my child grow up in an orphanage."

He blanched. His Adam's apple bobbed. "You're going to be fine, Mrs. Cole."

"Prom—"

The Ranger held up his free hand to quiet her protests. "There's nothing to worry about."

Jo scowled. "Never mind him. My ma can take the baby."

Elizabeth shook her head. Mrs. McCoy worked harder than ten men combined. She ran her household on a budget barely fit for a pauper. Heaven knew the overtaxed woman didn't need an additional burden. Not to mention the time and cost of rearing another child.

"JoBeth McCoy," Elizabeth scolded, "your mother has enough to worry about with five children at home. She doesn't need another mouth to feed."

Jo ducked her head, silently acknowledging the truth. Another violent cramp hardened Elizabeth's belly. She panted, clutching the Ranger's hand.

When the contraction eased, Mr. Elder refused to meet her pleading gaze.

She was pushing him, a stranger, to make a difficult promise. Even if he agreed, she would never know whether or not he had fulfilled his pledge. Despite the uncertainty, she needed him to say the words. She needed to clutch a glimmer of hope for her baby's future.

She wanted a better life for her child. "Promise me."

Jack turned. His hazel eyes shined in the dim light. "I promise."

His assurance released the floodgates of her emotions. She sobbed through another searing contraction, the most powerful yet. Black dots collected at the edges of her vision, growing larger. The room clouded. Voices came to her from a great distance, as if she were tumbling down a well. Down, down, down to a place where there was no pain, no loss, just darkness.

"Please, God," she whispered. "Save my baby."

Cold panic tore at Jack's insides. "Wake up, Elizabeth," he ordered.

He clasped her chin in his hand, humbled by the fragile bones. She was so delicate, so young to be facing this pain. Beneath his touch, her head rolled limply to one side. Her glazed eyes slowly cleared. His heart soared as dawning recognition focused her attention. She was still too pale, but a faint blush of color had infused the apples of her cheeks.

She drew in a breath, her shoulders rising and falling with the effort. Sweat beaded on her forehead, and her pale blue eyes had lost their luster.

"I can't do this," she sobbed.

"You're doing real good. It's almost over."

He said the words out loud, though he didn't fully believe them in his heart. There were no certainties for anyone. With only the two of them to assist her, if something went wrong, they were lost.

Alarmed to find his heart beating like a stampeding bull, he pressed the widow's hand to his chest, sharing his strength. His emotional reaction startled him. He'd paced the floor with his brothers, but not a one of his sister-in-laws' births had affected him this way.

Jack squared his shoulders. He was immune to suffering. He'd seen plenty of people die, men and women both. He'd buried children, marking their graves with rough wooden crosses or crude piles of stones. Nothing moved him anymore.

A shrill cry shocked him from his stupor. He swiped at his forehead with the back of his hand. He'd never felt so helpless. He was sweating as much as the widow now. All the comforting words he'd spoken to his brothers while their wives were in labor came back to haunt him. He blinked the perspiration from his eyes. What a bunch of inadequate nonsense.

Humiliated to be at the mercy of a prickly girl who couldn't be more than fourteen, he gave Jo a pleading look.

She met his gaze, her face revealing nothing. "The baby's head is crowning. I'll need a pan of water and some fresh linens."

He hesitated to leave the women alone.

"Sometime today, Ranger!"

Jack stumbled to his feet, clumsy and out of his element. He rushed to gather the supplies, grateful for something to do besides worry.

He fled to the kitchen and gingerly tossed the contents of a sturdy creamware bowl out the back door. His fellow Rangers often chided him on his cool, collected demeanor, saying icicles ran through his veins instead of blood. They'd eat their words to see him now. Returning to the sink, he pumped the lever arm to prime the well, his hands stiff and uncoordinated.

After filling the bowl, he pawed through his saddle bags, searching for the whiskey. Fear strummed through his body with each of Elizabeth's jagged cries. He yanked a handful of linens from the side cupboard, sending the rest of the neat stack tumbling to the floor. His arms full, he returned to the bedroom, then knelt beside the perspiring widow.

Jo glanced up. "Scoot in behind her and help her brace when she pushes. This baby's a might stubborn."

Beseeching him with her eyes, Elizabeth jerked her head in a nod. Her silent plea humbled him. She looked on him as if he might actually soothe her pain—as if he was something more than a giant lump of useless male. For a moment, he wanted to be everything she needed.

Jack snorted softly to himself.

Who was he fooling? He was about as much use in this situation as a handbrake on a canoe. He rubbed his damp palms against his pants' legs, wishing he'd never followed those bank robbers out of Texas. Wishing he'd stayed in town. Wishing that potbellied sheriff had directed him anywhere but here. Even as the traitorous thoughts filled his brain, he helped Elizabeth sit up, his work-roughened hand dwarfing her slim shoulder. He slid one leg behind her back, bracing his boot against the dresser as he hunkered down.

The pungent smell of alcohol stung his nostrils. Jo rubbed the whiskey on her hands, then wiped them clean with a dry cloth. The girl's fingers trembled, but she managed a wobbly smile. "When the next pain comes, I want you to push as hard as you can."

For a moment Jack didn't know who was more frightened—the widow, the kid or him. Like a battalion of warriors mustering for war, the three of them nodded in unison.

Elizabeth clasped his hand in a now-familiar gesture. He cradled her against his chest, willing his strength to infuse her exhausted body. Her blond hair had tumbled loose from its bun, catching on his coat buttons. He carefully untangled the strands, then brushed the silky locks aside.

"You know how to pray, Ranger?" Jo asked.

This time he didn't hesitate. "Dear Lord, if you're looking down on us, now would be a good time for some help."

"Amen," JoBeth murmured.

Elizabeth's body stiffened.

"You're almost there," he soothed. "You can do this, Elizabeth. You're almost done."

Curling forward, she squeezed his hand, her whole body straining with effort. Her agonizing shout of pain ripped through him like a bullet.

"Oh, my goodness," Jo cried. "It's a girl. It's a girl, Mrs. Cole! You have a beautiful girl."

Following her announcement, a heavy silence filled the room. Jack waited, hearing nothing but the sound of his own heartbeat thundering in his ears. Jo carefully wiped the child dry with a towel. Her worried gaze met his over Elizabeth's head. At the stricken message in her eyes, his heart seized.

The bundle squirmed. A lusty squall exploded from the infant, startling them all into relieved laughter.

Jo carefully placed the baby on Elizabeth's chest. The widow cradled her bellowing child, laughing and crying at the same time. "She's so beautiful." Elizabeth glanced over her shoulder, catching his gaze. "Isn't she beautiful?"

His eyes stung. He cleared his throat, recalling all the times he'd teased his older brothers for their weeping and wailing every time a niece or nephew was born. He'd never understood the vulnerable emotions those wet, froglike creatures inspired. Seeing Elizabeth's joy, her newborn, the miracle of life where there once was none, something in his chest shifted.

"Yes," he said, his voice husky. "She's beautiful."

While the two women laughed, awkwardly hugging each other over the baby, the walls crowded in around him. The air in the room turned dank and suffocating. His nerves tingled, warning him of an attack. He needed to escape.

This time, though, he feared the danger rested within his own heart.

Chapter Three

Elizabeth awoke in darkness to the clang of pots and pans and the mouth-watering aroma of frying bacon. Stiff and sore, she gingerly rolled to her side to check on the baby. The surge of energy she'd experienced immediately following the birth had plummeted soon after. A rare fatigue had overcome her, sapping her of strength and leaving her weak and listless.

Barely able to keep her eyes open, she'd mustered just enough energy to change out of her ruined dress with Jo's assistance. Her legs had proven too weak to hold her weight, so Mr. Elder had assisted her onto the bed. Silent and flushed red from his neck to his ears, he'd lifted her with treasured care.

He'd lingered to help Jo change the linens and tidy up the room, both of them waging a hushed, muttering war on the proper way to accomplish even the most minuscule task. Each time the Ranger had chanced a glance at Elizabeth, his cheeks had darkened to such a deep crimson, she'd feared he would burst into flames.

After ensuring the newborn was settled, a gown lovingly drawn over her body and crocheted yellow booties covering her feet, Elizabeth's two helpers had left mother and daughter alone in the hushed glow and hiss of kerosene lamps.

The infant had nursed voraciously, then stretched and yawned before falling into the peaceful slumber afforded only the very young, and the very old. Cocooned in a blanket of serene contentment, Elizabeth had been reluctant to surrender her gift from God. She'd dozed off with the infant cradled in her arms, her daughter's gentle breath whispering against her neck.

Swaddled tightly, the baby now rested beside the bed in a drawer Jo had extracted from the dresser and lined with blankets. Sighing, Elizabeth extended her hand over the edge of the mattress. She brushed the backs of her fingers over the supple, downy softness of the baby's cheek, then buried them in the shock of dark hair covering her head.

"How did I create something so perfect? So beautiful?" she whispered. "Thank you, Lord, for this is Your work."

Her heart swelled. Now more than ever, she needed to be strong. The awesome burden of responsibility weighed upon Elizabeth alone. Her daughter's survival in this wild, untamed land was at the mercy of her mother's courage. The prairie was brutal, especially for women and children.

Elizabeth glanced toward the darkened window, the glass panes frosted over like sugared candy. A tangle of memories pulled her into the past.

Her first month in Kansas, she'd stumbled between a cow and her calf. The animal had butted her to the ground, knocking the wind from her lungs. Will had been angry at her carelessness, chastising her for coming between a mother and her offspring. Elizabeth finally understood his warning.

The changes in her life over such a short time threatened to overwhelm her. In one short year, she'd been a wife, a widow and a mother. Last November she'd married Will after a three-week-long whirlwind courtship in New York and moved West. Three months later she was pregnant and three months after that Will was dead. The entire year had brought her full circle to this new life.

She might not know anything about raising children, but she loved her daughter already, had loved her since that first moment she'd felt the baby stirring in her womb. She'd die to save her child.

A child who currently had no name.

Elizabeth pressed her numb hands against cheeks burning with shame. How could she have been so thoughtless? She'd fallen asleep without naming her baby.

A vague memory took shape, Mr. Elder leaning over the infant, running his index finger reverently over the baby's cheek. "We'll name you tomorrow," he'd said. "When your mother has rested."

Gracious. Not only had she failed to name her child, she'd abandoned poor Jo to deal with the Ranger, alone. *So much for courage and fortitude.*

She'd abandoned those dearest to her to fend for themselves—while she *slept.*

A lump of regret clogged her throat. "Oh, baby," Elizabeth sighed. "What a mother you have."

She caught the sounds of someone puttering in the kitchen, whistling a merry tune. Perhaps she was being too hard on herself. Nothing awful could have happened for Jo to be so cheerful. With the baby nestled snuggly in her makeshift bed, and Jo busy in the kitchen, no one had suffered unduly for Elizabeth's absence. After all, she'd just delivered a baby. An exhausting task, to be sure.

As for their uninvited guest, considering the late hour,

Mr. Elder was probably long gone. Once a man wanted to leave, no one could stop him. She wouldn't be surprised if he was halfway to Texas already.

A twinge of loss stirred up her turbulent emotions. She recalled the way he'd held her hand, the encouraging words he'd murmured. How odd to think she'd never see him again.

She pressed a fist against her mouth to stifle uncontrollable sobs, alarmed by her inability to hold back the tears. She never cried, ever. Not when her father had died, not when she'd been escorted to the orphanage by two somber nuns while her mother looked on, not even when Will had left her for good. Yet over the past few days she'd been nothing but a watering pot.

Determined to quell the flood of emotion, she swiped at her cheeks. Weak women did not survive. Her baby was depending on her. She'd had enough trouble after Will's death, she couldn't let down her guard.

Heavy footsteps approached the door. A tentative knock sounded. "Are you all right?" a male voice called.

Her heart flipped. She absently smoothed her hair and tugged her heavy wrapper higher over her neck. Why was Mr. Elder still here? Had the weather changed for the worse? Had something happened to Jo?

She lifted the baby from her cozy nest, and cradled the bundle against her chest. "I'll be right out," she called, unable to disguise the quiver in her voice.

The infant's cupid-bow mouth opened and closed in a yawn, her tongue working. Elizabeth pressed her cheek against the baby's forehead, willing herself to be strong. Tears escaped her tightly clenched eyes, dripping down her cheeks. Frightened by her lack of control, she bit her lip. Another telling sob slipped out.

The doorknob rattled. "You don't sound all right."

A long pause followed while Elizabeth struggled to find her voice.

The door opened a crack. "I hope you're decent, because I'm coming in."

Mr. Elder swung the door wider, his gaze searching the room, his lips set in hard line.

"What's wrong?" he demanded.

"Nothing."

Elizabeth sniffled.

His fierce expression turned hesitant. He crossed his arms over his chest, then dropped them nervously to his sides before finally planting his burly fists on his hips. "I'll just be going then."

He reached for the exit, his feet still rooted to the floor.

She sniffled again.

One hand clinging to the doorknob, he sighed heavily. "If nothing's wrong, why are you crying?"

Tears dripped onto the baby's forehead, startling the infant. Sleepy eyes blinked open, catching Elizabeth's gaze. She stared into their depths, caught in the dark and mysterious vortex, fascinated. It was like looking at an old soul in a new body. "My baby doesn't have a name."

"Is that all? I thought something bad had happened."

"Well," she huffed. "I wouldn't expect a man to understand. A good mother would never fall asleep without seeing to her child first. I left Jo all alone with you and… and…" A fresh wave of tears spilled down her cheeks. "This poor child has been on this earth all afternoon, without a name."

His gaze swung between her and the baby as if he was puzzling out a great problem. "It's not like she understands the difference."

"Oh, you, you…" Elizabeth fumed. "I cannot say anything nice to you, so I am not going to say anything at all."

She clenched her teeth to prevent a torrent of angry words, so resentful, she wanted to lash out.

"No need to upset yourself." Mr. Elder hovered in the doorway like a wild-eyed buck poised for flight. "It shouldn't be too difficult to name a baby. Did you and your husband have any names picked out?"

Elizabeth choked back another sob. The only thing Will had ever called their child was a "nuisance." He'd ridden away the day after he'd discovered she was pregnant.

Her blood turned to ice. What if the child found out she was unloved by her father? Unwanted? Everyone deserved to be loved. All children deserved a name.

She cradled her daughter protectively against her chest. No one knew the truth about Will, and she'd keep it that way. Certainly plenty of people suspected her late husband of cheating at cards, and not a few had grown suspicious of his shallow, jovial smile. But no one knew his true character. He'd saved that part of himself for the people he no longer needed to impress. Like his wife.

Elizabeth had a safe, peaceful home now, and nothing else mattered. Not even an insensitive lawman. She canted a sideways glance at the baffled Ranger.

Mr. Elder hesitantly straddled the threshold—one foot in the room, one foot in the kitchen—as if he couldn't quite commit to his escape.

He pinched the bridge of his nose. "There are some beautiful names in the Bible. Rebecca, Mary. And, uh, some more I can't think of right now."

The infant stretched out a single, tiny hand. Her five perfect fingers opened to the world. Love shimmered in Elizabeth's chest. Instantly calmed, she stared in wonder, awed by this exquisite, fragile human being God had entrusted to her. This miracle of life.

"There's Rachel," Mr. Elder continued. "And—"

"Wait," Elizabeth cut into his mumbled list. "Rachel." She liked the way it sounded, the way the syllables rolled off her tongue. "This is my daughter, Rachel."

The name fit.

Peace settled over Elizabeth like a down comforter on a cold winter's night. "Thank you."

"You're welcome." He leaned forward to peer at the baby, still keeping his body half in, half out of the room. "You can always settle on a middle name later."

Her heart sank.

His stricken gaze darted to her face. "You don't need to make a decision now."

"I guess not."

"Okay." He nodded. "Glad that's settled."

"Don't let me keep you," Elizabeth muttered.

Mr. Elder groaned. Pulling his foot into the room, he leaned one elbow on the chest of drawers, then rested his chin on his fisted hand. "What was your mother's name?"

Elizabeth conjured up the one hazy memory she had clung to all these years. She pictured a blond-haired woman with kind, sad eyes. For ten years Elizabeth had clung to her anger and betrayal. Why had her mother relinquished her only child to an orphanage? Why hadn't she fought harder for Elizabeth? Perhaps it was time for forgiveness. How proud her mother would have been of her first grandchild. Right then, Elizabeth felt as if she could forgive anything. Even Will.

"Rose," she said. "My mother's name was Rose."

"Rachel Rose." He smiled, his teeth even and white against rugged, wind-chapped skin. "That sounds like the perfect name for a little girl." He turned on his heel to leave, then paused. "Are you hungry?"

Her stomach rumbled. In all the confusion she hadn't eaten all day. "Starving."

He chuckled, threading his fingers through his dark wavy hair, ruffling the neatly cut strands.

A sense of foreboding wiped the half grin from her lips. She'd never again trust a man who spent more time at the barber than he did with his own family. She'd learned that lesson the hard way with Will.

The Ranger smoothed his hair back into place. "I thought you'd be hungry. I'll fix you a plate."

"I'll help you." Scooting her legs to the side of the bed, she winced as her tender muscles screamed in protest.

"Don't get up," he admonished. "I'll bring supper to you."

His casual declaration kept her frozen for a long moment. Her eyes narrowed on his face. Was he sincere? Save for a hint of beard shadowing his jaw, Mr. Elder appeared as fresh and crisp as a spring crocus. He wore his dark gray shirt tucked into his trousers, his leather vest neatly buttoned, the gun holster conspicuously absent. Before she could protest, he ducked back into the kitchen.

"Wait," Elizabeth called. "Where's Jo?"

"She's in the barn, doing chores." He stuck his head around the corner. "That's one tough young'un.'"

"I didn't think you two were getting along so well."

"She's awfully opinionated for a youngster. But I'll let it pass since she took such good care of you. A lot of grown men don't have that kind of grit." He fisted his hand on the door frame, his head bent, his gaze fastened on the toe of his boot. "Are you sure you're all right? It's been a rough day."

A hint of blush tinged his handsome face, the scratch

on his cheek from his barn escape barely visible. Elizabeth suppressed a grin. She found his awkward attempt to inquire about her health painfully endearing.

"I'm fine," she said. "I'd like to think it's been a day full of blessings."

He exhaled a pent-up breath. "Yes, it has."

With a parting nod he disappeared again, taking with him the strange tension she felt in his presence. Bemused, she stared at the empty space he'd occupied. Though a large man, he carried himself with an easy grace. His gestures were spare and clipped, but he managed to speak volumes with his brief answers.

Her stomach rumbled into her musings.

She brushed her nose against Rachel's. "This should be a novel experience. Most men aren't interested in fetching and carrying for a lady unless they're courting. And we certainly aren't courting."

Elizabeth wanted to be annoyed with her frailty—she'd just declared her independence, after all—but the hunger gnawing at her stomach silenced her protests.

After pressing her cheek against Rachel's smooth forehead, she laid the baby on the bed. Twisting, Elizabeth fluffed the pillows behind her, sank her hands into the mattress and shimmied backward until she sat up straight.

She cradled her daughter in her palms. Rachel cooed, the sound no louder than the purr of a kitten. Tiny fingers worked in the air. Elizabeth kissed all ten tips, captivated by the miniature oval nails. She'd never seen anything so small, so absolutely flawless.

She inhaled Rachel's sweet essence, her heart swelling until she was sure it would burst right out of her chest. She'd been adrift for months, unsure of the future, and afraid to face the past. With Rachel, everything felt right. The way God had intended.

Mr. Elder returned a moment later with a steaming mug of coffee in one hand and a platter overflowing with food in the other.

"I can't eat all that!" Elizabeth laughed.

"You might be surprised."

Despite her protest, her gaze searched the plate, her mouth watering. He'd heaped a great mound of eggs next to a hearty slab of bacon. An enormous hunk of generously buttered bread balanced on the edge.

Worry dampened her enthusiasm. If this was what he had prepared for Elizabeth, how much had he eaten already? "Have you and Jo had supper?"

Purchasing more supplies didn't worry her. She had plenty of cash. Following Will's death, the somber undertaker had marched up to the house in his navy blue suit, his bushy salt-and-pepper eyebrows drawn into a fierce scowl. He'd slapped a fat wad of bills he'd discovered in Will's saddle bags into her limp hands. As if begrudging her the virtue of his honorable gesture, the disagreeable man had whirled and stomped away.

Money definitely wasn't the problem. It was the trip to town that had her stomach in knots. Traveling to Cimarron Springs meant facing the people who resented Will, even after his death. The people whose money and property he'd won in card games. The people who thought Will was a cheat. She'd felt the hot sting of their accusations as she'd run her errands on previous visits. The way the ladies had sniffed and swept their skirts aside when she passed, as if afraid of being tainted by association, was painfully burned into her memory.

Even the sheriff, a man who'd shared more than one raucous evening with Will, had accused her husband of being a cheat. He'd even threatened to seize her homestead if he discovered proof.

"I had a tin of beans earlier," Mr. Elder said, startling her from her gloomy thoughts.

Elizabeth blinked. "Wherever did you find those?"

"I packed them from town. I didn't want to deplete your food supply," he spoke matter-of-factly. "The weather has let up, but you never can tell in this part of the country. You've got enough to worry about without a full-grown man eating your winter supply. Might be a long season."

"Oh, yes, of course. I didn't think...."

Confounded by Mr. Elder's kindness, Elizabeth placed Rachel in the makeshift crib while he patiently held her supper. She accepted the plate from his outstretched hand. Their fingers brushed together. The dark hairs on the backs of his knuckles felt rough and foreign against her calloused fingers.

He set the mug on the nightstand. "Anything else you need?"

Surprised to note her quickened pulse, Elizabeth shook her head.

He gestured in Rachel's direction. "She appears to be healthy and all. No worse for wear."

"She's perfect." That same warm light shimmered around Elizabeth's heart. "Would you like to hold her?"

He shook his head, backing up so quickly his hip slammed against the dresser. "I'll pass."

With a curt nod at Rachel, he strode out of the room.

Elizabeth glanced around the room. Was something burning? Certainly a big, strong man like Mr. Elder wasn't frightened of a *baby*. Something else must have spooked him.

She shrugged off the Ranger's odd behavior and returned her attention to supper. The nutty aroma of fresh-brewed coffee wafted from the night table, mingling perfectly with the scent of freshly toasted bread. She speared a hearty chunk of bacon, her taste buds dancing in anticipation. Chewing slowly, she savored the spicy, salt-cured meat.

An unexpected stab of guilt dampened her enthusiasm. She felt as if she should apologize to Mr. Elder. But for what? For assuming he'd eat her food? It wasn't as if she'd actually accused him of anything. Still, no matter the circumstances, her lack of tolerance was unacceptable. So far, he'd been nothing but kind.

Her thoughts drifted back to the only other man who'd ever showed her the least hint of kindness. Hadn't Will started out in a similar fashion? She'd been sweeping snow from the walk outside the bakery where she worked in New York when he'd tipped his hat at her while strolling by. The gesture had stunned her. She couldn't recall a time when anyone had actually noticed her, much less acknowledged her with a greeting.

When he came back the following day, he'd called her "ma'am" and smiled so wide she'd blushed. By day three, she found herself jumping each time the bell chimed over the door, hoping he'd return. All day she waited, only to be disappointed. When she'd turned the closed sign for the evening, she found him lounging against the lamppost, his thumbs hooked in his pockets. Three weeks later they were married and on a train bound for Kansas.

He'd cared for her in the beginning, showering her with gifts and attention as if she were a shiny new toy. But after the novelty had worn off, he'd changed. Elizabeth was certain that the Ranger was no different. He'd reveal his true colors soon enough, and this time she wouldn't be taken by surprise.

Elizabeth attacked her food with a new vigor. Considering her appalling display of blubbering this afternoon, she must work harder than ever to prove her independence. In order to survive, she had to be strong. More than just blizzards and Indians threatened her home, and she had to be prepared.

Jack sucked in a lungful of frosty air, then kicked another enormous stump into place. Two days had passed during his self-imposed exile on the widow's homestead. Two days of letting the outlaw's trail grow colder. He stepped back, swinging the ancient ax he'd found rusting near the wood pile high over his head.

Exhaling a vaporous breath, he swung the tool in a neat arc, burying the blade three-inches deep into the dry wood. Repeating the motion, he circled the stump, kicking fallen pieces back into place until he had a satisfying jumble of split wood. His shoulder aching, he rolled another stump into position.

The physical labor, the satisfying crack of the blade, cleared his thoughts. The pile grew taller, but he didn't slow his pace. Driven by a need to accomplish a useful task, he forged ahead. Someone had already cut the smaller branches. The pie-shaped pieces were neatly stacked in a long, sturdy wall covered in oilcloth and mounded over with snow. But the unwieldy stumps had been heaped together to rot, wasted.

Jack didn't like waste.

The work put him in control, gave him a sense of pride and accomplishment. He swung the ax until his biceps burned and sweat trickled down his collar, until Elizabeth's screams of pain during childbirth stopped ringing in his ears.

He knew she was fine, but he couldn't shake his impotent rage at his own helplessness. He'd borne that same weight on his shoulders staring down at his sister-in-law's prone body. Doreen had done nothing wrong. She'd been running her errands when she'd arrived at the bank on the wrong day, at the wrong time. She'd walked right into an armed robbery, and the outlaws had shot her. The sense-lessness of the act had shaken Jack's faith, making him question God's plan. Why Doreen?

The dark-haired beauty had married his older brother when Jack was barely sixteen. When he'd decided to join the Texas Rangers instead of working the ranch like his older brothers, she'd been the only member of the fam-ily to support his decision.

After the shooting, he'd let his emotions overtake his good sense. When an enraged posse had tracked down a man named Bud Shaw and declared him guilty, Jack had gone along for the ride. Even when every instinct in his body told him the man was innocent. During the follow-ing weeks, he'd split his time between the family ranch and a Paris, Texas, jail. Questioning the imprisoned man at length had only cemented his doubts. There were two Bud Shaws roaming the central plains, and the man rot-ting in jail, waiting for his own hanging, was innocent.

Jack had pulled every favor owed to him by the local judge to buy the wrongly convicted man half a year's clemency. Three long months had passed since then. Every day without locating the real outlaw weighed heavy on his conscience.

His nieces and nephews deserved justice—but so did the innocent man sitting in jail. The one decent lead Jack had followed had led him to this isolated homestead in the middle of nowhere. Dawdling here wasn't going to bring justice for anyone. Jack had lingered over the widow and her newborn long enough. He was party to a grave injustice, and he couldn't rest until he set it straight.

He slid the last stump into place. Squinting at the horizon, he wiped the sweat from his brow with his leather-clad hand. The day looked to be overcast, but clear and calm all the same. If he left in the next hour, he'd be back in Cimarron Springs by lunch. His hands tingled with expectation. The familiar anticipation of embarking on another journey focused him, chasing away his lingering unrest. He had a goal, a purpose.

The widow and her child were none of his concern. Jo's family, the McCoys, would see to her well-being. Besides, a pretty woman was never alone for long in this part of the country.

The ax missed its target.

Jack windmilled his free hand, managing to right himself just before he tumbled into the woodpile. Straightening, he darted his gaze to the house. No mocking faces appeared in the square windowpanes. Satisfied his gaff had gone unnoticed, he slung the blade over his shoulder.

"Guess that about does it," he muttered to himself.

With his thoughts focused on the multitude of tasks to accomplish before his journey, he barely noticed the frigid, knee-deep snow on his trek to the barn. He'd saddle up Midnight, say his goodbyes and be gone. Simple as that.

A rare thread of regret tugged at his heart. He forcibly pushed aside the nagging concern. Mrs. Cole had survived this long on her own, there was no need to think she needed his assistance. He was a lawman, not a nursemaid. He had a job to do.

Jack slid open the barn door, relieved to find the cavernous space empty. He inhaled the pungent aroma of hay and feed. The scent reminded him of home, of his youth. He'd grown up mucking out barns, working from dawn till dusk on his family's cattle ranch. The familiar sights and sounds released an unwelcome longing to work with hands, to build something lasting, to recapture the camaraderie he'd once shared with his brothers.

Chickens clucked and a cow lowed. Midnight, one of two horses in the four stalls, whinnied.

A sound outside the usual barnyard racket caught his attention. Jack paused, tilting his head to one side as he heard it again. He recognized that sound all right.

His jubilant mood fled. Someone was crying. Not the pained howling of a body in agony, but a quiet whimper of despair.

Jack groaned. There was only one person on the homestead who'd hide in a stall rather than cry out in the open. Determined to slink away before he got sucked into another emotional conversation, he backed to the door. He'd already dealt with one weeping female this week. His problem-solving skills were limited to things he could shoot or arrest.

He had one hand on the door when another faint sniffle doused his annoyance. Compassion for Jo dragged his feet to a halt. The code of honor ingrained in him as a child reared its ugly head. He pressed two fingers to the bridge of his nose. He'd tackle this one last obstacle, and *then* he'd leave. After all, he'd comforted Elizabeth.

He was practically an expert on women now.

Chapter Four

Jack had an idea where to find the weeping girl. He crept through the barn, his boots silenced by the hay strewn over the floor. He should be saddling Midnight instead of chasing down the source of those muffled sobs, but his conscience drove him forward against his good sense.

Dust motes stirred in the shaft of light sluicing through the hayloft. The wind had blown the door open almost half a foot. No wonder he'd nearly frozen to death these past two nights. In his haste to escape Jo's trap, he hadn't fully latched the hayloft. He'd been so cold he'd almost hunkered down next to the milk cow for warmth.

He added another chore to his growing list. Better for him to climb that rickety ladder than risk having one of the women break a leg. The third rung from the top was nearly rotted through. Unfortunately, sealing his impromptu exit had to wait until he dealt with his current problem.

Stalling, Jack lifted his shoulders and stretched, easing the cramps from sleeping on the hard-packed floor. He tugged his gloves over his exposed wrists. The barn had given him shelter and little else. A feather bed in town called to him like a prayer.

He peered into the first stall, his gaze meeting the sloe-eyed stare of the caramel-colored milk cow. He inched his way to the second stall, glancing over the half door. Jo huddled in the corner, her thin arms wrapped around her legs, her forehead pressed against her bent knees. Two long braids brushed against the tops of her boots.

Midnight whinnied, stretching a velvety nose out the last enclosure. Jack saluted his companion with a finger to his brow. "Soon, I promise."

The girl jerked upright, her face averted.

Jack rested his elbows on the half door, chafing at the delay. He adjusted his hat forward before reminding himself this wasn't an interrogation, then set the brim back on his head in the "I'm friendly and approachable" position.

He didn't even know what was wrong, let alone how to fix the problem. Once again he cursed the mistake that had led him here. Why hadn't this homestead been teeming with hardened outlaws instead of weeping women?

He recalled Jo's mention of influenza. She was probably just concerned over her ailing family. Jack added the sheriff's failure to inform him of the influenza outbreak to his growing list of gripes against the incompetent lawman.

Sucking in a breath of a chill air to fortify himself, he contemplated his strategy. "Something bothering you?"

"Nope."

Jack bit back a curse. Didn't women love to talk? That's what all the fellows complained about, anyway.

As much as he'd like to turn tail and run, his feet refused to move. Frustrated, he reached into the stall, yanked a length of straw from a tightly cinched bale and twirled it between his fingers. "Seems like there's something bothering you."

She swiped her nose with an exaggerated sniffle. "You're touched in the head, Ranger."

The spark in her voice encouraged him. Rage was an emotion he understood, and inspiring anger in a touchy female was easier than shooting tin cans off a flat stump. "Then why are you crying?"

She threw him a withering glare. "I ain't no weeping female, so why don't you do something useful, like ride on out of here?"

"Maybe I will."

Undaunted by her harsh words, he continued to twirl the hay between his fingers. A chicken flapped through the barn, pecking at the dirt around Jack's feet. He let the oppressive silence hang between them. People generally didn't like silence. Most folks would rather fill up an empty space, even if that space was better left empty.

Jo kept quiet, a trait that won Jack's increasing admiration. At least she wasn't crying anymore, another positive sign. If she didn't want to talk, then he sure wasn't going to force the situation. Looked as if he was going to make it to town before lunch, after all.

She bumped her hand down the length of one dark braid, her gaze focused on the hay beneath her feet. "Mrs. Cole says you were chasing bank robbers when you barged in." She shot him a sideways glance. "What if you make another mistake? What if someone gets hurt?"

His fingers stilled. He had the uneasy sensation this conversation had nothing to do with bank robbers. "You make a mistake, you make amends. That's all the good Lord asks of us."

"How do you make amends for lying?"

He busted the straw in two pieces. *Everybody lied*, he reminded himself. *Just not for the same reasons.* "You make up for lying by telling the truth. You wanna start now?"

"I told Mrs. Cole I could deliver that baby. But I

couldn't." Her chin quivered. "I was so scared I wanted to run away."

Relief shuddered through him. He'd been expecting to hear something much worse. She was barely more than a child herself, no wonder she'd been terrified. He was making a fast slide past his thirtieth year, and he'd considered running away himself. "You delivered a baby. That's a grave responsibility. Being scared doesn't mean you lied, just means you're human."

"You ever get scared?"

"Every day." He barked out a laugh. "You wanna know a secret?"

She scrambled to her feet, brushing at the baggy wool trousers tucked into the tops of her sturdy boots. A voluminous coat in a dusty shade of gray completed the tomboy uniform. She flipped the braid she'd been worrying over one shoulder.

Her clear, green eyes searched his face. "What secret?"

"Truth is, I might have beaten you to the door. I wanted to hightail it out of that room faster than a jackrabbit out of a wolf den."

"Truly?"

He chuckled. How many times had he done the same? Judged someone's face, watching for subtle hints to test the sincerity of their answers? "I was terrified."

Midnight butted against the neighboring stall, reminding Jack of his purpose, of the unfinished business weighing on his conscience.

As Jo absorbed his confession, her shoulders relaxed.

He mentally patted himself on the back for his inspired handling of the situation. A few more words of assurance to wrap things up, and he could leave. He'd have to regroup in Cimarron Springs and interview the sheriff once more. Judging by the lawman's lazy work habits, the task of gathering information was going to take all afternoon, further postponing his trip.

He'd decided to visit Wichita earlier that morning. Every two-bit thief in Kansas wound up there at some point or another. The frontier city was the key to locating the outlaw, Bud Shaw.

"You're a brave girl for sticking it out," he encouraged.

He'd settled Jo's fears. He'd be in Cimarron Springs by this afternoon.

Jo looked him up and down. "You still chasing them outlaws?"

"*Outlaw.* There's only one left."

"What happened to the rest? How many were there all together? Do you always chase outlaws?"

Jack held up a hand, halting the deluge of questions. "There were three all together. They shot a…they shot a woman during a robbery in Texas. On their way out of town, the sheriff gut shot one of them, a man named Slim Joe."

"Did he die?" she asked eagerly.

"That kind of wound doesn't kill a person right off. Slim Joe had a lot of time to talk. He turned over his partners, Pencil Pete and Bud Shaw. We caught up with Pencil Pete right off and threw him in jail. Then we found Bud Shaw. Except, well, I think we made a mistake."

"Then Bud Shaw isn't one of the outlaws?"

"I think there are two men named Bud Shaw. I think the outlaw decided to take advantage of a man with the same name, and frame him."

Jack didn't want to expand, he'd already said more than he intended. Unease itched beneath his skin. There were two Bud Shaws, of that much he was certain. He'd discovered too much evidence to refute the fact in his own mind. Just not enough to convince the judge.

Jo glanced at him, her expression skeptical. "But what if something else *does* go wrong?"

"I'll cross that bridge when I get there." Jack threw up his hands. "Why are you worrying about something that hasn't happened yet?"

"What if you can't find him? What then?"

"Standing around here talking about the future ain't gonna change anything. Why solve a problem before it happens?"

"Don't get all riled up, Ranger. You're spooking the animals."

Jack pressed the brim of his hat tighter to his head with both hands. Women confounded him. He had one female concerned about naming a baby that was too young to answer, and another looking for a solution to a problem that hadn't yet occurred. What was a man to do?

Gritting his teeth, he forced a smile. "Well, you did real good delivering that baby."

"Better than you. I thought you were going to throw up."

"So did I," he retorted, his voice more forceful than necessary.

She tossed back her head and laughed at his shouted confession. Jack scowled and crossed his arms over his chest. Her infectious laugh soon had him chuckling. The sound rumbled low in his chest, rusty and neglected, then bubbled to the surface. He couldn't recall the last time he'd truly laughed, especially at himself.

He used to laugh with his brothers all the time—when they weren't beating the tar out of each other. They'd roll around in the dirt and blood, bent on killing each other, until one of them said something smart-alecky and the whole group erupted into raucous laughter. He missed that. Missed the camaraderie of his family.

Things had changed after their pa's death. His older

brothers had ceased brawling, and started slicking back their hair. Weddings had followed, and then a new niece or nephew every year after. His mother had reveled in her role as grandmother before she'd died. Lord knew they'd all been lost without her. Jack was too young to take over the ranch by himself, and too old to be ordered around by his brothers.

He'd joined the Texas Rangers instead, and Doreen had supported his decision. Jack pictured his sister-in-law the last time he'd seen her. How the white-linen pillow had framed her ashen face, the growing pool of red seeping through the bandages.

His smile waned. Three months, and he wasn't any closer to catching the real Bud Shaw than the day he'd ridden out of town. He'd failed the one person who had always believed in him.

"You okay, Ranger?" Jo asked.

"Yeah, sure."

"You look like someone just walked over your grave."

"Not mine," he growled.

He'd crushed all the joy from their exchange, but he didn't care. "How far does a man have to go to find some peace around here?"

He pivoted on his heel, stalking out of the barn. The sooner he brought the right man to justice, the better.

Elizabeth hoisted the empty laundry basket onto the bed. Her weakened body protested the exertion. The past two days had been so chaotic, so full of change, she craved a task to ground her. A mindless chore. Something familiar and comforting.

She turned, catching her disheveled reflection in the looking glass above the dresser.

"Oh, my," she groaned.

Her hair hung in a tangled mess down her back. Her cheeks were flushed a bright pink in stark contrast to her pale face. Dark circles rimmed her eyes. She looked no better than one of the beggars she used to pass on her way to work in the city. She lifted her brush from the dresser. Tugging the bristles through the snarls, she worked the knots loose. The heavy mass soon smoothed and shined.

Elizabeth didn't approve of vanity, but even she had to admit her hair was pretty. She had the same blond hair as her mother, thick and long. Wispy tendrils usually framed her face, falling in soft curls around her cheeks. The past days' toil had left her forlorn ringlets drooping and lifeless. She'd love nothing more than another thorough washing and a decadent soak in the galvanized tub, but that would have to wait.

She braided her long strands with practiced fingers, twisting the coil over the top of her head and securing the thick rope with pins. She rubbed her lips together to add a flush of color, unsure why she bothered. There was no one here to care about her appearance, least of all her sleepy daughter.

The extra effort buoyed her spirits, though, and she needed all her mustered strength to face the mess the Ranger had surely made while she'd been laid up.

She reached behind her for the basket, her gaze drawn to Will's trunk. The domed black chest sat just where he'd left it six months ago. He'd always been possessive of the battered piece of luggage. He never opened the lid in her presence, and he kept the hinge securely locked when he was away.

In the early days of their marriage she'd been obsessed with the contents, curious as to why he kept secrets from her. When the undertaker had delivered Will's personal belongings in a wooden crate, she'd expected to find a key.

Instead, the grim-faced undertaker had ignobly presented her with his grim bounty. An enormous sum of cash carelessly wadded together and secured with a band. The funds for Will's escape from domestic responsibilities.

Later, at the funeral, the undertaker had looked her up and down, suspicion in his lifeless gray eyes. The amount of money had been too excessive for a humble railroad worker, especially given Will's propensity for spending his paychecks before the ink had dried on the paper. Only a cheat could have acquired that much money, the undertaker's eyes seemed to accuse.

She'd decided then and there that what she didn't know couldn't hurt her. From that moment on, she lost all desire to peer into the trunk. The more details she discovered about Will's hazy past, the less certain she became of herself, of her judgment. By opening the trunk, she risked opening wounds that had only just begun to heal. Later, when she wasn't feeling so fragile, she'd delve into the skeletons he'd left behind during his hasty exit.

While Rachel dozed, she lined the laundry basket with another patchwork quilt she'd sewed especially for the baby, then laid the swaddled infant snuggly inside.

"A basket and a drawer." Elizabeth clicked her tongue. "We should have named you Laundry Day instead of Rachel Rose."

The baby blinked, her somber gaze trusting and innocent. A disarming tide of emotion rolled over Elizabeth. The awesome responsibility of shepherding this new life into the harsh world stunned her once again. She didn't know anything about babies. The years before her job at the bakery and then her marriage had been spent in an orphanage where the children were segregated by age.

While most of the older girls had chosen to work with the infants, Elizabeth had taken a job in the kitchens. Seeing those helpless babies, abandoned and alone, had been unbearable. She shuddered at the memory of sparse iron beds lined up against cold, bleak walls. The endless rules and constant chores. Thank heaven Rachel Rose would never have to suffer that life.

Elizabeth tipped her head to the timbered ceiling. "I think I know what you were trying to tell me. I was praying for myself when I should have been praying for others."

God had never been a presence in her life. Maybe that's why He hadn't answered her prayers. Mrs. Peabody from the orphanage had marched them to church on Sundays, their smocks pressed and their hair brushed smooth, but the service had been in Latin. Though Elizabeth had been entranced by the sheer beauty of the church, she'd never understood the words.

She'd been anxious to attend a service in Cimarron. Unfortunately, despite his earlier pious claims, Will had harbored an aversion to churches. They'd even been married by a justice of the peace. A ceremony so rushed, she'd barely registered the event before Will had whisked her to the train depot and settled them on a Pullman car bound for Kansas.

Elizabeth shook off the unsettling memories. Living in the past was a dull and lonely business. One thing was for certain, she'd never trust another man until she had seen a true test of his character.

She lifted Rachel's basket, then marched to the kitchen, her weary body braced for a full day of scrubbing. She raised her head, jerking to a halt. Every surface shined. Even the copper kettle gleamed in a shaft of light streaming through the clear glass windowpanes freed from the dimming oilcloth.

Her eyes wide, Elizabeth glanced around the room. Jo

must have been up all night to have accomplished such a feat. The brightly polished tin pots and pans hanging against the wall had been neatly arranged by size.

Setting Rachel on the worktable before the stove, Elizabeth made a note to give the girl extra wages this week. Will's money might as well benefit someone deserving of the blessing.

While she admired the spotless kitchen, Mr. Elder shouldered his way through the back door, his arms full of split wood, his hat set low on his head. A gust of frosty air swept a dusting of snow in his wake.

"I thought you'd be gone by now," Elizabeth blurted, astonished to find her heart thumping against her ribs. Certainly she wasn't afraid of him any longer. He'd shown himself to be honorable, if a tad overbearing. Heaven knew he'd had more than ample opportunity to take advantage of them.

His silver star caught the sun, reflecting light. The sight of the lawman's badge caused the memory of the sheriff's threats to explode in her head. There was more than one person in Cimarron Springs who'd like to recoup their losses with the sale of her belongings. Will had been a gambler, and everyone in town had lost money or property to him at one time or another. Yet despite the sheriff's threat to confiscate her property, he'd been too lazy to prove his suspicions.

She didn't need him spurred into action by another lawman.

Jack wiped his feet on the rag rug before stepping into the room. He jostled the wood in his hands for a better grip. "I didn't mean to startle you. I had some chores left." He jerked his head in the direction of the splintered hinges.

"That's very kind of you, but there's really no need...."

Their eyes met and held for a long moment. She'd thought Will handsome, but her late husband paled in comparison to Mr. Elder. While Will had been fair with washed-out blue eyes, the Ranger's features were bold, exaggerated, not at all perfect. His crooked nose indicated he'd broken it, more than once judging by the flattened bone. A faded scar ran the length of his strong jaw, visible through the stubble shadowing his chin. Deep lines creased his forehead between the dark slash of his eyebrows.

Taken separately, the imperfections should have lessened his attraction, but each one of those minor flaws worked together to lend him a rugged, earthy appearance. His scars revealed a man who had been tested and lived to tell the tale. The realization sent a tingle of apprehension down her spine. She sensed the Ranger's restless need to leave, his barely leashed discontent, even while he lingered, making minor repairs he might have abandoned with impunity. The discrepancy confused her.

Unsure what else to say, she tore her gaze away. She opened the oven door, and stoked the scarlet embers before setting a pan on the stove and pouring in a measure of fresh milk to warm.

Mr. Elder trudged through the kitchen three more times while she arranged her workspace, his arms heaped with a new batch of wood on each trip. She dusted her hands together and shook her head. At this rate, she wouldn't need to refill the woodpile until next fall.

Grasping a tin scoop, she heaped flour along with two generous pinches of salt into an enormous creamware bowl, then pressed her fingers into the mound, digging a hole. After brushing her hands on her apron, she reached into the pie safe and pinched off a corner of yeast, crumbling the moist leaven into the center of the flour. With the milk properly scalded, she added a dollop of bacon grease, stirring until the ingredients melted together.

While the mixture cooled, she wiped down the table with a damp rag. Once she'd gingerly tapped the side of the pan to ensure a lukewarm temperature, she poured the thickened milk into the well of flour. Waiting for the yeast to dissolve, she gradually added a generous handful of sugar.

The Texas Ranger pounded on the back door as she worked. Elizabeth winced at the hammering. Rachel barely stirred.

He paused his work at one point, stepping into the snug kitchen with his hat in his hands. "Is the noise too much? Am I disturbing your daughter?"

Her heart jolted. Hearing someone else call Rachel her daughter made the whole experience real. *This is my family.* Something no one could take away. "Looks like this child would sleep through dynamite."

He gestured toward her face. "You've got a bit of, umm, flour on your..."

Elizabeth's hand flew to her warm cheek. She scrubbed at the mark. "I didn't notice."

His own cheeks red and chapped with cold, he cleared his throat with a curt nod, then backed away to resume his work inside. She took in his appearance, smiling at the way his expensive wool coat with a fresh tear in the shoulder stretched over his broad shoulders. He was a large man with an enormous chest tapering down to a lean waist, but he kept a respectful distance, never using his size to intimidate.

He glanced over his shoulder on his way out, catching her curious regard.

Confused by the fluttering in the pit of her stomach, she ducked her head to tighten the apron around her waist. With the Ranger gone, she focused her attention on the liquid mixture foaming merrily in the center of the flour. Satisfied she'd waited long enough for the yeast to develop, she folded in the dry ingredients, invigorated by the familiar process. Making bread was her favorite chore.

She loved the silky texture of the flour, the way the dough gradually came together beneath the heels of her hands to form a smooth, elastic ball. The way the yeast smelled like a summer's day, warm and comforting.

Mr. Elder returned again, his saddlebags slung over his left shoulder. He'd packed to leave. To her chagrin, that curious fluttering resumed.

He snatched off his hat. "I replaced the hinges. You shouldn't have any problems."

"I appreciate that."

"I cut the stumps for kindling."

"Thank you."

An emotion she couldn't quite read flitted across his face. "Well, then. I filled the woodpile in the parlor."

The barren room was hardly a parlor, but she appreciated his concern. "I saw. Was there any room left to sit?"

He flashed a lopsided grin. Not the charming smirk he'd plastered on his face that first night to put her at ease, but a genuine smile. "Just enough."

She was struck by how young he looked without his usual scowl. His abashed expression softened the lines of his face, smoothing the customary crease of worry between his eyebrows. His hair wasn't black, as she'd supposed that first night, but more of a deep chocolate. His hazel eyes sparkled with flecks of gold around the irises, lightening the somber effect of his austere demeanor.

She was unaccustomed to such relaxed behavior in a man. Though he'd been delayed on his journey, he didn't prowl around the house like a caged animal, or burst into action with unleashed energy. He held himself straight and tall. Even when he feigned casual indifference, she sensed a stiffness in his spine, a certain resolve in his stance.

A sudden need to capture this moment overwhelmed her. She wanted to remember the way he circled the brim of his hat in his hands, the way he kept peeking at Rachel when he thought she wasn't looking.

There had been so few moments in her life she had tucked away, saving like priceless treasurers. Why this one? She glanced at Rachel Rose, swaddled in peaceful slumber. This unfamiliar emotion bubbling to the surface, this sensation of warmth and safety wrapping around her like a velvet cloak must be attached to the infant.

Elizabeth floundered for something to say, anxious to avoid the troublesome feelings Mr. Elder aroused. It was best he left now, before she was disillusioned, before time and familiarity revealed the cracks in his facade.

He stuck his hat on his head, lowering the brim to shield his eyes. "I should be going."

Elizabeth busied herself with separating the dough. "Thank you for everything you've done. Someday I'll tell Rachel the story of her birth. How you thought I was a bank robber."

They both chuckled, her own forced laugh hollow and strained.

When the awkward silence fell once more, he peered at her from beneath the brim of his hat. "When I tell the boys this story, I'll be painting a more heroic picture of myself."

"You did just fine, Mr. Elder."

"After all we've been through, I think you can call me Jack."

Suddenly shy, she met his sheepish gaze. The name suited him. It was strong and solid. Elizabeth let her gaze skitter away from those compassionate, hazel eyes. "Goodbye, Jack."

"Goodbye," he replied. "I'll just be going."

Neither of them moved.

A sharp sorrow robbed her of breath. She attacked her kneading with renewed vigor.

"Jack," she spoke, prolonging the moment, "can you check on Jo? I don't know what's taking her so long with chores."

"I saw her in the barn earlier." His boots scuffed the floor.

Elizabeth suppressed a grin. He probably didn't even notice his own nervous fidget, the boot scuffing that reminded her of a young boy, but she found the gesture charming.

Her somber mood lightened like a leavened pastry. "Tell Jo I'm making bread."

She squelched the urge to slap her forehead. Of course she was making bread. Why had she said such a silly thing? What was wrong with her? She was behaving like a giddy schoolgirl.

Jack cleared his throat. "I will."

"Where will you go after this?"

She didn't even know why she'd asked, except that talking meant he wasn't leaving just yet, and she missed the company of another adult.

"I've got to see the sheriff."

Her effervescent mood plummeted. Clearing her throat, she stood up straighter. "Tell him we're doing fine. Just fine."

He nodded.

Another moment laden with unspoken words passed

between them. She grasped for an elusive farewell, a way to thank him that encompassed her diverse emotions, but no words came. Jack pinched the brim of his hat between two fingers, tipping his head in a parting gesture before the door closed quietly behind him.

She pressed the back of her hand to her brow. The temperature in the room seemed to drop. Those pesky, annoying, infuriating tears were clogging her throat once more. What on earth was wrong with her?

A lank strand of hair had fallen across her forehead, and she shook it away with a sigh. She was tired, that was all. Rachel had awakened three times last evening to be fed and changed. All this weeping must be due to her exhaustion.

The growing fatigue pulled her to slump on the stool before the worktable. She didn't need a man around the house.

Rachel's face pinched up a like a dried apple, her lips trembling in distress. The infant's faint mewling reverberated in Elizabeth's chest.

Better that Jack left now. Keeping this home meant keeping her family together, and a wandering lawman asking questions about her past didn't bode well. She was glad he was gone. For good. She was doing *just fine* on her own.

Just fine.

If she repeated the mantra often enough, maybe she'd even believe her own lies.

Chapter Five

If Jack hadn't been so furious, he might have seen the humor in his current situation. First off, he'd never seen a man so partial to drab brown—the exact color of the hindquarters of a bay mare. Dressed head to toe in the unflattering hue, Cimarron Spring's sheriff resembled a great mound of lumpy, oozing mud.

The older man's dirty-blond hair was saturated with gray, and his eyes mirrored the washed-out beige of his stained and wrinkled shirt. An extra-long pair of suspenders stretched over his shoulders. A leather belt hooked on a freshly notched hole, perilously near the ragged tip, strained to cinch his spreading waist. Ferret-like eyes took Jack's measure.

The sheriff smacked his flabby lips together. "You shoulda told me you was lookin' for a *live* horse," he cackled, his enormous belly undulating with laughter. "Now, that's a different story."

Clenching his teeth, Jack let his molten anger cool into hardened steel. He failed to see the humor in sending a fellow lawman on a wild-goose chase. "I'm looking for a *live* horse and a *live* man. A man who murdered a woman during a bank robbery."

Jack had been in Cimarron Springs for several days, waiting for a meeting. Both the sheriff and the town doc had been unavailable. While Jack understood the doc's busy schedule causing a delay, he'd yet to discern the cause of the sheriff's stalling. As far as Jack could tell, the only pressing item on that man's schedule was his next meal.

Under Jack's unyielding scowl, the jovial smile on the sheriff's face gradually dissolved into a blank stare. "Don't get all uppity on me, Ranger," the man spoke, his tone defensive. "I've got a lot going on here. There's a flu epidemic crippling the town. We've had six deaths already. The undertaker had to pile the bodies in the lean-to. Good thing it's winter or we'd a had a putrid smell."

The sheriff thoughtfully rubbed at his drink-reddened cheeks. No doubt concerned about the effect of such a noxious odor on his appetite.

"I'm sorry for the town's losses," Jack replied, though nothing in the sheriff's demeanor suggested he had suffered unduly. "But you knew I was searching for outlaws, and you sent me to a homestead."

Jack kept out the part where he'd aimed his gun at a woman in labor—for Mrs. Cole's privacy, and his own credibility. He might have lived an uncommitted life, never staying long enough in one place to let the gossips sink their teeth into his hide, but Elizabeth didn't have the luxury of escaping a scandal generated by his stay on her property.

"You asked about a horse," the sheriff pointed out. "I told you the truth. Will Cole was partial to a distinctive bay mustang." The older man snorted. "'Course, they're both dead now."

Jack reigned in his growing frustration. Incompetence was no excuse, and the sheriff's feigned ignorance had his teeth on edge. Elizabeth's husband certainly wasn't a bank robber. Enough money had been stolen during the Wells Fargo job to leave a man set like a king. Jack had yet to meet a thief capable of restraining his natural desire to immediately spend his ill-gotten gains. A fellow with that much money didn't live on an isolated homestead with only one milk cow and a bunch of scrawny chickens.

This trip to town had been a waste, and the trail out of Cimarron Springs had dried up, yet he found himself loitering in the sheriff's stale office, surrounded by walls yellowed with cigar smoke, as his growing defeat warred with his burgeoning curiosity. Jack had discovered long ago that if he let people talk long enough, they let down their guard. That's when his job got interesting.

He kicked back in his chair, forcing himself to link his hands behind his head. Gossip was a good lead into more important matters—like outlaws and stolen money. Of course his renewed interest in interrogating the sheriff had nothing to do with the widow and her newborn. This exercise was strictly related to the Wells Fargo job.

"What happened to Mr. Cole?" Jack asked.

"I miss that Will."

Jack's sudden consternation at the mention of Elizabeth's husband startled him. Before now, he hadn't actually thought of her late husband as an actual flesh-and-blood man with friends and family. Will Cole had been a shadow figure, undefined, relegated to the past. Talking with the sheriff about Will made him real. Jack had a sickening realization he wasn't going to shake the dead man's presence any time soon.

"You miss Will?" Jack asked noncommittally.

"He was a man who appreciated a good joke." The sheriff shot Jack a telling look, as if sending a fellow lawman into a snowstorm was some sort of great lark, and Jack was a spoilsport for not appreciating the humor.

Jack forced himself to concentrate on the droning conversation while the sheriff touched on a multitude of subjects with the mentions of Will Cole spread out sparsely in between. The way the sheriff carried on about everything from the weather to the lack of tasty licorice at the dry goods store, Jack figured he'd see the spring thaw before an insightful piece of information spilled.

The sheriff spat a wad of tobacco juice into the spittoon at his feet. "That Will Cole sure was a charmer. Came into town every night when he wasn't traveling. Had a job with the railroad, ya know."

"The railroad, huh?" Jack encouraged. So far, the sheriff had bragged about all of Will's dubious attributes—his gambling, his drinking, his roving eye. The last transgression bothered Jack most. He wondered if Elizabeth knew, and prayed that she didn't. What kind of man dishonored his wife that way? If Jack had a woman like Elizabeth waiting for him, he wouldn't be hanging around rancid saloons.

He recalled the humor in Elizabeth's clear blue eyes as she'd thanked him for his help. She had a way of looking at him, really looking, as if nothing was more important than listening to what he had to say. When she'd smiled at Rachel, her face had lit up like the sun rising over the Rockies. He'd never seen anything like it.

The sheriff scratched at his domed belly. The unwelcome grating of his overly long fingernails against coarse cotton interrupted Jack's fond recollections of Elizabeth.

The potbellied man wiggled his upper lip to adjust the wad of chew tucked between his cheek and gum. "That Will sure had a lot of luck with gambling. Real generous, though. Always bought a round of drinks before he left."

Elizabeth's fearful words echoed through Jack's head. *You won't bring whiskey into this house.*

She might not have known every disreputable detail about her late husband, but she knew plenty. Did she know that her husband had most likely supplemented his income as a card cheat? Professional sharps often gave away just enough of their winnings to keep the other players from growing suspicious.

Jack stared at a spot of cracked plaster scarring the wall above the sheriff's head. "What happened to Mr. Cole?"

The sheriff's expression grew somber. "Will and his horse slid down a gully sometime early summer. Must have been the end of May or the first part of June. Can't rightly remember. We had a real bad rain. Just kept pouring down for over a week. I was about to build an ark myself." The sheriff cackled at his own joke.

Jack forced a grin to keep the sheriff talking. He'd rather be anywhere than listening to the painful details of Elizabeth's troublesome past, but shying away from cold, hard facts never solved a problem.

"Anyway," the sheriff continued, "Will was riding over by Hackberry Creek. His horse slid down an embankment, broke its neck. Landed right on Will's leg. The poor guy must of drowned when the creek water rose." The sheriff leaned forward. His overburdened chair groaned in protest. "We kept that part about his suffering from his missus. I told her he died right off. She's one of those greenhorns from back East. Real weak little thing. I figured she'd die within a year. Most of those city folk don't survive long out here."

The sheriff's remarks had Jack's hands curling into fists. He recalled Elizabeth's accent, the slight lilt in her voice that gave her words a lyrical quality.

"She from Boston or something? She's got a particular way of talking."

"New York, maybe. Leastways, that's where Will found her. Real whirlwind courtship from the way he told it. She was some sort of orphan working for scraps in a bakery, when Will saved her. His job with the railroad took him all over the country. I think maybe her parents came over from England. Can't say for certain. She wasn't much for talking. Hardly came to town at all. Not even for church."

Jack muffled his snort of disgust. From what the sheriff had just said, her husband came to town often enough for the both of them, and his activities weren't conducive to attending services on Sundays.

What kind of a fellow left his wife all alone for weeks on end, this close to Indian territory, then took off again to gamble just as soon as he'd arrived home? Life on the plains was too dangerous for that kind of self-centered idiocy.

Jack adjusted in his chair. "Mrs. Cole shouldn't be out on that homestead all alone."

"I talked to her after Will died. Told her she was a fool to stay." The sheriff lowered his voice to a conspiratorial whisper, "I even offered to marry her myself."

Jack's heart skidded to a halt. "You what?"

"Offered to marry her. Women around these parts are harder to find than an Irishman at work. Not that I care to raise another man's brat, but sometimes you gotta take the wheat with the chaff."

"I see."

Jack gritted his teeth at the insult to Elizabeth. He wasn't a man who liked violence; most problems could be solved amicably with subtle negotiation, but some people were just too pigheaded to listen. That's when a man had to use force.

The sheriff brought his hand to his cauliflower-shaped ear and buried one finger up to his grimy knuckle. "Never could figure out why a man with that much to live for would be down by the creek that day. Doesn't make any sense."

His casual declaration finally piqued Jack's interest. "What doesn't make any sense?"

The older man continued working his finger back and forth in his ear. He scratched so deep, Jack figured his brain must itch.

"Will was awful fussy about his appearance. He wasn't much for dirt or mud. Kept his hat dry and his boots clean. His buttons shined so bright, they'd darn near blind a man."

Jack felt himself flush. Hadn't his own brothers mocked him for his fussy way of dressing? He'd ignored their ridicule because they didn't understand life outside a cattle ranch. A Texas Ranger mingled with people from every walk of life. Jack had discovered early on that men respected appearance before they respected words. His dress wasn't vanity, it was survival.

Elizabeth's sweeping assessment of him that first day flashed in his mind. Her gaze had lingered on his coat. Had she been thinking of Will? Was the disappointment blazing in her pale blue eyes directed at Jack, or at her late husband?

His mind lost in thoughts of Elizabeth, Jack snapped back to the present when he realized the sheriff had spoken.

"You touched in the head, Ranger?" the sheriff all but shouted.

Beginning to wonder himself, Jack bit back a sharp reply.

"I said, where are you going from here?"

"Thought I'd make my way to Wichita," Jack said.

"Yep. If I was a bank robber, I'd travel on up to Wichita." Spittle ricocheted into the spittoon. "There's more money to be had in the big cities."

"If you were a bank robber, my job would be a whole lot easier."

The sheriff started to laugh, then thought better of it and stuttered to a halt. "You mean something by that, mister?"

"Not at all," Jack soothed. "Just means you're a lot handier, being as you're sitting right in front of me and all."

"That's what I thought you meant," the sheriff replied, mollified for the moment.

Jack assumed the "hey, we're all friends here" smile he used when gathering information. "You've been real helpful, Sheriff…"

"Stanton."

"Sheriff Stanton. Don't suppose I'll ever forget that name."

Jack forced his hands to unclench. Pushing off from the arms of his sturdy wooden chair, he stood. "It's been real nice to meet you, Sheriff Stanton. I've got to visit the doctor before I leave. If you think of anything else that might be useful, that's where you'll find me."

The sheriff struggled out of his chair, his lumbering rise to his feet accompanied by the crackle and pop of his joints. Straightening, he hoisted his muddy brown trousers over his potbelly, then shook them back down into place.

Jack had never been so grateful for the double security of a belt and suspenders.

The sheriff picked at his yellowed teeth. "Think I'll head over to the saloon. Get something to eat, maybe something to drink, then call it a day."

Jack added gluttony to the sheriff's growing list of sins. The clock hadn't even struck the noon hour, and here the man was ready to start drinking. Spending only twenty minutes a day on the job didn't leave much time for work. The next time Jack needed a lawman in Cimarron Springs, he'd know better than to count on Sheriff Stanton.

Too dense to pick up on Jack's disgust, Stanton droned on about how much the community paid him to play cards. Jack cut short the pleasantries and stepped into the gray afternoon.

A young couple bumped past him, bundled against the cold. The gentleman took his companion's hand as they traversed an icy patch. The woman smiled shyly.

A flurry of memories drew Jack to a halt. He hadn't thought of his parents in years, but something about the couple brought them to mind. How many times had his own father displayed the same courtly manners with his mother? Held her elbow to cross a rocky patch of ground, or stepped forward to hold open a door? Jack recalled their private looks over the dinner table, their shared jokes.

He'd never thought of his parents as anything but two ordinary, middle-aged folks raising a family. But a newer, more mature understanding dawned on him. His parents had been young once, like the couple he'd just seen. Young and courting. The novel idea kept him rooted to the spot.

"Someone nail your feet to the boardwalk, Ranger?"

The sheriff nudged him out of the way. "Looks like the doc's heading for his office. There's another sawbones farther down the road, but I wouldn't recommend him. Takes a little too much of his own tonic." The sheriff held his pinky in the air and touched his thumb to his lower lip. "If you get my meaning."

Jack gave a curt nod. With every other person in this town drunk or loafing, he wondered how any work got done.

Focusing his attention on the tall, slender man the sheriff had indicated, he crossed the snow-packed road. Crystalline flakes caught on Jack's eyelashes and stood out like dandruff on his wool coat.

He squinted at the ominous sky. *Great.* Just what this day needed, more snow.

Brushing the flakes from his shoulders, he stalked toward the gentleman sporting a black bowler and clutching a crisp, leather satchel.

"You the doc?" Jack asked abruptly.

The man glanced up, his sharp gaze annoyed at the interruption. "Yeah, that's me, Doc Johnsen."

The fair-haired doctor was younger than Jack had expected, with translucent blue eyes indicative of the Norwegian populations farther north. Blond hair curled beneath the brim of the doc's bowler. While Jack sized up the man, two well-dressed young women paused on the boardwalk. One of the women pointed a gloved finger at Doc Johnsen, whispering to her companion. They both giggled, holding hands to their mouths before scurrying away.

Jack tugged his hat lower over his dark hair. You never could tell what women found attractive. What did looks matter when there was work to be done? A head full of curly golden locks never stopped a bullet. Besides, the doc still had the "wet behind the ears" appearance of a body too young to be seasoned by life.

Then again, something in the way the younger man sized Jack up with one long sweeping gaze told him he'd be able to survive the West with his wits intact. Glancing down the street, Jack sighed. What other choice did he have? The doc might be young, but at least this fellow wasn't imbibing his own tonic.

Jack stuck out his hand, his faultless instincts urging him to trust the man. "You're just the person I wanted to see. I'm Jack Elder. I was wondering if you could check on Mrs. Cole. She delivered her baby on Sunday. I'll pay you double your usual fee to check on the widow and her baby."

"I'll be." Doc Johnsen gave Jack's hand a brisk, solid pump. "I just checked on the McCoy family a few days ago. I planned on visiting Mrs. Cole on my way back, but the weather changed, and I didn't want to risk the trip. I hope she was able to get help. It pains me to think of her out there all alone."

Jack had been so focused on locating the doc, he hadn't thought of how he would explain his own involvement. "Well, Jo—uh—Jo McCoy was with Mrs. Cole last I knew."

Those translucent blue eyes narrowed with curiosity. "You don't say."

Forced to elaborate on his role, Jack paused, searching for an answer that wouldn't incite more questions. The emotions attached to those events were still too raw, too slippery to share with a stranger. "I, ah, passed by on the way to town." That was the truth. Not as if he was lying or anything. "Jo was there with Mrs. Cole. The baby seemed healthy."

"Well, then. I'm sure everything is fine. Mrs. McCoy

is about the closest thing we have to a midwife around here, and Jo often assists her. If need be, Jo's smart enough to send for help."

Jack's stomach contracted into a tight ball. How would Jo send for help? The widow's swayback mare probably scraped the snow drifts with its distended belly. What kind of fool lived on the prairie without a decent horse and wagon? He gave himself a mental shake. The same kind of fool woman who stayed on a homestead, alone, when she was nine months pregnant. That's who.

His heart rate quickened with anger before he hardened his resolve. The widow was someone else's problem now. "How are the McCoys?"

"There's a whole lot of McCoys leaning over chamber pots." The doc chuckled. "They're a strong lot, though. The fever has gone through two of the older boys. Should take another week or so before everyone is healthy again."

"Is that the worst of it?"

The younger man gave him a knowing look. "We've had deaths in town, to be sure, but mostly the elderly and the infirm." He switched his satchel from one gloved hand to the other. "There's not an elderly or infirm McCoy in fifty miles. They'll need some time to recover, but I'm confident of the outcome. I'm sure they'll be out to see Mrs. Cole soon enough."

"Confident, are you?" Here was another person with a total disregard for the dangers Elizabeth and her newborn faced. Almost everyone he'd talked to so far acted like a lone woman with an infant, living on the plains, was just a matter of course.

"Mrs. Cole shouldn't be living out there by herself," Jack snapped. "Someone ought to talk some sense into her."

The blond man shrugged. "It distresses me, too, to

think of Mrs. Cole doing all that work, especially with a baby to care for. Don't see how we can stop her, though." Doc Johnsen stood up straighter, his neck flushed. "I offered to marry her myself after Will died. She turned me down so politely, I almost felt bad for asking."

Something hot and ugly rolled in Jack's stomach. "Really? Seems like I heard something similar from someone else."

The snow must have covered the divots left in the road by the town's bachelors in their treks to and from the widow's door after Will's funeral. While it wasn't unheard for a woman living out West to marry within weeks after her husband's death, Elizabeth had turned them all down flat. She'd chosen to remain a widow, rather than remarry. Had she loved her husband that much?

The logical conclusion nearly bowled him over. She'd wasted her love on that fool, and Jack didn't like waste. He also didn't like the way his own emotions had tipped upside down. Instead of anger at her refusal of the handsome doctor's perfectly reasonable offer, the only feeling he could muster was cold relief.

Lack of sleep must be driving him mad. The boarding house in town had played host to a crowd of rowdy cowboys until the wee hours of the morning. Whatever the cause of his unrest, he vowed to leave all thoughts of the widow behind and concentrate on the present. Jack reached into his pocket for payment, but the doc waved away the proffered bills.

"No payment necessary. I was heading in that direction, anyway. I'd best be going, the day's half over already. Nice to meet you, Mr. Elder."

The doc continued his brisk walk in the opposite direction. Jack turned on his heel to follow, drawn to say something more, to send a message. He slowed his pace.

His job was not to babysit the woman, his job was to pick up on the outlaw's trail.

He'd heard from another man in town that a foot of snow had fallen up north. With any luck, the killer was holed up in Wichita because of the weather. Jack's brothers were counting on him, and he never let family down—not for anything, or anyone. Not even a pretty little widow with laughing blue eyes.

After all, she'd been fine on her own up to now.

She was a failure. In six short weeks, her life had descended into bedlam.

Elizabeth glanced around the chaotic room, taking in the overwhelming mess. Recently laundered rags set to dry littered every available surface. Tin plates and cups overflowed the sink. Dirt tracked in by muddy shoes streaked the floor in spokes away from the back door. A pan of fragrant winter-vegetable stew bubbled on the stove.

She laid Rachel against her shoulder, patting the infant's back. The baby had been crying for almost twenty minutes. Not the sweet mewling sounds from previous weeks, but great squalling sobs that had Elizabeth's stomach churning. What if something was wrong with her daughter?

The firewood Jack had left for the stove, the supply she'd thought would never end, had dwindled. She needed to gather more kindling to keep the house warm enough for Rachel, but each time she began a task, a fresh crisis distracted her.

The doc had stopped by several weeks before, giving Rachel a clean bill of health. He'd also hinted that a certain Texas Ranger had been asking the sheriff a lot of questions about Elizabeth's late husband and her living situation. She'd spent the days after Doc Johnsen's visit on pins and needles, terrified the sheriff would start threatening her ownership of the property again.

As if sensing her tension, the infant wailed louder. Elizabeth gently rocked the baby. "Shh, shh, shh," she cooed.

She bent to set down Rachel, determined to remove the boiling stew from the stove before dinner burned. While she suspected the sheriff was using his threats as leverage to marry her, she still feared his retribution at her continued refusal.

Alarmed to note Rachel's face turning a brilliant shade of red, Elizabeth paused midair.

What in heaven's name did that mean? Had the infant taken ill? Gracious, fourteen-year-old Jo knew more about babies. But with all the young McCoy boys full of unleashed energy from their forced confinement and causing mischief, Jo had been too busy at home to tutor Elizabeth on child rearing.

At least the younger girl had managed to slip over this afternoon to help with chores. The assistance was invaluable, and the company kept Elizabeth sane.

She rose wearily to her feet, doing the only thing that seemed to work to quiet Rachel. Back and forth she paced, patting and shushing. Her steps chewed up the distance between the kitchen and the parlor. No amount of soothing comforted the infant.

Exhausted, she slumped onto a chair and attempted to feed the baby, but Rachel wouldn't latch on. Elizabeth set to pacing again, tears of frustration gathering in her eyes.

Jo stepped through the back door, an armload of kindling in her hands.

"I was going to do that," Elizabeth grumbled over Rachel's howling cries.

"That baby sure is squawking. What's wrong with her?"

"I was hoping you would know. I've tried everything, but nothing soothes her."

"She might be colicky." Jo raised her voice to be heard over the wailing infant.

"What's colic?"

"It's when their stomach gets upset."

Certainly if the problem had a name, there was also a solution. "Is there a cure?"

Distracted by their conversation, the baby's sobs relaxed into snuffled hiccups.

Jo shrugged, not pausing on her way to the parlor. "I can't rightly remember. I'll ask my ma when I go home tonight."

Rachel burped. The baby brought her fist to her mouth with a contented coo, and snuggled into Elizabeth's shoulder.

Elizabeth blew out a sigh of relief. Who knew there was more air in that tiny body? She'd already been burped before. Elizabeth did everything on a schedule. Unfortunately, her daughter didn't seem to like schedules. Everything Elizabeth knew about child rearing would fit into a thimble, and she'd exhausted her limited knowledge weeks ago. She hadn't realized raising an infant was so intense, so grueling. She had to learn faster. Rachel Rose was depending on her.

A pungent odor teased Elizabeth's nostrils. She glanced up to find a haze of smoke floating near the ceiling. Something in the kitchen hissed and popped.

The stew!

She dashed to the stove and found dinner bubbling over. Dark brown blobs streaked down the sides of the pan, igniting in the grate.

Elizabeth whirled, colliding with Jo.

The girl rolled her eyes. "I'll take care of it."

Jo snatched a flour sack off a loaf of bread, then wrapped the cloth around her hand before reaching for the pot. Grasping the handle, she scooted to the exit. Elizabeth balanced Rachel on one shoulder, holding open the door with her free hand.

Jo crossed the threshold, searching for a place to drop the scalding pan. She stepped off the landing to her left. Her toe skidded along a patch of ice. Her feet slipped out beneath her. Limbs flailing, Jo struggled to right herself. The pan flew into the air. Vegetable stew rained down, splotching into the snow like blobs of mud.

A sickening thud accompanied Jo's shriek of pain.

Chapter Six

The forlorn town of Cimarron Springs huddled in the distance beneath dismal clouds signaling yet another snowstorm. Jack reined Midnight to a halt on a ridge overlooking the Arkansas River. The horse's muscles bunched beneath him as the animal stomped and snorted.

Thoughts of the pretty widow buzzed relentlessly in his head like fireflies trapped in a Mason jar.

Nervous anticipation scratched beneath Jack's skin the closer he traveled to Cimarron Springs. More than a month had passed, and he had nothing to show for his time. Plenty of the locals around Wichita knew of Bud Shaw in passing, but no one had seen the outlaw in months.

He teetered infuriatingly close to a capture, yet the killer eluded him. Compounding his difficulties, only a few hundred dollars had been recovered from the Wells Fargo robbery. If Bud Shaw maintained control of the balance, there was no telling how far and how fast the outlaw had run.

With the threat of snow hanging heavily in the air, he couldn't afford any delays. Even if he wanted to linger in Kansas, an innocent man faced certain death if Jack dawdled over a blue-eyed widow and her infant like a lovelorn fool.

"Lord," he spoke, his voice lost in the blustery wind. "If you're looking down on me, now would be a good time for some help."

Midnight stumbled over a slick patch of ice. Jack tugged on the reigns, struggling to regain his balance in the saddle. "Don't worry, old boy. My ma always used to say, 'God doesn't mind if your prayers are long or short, He hears them all.'"

The horse snorted a vaporous breath as it skittered over slick, packed snow, jerking to a halt where the wagon tracks split. One road stretched west, to Cimarron Springs. The other meandered south, over the border into Indian territory. Jack urged the horse forward. Midnight shied, dancing to one side.

Reaching back, Jack slapped the obstinate animal's hindquarters. "No more stubbornness. We have a long way to go before there's rest for either of us."

Midnight pawed at the frozen ground. Jack sighed. At least the delay gave him another opportunity to study Cimarron Springs. Black smoke drifted from the multitude of chimneys burning coal and wood against frigid north winds.

An elusive thought teased his brain. A piece of the puzzle that didn't quite fit. What was he missing? Rubbing at his eyes, Jack sucked in a deep, icy breath. He'd seen the gaudy innards of so many seedy saloons, the stench of rancid cigar smoke still clung to his coat.

He needed something—anything: a name, a rumor, even another sighting of that bay mustang. The next best thing to Bud Shaw was someone who knew the outlaw well—someone who knew where the killer had holed up. Outlaws weren't known for their honor.

According to Sheriff Stanton, Elizabeth's husband had run with coarse company, and a lot of it. Gamblers were bound to cross paths. Perhaps Will Cole had mentioned his card-playing buddies to Elizabeth.

The hairs on the back of Jack's neck stirred.

She hadn't recognized Bud's name all those weeks ago, but she'd been awfully distracted. It was a long shot, but what did he have to lose? At this point, he was desperate for another lead. Anything but these infuriating dead ends and false starts.

Jack studied the cluster of buildings.

There had to be a reason why every clue led to this sleepy little town. His plan wasn't totally without merit. Cimarron Springs was the last place Bud Shaw had been spotted, and where the trail had grown cold. And if Jack was wrong, Kansas was as good a place as any to rest. After sending out a few telegrams, he'd pay a visit to Rachel Rose and her mother.

A new plan formed in his mind, the steps laid out like a bricked path in his brain.

His plan served two purposes. Inquiring about the widow's late husband gave him a legitimate reason to check on her and the baby. If her husband had played cards with Bud Shaw, she was a link to the killers and their stolen loot. She might even be in danger.

The outlaw was a braggart, and there was no telling who else was looking for that money—or who else was following the same leads.

Jack's gut twisted. The face of every victim he'd ever buried, every child whose grave he'd marked with piles of stones flashed in his mind. A sudden image filled his brain. He pictured the smudge of flour on Elizabeth's cheek, and a new urgency drove him forward. Kicking

Midnight into a canter, he gave in to his growing impatience.

This surge of anticipation had everything to do with finding Bud Shaw, and nothing to do with his rampant worry for a tiny infant girl and her beguiling mother.

Elizabeth bent her head against the ferocious wind. How long had she been walking? Over an hour at least. The deep wagon ruts she usually followed to the McCoys had been whipped smooth with snowdrifts, forcing her to search for familiar landmarks, instead. Only the spindly cottonwood trees lining the creek bed kept her from straying completely off track.

She pressed her mittened hands to her face. At least the painful stinging in her cheeks had faded into a dull ache. No matter the discomfort, she had to keep moving. Thoughts of Jo and Rachel drove her forward. They were depending on her, and time was running out. Elizabeth concentrated on lifting her numb feet, placing one foot in front of the other in a relentless march through white oblivion.

A flash of light caught her attention. Rubbing her eyes, she squinted, then glanced behind her. Nothing appeared on the horizon. Probably just the wind playing tricks on her. She yanked her hat closer over her ears, forcing herself to focus on moving from one landmark to the next, rather than crossing the whole overwhelming distance.

Rippling hills of relentless snow and ice stretched on forever. Studying the flat terrain kept her thoughts from wandering into all the frightening consequences of her perilous journey.

Her scattered thoughts drifted back to her journey West only a year ago. This was how the prairie had looked when she'd first arrived from New York—the grasses flattened and windblown. After the bustling crowds of the city, the barren landscape had overwhelmed her with its lonely visage.

When the golden mantle of spring had finally settled over the desolate prairie, she'd practically wept with relief. By mid-summer, stalks of wheat grasses had rippled in the wind, moving like golden waves on the ocean.

Spring seemed an eternity away. No matter how far she walked, the distance to the next rise refused to shrink. She longed to sit and rest, just for a moment. Time had become her enemy.

A low rumble vibrated beneath her feet. Thoughts of Indians and outlaws robbed her of breath. Heart pounding, she jerked around to find a great black horse charging across the plains. Elizabeth froze. The apparition galloped over the white snow, chewing up the distance. Her brain told her to move, but her feet refused to obey.

At the last moment she stumbled to one side. Covering her face, she braced for a blow from those enormous, coal-black hooves. The horse skidded to a halt, kicking up a shower of snow. A great bear of a man in a familiar dark wool coat leaped down, stalking toward her as if he'd materialized straight out of the blowing storm.

Elizabeth backed away, terrified by the low menace in his approach. He raised his arms. Her hands flew to her face in a protective gesture.

"Fool woman," Jack shouted over the wind.

Something heavy wrapped around her shoulders. She peeked with one eye to find her shoulders swathed in a tartan fabric. He'd covered her with a wool blanket. Her apprehension waned a notch.

"What are you doing?" Jack demanded.

Fear, relief and annoyance jumbled together in a confusing churn of emotions. "Getting help," Elizabeth snapped back through chattering teeth. "Jo fell. She's hurt her foot and her ribs. I think she's broken her ankle."

Tightening the comforting blanket around her shoulders, she noted how the cold had seeped through her coat. With the Ranger's sudden appearance, all of her physical discomforts came rushing back.

Jack grunted. Only his eyes showed between his hat and his muffler, but those hazel orbs sparked with exasperation. "You were fool enough to walk out in this weather?"

"It wasn't snowing when I started."

"You left an injured kid to mind your baby. What were you thinking?"

The obvious censure in his question sent her stumbling back a step. "R-Rachel was sleeping. I wasn't going to be gone that long."

Her first instinct had been correct. He wasn't annoyed, he was furious. Anger radiated from his enormous body like steam rising from a hot spring. For the first time since he'd barged into her life, she feared him.

He looped the reins around his leather-clad hand with a scowl. "You're going home."

Afraid or not, he had no right to order her around.

"I'll do what I please." Elizabeth ducked away from his outstretched arm. "You go back to town and fetch the doctor. I can walk home on my own."

"You'll ride with me." His expression dared her to disobey his order. "Then we'll decide if Jo needs a doctor."

"You're not in charge of me."

"As long as you're behaving like a lunatic, I am."

Trembling with the accumulated tensions of the past days, Elizabeth knotted her fists at her sides. "What did you just call me?"

"You heard me. You left an infant and an injured kid

alone so you could freeze to death in a snowstorm. That's a lunatic decision if ever I heard one."

"How dare you question my decisions? What else was I supposed to do? Send the milk cow?"

He hooked one finger into his woolen muffler, tugging the material down to reveal the full force of his disapproving glower. "Look, lady. If you die, Rachel is an orphan, and we both know how you feel about that option. You coming or not?"

A stubborn denial sat on the tip of her tongue. Swirling flakes battered her face. Searching the distance, she was shocked to discover the group of trees she'd been aiming for completely obscured by churning snow.

She pictured her daughter's wise, trusting eyes and Elizabeth's stomach sank. The Ranger was correct, her life was no longer her own to gamble. Pride clogged the words in her throat.

"Let's go," Jack declared, softening his demand to a brisk instruction. "I've already checked on the house, and Jo and the baby are fine."

"You what?"

"How do you think I found you? I stopped for a visit on my way out of Cimarron Springs. By the looks of the place, I assumed something awful had happened."

Elizabeth huffed. Of course he'd already been to the house. Hadn't he mentioned that Jo was minding the baby? Nettled, she refused to dignify his remark with an answer. The condition of her home was none of his affair. He wasn't exhausted from raising an infant. She'd like to see how well he'd fare after taking care of a baby all alone with only a few squandered hours of sleep each night.

He hoisted himself onto the horse, holding out a hand. Floundering in the gathering snow, she shook her head.

The thought of climbing atop that enormous animal terrified her almost as much as the man sitting astride it.

He beckoned impatiently. "Put your foot in the stirrup and I'll pull you up."

"I don't need your help."

"'When pride cometh, then cometh shame. But with the lowly is wisdom.'"

"Are you mocking me?"

"The Bible isn't meant to mock you, Elizabeth."

Once again, her own ignorance condemned her. She'd opened her Bible plenty of times. The worn copy had been bestowed upon her by Mrs. Peabody from the orphanage. Banished to find work in the city at sixteen, all the girls had received a Bible and two dollars. The orphanage had given her plenty of training in working hard, and little else. Elizabeth had treasured the book, one of her few possessions, but she hadn't studied the scriptures as much as she would have liked. Sure of her unworthiness, she'd been humbled by the wisdom the book contained.

There hadn't been much time to learn, anyway. The hours at the bakery had been from dawn till dusk. The family who owned the shop had insisted she stay behind on Sundays in order to prepare the kitchen for busy Monday mornings. During her three-week courtship, Will had promised to accompany her to services. He'd broken that promise along with so many others.

Jack reined his horse to a halt before her, effectively blocking her flight. "If you won't think of yourself, at least think of Jo. She was sick with worry when I left to find you."

"How dare you judge me." Her voice broke. "I did the best I could while you were gone."

Suddenly another man stood before her. Another man

who had left her, again and again, until at last he'd been so disappointed, he'd left for good.

"I'm here now."

Jack nudged the horse closer. A cutting wind brought moisture to her eyes. Numbing cold penetrated the tartan blanket around her shoulders. Uncontrollable shivers racked her body.

If she refused, he'd know she couldn't ride. Drained of fight, she focused on a glimpse of the scrollwork design stamped into the pommel of his leather saddle.

Constantly living in fear was exhausting. From the moment her mother had abandoned her at the orphanage, the grueling emotion had ruled her life. Even her marriage had been fraught with fear—fear that Will might never return from one of his many trips—and fear that he would.

She didn't want to be afraid anymore. She didn't want to be a disappointment to anyone, especially herself.

Elizabeth grasped the Ranger's hand. The coarse threads of her woolen mittens dug into her fingers as he squeezed. Gathering her courage, she lifted her booted foot. The leather stirrup loomed impossibly high.

"The other foot," Jack grumbled.

Fuming, she shifted her weight. Her skirts stretched over her knee as she drew her leg higher, finally sinking her toe into the narrow loop.

He effortlessly tugged on her arm. She managed to swing her leg over the back of the animal. Matted snow clumped wetly to her hem as her skirts flapped over her calf. Seated precariously, Elizabeth wrapped her arms around Jack's waist and hung on for dear life. His large body sheltered her from the worst of the buffeting wind.

Glancing over his shoulder, Jack caught her gaze. "You set?"

Her heartbeat raced. She nodded, not trusting herself to speak. His face loomed so close she noted the flecks of gold surrounding his irises. Heat emanated from his body, enveloping her in warmth. Her bone-rattling shudders stilled.

"We'd best get back home, then," he muttered brusquely. Despite the urgency in his voice, he gently nudged the horse at a sedate, slow ramble.

Elizabeth glanced down, quickly pinching her eyes shut again. The hard ground rushed by a great distance away. She fisted her hands in his coat, hugging Jack closer. The rough wool abraded her cheek with the horse's uneven gate.

The muscle along his strong jaw clenched and unclenched, as if he was biting back his fury. With every step that brought them closer to home, her initial annoyance at his high-handed behavior blossomed into outright resentment. She didn't want to be afraid, but she didn't want to be ordered about or subjected to this seething resentment.

The horse stumbled, sending her teetering to one side. Shrieking, she fumbled to regain her balance.

Jack pressed his leather-clad hand over her woolen mittens to hold her steady. "I've got you."

His protective gesture acted like a bucket of ice water on her smoldering anger. Elizabeth sighed. The lawman was simply a convenient target for her irritation. In truth, she wasn't angry with Jack. She was disappointed in herself. Once again, an impulsive decision had proven disastrous. Going for help had been the wrong choice. She hadn't known it was going to snow.

A sharp wind kicked up, tearing at the tartan blanket. Jack leaned forward, urging the horse to a quicker pace while still keeping a firm hold on her arm.

The faint outline of her homestead appeared in the distance. Three modest buildings clustered beneath the branches of red oak, sugar maple and linden trees planted by settlers long since gone. The protective copse of trees stood guard against the maddening winds that drove across the plains from season to season.

The bunkhouse appeared first, with the barn set farther back and to the left. The one-story main house with its covered porch sat closest to the road to town. Those buildings represented everything she owned, every piece of her desolate history. Her only hope for the future.

Here was the one piece of security she'd managed to cling to despite the relentless forces buffeting her safe, ordered world. Here was the only property she'd ever owned, the only home that had ever truly belonged to her. Her heart had soared the first time she laid eyes on the modest spread. Now she waited for the familiar surge of possessive emotion.

Nothing.

Her stomach plummeted. She clawed for purchase on a slope of conflicting emotions, but the drab structures failed to inspire anything but apathy. There was no life in the wood, mortar, brick or glass. The absence of her usual giddy pleasure unsettled her. Instead, she felt trapped. Without those steadying markers, what did she have?

Rocked by the loss, she clung to Jack, letting his body shield her from the driving snow while she absorbed his comforting warmth. She could pretend, just for a moment, that she wasn't alone any longer. Rachel's birth had driven home how desperately she needed someone to confide in, to lean on.

Her cranky rescuer veered away from the barn, continuing on a path toward the house. He reined the horse to a halt before the front porch. Jack turned his head, bringing his profile into view.

Without speaking he held out his hand. Elizabeth grasped the offering, swinging to the ground. When her feet hit the solid earth, she feared her legs would buckle. As if sensing her distress, Jack held her mittened fingers until she steadied herself.

Glancing up, she recalled how he'd looked the night Rachel Rose was born. Her pulse quickened. What a blessing that evening had brought. The memory had her heart opening like the first crocus of spring, new and reborn.

Finally, here were the feelings she'd been searching for.

Anxious to ensure Jo and Rachel's safety, she whirled, racing up the shallow, slippery steps to yank open the door.

She dashed to the bedroom and discovered them both sleeping peacefully. Jo with the blanket tucked beneath her chin, Rachel in her makeshift crib. Elizabeth pressed a hand to her chest. *Thank the Lord.* No one had suffered for her impetuous dash for help. She took several deep breaths as her thundering heartbeat gradually slowed. Backing out of the room, she crossed to the pantry. Embers sparked in the stove's grate. The fire's warmth chased away the last of her frosty chill.

With her fear for Jo and Rachel eased, the Ranger's sudden appearance in her life troubled her. What did he want? Why had he returned? If she was truthful with herself, she was just as disturbed by her flustered reaction to him. She'd best guard her heart against softening to him. For all she knew, he'd come to check on her at the sheriff's bidding.

Preparing for a long talk, she reached for the tin coffee kettle. She didn't know why Jack had wandered back into her life, but she was going to find out. One thing she did know for certain.

His return meant trouble.

"You can't handle an injured girl and newborn baby all by yourself," Jack spoke, dizzy from talking in circles with the mule-headed widow for the past twenty minutes.

Upon his return from the barn, Elizabeth had laid out coffee and pulled peach-filled kolaches sprinkled with crystallized sugar from the oven warmer.

He surreptitiously reached for another pastry. "There's too much work to be done."

"And what do you suggest I do?" Elizabeth countered. "Jo can't be moved."

He licked a spot of jam from his thumb. Problem was, he kept getting distracted when he should be trying to outwit her. Not that his distraction was entirely his fault. She was even prettier than the last time he'd seen her. Her lustrous hair was braided into an elaborate knot at the base of her neck, highlighting her slender throat. Her pale blue eyes had grown more vibrant, a charming hue that reminded him of a clear summer's day. Only the faint circles of exhaustion darkening her eyes like bruises indicated her exhaustion.

She wore a crisp white shirtwaist tucked into the wide band of her blue gingham skirt. Looking at her, he could hardly believe this was the same round woman he'd burst in on weeks ago.

A woman that pretty shouldn't be risking her life. "If you're in trouble, send for help."

She grasped the baking sheet with one hand, slipping her spatula beneath two more kolaches.

She slid the pastries onto his plate with a scowl belying her thoughtful act. "I believe that's what I was doing when you referred to me as a lunatic."

Abashed, Jack studied his calloused hands. He absently flicked a crumb from his palm. "I apologize for that remark. I was, um, concerned, and might have let some emotion leach into the situation."

"Gracious, I don't believe I've ever heard you string so many words together into a sentence." She wiped her hands on the crisp, white apron knotted around her waist. "That was an articulate, almost heartfelt apology."

He scowled, not knowing if all those showy words added up to a good thing or a bad thing. To cover his confusion, he bit into another luscious pastry, then groaned in delight as peach filling enveloped his upper lip. Right then he didn't care if she was praising him or insulting him. As long as he was eating her tasty baking, nothing else mattered.

"Your apology is accepted," Elizabeth grudgingly offered. "You may stay for supper."

"That's mighty kind of you." Where did she think he was going, anyway? "You didn't happen to look outside recently? It's a whiteout. You and I are going to be sharing more than supper together."

Watching her cheeks flush a becoming shade of pink, he immediately regretted his words. "I meant to say, this snow is forcing me to hole up here for a few days until the weather clears."

She crossed her arms over her chest and glared at him. "You might as well be truthful. Did Sheriff Stanton send you out here?"

"What's that supposed to mean?"

"You—"

Rachel let out a shrill wail. Jack started, surprised to hear such a robust noise from such a tiny package. The widow's face clouded with worry as she lifted the crying baby from her woven laundry basket. To his astonishment, the child appeared to have doubled in size in the weeks he'd been gone.

"Mrs. Cole," Jo called from the other room.

Elizabeth's attention swung between the red-faced baby and the bedroom, torn between the two demands. "I need to check on Jo."

Quickly wiping his sticky hands on his pant legs, Jack rose to his feet. "Let me hold Rachel."

Elizabeth hesitated.

He quirked an eyebrow. He'd been present for the delivery, certainly she trusted him to hold the infant for a few minutes? "She's already crying. I'm not going to make it any worse."

As she cautiously handed over the baby, the widow caught her lower lip between her teeth. The impossibly light bundle fit perfectly into Jack's outstretched arms. Adjusting the blankets, he tucked Rachel close to his chest. The baby's distraught howling ceased. Peaceful silence filled the room.

Elizabeth's jaw dropped. "What did you do?"

"Nothing." He shrugged, secretly pleased with his success. "Check on Jo. This isn't the first baby I've ever held, you know."

Her eyes narrowed.

"I have nieces and nephews, remember?"

Another crimson flush spread over the apples of her cheeks. "Of course."

She spun away from his mocking regard, tugging her apron strings loose on her way to check on Jo.

Jack blew out a long, relieved breath. "I'm not much good at talking with the ladies."

He studied the baby, her perfect Cupid's bow mouth, her dark, solemn eyes. An unfamiliar contentment seeped through his veins like warm molasses. He'd spent the last decade of his life immersed in the filth and human muck littering every dark corner of the American West. He'd grown so accustomed to dishonesty, he expected most men to tell a lie even when the truth would suit them better. Yet here in his arms rested an innocent human life, completely reliant and trusting.

His chest tightened. He felt as if he'd betrayed the child by leaving, though his guilt made no sense. This rag-tag group was none of his concern. He'd done far more than most men in his position would have.

He caressed Rachel's cheek reverently with his finger. Her mouth worked, rooting toward his touch. A protective instinct banded around his heart. One minuscule hand stirred beneath the blankets, a seeking arm struggled free. Five pudgy fingers wrapped around his knuckle.

Rachel's mouth spread into a wide, toothless grin. His heart brimmed with awe. They were connected. He didn't know how or why, but his fate was irrevocably linked to this child and her impossible, beautiful, infuriating mother.

And he didn't like it.

He didn't like it one bit. Caring meant risking loss. He'd seen too much in his career as a Ranger to convince himself otherwise. He'd witnessed enough of other people's suffering to know he never wanted to risk such sorrow in his own life. He never wanted to suffer the way his brother had after Doreen's death.

If the Lord had brought him to this place and time for a reason, he had to trust the Lord to guide him still.

"'Great is our Lord, and of great power,'" he whispered to the infant cradled in his arms. "'His understanding is infinite.'"

Jack prayed he was worthy of that understanding.

Chapter Seven

Jack rubbed his eyes, appearing as unbearably weary as Elizabeth felt.

"Have you ever fired a gun before?" he asked.

"Once," she replied.

If you could call Will grabbing her hand and pulling the trigger actually firing a gun. Then, yes, she had. It wasn't an event she liked to recall. Will had been unsympathetic to her bruised shoulder, even belly-laughing at her pain.

"You can't live on the prairie without knowing how to shoot a gun."

Elizabeth scowled.

Jack paused in his lecture.

They stood in a clearing several hundred yards from the main house. Jack had scoured the barren landscape before deciding on the safest area to test fire her shotgun. While snow had mounded in six-foot drifts along the gentle dips in the ground, this section had been swept smooth by fierce winds. Tufts of grass spiked through the white frost as if Mother Nature had given the whole prairie a bad haircut.

Jack had instructed her on how to clean and load the

unwieldy firearm earlier. Now the moment she'd been dreading all morning loomed before her.

She sucked in a fortifying breath. "I'm ready."

Gripping the cold metal barrel, she clamped her jaw shut. She loathed guns, the noise and the violence. Despite her fear, she steeled her resolve. Her fledging independence required her to learn, no matter how repugnant the task.

"You've got only one chance with this particular shotgun," Jack said. "So you have to make your shot count."

Elizabeth chanced a sidelong glance at her reluctant instructor. His double-breasted coat stretched taut over his broad shoulders. His dark hat sat low on his head. Her cheeks warmed. He stuck his left foot slightly forward and angled his body.

His woolen overcoat with its wide lapels resembled the pea jackets she'd seen on dock workers near the harbor. She pictured Jack on the bow of a ship, strong and sure, the wind whipping through his hair.

"Here's how you stand." His deep-timbered voice intruded on her musing.

Shaking away the fanciful thoughts of rolling waves and unfurled masts billowing in the breeze, Elizabeth mirrored his stance, inordinately pleased at his curt nod of approval.

"Raise the barrel like this." He lifted both hands as if he held a phantom gun, his left eye squinting into the distance.

Once again she mimicked him, raising Will's ancient shotgun to level the sight at a stray line of brush on the horizon.

"That's not quite right," Jack murmured, rubbing his chin in thoughtful consideration as his gaze swept over her stiff form.

He circled to stand behind her. Elizabeth tensed. He wrapped his arms around her upper body, not quite touching the nap of her coat. He leaned forward. His breath fluttered against her cheek. His right hand covered hers, their skin separated by layers of leather and the thin cotton gloves she'd donned this morning in anticipation of the firing lesson. Gently nudging, he adjusted the barrel to rest more firmly in the crook of her shoulder.

"Like this," he said.

Her stomach performed an unexpected flip. Elizabeth jerked her head in a nod.

His left arm came around her body, guiding her with surprising gentleness to rest her stiff fingers on the smooth, mahogany forestock. "That's better," he said. The vibration from his baritone voice tickled her ear. "You're shivering. Are you cold?"

"A bit," Elizabeth gasped, hoping her quivering voice hadn't betrayed her.

This uncontrollable trembling had everything to do with the large, warm male cradling her in his arms, and nothing to do with the weather. To her shame, she ached to close her eyes and rest her head in the hollow of his shoulder. To feel safe—just for a moment. To forget that he might very well be here at the sheriff's bidding, ready to snatch the rug from beneath her fragile security. After all, why else would he have returned?

Elizabeth straightened her spine. "What next?"

"Squint your left eye, and focus your right eye on that shrub in the distance. You've got a near sight on the barrel, and a far sight on the muzzle. Line them up against your target."

She concentrated on his instructions, willing her thudding heart to slow. The wind kicked up again, ruffling her skirts around her ankles. Focusing her attention on the target, she ran the tip of her tongue over her parched lips. The arm holding her steady stiffened.

Jack audibly cleared his throat. "That's it. Now bring your cheek to rest on the stock and line up the sights."

His scent enticed her—a distracting combination of wood smoke, shaving lather and something musky.

"There's going to be a kick when you pull the trigger. Keep the stock tight against your shoulder, or it's going to hurt."

"Okay," she replied, blinking against the wind.

Her courage drained away as the memory of her last experience returned with startling clarity. How her ears had rung from the thunderous report. The way her shoulder had stung for a week. Elizabeth pinched her eyes open and shut a few times to release the tension, then shifted her feet.

"Take your time," Jack murmured.

He waited patiently while she gathered her nerve. When she nodded, he released his hold on the gun, letting her steady the weight while still maintaining his comforting position behind her. She felt his chest move with his deep, even breathing. Her sporadic heartbeat grew more even. She concentrated on the present, clearing her thoughts to focus on the target.

Anticipating the kick, she tightened her grip, then slowly squeezed the trigger as Jack had instructed. Buckshot roared from the barrel with a thunder-clap burst. Fire exploded in her shoulder, launching her backward. She stumbled hard against Jack's chest.

He steadied her with a hand to her hip, then reached around to pull the smoking barrel from her limp hands.

Elizabeth pressed icy fingers to her ears. How she loathed loud noises. Jack appeared before her, propping the gun against his leg before tugging her stiff hands away from her head.

"That's enough for today." He rubbed warmth into her raw fingers. "You need better gloves."

"I thought these would make it easier to pull the trigger." Her teeth chattered. "I've got my m-mittens in my pocket."

She drew back her hands, but he held firm, cupping them in his palms. He tipped his head forward, blowing a warm burst of air over her tightly clenched fists. A shudder coursed through her body.

"Is that better?"

His tender voice slipped over her like a caress. She jerked her head in a nod.

He nudged her chin up with his gloved hand. "You did well."

She had to pull her lower lip between her teeth to keep it from trembling.

Her heart pounding, she met his steady gaze. His eyes fascinated her. In the dim light of the cabin, they appeared dark and mysterious. A vague brown. In the hazy afternoon, his irises flared over the brown-and-gold flecks, highlighting the green edges. Whiskers already darkened his cheek, though a blot of red dotting his chin indicated he'd nicked himself shaving that morning. How quickly his beard must grow.

Elizabeth tilted her head to shake the spell. "The prairie is fascinating, isn't it? In the city, I never noticed how the clouds roll in for a thunderstorm like black smoke puffing from a train engine. Out here, you can see a storm coming for miles." The nervous words tumbled off her lips.

"I don't know." Jack shook his head with a sigh that

sounded suspiciously like self-reproach. "Sometimes a downpour sneaks up when you least expect it."

His eyes filled with a curious sorrow, Jack stepped away to crack the shotgun and rest it over his horse's saddle. He returned to stand before her, his arms crossed over his chest.

A peaceful calm settled over Elizabeth. For the first time in a long while, she *was* all right. She was shaken, but proud. Proud of herself for taking aim and firing. Proud of herself for overcoming her fear. Giddy exhilaration stirred in her chest. "I did it!"

"You did real good." He smiled, the corners of his eyes crinkling. "You killed that bush dead."

Suddenly jubilant, she raised up on her tiptoes and quickly bussed him on the cheek. That might have been the end of it, except he turned his head at the last moment, and instead of finding the rough stubble of his cheek, their lips collided. His mouth was firm, but surprisingly soft. Shock held her immobile for a beat.

She leaped back, groaning in embarrassment as he blinked at her spontaneous gesture. "I'm so sorr—"

The intense look in his eyes silenced her apology. Jack caught her around the waist, splaying his hand over the small of her back. He gathered her close to him, gently, ignoring what was only a halfhearted resistance. A muscle in his jaw ticked, the fisted hand at her back tightened.

Blood roared in her ears. She tipped her head back, craving the comfort of his embrace. Her lips parted.

With an abrupt grimace, he thrust her away. "We should get back."

His gaze didn't quite meet hers.

"Yes." His rejection stabbed her heart, hurting more than the throb in her shoulder from the gun's kick. "Of course."

What on earth had come over her? No longer cold, her flaming cheeks could melt the frozen tundra. Kissing Jack had felt like the most natural thing in the world, as if she'd been anticipating this moment her whole life. Knowing he didn't share her feelings sent a hard knot forming in her chest.

She'd been tempted to kiss two men in her twenty-three years, and neither of them had truly wanted her affection. The realization stung.

Desultory small talk accompanied their return to the house, each of them attempting to cover the embarrassment of Elizabeth's spontaneous, foolish behavior. Knowing the day couldn't get any worse, she removed Will's revolver from its place in the empty lard tin and held the stock with two fingers, the barrel dangling to the floor.

"Will you help me load this, too?"

"Careful with that." He accepted the gun, flipped out the cylinder, then gave it a spin. "This gun has never been fired. There's not even a speck of grease on the cylinder. Still, you have to remember the first rule of gun safety. Treat every gun as if it's loaded."

Elizabeth rolled her eyes. That was the whole problem in a nutshell. "Not this one."

His expression grew thunderous. He rested the gun on the table with a grim twist of his lips. "You have a child in the house now. Every gun is loaded. Period. You treat every weapon you pick up, put down or point at someone as loaded."

Cords of tension formed in her neck. She willed herself not to shrink away from his censure. "Fine. It's loaded."

"Excellent." His gaze slid over her face. "I didn't mean to snap at you, but with a baby in the house we can't be too careful." He nodded to the back bedroom where Jo rested and Rachel napped. "Where are the bullets?"

"I—uh—I don't know."

Frowning, he flattened both palms against the table. "I thought you wanted me to load this?"

Elizabeth immediately regretted her impetuous decision to request his help. No matter how hard she tried to forget, every corner of the house was fraught with reminders. Even searching for bullets stirred up recollections of a past she'd rather forget. Will had always been so possessive about his property.

Though he'd been gone for more than eight months, longer even than they'd been married, she still felt his disapproving presence each time she searched his belongings. Her time with Will had been blessedly short, but the echoes lingered. Folding her arm across her stomach, she unconsciously touched the arrowhead scar on her arm over her sleeve.

Will was gone, she reminded herself. He had hurt her for the last time.

If she wanted to maintain control of her home and her property, she had to learn how to defend herself. Considering Jack's dramatic entrance all those weeks ago, she had to force herself to learn a new skill, even if she was mocked for her ignorance. The next stranger who visited might not be a Texas Ranger with chocolate-brown hair and hazel eyes. She had her daughter to think of now. If it took her all winter, she'd perfect the skill.

Memories or not, it was time to face her future. "I think the bullets are in here."

Heart thumping, she crossed to the pantry, then let her hand linger on the knob. Taking a deep steadying breath, she pushed open the door. Neat rows of mason jars lined the shelves; apples, peaches, pickles and a rainbow selection of various other preserves. She took down the heavy galvanized bathing tub that hung on a hook on the outside wall.

"Odd time to take a bath."

Shrieking, her hand flew to her chest. The tub banged to the floor with a metallic clang. "You startled me."

"I see that." He quirked an eyebrow, reaching for the tub. "You want me to put this some place for you?"

"No, no." Elizabeth shook her head. "I need to stand on it. I think the bullets are up there." She indicated a crude wooden crate teetering on the top shelf.

He easily reached over her head, dwarfing her with his superior height. Crowded together in the confined space, his unique male scent enveloped her once again. Without his coat she caught a clean, crisp scent like freshly washed sheets. A lock of hair fell across his forehead, lending him a rakish appearance. She envisioned him as Mr. Darcy in the Jane Austen novel her mother had loved. Yet she couldn't picture Jack sipping tea in an ornate parlor. He belonged on the open range, herding cattle, not confined indoors. He exuded a strength and assurance at odds with his cautious gentleness.

Her breath quickened. She was hot and cold at the same time, the sensations nothing like fear. An anxious anticipation stirred in her limbs. She needed something, wanted something from him, but the yearning was elusive, ethereal.

He grasped the box, turning on his heel in one swift motion to exit the room. She blew out a long breath, shocked at the way her blood surged through her veins. By the time she'd gathered herself enough to follow him out, he'd set the box on the sturdy worktable.

The forlorn sight of Will's legacy robbed her of breath. Here was an emotion she understood. Sorrow. The color of the leather had leached away, giving Will's saddlebags a dull, lifeless appearance. How quickly the vibrant material had faded.

Jack cleared his throat, startling her back to the present. Her numb fingers tugged the buckles loose.

Hooking his thumbs into his belt loops, Jack lowered his head. "How long has your husband been gone?"

Her mind slid over the memories. "Just over eight months."

"I'm sorry for your loss."

She couldn't force her gaze higher than the mother-of-pearl buttons at his chest. "Thank you," she replied simply.

How did she explain this confusing whirl of emotions to Jack when she didn't even understand the feelings herself? "We were married for only six months. It's strange to think he's been gone longer than we were together."

Avoiding Jack's sympathetic gaze, she lifted out each item, a dismal accounting of Will's life—a knife, matches, the hollow swish of liquid from his engraved flask, a deck of cards and finally the paper-wrapped bullets. What must the Texas Ranger think of the telling assortment?

The second bag bulged with a large object. Feeling safe in the Ranger's presence, she checked inside to discover a Bible. She paused, her hands trembling. She'd never thought of Will as a man to carry around a Bible. He'd never gone to church once in the entire time she'd known him. She recalled all his promises during their whirlwind courtship. He'd talked of God and church, but his words had been brisk and shallow. She'd thought he would guide her on her faith journey, but his wisdom had proved false.

Jack rested a warm hand on her drooping shoulder. "I didn't mean to bring up sad memories."

Tears burned behind her eyes. "They're not sad, so much. Not like you'd think. In some ways, it's like he's on another trip."

Jack let his hand drop back to his side. "He traveled a lot?"

"For his job with the railroad. Even after he died, I felt like I was waiting for him to come home after another long absence."

Crushing guilt erased her prepared speech. The one she'd murmured to the few kind ladies from town who'd braved their husbands' censure and brought her cakes and condolences after Will's death. She'd been so alone for so long, that all her dammed up conversation jostled to be unleashed.

She cleared her throat, driven to talk to someone, anyone. "I had to get used to him being gone, you see. I must have gotten too good at forgetting."

"I think I understand."

Elizabeth started at his revelation. She'd expected his censure, his disgust at her admission. "You do?"

"I felt that way when I first left my family's cattle ranch. When you're away from the people you love, you have to lock away those feelings, or the memories eat away at your joy until you're not happy any place."

His deep voice soothed her battered senses. His quiet understanding drove her to speak of the long buried memories. "Once I forgot to set a place for him at supper. It was a habit, you know? One bowl, one plate, one spoon. I didn't even realize what I'd done until he came in to wash up."

Jack scuffed the toe of his boot along the braided edge of the rag rug beneath the worktable. "What did your husband do when he realized he didn't have a plate?"

"He didn't even notice. He just sat down to eat. I guess

he thought I wasn't hungry." She glanced up, quickly ducking away from the pity shimmering in the Ranger's eyes. "You can teach me how to load the gun another time."

In truth, even when Will had been home, he'd never truly been there. He was always off to town, always making grand plans for the next adventure. She'd told him time and again that she was satisfied with their little slice of the prairie, but she hadn't been paying attention to his unspoken replies, his restless need to escape her. She'd thought she'd done everything to be the perfect wife, but she hadn't done nearly enough. Will was never going to be satisfied. Especially not with her.

Jack donned the fake smile she had begun to think of as his Texas Ranger grin.

Her confession had obviously made him uncomfortable.

"I really should teach you how to load this gun," he said. "No time like the present."

A yeasty smell teased her nostrils, providing her with a much-needed distraction. "I need to check my baking."

Brushing past Jack, she plucked a fragrant loaf from the warm oven. Carefully holding it in a towel, she tapped the golden-brown crust, satisfied with the hollow report. "It's perfect."

Jack's face lit up at the sight. "Ma'am, I don't think I've ever eaten so well, and I've traveled all over the country."

His praise ignited a warm glow in her chest. She couldn't remember anyone actually complimenting her. "I should bake well. I must have baked thousands of these when I apprenticed in New York."

"Mind if I have a slice?"

"Buttered?"

"Is there any other way?"

She laughed at his horrified expression. "I guess not."

Leaning one hip against the worktable, he crossed his arms over his chest. "What's it like, New York?"

"Crowded." A delicate shudder sent the serrated knife in her hand trembling. "You can't believe all those people live in one place. The noise and commotion never stop."

"Must have been quite a way to live."

"In some ways, it was more lonely than living out here. When you see people together, families and married couples, friends, it reminds you of what you don't have."

She'd thought she'd conquered the loneliness, making do with Jo's company and the occasional visit to town or a trip to the McCoys.

But she missed this, talking to someone. Just talking. "All I ever wanted was a family. Something to call my own that couldn't be taken away. But nothing lasts forever, right?"

His eyes darkened. "You have to hold on to the memories. The Bible says, 'All go unto one place, all are of the dust, and all turn to dust again.'"

"I like that." She considered his solemn visage. "That's all we really have, isn't it? Our memories."

The corner of his mouth tipped up. "The good and the bad. Seems the longer I stay away from home, the more I cleave to the fond memories. The bad ones seem to fade away in their place."

"I wish I could say the same." She sighed.

Exchanging this easy banter unleashed a yearning for human companionship. She wanted to immerse herself, to hang on to the light and never let go.

"Where are you from?" he asked. "Originally, that is. You still have an accent."

"My father would be proud to know that I still carry

a piece of his homeland." She thought back to her own fond memories. "My family is originally from Bucklebury, England. We lived with my uncle just outside the village. My father was a baker, but as the youngest son, there wasn't much room for him in the family business. We traveled to America when I was five so he could open his own store."

She hadn't thought of England in years, but images came flooding back like pictures behind a scrim, hazy and diluted. She envisioned the rolling green hills, the misty fog that hung over the fields at first light.

She slathered butter onto the steaming, soft bread. "My father started a pastry shop in New York. For a few years he worked from dawn to dusk. When I was nine, a fire burned down the whole block. We lost everything. My—uh—my father went to work for someone else after that." She let her voice trail off.

Better to end the story there. She had been too young to understand. Too young to realize that her whole life was about to change, forever.

Jack accepted the slice of bread, studying the melted butter as it pooled into the fluffy air pockets. "Why don't you move back to New York? Live with your parents? Raising Rachel Rose with your family would be better than living out here all alone."

She pondered her answer, wondering how much to reveal. "My parents are both dead. After my father died, my mother was sick, and then…and then she died, too. I spent several years in an orphanage." She skirted around the truth. Not quite lying, but not telling the whole of it, either. "All of the girls had to have jobs and I, well, I chose to work in the kitchens. The task helped me feel closer to my family, to my roots. When I was too old for the orphanage, I even took a job at a bakery. That's where I met Will."

She glanced up, startled by the stricken look on his face.

"I'm sorry," he muttered. "I didn't realize."

There was more to her story, but she couldn't bear to reveal her pain. Not when he appeared so horrified to learn she'd spent half of her life in an orphanage. "Other people have suffered far worse than I."

He made a noncommittal sound in his throat. "Why don't you at least move to town, open your own bakery? I'm sure there are plenty of people who'd devour your cooking."

"I couldn't," she protested with a nervous laugh.

"Why not?"

"Well, I, uh—" She paused. "I guess I never thought about it before. I don't know if I could handle the work alone."

"Hire someone to help out. There's always a body in need of work. 'The hand of the diligent man maketh rich.'"

A bakery. Elizabeth pictured a warm kitchen, a bell tinkling over the door to indicate a customer. A place of her own where people gathered. A place where people knew her. How well would the people in Cimarron Springs greet Will Cole's widow? The warm image dissolved. If the scathing stares they shot at her on her rare trips to the mercantile were any indication, not very well. Even after Will's death, his legacy haunted her. Memories were long, and she'd always be Will Cole's widow. Elizabeth's heart sank. The homestead that had saved her, trapped her at the same time.

She briskly chafed her hands together, rubbing off the last bit of flour dust. "It's time to prepare supper. Do you mind keeping Jo company while I work? She's getting real antsy being cooped up in there."

"After another fortifying slice of bread."

Running a bakery sounded heavenly compared to running the homestead. She'd barely survived the autumn, working eighteen hours a day to prepare for winter. The long cold months had given her a brief reprieve, but spring loomed just around the corner. With the change in weather came planting the kitchen garden and all the other repairs neglected over the winter.

Elizabeth pressed the heels of her palms against her eyes. The rare glimpse of hope at a new future had left her longing for things that could never be.

How did one pray for an answer, when the question remained elusive? "Are there any Bible verses on hope?"

He chewed thoughtfully. "I don't know. I seem to recall something about 'in His word do I hope.'"

"'In His word do I hope,'" she repeated. "Amen."

Hope was a dangerous thing. A luxury she couldn't afford.

Jo winked at Jack. "You're a real charmer, aren't you?"

He cradled his forehead, warding off the stinging pain that pierced his brain each time Jo spoke. Her constant jabs wore on him. "I thought you broke your ribs, not your lips. Why am I sitting here reading to you, when reading is probably the only thing you *can* do?"

"Because Mrs. Cole told you to keep me company." She smirked. "Now, let's see, was that before or after you brought up her late husband and her life in the orphanage?"

"If you minded your own business as well as you mind mine, you wouldn't have two cracked ribs and a sprained ankle."

"You're getting sloppy with your insults."

Jack blew out a frustrated breath. He was still kicking himself for his awkward handling of the situation earlier. Jo's probing questions delved too deeply into his wounded dignity. "*Pride and Prejudice* is an odd name for a book."

"Mrs. Cole said her mother brought it over from England. It's one of her favorites."

"I don't see why. Nothing happens." Unless you counted people doing an awful lot of talking about their feelings, and not doing a whole lot of action concerning those feelings.

"It's very romantic."

Jack turned over the book to check the back. "Am I missing something?"

So far, the main character had insulted the heroine, and the heroine had insulted him right back. Where on earth was the romance in that?

"It's about a cranky fellow who can't seem to get along with anyone." A sly grin coasted across Jo's face. "Should be right up your alley, Ranger."

The barb struck home with deadly accuracy. "You sure you wouldn't rather take a nap?"

"I've been sleeping all day." She plucked restlessly at the quilted comforter, clutching her side as the movement jostled her sore ribs. "Why did you come back?"

"It was on my way home." He flipped open the book to a random page. "Now, where were we? I'm sure Mr. Darcy is about to do something romantic like tossing Miss Bennett into the river."

"Where do you live, Ranger? This place isn't on the way to anywhere."

His temper flared. Trust Jo not to let a sleeping dog lie. It was none of her business why he'd decided to check on the widow. "Do you want to flap your lips, or do you want me to read?"

"You're crankier than usual." She appeared almost gleeful in her assessment. "Guess you didn't catch that outlaw."

"No." He snapped shut the book. "I didn't."

Rachel stirred restlessly at the commotion. Jack lifted her from the cozy nest of blankets, and tucked the infant into the crook of his arm. She cooed. His chest expanded with pride. No matter how upset the baby was, she always calmed in his arms.

"That day in the barn," Jo continued. "You told me you were chasing a bank robber, right?"

"Yep."

"I been thinking about what you said, but I still can't figure out why you ended up here. How did you stumble onto this homestead? This place ain't on the way to nowhere."

Jack hesitated, but talking about his case was a whole lot better than reading Elizabeth's "romantic" book. "The man I was chasing—"

"Bud Shaw?"

"Yeah, that's him. He disappeared along the train route, but his horse didn't. People remembered the mustang. That animal caused a lot of trouble along the way. When I arrived in Cimarron Springs, the sheriff said a fellow living out here had a feisty bay mustang. The whole thing seemed logical. Made sense that the fellow got off the train at Cimarron Springs and headed home."

"Didn't the sheriff tell you that mustang belonged to Will Cole, not that fellow you were looking for, Bud Shaw?"

"Could have been a lot of explanations for that. Maybe Bud Shaw had a partner we didn't know about. Maybe he was using another name to throw us off the trail. Criminals aren't exactly known for making things easy."

Jo snorted. "Still, if you thought a lightweight like Will Cole was a bank robber, I'd hate to see what kind of other fellows you've chased in your career."

Jack glanced furtively over his shoulder. "Keep your voice down. Mrs. Cole has dealt with enough painful reminders today."

"Don't worry. She's off to feed the animals while you're in a nice warm house loafing around and playing nursemaid, remember?"

This time the barb bounced off his thick hide. Jo was hiding her pain with her sharp words. Jack smoothed the blanket over the infant, using the distraction to sneak a look at Jo's exhausted face. Her two braids hung listlessly over her shoulders. Lines of fatigue showed at the corners her mouth. Her green eyes stood out against her ashen face. She was putting on a good show, but he could tell she was hurting. What was wrong with him, snapping at an injured girl?

"I'm telling you, Ranger," she continued. "Mr. Cole could hardly pluck a chicken let alone rob a bank. He reminded me of this snake-oil salesman that came to town last spring. He talked up a real storm, but once you got past all the hot air blowing through his lips, there was nothing to him."

"Really?" The question slipped out.

"Yeah. Maybe that snake-oil man is your bank robber. Maybe his secret ingredient is stolen money. That's about as good of a theory as Will Cole."

She chuckled at her own joke while Jack remained thoughtful. He'd heard enough gossip about the widow's late husband to last him a lifetime. He was growing heartily sick of how the conversation kept circling back around to the man. Will Cole might as well be standing in the room, not six feet under. "It's not appropriate to talk about Mr. Cole."

"I'd say it's more appropriate than kicking down a dead man's door, isn't it?"

The shooting pain in his temple intensified. "We've gone over this already. I was looking for Bud Shaw." He braced his free hand on the seat of his chair, the book pressing painfully into his palm. "If you don't want me to read to you, maybe I can pull out one of Mrs. Cole's samplers and you can stitch us a pretty flower hanky."

"I'd rather poke my eye with a stick."

"That's what I thought."

Pleasant sounds from the kitchen indicated Elizabeth's return. She stepped into the room, her eyes sparkling with health.

Rushing to his side, she reached out to run her knuckle along Rachel's cheek. "Good morning, beautiful."

His breath snagged in his throat. He caught a tantalizing hint of sweetened vanilla and lavender. Tendrils of golden hair framed Elizabeth's face, curling along her cheek. Her hair wasn't simply blond, as it appeared at first, but a curious mixture of aged gold, flaxen and an alluring hint of bronze.

His blood pounded. He longed to reach out and loop one of those charming ringlets around his finger, just to see if it felt as soft as it looked.

Elizabeth's gaze swung between him and Jo as she flashed a hopeful grin. "Everything okay in here? Are you two getting along?"

"Couldn't be better."

"Like beans and ham."

"Excellent." Elizabeth brought her hands together with

a clap. "It's so nice to see the two of you mending fences so well."

She smiled so wide he caught a rare glimpse of the place where her eyeteeth overlapped her front teeth ever so slightly. He found the modest imperfection delightful, especially since it was only visible when she smiled the widest.

She turned her radiant gaze on him. "Can you hold Rachel for a few more minutes? I'd like to start supper."

Swallowing hard, he nodded.

Heaven help him. She had him tongue-tied and tangled in knots. Returning to the homestead was a mistake, a mistake he'd soon remedy. The longer he remained, the more his emotions became entangled with the plight of this ragtag bunch. Tonight he'd complete the task he'd come here for in the first place. He'd show Elizabeth his newspaper clippings, and see if she recognized any of the wanted posters.

"Mrs. Cole?"

She raised an eyebrow.

His mind went blank. What was he supposed to say? *By the way, did your husband ever gamble with outlaws? Did he happen to mention their names?*

"Nothing. Never mind."

She shrugged and turned away.

Jack grunted. His entire plan was ridiculous. This whole delay had been an excuse to see Elizabeth again. And what was wrong with that? There was no harm in ensuring her health. After aiming a gun at the poor woman, and practically accusing her of lying, it was the least he could do.

Jo caught his attention, a mischievous glint in her green eyes. After Elizabeth rounded the corner, safely out of view, the little bugger had the audacity to stick out her tongue at him.

Jack rolled his eyes and prayed for a break in the weather. The sooner he found the real Bud Shaw, the better. Staying here was stirring up more problems than he could solve. Even as he itched to resume his journey, he couldn't shake the feeling that he'd been drawn here for a purpose.

Jack rubbed his chin while pots and pans clanged in the kitchen. The widow was too serious by far. She had a perpetual frown of worry between her eyes, and saved her smiles like precious coins. She needed to relax and let a little fun into her day. Maybe that's why the Lord had brought him here, to bring some laughter into her life.

But his time was running short. How did he distract from her rigid schedule, and self-imposed rules long enough to discover the joy still left in the world? He glanced out the window. A grin spread across his face. Staring at the snow gave him an idea.

Chapter Eight

"Gracious, what's that man doing?" Elizabeth stretched over the bed and scratched a hole in the frost-covered window.

"I don't know," Jo replied. "He pulled off the oilcloth earlier. He's mighty busy doing something, but I can't figure out what."

Elizabeth stood, knotted her muffler tighter around her throat, then tucked the fringed ends beneath the collar of her woolen coat. "Just like a man to fuss around when there's work to be done."

She knelt and adjusted Rachel's blanket. The infant's toothless grin filled her heart with wonder. "Did you get more precious last night? Did you? You sweet little thing."

Jo made a gagging sound in her throat.

Elizabeth rolled her eyes. "You'll feel differently when you have your own babies."

"Never. I'm not having any brats. Not after what you went through."

"It's all worth it."

"I don't plan on finding out."

Elizabeth ducked her head to hide her knowing grin.

"I'm off to gather eggs for supper. If Rachel gets fussy, I'll be back shortly."

"We'll be fine. Now stop running yourself ragged."

"Don't be silly." Elizabeth pressed the back of her hand to Jo's forehead, relieved to find the skin cool and dry. The more days that passed without a fever, the more Elizabeth's relief grew. Jo was making a blessedly quick recovery. "Mr. Elder was able to get a message to your family. You'll be happy to know they're all praying for your health."

Elizabeth managed to keep her irritation hidden. What were the McCoys to think of a Texas Ranger hanging about? Mr. Elder hadn't shared how he'd explained his presence to the neighboring family. "Your brothers miss you. Once the weather warms a bit, I'm sure they'll be tracking over here to see you."

Jo snorted. "Not like I'm going anyplace."

"You'll be up and about in no time. Jack—Mr. Elder said your ankle isn't broken. Just a sprain and some cracked ribs."

Jo rubbed her leg and groaned. "This is one winter I'll never forget."

"You and I both."

Elizabeth chuckled dryly. With a last lingering glance at Jo and the baby, she stole from room.

Safely out of view, she scowled. Mr. Elder had taken word to the McCoys without even a by-your-leave to Elizabeth. She'd discovered him missing when she'd wandered into the barn half asleep, groggily attending her chores, only to discover his jet-black horse missing. After taking several deep, shuddering breaths, she'd set about her chores, determined to push him out of her thoughts.

Jack had returned hours later, casually relating his trip to the McCoys. As if rambling in and out of their lives had no consequences. Elizabeth expressed her frustration under her breath. At least Will had taken the time to say goodbye when he'd left.

She glanced out the window, annoyed to find the bunkhouse chimney billowing smoke. Jack had taken charge of a whole lot of things in the past forty-eight hours. After declaring the barn unfit for sleeping, he'd moved his belongings into the bunkhouse, setting up shop like he planned to stay all winter.

Elizabeth tugged on her woolen mittens. She vowed to speak with him that evening. If he could travel to the McCoys, he could travel to town. There was no need for him to stay any longer. A strange man shacked up in the bunkhouse was bound to draw attention.

Reaching for the doorknob, she considered the other reason he had to leave. She couldn't afford to let anyone know how accustomed she'd grown to his comforting presence—a reassurance that was as dangerous as it was foolish. The more she grew to depend on him, the more difficult her life would be when he was gone.

With a resolute huff, she pushed open the rear door, relieved to find the wind had calmed. The orange-ball sun had made a rare appearance through the clouds, turning the rolling prairie into a blinding, sparkling wonderland.

She had just reached the bottom step, when something wet and cold pelted her from the side.

"Just the person I wanted to see," Jack called from her left.

She turned. He stood there smiling, as though he was impervious to the frosty winter air.

Elizabeth dusted the white from her shoulder. "Did you just throw a snowball at me?"

"I need your help."

She searched his face for any sign of guilt. Not even a

suspicious twinkle showed in his hazel eyes. She slanted a glance upward. Icicles hung like frosting from the eves above her head, turning the house into a gingerbread confection.

Perhaps a bit of snow had melted from the roof. "Why do you need my help? I'm fetching the eggs."

"Already done."

He jerked his head. A wire basket full of eggs rested in the snow near the corner of the house.

She ground her teeth together. She didn't like how he was taking over all the chores. He was disturbing her schedule once again.

"Stop fussing over your routine." He grinned. "Follow me."

The accusation stung. "I do not fuss. I have a certain way I like things done. A certain order to my chores that maximizes efficiency."

"You're definitely fussing now. Why don't you help me finish the snowman?"

Crossing her arms over her chest, she tapped her foot on the packed snow. "A what?"

"Haven't you ever built a snowman?"

Elizabeth gaped at the fool man. *No one built snowmen, did they?* While she pondered the question, Jack disappeared around the corner.

With a weary sigh, Elizabeth trudged in his wake. Since the eggs had been gathered, she *did* have a few extra minutes this morning. Perhaps if she indulged him for a moment, he'd leave her alone to finish her chores.

Perhaps she'd simply watch his antics. She hadn't managed more than a few hours of sleep at a stretch in months. For weeks she'd existed in a blurry fugue. This morning, in an exhausted haze, she'd stumbled right into the doorjamb. Frolicking around in the snow was not on her to-do list.

As she rounded the corner, another snowball hit her on the opposite shoulder. "What are you doing?" she sputtered.

"It's a snowball fight. You're supposed to hit me back."

"I will not." She knew full well how these games went. He'd use the opportunity to show off his superior strength and skill, humiliating her in the process. "Have you been drinking your *medicinal* whiskey?"

He shrugged. "I'm having fun."

Since when did he have fun? He was always frowning and serious. "Are you ill?"

He stared at her as if *she* were the one acting like a fool.

"Some of us have chores." Elizabeth glared at him, one hand shielding her eyes from sunlight sparking off the shimmering, white snow. "Enjoy your fun. I'm going back in the house."

She pivoted on her heel. A soft explosion shattered over the back of her head. Chilly blobs trickled down her neck. "You—why—you."

Fuming, she bent to gather a handful of snow. If he wanted a fight, she'd give him one. She packed the frozen material together, cocked back her arm and let the ball fly. White exploded over his face.

"You have good aim," he said with an ice-covered grin.

"And you called *me* a lunatic?" Gracious, the man didn't even have the good sense to be annoyed. The time for fun and games was over. "I don't have the energy for this. You and I need to have a conversation, Mr. Elder."

His jubilant expression fell. "So it's like that, is it?"

"Yes." She didn't care that her words had wiped the

joy from his face. She didn't care at all. She didn't even know what he was insinuating with his cryptic declaration and hangdog expression. "It's like what?"

"Never mind." He brushed the snow from his hands. "Let's have this talk."

She stole a furtive glance at the window. No doubt Jo was watching them with rapt attention. "Not in the house. I don't want Jo to overhear."

He quirked an eyebrow. "The bunkhouse, then?"

Warmth crept into her cheeks. His temporary quarters were closest to where they stood, but she shied away from his offer. "It's not proper. How about the barn?"

She waved in the opposite direction.

"What's more proper about the barn?"

A lump of snow had caught between her boot and her stocking. The ice was starting to melt, sending a stinging cold trail down her ankle. She shifted her feet. "There's more activity in the barn."

"I guess I see your point." He wiped the snow from his face with a bandanna he'd unfurled from his pocket. "But the pig isn't going to be much of a chaperone."

"Fine." She gritted her teeth. "We shall conduct our conversation in the bunkhouse." Straightening her collar, she assumed her most disapproving frown. "But only because I left my rosetta iron in the cupboard last summer."

"Your English is showing, Miss Prim and Proper," he teased.

"Well." The nerve of the man! One minute he was pelting her with the snowballs, and the next minute he was mocking her heritage. "The English are very fine people. I take that as a compliment."

He winked at her. "As intended."

"Oh," Elizabeth huffed. She really didn't have time for this foolishness. Tossing him off her property was going to be so much easier since he had reverted to this annoying behavior.

She marched to the bunkhouse and yanked open the door with too much force, then leaped out of the way as the heavy wood ricocheted, nearly taking off the end of her nose in the process.

Good heavens, this wouldn't do at all. She was accustomed to being in control. He had her huffing and grinding her teeth like a fishwife. Pausing for a long beat, she took a deep, fortifying breath. While her pulse slowed, she studied his temporary quarters, struck by how clean and tidy the space appeared.

The bunkhouse had replaced the original sod homestead years before Elizabeth and Will had arrived. The long narrow room had five empty cots lined up along either side of the center corridor. A sturdy pine box capped the end of each bed for the worker's storage. The previous owner had been a wealthy adventurer from back East with grand schemes for improving the land. His dreams had fizzled beneath the relentless prairie winds and his wife's discontent.

She rarely used the space except for cooking occasionally in the summer months to keep the heat out of the main house. An enormous cast-iron stove used for heat as well as cooking dominated the center of the room. Unbidden, images of the orphanage came rushing back. A familiar wash of loneliness clouded her vision. She recalled staring at the ceiling, night after night, praying for the loneliness to end.

She wanted to run to Rachel and cradle her baby, never letting go. What a tragic choice her mother had had to make, surrendering the care of her only child. Elizabeth curled her hands into fists. That would never happen to her. She'd fight a grizzly with her bare hands to keep her baby.

A gentle hand touched her sleeve. "Are you all right?"

"Of course."

She shook off the gloomy feeling along with the last of the melting snowflakes. Lingering in the past was a dull and lonely business.

Clearing her throat, Elizabeth squared her shoulders. "You're going to have to leave. It isn't proper for you to be here. The McCoys know you're back. They're a nice family, but I don't want word of a single...of a man...of *you* reaching Cimarron Springs."

Jack leaned one shoulder against a sturdy support pillar and crossed his arms. "Mrs. McCoy didn't strike me as the kind of woman to gossip."

"Be that as it may, gossip has a way of spreading like wildfire during a draught."

Chilled from her trip outside, she sidled down the narrow center aisle toward the cast-iron stove. She stole a discreet glance at Jack's belongings. He'd taken the bunk nearest the warming fire. His saddle bags and other paraphernalia were neatly laid out on a small side table. Each item had been carefully arranged—razor, mirror, pencil and paper. How different from what Will had carried, and yet how similar. They were both drifters, men who preferred to live their lives unencumbered.

Nothing encumbered a man more than a wife and child.

She'd already made one mistake concerning a man. She couldn't afford another. She wouldn't let the Ranger's laughing hazel eyes lure her into a false sense of security.

"Listen, Mrs. Cole," he spoke. "I'd like to leave. I have work to do. But I can't abandon you to care for Jo and Rachel all alone. It just isn't right."

"We managed quite well on our own."

"Yeah. That's why I found you half frozen in a blizzard." He raked his hand through his hair. "You're a greenhorn with no idea what you're up against. You haven't an inkling what you're risking."

He crossed the length of the room, crowding her until they stood inches apart.

A shiver of panic snaked down her spine. She refused to back away, even when she had to tip back her head to meet the raw fury glittering in his steady gaze. "What happens to us is none of your concern."

"You don't have enough wood cut to make it through the rest of the month, let alone the rest of winter. What are you going to do then?"

His accusation straightened her spine. She was all the more determined to prove him wrong. "I'll manage. I always do."

"Yes, but it's not just you anymore, is it?" His freshly shaven face flushed with anger. "You have your daughter to think of now."

She felt heat creep up her cheeks. "Are you insinuating something?"

"No, I'm telling you. Move to town. Be near people. Then I'll leave. If you don't care enough to save yourself, at least have the decency to think of your child. She doesn't have a choice. You do."

He could question her skills all he wanted, but he'd better steer clear of her mothering. "How dare you question my devotion. I can protect my daughter. I can protect my home. This is where I belong."

"Prove your devotion. Sell the buildings. Move to town."

She swallowed around the lump in her throat. If only things were that easy. She didn't want Rachel to live under the townspeople's scorn, and she didn't know where else to go. Right then, the homestead was the safest place for them.

"It's not that simple."

"'Course it is."

"This is none of your business."

Anger swelled in her chest. He was a threat. A threat to her home, a threat to her reputation, and a threat to her peace of mind. "What does a drifter know?"

Hurt flicked in eyes, passing so quickly she might have imagined the emotion if not for the agitated tic in his cheek. "I'm not a drifter, I'm a lawman. I have a purpose."

Suddenly, she wanted to hurt him as much as he'd hurt her. "Really. Then where is your home? What is your purpose now—besides threatening me?"

"*Threatening* you? I saved your hide. Twice." His boots scraped the floor as he pivoted away. "And this isn't about me. This is about you living on a homestead without even a rifle."

"I have the shotgun and Will's revolver, remember?"

"You've fired the shotgun twice. And you've never fired the revolver. How are you going to react in an emergency? That's not your only handicap, and you know it. You've limped through half the winter, but once spring comes, you'll never be able to keep up. How are you going to climb on the roof and clear the chimney? How are you going to cut hay, chop wood and still care for Rachel? You can't handle all the work on your own."

Elizabeth narrowed her eyes. She was well and truly tired of being told what she could and couldn't do. She'd done a fine job of caring for the homestead while Will was away, but he'd never once complimented her abilities. Instead, he'd search until he found something out of place, a frivolous chore she'd failed to accomplish, then he'd pounced. She didn't need a man to criticize her efforts. Jack wasn't so perfect, either.

"It's not safe," he continued. "You don't have any idea what I've seen. You have no understanding of the dangers facing a woman." He stabbed his hand through his hair again, appearing to reconsider his tact. "And it's not practical. If you want me to leave, you'll have to prove you're capable."

He splayed his hands, pained frustration glittering in his eyes. "Don't you miss the company of other people?"

"That's none of your business," she spoke, her voice pinched. "I don't have to prove anything to you."

She'd never confess her insecurities, but his words eroded all her rationalizations. Her head ached at the thought of the insurmountable tasks awaiting her in the spring. She needed more time to think, to plan.

Rubbing her temples, she blew out a long breath. Those problems were months away. She'd figure something out, she always did. "Why do you care? You'll be gone. Back to Texas."

"I'm saving somebody else from the trouble of cleaning up your mess."

"I've never been a burden to anyone."

She'd love nothing more than to report him to the law for trespassing, but involving the sheriff risked drawing attention to herself.

"Say something," he demanded. "Defend yourself. Tell me how you're going to cut enough wood to keep the house warm for the next three months. Tell me what you're going to do if there's an Indian uprising."

"God will take care of us. 'Consider the ravens. For they neither sow nor reap. Which neither have storehouse nor barn. And God feeds them. How much better are we than the fowls?'"

"You're a naive fool who never should have left New York. This isn't a page from a penny tale, this is the real thing. Do you want to know what it's like out here? Really like? I once saw a man hanged for shooting his whole family. You want to know why he murdered them?"

His implacable expression unnerved her. "You're just trying to frighten me with these petty parlor tricks."

"He shot them because he couldn't stand to watch his family starve. Is that what you want? Do you want to watch Rachel starve? To see your own flesh and blood waste away in misery before your eyes?"

Elizabeth pressed her hands to her ears. "Be quiet. You don't think people starve to death in the city? They die in the gutter while people step over their bodies like so much garbage. No place is safe. You don't frighten me."

How dare he intimidate her. This was a home. Land. A roof over her head and the prairie stretching out to the horizon. If she lost this house, she had nothing. Here on the homestead she had shelter, a sustainable source of food and the possibility of a legacy for her daughter. She had a future.

He paced the narrow aisle. "I'm not going to quit until I talk some sense into you. If you keep on the way you're going, you'll end up a pile of stones on the prairie. Is that what you want for Rachel? No one will even remember your names."

She froze, numbed by the thought of the anonymous piles of stones littering the prairie. "This is pointless."

Drained by the frustrating conversation, not to mention more exhausted than she'd ever been in her whole life, Elizabeth spun on her heel for her dramatic exit.

Instead, she stubbed her toe. "Ouch."

With tears of frustration pricking behind her eyes, she rubbed her foot. "What else can go wrong today?"

Jack lifted the heavy metal box she'd collided with onto the bunk. "Since you're not going to take my advice, it looks like I'll be staying a few more days. At least until Jo is up and about."

Her annoyance suddenly felt like relief. That was absurd. Of course she was mad. She was furious.

"Where on earth did the box come from?" she asked to cover her confusion.

Certainly he hadn't dragged the heavy object around on the back of his horse.

He wrestled the box into position. "I found this in the bottom of one of the lockers. You might as well take it back to the main house."

Startled by the abrupt change in conversation, she touched the lid. "I don't recognize this."

"It's yours now. I found it on your property."

The metal shape was vaguely familiar. Had the box belonged to Will? She had a hazy recollection of a furtive trip to the bunkhouse last spring.

Jack stared at her expectantly. Her hands grew cold. Dare she open the box in the Ranger's presence? Certainly Will hadn't left behind anything of value. He'd cleared the house of valuables before he left.

She pinched off her mittens. If she didn't reveal the contents, Jack would only be more suspicious. She couldn't afford him asking any more questions, or worse yet, reporting back to the sheriff.

As she vacillated, Jack's expression stilled and grew serious. She sensed the return of the Texas Ranger in the speculative gleam of his eyes.

Her resolve crystallized. There was no reason to assume the box held anything worth worrying about. If Will had left anything valuable, he'd have left it in his trunk in the house.

She licked her lips, tentatively stretching out one hand. Flipping open the lid, she sucked in a breath. Jack loomed behind her. She glanced over the contents. Several crumpled bills, four gold watches, a money clip and a revolver nestled in the box. She poked around with one finger, brushing the bills aside to reveal two thin gold rings.

Inordinately relieved to find the box filled with harmless objects, Elizabeth sighed. "This must have belonged to the previous owners."

"These items don't belong to you?"

She shook her head. "I told you. They must belong to the previous owner. A man from Pennsylvania lived here for years. His wife never could adjust to the prairie, so they moved back East. They must have left these things behind."

"Why didn't someone discover the box sooner?"

"Will kept a few hired hands when we first moved, but they took off."

Much to her relief, they hadn't returned. She'd never been partial to the company Will kept, and she definitely didn't like being alone with them when Will traveled.

Jack frowned. "How many watches does one man own? It doesn't seem right."

From the corner of her eye, she studied the objects. Fear pooled in her stomach. Another explanation dawned on her, one that she didn't want to share. "I don't suppose we'll ever know for sure."

The more she thought about it, the more certain she become of the objects' origins. If Will had won the personal items on one of his many gambling binges, he wouldn't have told her. He'd known she didn't approve of his card playing. But like everything else in their brief marriage, her opinion hadn't mattered. He'd done as he pleased, no matter how much his actions hurt her.

Another worry pressed on her. She recalled how the sheriff had threatened to seize her land if he found out the property was purchased with illegal money. Gambling wasn't illegal, but cheating was—and most people in town were suspicious of Will's propensity for winning.

Before Will's death she'd gone to the mercantile and the clerk had refused to serve her. The man was angry because Will had won his best horse in a card game. Fearful of another tense encounter, she'd curbed her trips to town.

Jack lifted a watch. "If they don't belong to you, I'll turn them over to the sheriff. This looks mighty expensive. Someone is missing this fancy piece."

Elizabeth thrust out her hands. "No!"

This was proof, leverage to use against her. If she lost her home, the land, she lost everything.

Guilt and fury ground together in her stomach. She couldn't afford to have the Texas Ranger around any longer. He had to leave. Her decision made, she tugged on her mittens. She'd handle this on her own. She didn't care how much Jack's eyes reminded her of the flaxen and emerald grasses sweeping across the plains in spring.

She pointed a finger at him, the irritated gesture lost in her enveloping mittens. "I expect you to be gone in one hour."

"Why are you mad at *me?*" he asked, his tone placating. "Can't you see I'm trying to help you?"

"I don't need your help."

"You're too stubborn for your own good, Elizabeth Cole."

"Maybe I am, but it's my decision. And I'm asking you to leave."

"I have a job to do, and no one is going to stand in my way. Not even you."

"Your job has nothing to do with us. Coming here was an accident. A mistake."

"I'm not so sure anymore."

Fear swept over her like a chill wind. "All the more reason you should go."

She slammed the door behind her.

Jack rested his fisted hand on the bedrail while he inhaled the lingering scent of lavender and vanilla. Last night, he'd asked himself the same questions Elizabeth had demanded of him. What *was* his purpose? Were his suspicions founded in logic, or based on emotion? Why was he still here when the widow's problems were none of his concern? More than once he'd packed his bags, preparing to leave, only to find his footsteps dragging.

The truth, he'd finally admitted to himself, was that he didn't know why he was still here. He thought he'd conditioned himself to ignore petty human emotions, but all his conditioning had deserted him. The widow's needs had become his own. Her fears had become his fears. Her fate had become his responsibility. He was torn between honor and affection.

He finally understood his purpose.

When a bank was robbed, the outlaws often took more than money. They stole from the patrons, as well. Valuables such as watches, rings and pocket change. Exactly the sort of items floating around in that box. He opened the lid and lifted out the four watches. The hairs on the back of his neck stood on end.

He'd tracked the outlaw to Cimarron Springs, and the trail had grown cold at the widow's front door. He'd tracked a bay mustang and a man with cold eyes and a charming smile from Colorado to Kansas. From one livery to another he'd relentlessly pursued his prey. His instincts had led him here for a reason, and Elizabeth had tripped right over that reason.

Jack flung open the heavy stove door and tossed another log onto the dwindling fire. The widow feared the sheriff, and Jack was starting to wonder why.

Like other men smelled trouble, Jack recognized the distinct odor of fear. He didn't think the widow knew the origin of the items, but she knew enough to be frightened.

Her late husband must have been involved with the outlaws. The question remained, how much did she know? Elizabeth didn't strike him as the kind of woman to condone that sort of activity. Then again, people did all sorts of things he'd never thought possible. Could he really trust her?

Had his emotions clouded his judgment? There was no such thing as being a little bit guilty. She was a party to a crime or she wasn't. Simple as that. Either way, she was hiding something. He hadn't looked any deeper, because he hadn't wanted to know the truth.

Unbearably weary, he pinched the bridge of his nose. If he ceased pursuing justice, if he let an innocent man hang, he lost everything that made him a man, everything he believed about himself.

He'd have to pressure her until he learned the truth. No matter what the personal cost, until he knew where the widow placed her loyalties, he had to treat her as a suspect.

Jack rubbed at his chest. Why did he feel as though someone was tearing out his heart?

Chapter Nine

Elizabeth eyed the loaded revolver on the worktable. Short of shooting the Ranger, she didn't know how else to get rid of the man. Tempted though she was, she'd never resort to violence. Too bad her options were appallingly limited. Involving the sheriff would only cause more problems, and asking Mr. McCoy for help was out of the question. What would she tell them, anyway, "There was a Texas Ranger on my property. He was cutting wood and taking care of chores, so I shot him?"

Elizabeth snorted.

Since their argument that morning, he'd holed up in the bunkhouse. Perhaps he'd simply leave on his own. She knew his food supply must be getting low. Better for her if he scampered off to town because he was starving. Better than having to admit that her husband was a card cheat. Better than risking her ownership of the homestead by revealing the truth. Jack was nothing if not a lawman, and he'd have to do the right thing. Even if the right thing left Elizabeth homeless and penniless. She'd expect him to do no less.

As if conjured from her thoughts, Jack appeared on the horizon, his rifle slung over one shoulder, an enormous turkey dangling behind him from a leather strap. *So much for starving him out.* He cut through the dry brush edging the creek bed with long strides, his broad shoulders grazing the barren tree limbs. A dark hat shadowed his eyes.

Her heart did a little flip, but she quickly squashed the emotion. Angry with her weakness, Elizabeth stomped to the barn, setting about her chores with angry vigor. She didn't even bother to look up from the grain bin when the heavy panel door creaked open. He had to leave, didn't he? He had a case to solve.

"Thought you'd like fresh meat for supper," Jack called.

She peered at his catch from the corner of her eye. Her mouth watered.

"I'll dress this," he declared, tossing the plump bird onto a worktable beside the sandstone sharpening wheel.

Ignoring his peace offering, she scooped a dipper of feed and dumped the contents into the burlap sack slung over the milk cow's stall. Unable to resist, she canted him another sideways glance. Jack flicked the pad of his thumb over a shiny silver knife, testing the edge.

His hands snagged her attention. They were sturdy and strong with a dusting of dark hair over the knuckles. Those hands could break a man's neck, yet she'd never seen them raised in anger. He held Rachel with an aching tenderness belying his superior size. She recalled clinging to his hand during Rachel's birth, the feel of his calloused palms, how his strength had been both alarming and comforting. She marveled at the combination of size and grace.

The milk cow bumped against the stall, startling Elizabeth from her reverie.

He was up to something. She'd starve before she accepted Jack's offering of dinner. "There you go, Betsy."

The cow snuffled in response.

Elizabeth noted the empty pan of milk she'd set out for the feral cat that had taken up residence in the barn. She splashed a few drops from the pail into the dish. The cat had proved useful in keeping rodents out of the grain bin. While the mangy thing was mean, ornery and ugly, the cat served a useful purpose and Elizabeth was content to keep her homely little mouser happy.

Setting down the pail, she wrinkled her nose against the pungent scent of manure. Time to clean out Betsy's stall. That chore meant climbing into the hayloft for bedding. While Elizabeth wasn't exactly afraid of heights, climbing the rickety ladder was not her favorite activity. Instead, she puttered around the barn, putting off the task as long as she could.

A half hour passed while she stalled, avoiding Jack as he efficiently divested the turkey of feathers. At last, chiding herself for being a frightened ninny, she grasped the rails and carefully set her booted foot on the first rung. The ladder creaked and groaned with her careful ascent. Hoisting herself over the ledge, she stood, then brushed her hands together with a relieved sigh. She'd survived the climb one more time.

Dust motes floated in the beams of light shafting through the loft door. The faulty latch never stayed shut. One strong wind was enough to blow the door open a crack. Elizabeth glanced over the ledge, catching sight of the top of Jack's head. She had a fair idea how he'd escaped the barn that first night. No wonder he'd been so grumpy. Even if he'd dangled his whole body out the loft door, he still had a good five foot plunge onto the snow below. The fall must have bruised his dignity *and* his hide.

Served him right for kicking down my door.

She crept forward, only to be yanked to a halt. She glanced down. Her hem had caught on a splinter. Tugging her skirts free, she continued on her way, her arms outstretched for balance as she tiptoed to the open door. Maintaining a safe distance from the ledge, she stretched one hand and heaved the door shut.

Blood pumping, she scurried away from the edge, then faced the dwindling stacks of hay bales. How different the space appeared from last spring when Will had hoisted the bales from Mr. McCoy's sturdy wagon and stacked them to the ceiling. Winter was only half finished, and she'd used her stores more rapidly than she had anticipated.

Another problem she'd have to deal with soon.

Discouraged by the thought, she yanked a heavy rectangle off the stack, then kicked the tightly bound straw bale over the side to the barn floor. Betsy snuffled at the disturbance.

"Oh, be quiet, you grumpy old thing," Elizabeth called.

Turning, she grasped the ladder rails and stretched her left foot to the first rung. Adjusting her hold, she reached for the second rung and pressed the ball of her right foot onto the slat. A crack sounded. Her boot broke through the splintered wood. She lost her balance, flailing her leg to find a solid purchase. The jerky movement sent her left foot skidding off its rung. Clutching the rails, she arched backward, her feet dangling.

"Help!"

"Don't let go!" A deep voice called from behind her.

"I hadn't planned on it," she bit out through gritted teeth.

Boots scuffled, indicating Jack's hasty dash to assist her. Arms burning, she strained to hold herself aloft. A bead of sweat trickled down her cheek.

She felt the ladder strain, a telling creak sounded near her ear. She gasped in horror as one of the nails separated from its anchor. A hand snaked around her calf. The nail slid out another half inch.

"Don't come up!" she shouted. "The ladder won't hold us both."

She glanced down, quickly squeezing her eyes shut. Ten feet remained between her and the hard-packed dirt below. She'd surely break her leg if she let go now. "Pull that bail beneath me. I'll jump down."

"It's too far. You'll break your leg."

"Maybe I'll break my left leg," she gasped. "Together Jo and I will be one whole person."

Scrambling, she hoisted her leg to reach the first rung, but her booted heel caught in her petticoats. Jack clambered up behind her. The ladder sagged. Desperate to counter his weight, she tore through the cotton fabric to release her heel and leaned forward, pressing her forehead against the dry wood. "Get down."

A hand snaked around her waist. "I've got you."

"But who's got you?"

He chuckled, the vibration sending the nail sliding further from its mooring. "You can let go."

She gently shook her head so as not to agitate the overburdened ladder. Her fingers strained. "I don't know how much longer I can hang on."

"Let go."

She hadn't heard him use his brisk tone of voice since that first night so many weeks ago.

Fear surged through her veins, giving her strength. Even if she had wanted to release her grip, he was still too far below her. When she dropped down, the loss of balance would send them both plunging to the ground. "I can't let go."

The arm around her waist tightened. "You're going to have to trust me."

"No!"

He heaved back, yanking her with him. Her fingers wrenched from their hold. Her mittens snagged on the rough wood and slipped from her stiff hands. With a shriek she fell, pitching backward to the packed dirt below. Jack's feet hit the ground first. The force of their fall sent him stumbling backward.

Together they tumbled to the floor. Jack cushioned her landing, holding her tight against his chest. A cloud of dust billowed around them.

Too stunned to move, she stared at the timbered ceiling. His solid body protected her from the chill ground, warming her back. Adrenaline still rushing through her veins, she flipped over. A chicken flapped in the dust just behind Jack's head.

Realizing they were still intimately entangled on the floor, Elizabeth scrambled to one side. She ignored Jack's muffled grunt of pain when her knee dug into his thigh.

"Why did you do that?" she demanded. "We could have both been killed."

With a casual grin, he pillowed his hands beneath his head. "Mighty sore maybe, but not killed."

"Oooh, you daft man."

He quirked an eyebrow. "Daft?"

"Yes, daft," she replied, the indignation leaching from her voice.

She cut a glance at the broken ladder. The *daft* man was correct. The distance had seemed much more dramatic when she was dangling from the ledge. She hung

her head in her hands, willing her hammering heart to
slow. The tension gradually drained from her body, replaced by a curious lethargy. When her breath ceased
coming in sharp gasped, she chanced a peek at Jack.
His gaze rested on her face, somber and concerned. She
knew she should be angry, but his eyes captivated her.
The way the color grew darker nearer the rims.

She pressed her palms against his chest to leverage
herself upright, then paused. His heartbeat thumped solid
and sure, but rapid all the same, against her outstretched
fingers. He wasn't nearly as unaffected by their contact
as he feigned.

He kept the half grin on his face, his hands firmly
locked behind his head, but she sensed his coiled tension, a subtle shift in his attitude. Tilting her head, she
considered his casual pose.

She sensed if she pulled away, he wouldn't stop her,
but she had no desire to test her theory. There was something alluring about the way he never rushed a moment.
Surrendering to the urge, she ran her thumb over the
rough surface of his stubble-covered cheeks, letting her
finger linger on the thin white scar barely visible along
the length of his jaw. The slight disfigurement gave her
a glimpse into his checkered past.

She savored the rare quiet moment. Even though he
threatened to stay, eventually his case would force him to
leave. She couldn't forget he'd rescued her. Three times.
His hazel eyes evoked a warm longing. As if her soul had
been searching for refuge, and Jack held the map. A rare
impulse took hold of her. She wanted to know everything
about him. His home, his past, his future.

Had he ever been in love before? Had he ever wanted
to give up his job and settle down?

She grazed the scar with her finger. "How did this happen?"

He turned his face into her hand. "Mule kick."

His lips tickled her palm, sending shivers down her spine. She felt buoyant, brave and invincible. The stubborn tilt in his chin gave her the courage to tease him. "Was this mule an animal, or one of your brothers?"

He grinned, and she felt the movement all the way to her toes.

"You're a very perceptive woman. I come from a long line of stubborn men."

At the husky sound of his voice, her heart quivered.

Her feelings for Will had been bright and intense, like lightning bursting in the sky. But they'd faded just as quickly. She'd never been in love with Will, but at least she finally understood his draw. She'd been in love with the way he made her feel. For someone who had been alone most of her life, his attention had been intoxicating, and brief. If their courtship had been even a week longer, she'd have seen the chinks in his respectability.

By the time she'd noticed the signs of his cruelty, they'd boarded a train bound for Kansas. There was nothing for her to do but stay, and face the consequences of her rash behavior.

With Jack the sensations felt like a summer shower—unhurried, light and enduring. The juxtaposition of the two men was startling. Spring rain brought daffodils and crocus, while thunderstorms flattened the prairie grasses and uprooted trees.

Fighting his attraction taxed her resolve. Especially when he made her insides melt like warm butter. Why did Jack have to threaten everything she held dear? She didn't want her well-ordered existence to change any more than it already had. Whatever Will had done was in the past, but she didn't know if Jack would see it that way.

She'd carved out a life for herself and a future for her daughter, a carefully maintained, brittle sense of safety. But Jack chipped away at the foundations of her security with his lack of faith in her. No matter what happened, she didn't want to be wrong about a man again. She couldn't risk her own heart, and she definitely couldn't risk Rachel's affection.

"Why won't you just leave?" she whispered, blinking frantically against the sting of tears behind her eyes.

He studied her for a moment, then offered a tired smile. He tugged one hand from behind his head and gently brushed away the moisture from her cheek with the pad of his thumb. "I can't. You know why."

Her heart turned in response to his gentle caress. Being here like this wasn't proper. She should flee, but her limbs refused to budge. Jack was right again. The pig wasn't much of a chaperone.

"What about your case?" she asked, hoping to change the subject, to dissipate this frightening intimacy.

"For the first time in my career, I've failed." A shadow flitted across his eyes. "I've run out of leads."

His obvious distress struck a chord. He'd helped deliver Rachel, he'd chopped wood and shoveled snow. He'd even mucked stalls, and she had never once thanked him for his help. There was no way to repay him, unless...

An idea sprang into her head. "What if I help you? I'm good with puzzles. I've seen your newspaper clippings." The more she thought about the idea, the more enthused she became. "Perhaps I can discover a pattern."

He rolled his head from side to side in a negative motion. "There's nothing you can do. I've been looking at those clippings for months. What makes you think you can find a connection?"

She braced her hands on either side of his head, daring him to hold her gaze. "What makes you think I can't? I'm a fresh perspective and I don't have any emotions attached to the case."

His eyes narrowed in thoughtful consideration. Another emotion she couldn't define flitted across his face. "I guess it wouldn't hurt to let you try."

She grinned, pleased with the opportunity to prove her abilities. The idea was inspired. If she found a new lead in his case, he'd be forced to leave. Without his interference she and Rachel returned to their safe, orderly world.

After seeing the box, she feared he suspected the truth about Will's gambling. Perhaps if Jack solved his case, he'd forget all about the watches. "Bring your newspapers to the house this evening. We're having turkey for supper."

"My turkey?"

"*My* turkey. I'm assuming you shot it on my land."

Elizabeth's coat sleeve had torn during her ordeal, and the frayed material parted to her elbow. Jack caught her arm, turning her hand to reveal the arrow-shaped scar on her skin. She quickly brushed her sleeve down to cover the mark.

"How did you get such an odd scar?"

"It was a long time ago," Elizabeth mumbled.

The escaped chicken pecked at the ground near Jack's head.

"Myrtle," she called to the chicken, shooing the bird away with her outstretched hands. "Back to the henhouse with you."

She glanced down to discover her skirts draped intimately over Jack's legs. She quickly brushed them aside, but not before he quirked an eyebrow at the hasty motion.

Rolling to one side, Jack stood, then brushed the dust from his pant legs. "You name your chickens?"

He pulled her to her feet and quickly dropped his hand to his side. She noted how he flexed his fist a few times, as if disgusted with the contact. Her heart sank.

Elizabeth knelt before the brick of hay, tugging the bailing twine free. "That hen is very memorable. I call her Myrtle the Mouser because she's always escaping the chicken coop to chase down mice with the barn cat."

"Please tell me you're joking."

"I'm perfectly serious."

She scooped Myrtle into her arms, then whirled to face the Ranger. He towered above her, an incredulous grin on his handsome face. She had the distinct impression he was laughing at her and not the chicken.

"Here." She thrust the bird at his chest. "Make yourself useful and put Myrtle away. I'll get the turkey started." She patted the chicken's feather-soft head. "I'll clean your cage tomorrow."

"Not tomorrow." He juggled Myrtle in his hands. "It's the Sabbath."

"Of—of course," Elizabeth stuttered, not sure of the reference, but afraid of looking foolish. "I guess I just forgot."

Myrtle struggled, feathers flapping in the Ranger's face. Grimacing, he shrugged. "It's hard to keep track of the days."

"Yes, well, I'd best get back inside. I've left Rachel alone for too long already."

She paused, unable to tear her gaze away from the tall man. At his murmured assurance, Myrtle settled into his arms. Jack had an affinity with animals and children. A way of charming them with his amiable smile, though she knew a layer of steel rested beneath that friendly grin.

"Supper is at six," she said hastily. "And don't forget your newspapers."

She had stumbled upon the perfect solution. Reviving his interest in his case would surely focus his attention on something other than her. The sooner he moved on, the better.

Right?

Jack dunked his face into the bucket of ice-cold water, quickly straightened, then flung back his head, sending a shower of water droplets raining over the floor.

He ran his hands through his drenched hair, smoothing down the mass. Rubbing his face, he groaned at the stubble already covering his chin. Perhaps he should shave again. He shook his head. No, that was foolish. He wasn't attending a church social. Then again, this was the first invitation he'd received to dine in the house since his return, and his beard *was* a bit long.

Reaching for his shaving kit, he studied his face in the tiny mirror. The reflection showed a man in his early thirties, not handsome certainly, but not ugly, either. There was nothing fundamentally wrong with any of his features. Certainly no one would call him handsome, but women had fawned over his older brother, Robert, and people often said the two of them bore a passing resemblance. The comparisons had to mean something.

A glint of sliver caught his attention. He squinted, tilting his head farther to the right. Several gray strands stood out in stark relief. His fears realized, he whipped around to the left and studied the opposite side of his head. He was graying at the temples! When had that happened?

With one calloused finger, he smoothed down the offensive outcropping. Surely he wasn't old enough for gray hair. Thinking back, Jack mentally ticked off the years. His father had been forty-five with a full head of silver when he died.

But his father had been *old*. Not much older than Jack was now, though.

The realization stunned him. He arranged a hunk of hair over the gray spot, then brushed it back into place again. He wasn't old, he was seasoned. The look was distinguished. He squinted into the mirror. Besides, who wanted to be young and impulsive?

With that thought firmly in place, he reached for his shaving kit again. He lathered his face and carefully pulled the razor over his rough beard, idly wondering how the widow thought of him. Did she see him as mature? Or old? He stilled his hand. He'd never considered Elizabeth's age, but she was definitely younger than him. In her early twenties perhaps.

She had a brisk, efficient way about her, a maturity beyond her years. The thought of her living in an orphanage sent his stomach dipping. She had such a wide-eyed innocence about her. As if she refused to be broken by the evil she witnessed in the world.

A pot of water boiled merrily on the stove to his left. The steam drifted over the shirt he'd hung from the center beam, smoothing out the wrinkles. Jack grunted at the sight. His fellow Rangers would have a heyday if they saw him now, primping like a debutante for her first dance.

He studied his face in the mirror again, checking every angle for missed whiskers. Satisfied with the results, he wiped the excess foam from his face. Of their own volition, his hands went to the minuscule vial of aftershave tucked in the corner of his bag. A gift from his sister-in-law, though he couldn't recall which one.

He did remember the gift had been accompanied by a whole lot of ribbing from his brothers, and not a few hints from his mother that she was ready for another daughter-in-law and a passel more grandchildren.

Embarrassed by his uncharacteristic vanity, he dropped the vial, snatched his shirt from its perch, then snapped out the last of the wrinkles. He swiped a drop of cologne on his pant legs. It was a turkey dinner, not an audience with Queen Victoria.

He had to stay focused. Elizabeth's offer of assistance had haunted him all afternoon. Why had she finally decided to help him? This dinner was about finding out how much she knew, and questioning her about her husband's activities. It wasn't as if he was going courting or anything. This was business.

He strode across the clearing to her door, not bothering to don his wool coat for the few steps to the widow's house. His gaze lingered on the shiny, unweathered hinges he'd replaced only weeks before. He knocked sharply. His job was to free an innocent man from the hangman's noose, not deliver babies.

The door swung open. A puff of warm air scented with roasting turkey sent his mouth watering. He glanced up. His heart jolted. All thoughts of outlaws and interrogations fled his brain. He'd just seen Elizabeth hours ago, yet she'd done something different with her hair, or maybe it was a new dress. She was so beautiful, she'd rooted his feet to the floor. Jack swallowed. Doing his job had just gotten a whole lot more difficult.

Chapter Ten

Elizabeth soon discovered one thing about the lawman—he sure knew how to eat. She heaped a third helping of apple pan Dowdy onto his scraped-clean plate while he looked on with rapt interest.

"I couldn't possibly have any more," Jack protested, drawing the plate closer to his chest, his fork poised in the air. "But since you've already served some up, I'd hate to see it go to waste. I've never eaten a finer meal, Mrs. Cole."

His formal address set her back a notch. "You're welcome."

He'd been different all evening, though pinpointing the exact difference eluded her. His manners remained impeccable, yet a hint of solemnity colored his actions. His conversation stayed smooth and rigidly correct—almost too correct. Perhaps that was the problem. On the one hand, his deference made her feel important, cherished. On the other hand she felt as if he was holding something back, keeping a part of himself hidden.

The change in his attitude had her off balance, unsure how or why their relationship had altered. Instead of alleviating the tension between then, their encounter in the barn had heightened the strain.

She fussed with her apron, smoothing a nonexistent wrinkle from her skirt. "My mother always insisted on starting at the beginning whenever there was a problem. Let's review what we know for certain. You're looking for a man named Bud Shaw because he's a bank robber."

"There's more to it than that." Jack's knuckles whitened where he gripped his fork. "I put the wrong man in jail. If I don't find the real Bud Shaw, an innocent man will hang. I can't live with his death on my conscience."

Elizabeth's hand flew to her chest. His raw confession lent her a rare glimpse into his vulnerability. He sat stiffly, as if waiting for her to accuse or berate him. But for what? She certainly wasn't his judge and jury.

After a moment she asked, "How can Bud Shaw prove this man's innocence? I thought he was an outlaw."

"Because Bud Shaw is also in jail."

Elizabeth widened her eyes. "You're searching for Bud Shaw. And Bud Shaw is in jail?"

Jack pushed his empty plate forward, set his forearms on the table and clasped his hands together. His somber gaze fixed on a point just above her left shoulder. "I'll start at the beginning." He exhaled a heavy breath. "There was a string of bank robberies from Kansas through Colorado last year. They crossed into Texas sometime during the spring. My brother's wife was shot during one of the robberies."

"Is she all right?"

The stark agony in his exotic hazel eyes rocked her. He must have been close to the woman for such a reaction. An unexpected shaft of jealousy stabbed her. She pressed her hand tighter against her chest, quelling the hateful emotion. What kind of person was jealous of an injured woman? What was wrong with her?

Certainly she was no stranger to jealousy and envy.

Growing up she'd watched other families with yearning in her heart. She'd even noticed how Will had paid particular attention whenever a pretty woman passed by, but she'd never experienced this sort of spite in her heart.

Jack seemed to gather himself, shrugging his shoulders as if divesting himself of the somber memories. "No. She didn't make it." He cleared his throat. "Emotions got involved during the initial hunt for the outlaws. People wanted justice, and they wanted it fast." He finally met her sympathetic gaze. "In our rush to capture the outlaws, we made a mistake. There's an innocent man set to hang, and I can't save him."

As if physically weighted by the burden, his shoulders sagged. The gesture touched a place deep within Elizabeth's heart. She understood the wearing pressure of guilt.

She lowered herself to perch on the edge of her chair and leaned over the table. While she longed to reach out and press her hand over his, to absorb his pain, instead, she said, "Why do you think this man is innocent?"

"Instinct."

She dug her fingernails into her palms. How nice it must be, to trust in one's self. She'd lost that confidence the moment she agreed to marry a man who cared more for personal appearance than he did for his wife. She missed the sure knowledge of right and wrong, and her ability to judge the difference.

"Did you investigate the other robberies?"

He shook his head.

"Why not?"

"I only got involved because of my sister-in-law Doreen. My brothers are ranchers. I'm the only one in the family who had the background to investigate. Except that it's not really what I do. I'm more of a negotiator.

I'm good at tracking." He stared at his hands. "At least I used to be. As for the other robberies, the Rangers had already done their job. Wasn't much more I could do."

He appeared reluctant to elaborate on his job duties. Though she didn't understand why, she decided not to pressure him. "Tell me what you think happened."

Jack cleared his throat. "We captured the wrong Bud Shaw."

"Two men and one name."

"Yes, but only one of them is a killer."

"It says here the Texas Rangers captured two outlaws." She glanced at his jotted notes. "Certainly they can identify each other."

"Pencil Pete says the man sitting in jail is Bud Shaw, all right. Says Bud is the one responsible for shooting a clerk up in Colorado Springs, too." Jack's eyes grew cloudy, distant. "But I don't buy it. Old Pencil Pete is too gleeful, too fired up about selling out one of his own gang. I've put plenty of men away for doing crimes. I've watched them trample each other to cut a deal. But I've never seen a man so eager to identify one of his own with nothing in return. Something isn't right."

Heat from his simmering frustration washed over her in waves. She'd been around him long enough to see the subtle signs of his distress. The way he kept his palms flat on the table. The muscle that ticked along his jaw.

She forced her own tightly clenched hands to relax. "Then we'd best find the killer. I owe you that much."

Whether she wanted to admit it or not, he'd been a help around the farm. He'd cut wood and mucked stalls. He patiently instructed her on loading Will's gun, he'd even kept Jo company, distracting the younger girl from the crushing boredom of laying in bed all day.

Elizabeth hadn't asked for the Ranger to barge into

her life, but he'd made himself useful none the less. Assisting him in discovering a new lead served two purposes—she'd repay her debt, and she'd remove his reason for staying.

She forcibly squelched the nagging doubts that sprang up each time she thought of Jack leaving. This was the right thing to do. He was a drifter and a loner. Men like that didn't change.

If her thoughts lingered over the way his voice gentled when he talked to Rachel, or the way the baby seemed to instantly calm in his presence, then she blamed the weather. The long winter had left her fatigued, and more prone to melancholy. Things would be better in the spring. There'd be more people around. Life on the homestead would be less lonely.

The longer Jack stayed, the less she'd want to let him go. "Let's start with the bank robbery."

She stood, crossed to the kitchen cupboard and swung open the door. For the first time in a long while, she had a concrete goal. A purpose. Her thoughts raced as she pulled down a lead pencil and one of her precious sheets of paper. "We'll start with the last robbery. How many outlaws were involved?"

"Three."

"How many people were injured?"

His lips drew into a thin, white line. "Just Doreen. She was reaching for her reticule. One of the men spooked at the movement. He shot her."

She gave his hand a quick squeeze. "I'm so sorry about your sister-in-law."

"Thank you," he replied, his voice husky.

To ease the tension, Elizabeth jotted down several notes before flipping over the paper. "Sketch the inside of the bank and where everyone was standing. To the best of your knowledge at least."

"I don't see what—"

"Please," she implored. "I need to know everything. I need to get a picture in my mind of what happened."

Reluctantly complying, he concentrated on the sketch. With his head bent, he drew a remarkably detailed outline of each chair, desk and window. A lock of hair fell over his eyes, and he swatted it away. Her fingers itched to smooth the chocolate waves back into place.

His hair had grown. With his face cleanly shaven, he appeared even more dangerous than the first time she'd seen him. The impulsive side of her, the part that had led her to Kansas in the first place, was drawn to that danger. How tempting to rest her burdens on his strong shoulders, to share her fears and insecurities, to let the low rumble of his baritone voice soothe her.

Elizabeth started, ashamed of her wayward thoughts.

While she struggled to force her attention back to the robberies, Jack indicated the locations of the three outlaws and the four civilians.

"What's that?" She indicated a box drawn near the edge of the picture.

"That's the safe."

Their fingers brushed together. The touch struck a vibrant chord within her. Their gazes locked. His hazel eyes sparked with an inscrutable emotion.

Her heart jolted and her pulse pounded. A plaintive cry from the bedroom sent Elizabeth stumbling to her feet. "While you're finishing that, I'll fetch the baby and check on Jo."

He jerked his head in an absentminded nod, his attention once again focused on the sketch. Elizabeth paused, wondering if she'd imaged the flare of emotion in his eyes. Another lusty cry from the baby yanked her from her contemplations.

She fed and changed Rachel while Jo twirled one mahogany braid and frowned over a dog-eared copy of *Pride and Prejudice*.

Elizabeth's chest constricted at the forlorn sight. "Would you like me to sit with you? Keep you company? You must be getting lonely."

The girl glanced up and smiled, dropping her braid to shoo away the interruption. "This is a good part," she whispered. "I'm almost finished."

Elizabeth quirked an eyebrow. *So much for entertaining the invalid.*

Her guilt assuaged, she flashed a knowing smirk at the top of Jo's head. The very proper English romance certainly had her tomboy helper engrossed.

Rachel fussed in her drawer, kicking away her blankets to reveal her darling, stocking-clad feet. Elizabeth picked her up and cradled the baby to her chest. There was something grounding about holding Rachel to her heart, feeling her daughter's warm breath rustling against her neck. For a moment everything was possible, the future wild and free.

Elizabeth closed her eyes, letting herself imagine her life if Will had loved her even half as much as Jack loved his family. Tears pricked behind her eyes. She surreptitiously wiped them away, relieved to find Jo too engrossed in her book to notice. They'd love each other, she and Rachel, and that would be enough.

With the baby propped against one shoulder, Elizabeth returned to the dining table, then struggled to clear the plates with her free hand.

"I'll hold Rachel," Jack offered. "I've finished with the drawing."

Elizabeth rested the infant in his outstretched arms. His enormous hands dwarfed the growing baby. He tucked Rachel into the crook of his elbow where she stared at his face in curious wonder. Lost in a private world, the two made faces at each other.

The stern Texas Ranger melted away, leaving in its place an affectionate, openhearted man with an affinity for fatherhood. The sight warmed Elizabeth's heart.

Jack touched the infant's nose, assuming a mock expression of stern disapproval. "I hope you haven't been giving your mother any trouble."

The infant's mouth worked, as if she were struggling to form a reply. A tender affection stirred in Elizabeth's chest, a glowing circle of light seemed to grow and expand around her heart. She had dreamed of this moment, in the deep recesses of her heart where the harsh light of truth failed to penetrate. She had imagined this event in her waking dreams. A home, a family, the soft haze of firelight chasing away the evening gloom. The fresh smell of baked apples wafting around her. Of course, she'd pictured the man to be her husband, not a Texas Ranger who'd burst into her life with his gun drawn.

"You're smiling," Jack said. "What are you thinking about?"

"Nothing. Nothing at all. Now where were we?"

His smile faltered. "The newspaper clippings are all here." He indicated a neat stack of folded papers. "I've circled the relevant articles."

"Excellent." She assumed a brisk efficiency. "First though, tell me about the man you captured. Tell me about the Bud Shaw you jailed."

Jack absently rocked the infant, his eyes thoughtful. "He's quiet, I guess. Just an ordinary fellow. He had some problems as a kid, rustling cattle with his father and the like, but nothing violent. He's just ordinary."

Elizabeth sighed at his frank reply. Jack didn't consider her questions silly or unimportant, he simply answered them with his usual straightforward, direct responses. As if they were equals. The cozy room took on a misty shimmer from the kerosene lanterns, softening the homestead's rough edges. For the second time in so many weeks, she wanted to stretch out time and capture this moment in her memory.

She sat up in her chair, pulling away from his magnetic draw. "Why do you keep saying he's ordinary?"

"Because the real Bud Shaw is larger than life. People describe him as handsome, gregarious, a gambler and a fellow all the ladies clustered around." Jack adjusted Rachel to the other arm. The baby kicked and cooed in delight. He dropped a kiss to her forehead. Elizabeth's heart stuttered at the unconscious gesture.

Unaware of the havoc he wreaked on her senses, Jack continued, "The fellow serving time in a Paris, Texas, jail doesn't strike me as that sort of man."

Elizabeth crossed her arms over her chest. She couldn't help but think of another man who fit the description of gregarious lady charmer. As far as she could tell, leopards did not change their spots. At least not for long.

"Did Bud Shaw do the shooting?"

He shrugged. "We believe so."

Elizabeth blew out a relieved breath. The description had been so similar to Will. Yet Will's gun had never been fired. He'd carried the flashy piece like a badge of honor, but even Jack had noted the gun's pristine condition. "How much time have you spent with the Bud Shaw in jail? Could he be acting?"

"I spent two weeks in Paris helping my brother with

the arrangements after Doreen's death. I didn't see any behavior to indicate the man was anything but a quiet, conscientious worker who'd run into some trouble in his youth."

Jack smoothed his thumb over Rachel's eyebrow. The infant captured his index finger, tugging it toward her mouth. He grinned, a dimple appearing on his left cheek. The baby explored his hand, even taking a tentative bite at his thumb. Jack held Rachel as if it were the most natural thing in the world. As if he were meant to serve the role.

Rubbing her hands over her eyes, Elizabeth dragged her attention back to the clippings. "What led you to this man in the first place?"

"Slim Joe was gut shot during the last escape. Before he died, he gave me the names of Pencil Pete and Bud Shaw. Slim even told me where Bud lived. His name and address matched a signature at the hotel the night before. We went to his spread and found part of the money hidden behind his woodshed."

"Sounds like Bud is guilty."

"To you and everyone else. Even the other witnesses aren't certain. He looks close enough to the description to be the man. But something isn't right. He doesn't act like a criminal. He doesn't even seem the type."

Elizabeth suppressed a grin. The frustration in his voice was incongruent with the silly faces he kept flashing at the infant to make her gurgle in delight. "Does anybody else share your conviction?"

Jack barked out a laugh, startling Rachel. The baby's face pinched as if she might cry. He crossed his eyes and stuck out his tongue. A smile stretched across her round face. "Not hardly. Bud Shaw would be dead and buried already if it weren't for me. I talked the sheriff into giving me six months to find the real outlaw. I'm running out of time, though. More important, Bud is running out of time."

"You've gone to an awful lot of trouble based on your instinct."

"That's all I've got."

In that second, she understood his purpose. The pursuit of justice consumed him. She was right to focus his attention on the case once again. The sooner he found a lead, the sooner he'd be on his way. Discovering the truth drove him forward. The same way having a permanent home drove her to stay on the homestead, despite the obvious danger.

A chill breeze swept through the room, ruffling her papers. Elizabeth mustn't let regrets fill her heart. The past could not be changed. Jack had not appeared in the bakery all those months ago, sweeping her off her feet. Will had. Any longings that might sneak into her heart, any wistful dreams of a handsome Texas Ranger whisking her away, were foolish and dangerous. Everything she had rested on this desolate slice of prairie. This endeavor wasn't about watching Jack putter around the room, Rachel in his arms.

Her goal was to remind him of his duty, and motivate him to leave. "Why don't I read through these newspapers? See if there's anything interesting?"

Jack settled himself in the chair nearest the roaring fire he'd started in the grate. "It's your time. Do you have something I can read?"

Elizabeth stood and crossed to the bedroom. Jo had dozed off with the book slack in her hands. Elizabeth opened the top dresser drawer and dug beneath her clothes. She returned to the hearth room and handed Jack a book.

He propped the Bible open on one knee, his ankles crossed on a three-legged stool. Rachel sprawled over his chest. Elizabeth's gaze swung between Jack and the rear door. There really was no reason for him to be here. Why didn't she just demand that he return to the bunkhouse and save herself this torture? Save herself from the dream come to life? After all, the truce had been for dinner only.

Yet Rachel appeared so content in his arms. The baby struggled to lift her head, reaching out to grasp his silver star. The pin tugged at his shirt. Jack's mouth kicked up at one corner.

Elizabeth's soul crashed and soared at the same time, torn between the truth and what might have been. Despite the pain, she couldn't tear her gaze away.

Jack returned his attention to the Bible, studying the pages, his brow furrowed in concentration. Why disturb them to selfishly save her shattered heart?

Elizabeth spent the next forty minutes poring over the newspaper articles and making notes. She sketched out dates and times in one column, the bank locations in another. Below Jack's picture of the last bank robbery, she traced the route the outlaws had taken through the western territory. She lined up the wanted posters, but they offered little help. The outlaws had worn bandannas over their faces to protect their identities. Even the witnesses had given conflicting accounts of their heights and weights.

The crimes appeared to be random, like spokes on a wheel. There was no obvious trail, no distinct line from point A to point B. The times didn't match up, either. The outlaws struck at random intervals, giving no clue as to why they chose the particular banks to rob.

Stumped, she wrote down the events happening in the

towns. There were church socials, local festivals and the occasional marriages and arrests. Her eyes drooping, she rested her head on the table. Something about the towns piqued her curiosity.

Jack woke with a start. Disoriented, he searched the still cabin. Rachel dozed in his arms, her tiny fists bunched beneath her chubby chin. Banked embers glowed red in the hearth. Alarmed by the unnatural quiet, he searched the room, then heaved a sigh of relief to find Elizabeth sleeping at the table with her head cradled in her arms. Escaped tendrils of blond hair curtained her face.

He rolled the baby into the crook of his elbow. Standing, he raised himself up on his toes to stretch his stiff leg muscles, then bustled around the cabin. He placed a dozing Rachel in her bed before clearing away the rest of the dishes. As quietly as he could manage, he gathered his newspapers and stacked them neatly atop Elizabeth's notes. Curious, he slipped her papers free. Her handwriting was neat and precise, her organization of the facts logical.

Jack rubbed the back of his neck with a sigh. The futile endeavor hadn't been a complete waste. He'd gotten his first decent meal in weeks, and his brief nap had left him more rested than he'd felt in a month of Sundays. The company of the pretty widow hadn't hurt, either.

He'd forgotten the soothing comfort of women. The tiny details that made a house a home. Elizabeth had set the table for company, just like he remembered from his youth. She'd even pressed the butter into decorated pats. A stamped cow adorned the yellow disks. A tablecloth embroidered with delicate pink roses draped the table.

The frivolous touches stirred up memories he thought he'd buried long ago.

Rare longings for a home of his own surprised him with their intensity. He'd didn't want a family, a permanent place to live. He was content with his work, satisfied with his contribution to society. But the widow had him picturing a life where he returned home every night to enjoy a hearty meal before a roaring fire. A home where he watched his own children grow.

He stretched to release the painful knot throbbing in his neck. He'd chosen his given profession for a reason. He didn't want to be tied to the family ranch like his brothers, buried beneath the uncertainty of droughts and blight. Held prisoner by weather and fate. He controlled his own destiny. And, right now, he controlled the destiny of an innocent man. If he forgot that, he surrendered his honor.

Elizabeth and her daughter had unleashed his protective instincts, that's all. These unsettling emotions were a reaction to his failure to locate the real Bud Shaw. The delay presented an opportunity to feel useful, needed. Nothing more. He'd quiet these disturbing yearnings for home and hearth once he found proof that Elizabeth's husband had been involved with the outlaws. There was something here. He just knew it.

If he found his gaze lingering over Elizabeth's soft lips, his heart catching at her infectious laugh, his reactions were the natural result of a man isolated from the comfort of a woman's company for too long. He'd steeled himself from the crushing loneliness of life on the trail before, and he'd harden his feelings once again.

When he could avoid the task no longer, he touched Elizabeth's shoulder. She blinked at him, her eyes sleepy and unfocused.

His hands trembling, he brushed the hair from her forehead. "It's late. I'll see you tomorrow."

Her eyes flew open. She stumbled to her feet. He reached out a hand to steady her. Swaying, she leaned into him. Her gaze searched the room while she pressed a hand to her forehead. "Where is Rachel?"

"She's snug as a bug in a rug."

Elizabeth blinked sleepily, brushing the wrinkles from her skirt. His mouth suddenly felt as dry as the west Texas desert. With her eyes blurry from sleep, her shirt-waist rumpled and her hair tumbling loose, she was the prettiest thing he'd ever seen. Loose waves of hair framed her face in a halo of light. A becoming hint of pink tinged her cheeks. A thousand different words came to mind, but not a one of them lent her justice.

"Gracious, I must have fallen asleep." She ran a hand over her eyes. "Rachel is probably due to be fed and changed soon."

A lump of regret lodged in his throat. Not trusting himself to speak, he nodded. He vowed never again to torment his older brothers about their fierce devotion to their children. For years the thought of being tied down to kin had struck him as stifling and restrictive. He finally understood.

Standing here, staring into Elizabeth's questioning blue eyes, the thought of living in one place for the rest of his life didn't seem so threatening anymore.

She blinked at him expectantly, as if waiting for him to say something.

"I'll, uh. I'll just be going. Thank you for dinner."

"You're welcome."

She smiled then, wide enough to reveal those overlapping teeth. His heart hammered against his ribs. Sleep had washed away her usual reticence, leaving her open and vulnerable. A very male part of him wanted to sweep her into his arms, to wipe away the lines of worry that furrowed her brow each day, to care for her. He yearned to be the man she leaned on.

Jack fisted his hands. He wasn't a rancher or a farmer. He was a man whose whole life revolved around travel. Even if he trusted the widow's motives completely, he was still a Texas Ranger. Wandering and family life didn't mix well. Jack had no rights here.

He had to remind himself of his purpose. His instincts had never failed him before, and every nerve in his body screamed that the answers to his questions were hidden on this isolated homestead. If her husband had been involved, if he had financed their marriage with stolen money, then the truth threatened to shatter her world.

He didn't want to choose between Elizabeth and Bud Shaw, but the answer was obvious. This wasn't about love and land and a tiny baby girl. A man's life dangled in the balance.

He caught sight of a knitted blanket draped over the back of the kitchen chair, Rachel's basket sitting on the seat. There was one thing he needed to do before he left for good. Before the decisions he had to make destroyed any chance of peace for either of them.

Chapter Eleven

Elizabeth knew something was wrong the minute she reached the bottom step out the back door. An eerie hush had settled over the prairie. Not even the wind blew to rattle the hook dangling from the hayloft. She stumbled back up the step again, leaning one hand on the railing as she peered into the distance.

No shadows stood out on the horizon, no ominous clouds hung in the distance. A muffled thump sent the hairs on the back of her neck standing on end. She waited. When nothing out of the ordinary appeared, she took another cautious step.

A crack sounded overhead followed by a shower of snow. Elizabeth shrieked, slipping and stumbling until, in her haste to escape, she teetered backward, flailing her arms and sitting down hard on the first step. Heart pounding, she scrambled to her feet.

Her gaze snagged on a broken tree branch dangling above her head. The heavy weight of snow had snapped the limb. She pressed a hand to her breast with a sigh, slumping against the handrail. "Gracious, I've become a simpering ninny."

Feeling foolish for her cowardice, she retrieved her

pail and set off for the barn. She'd had a revelation the night before, and she was anxious to share her newfound discovery with Jack. Her footsteps quick and light, she almost missed the trail of red splotches crossing the freshly cleared path.

Paw prints accompanied the bloody trail, disappearing around the edge of the barn. *The chicken coop!*

Elizabeth lifted the hem of her skirts and set off at a run. The prints looked fresh. A stray dog most likely. She rounded the corner and stumbled to a halt.

Myrtle's brown feathers with their distinctive white tips littered the ground in a sodden mass. "Oh, you naughty thing," Elizabeth sniffled. "I told you escaping the coop would only get you into trouble."

She dug her nails into her palms. Myrtle might have been an annoying nuisance, but the poor thing didn't deserve to end her life as dinner for a stray dog. Elizabeth straightened and stomped around the chicken coop, her boots crunching through the icy drifts, determined to scare away the beast that had eaten her mischievous bird.

She lifted her pail. A dark form crouched in the snow. Her heart leaped into her throat, strangling her angry words.

An enormous gray wolf bared its fangs as a low growl reverberated in its throat. Elizabeth took an involuntary step backward. A mammoth dusky paw inched closer. Her frantic gaze skirted the clearing. She had nothing to defend herself with except the flimsy tin pail clutched in her mittened hand.

She'd encountered enough ruffians in New York to realize bullies sensed fear. Drawing herself up to her full height, she sucked in a shaky breath. "Go away," she hollered. "Bad wolf."

The beast snarled in reply.

"I said shoo!"

Another beefy paw moved toward her in the snow. The animal slunk forward, its belly scraping on the frozen ground.

So much for acting fearless.

She gauged the distance to the barn door. How desperate and hungry was the wolf to be searching for food this early?

Myrtle's crimson blood darkened the animal's snout, chilling Elizabeth. Where was the rest of the pack? Had this one become separated? Was it rabid?

Her mind raced with possibilities. If she dashed to the safety of the barn, she still had to lift the heavy T-bar and shove aside the bulky door. The mangy beast would have her in shreds before she accomplished the task.

A furtive movement caught the corner of her eye.

The barn cat hissed.

The wolf swung its scruffy head at the distraction.

Elizabeth whirled, floundering in the deep snow, hampered by her long skirts. Not risking a look behind her, she dashed away from the barn. When the wolf's fierce yelps didn't sound any louder, Elizabeth chanced a glance over her shoulder. The cat had clawed its way up the side of the henhouse to perch on the roof. Beneath the overhang, the wolf danced in the snow, bounding from side to side, jaws snapping.

Elizabeth skidded to a halt on the cleared path. Gasping, she pressed a hand to the stitch in her side. The house sat to her left, the bunkhouse and Jack farther to the right. Dare she lead the wolf to the house, even though the distance was shorter?

The unmistakable gallop of padded feet pounded behind her, coming up fast.

A plaintive howl spurred her into action.

* * *

At the sound of Elizabeth's scream, Jack dropped his level and leaped over the carved wood pieces littering the floor. He fastened his gun holster around his waist while bolting to the door. In one swift movement he grasped his rifle from its perch and burst onto the porch.

He slammed into Elizabeth with enough force to send them both sliding toward the shallow stairs. He caught her around the waist as they stumbled to the floor. Unable to cushion her fall, he jerked to lessen their blunt landing. Angling his body, he cracked his elbow against the wood, his sights focused on the animal bounding toward them. Ignoring Elizabeth's cry of pain, he aimed the rifle and fired.

The wolf yelped, its forward momentum halted as if it had smacked into a brick wall. Jack glanced around the uneven clearing formed by the three homestead buildings, searching for the rest of the pack. Where there was one animal, more were certain to follow.

With raw fear rushing through his veins like a river current, he jerked Elizabeth to her feet. Half leading, half carrying the stunned widow, he dragged her into the shelter of the bunkhouse.

Only when the door was safely closed and the latch firmly in place did he allow himself to search her trembling form for any signs of injury. Tears pooled in the corners of her eyes.

Jack ran his hands down her arms. "Are you hurt?"

"I'm fine, but—"

Relief shuddered through him. He folded her in his embrace, wanting to wrap her in his warmth. With a muffled sob, she buried her head in his shoulder. Rocking her gently, he murmured soothing words against the delicate curve of her ear.

"I must see to Rachel and Jo," she said, her voice muffled against his shirt. She wrenched free of his arms.

He managed to reach over her shoulder and slam the door before she exposed them both to certain danger. "You can't go outside. Where there's one wolf, there's bound to be more. We have to be sensible about this."

"That wolf killed Myrtle," she declared.

He pressed his forehead against hers. "I'm sorry about Myrtle."

"I'm just so mad."

She actually stomped her foot.

Sighing, Jack let her collapse against his chest. "I bet the old thing stuck in that wolf's craw and choked him. Don't cry."

"I refuse to cry. I didn't ever used to cry." She tipped back her head, her pale blue eyes standing out against her ashen face. "Having a baby has ruined me. I haven't stopped crying in months. It's ridiculous."

"You're tired, that's all. Things will look better when you get some rest."

"No. I'm not going to think like that any longer. Things have to change, now, or not at all. From this moment on, I will no longer be a simpering watering pot."

She set her chin in a stubborn line.

"You're the bravest woman I've ever met." Once again he found himself wanting to rid the earth of every wolf and every danger that dared threaten her safety and peace of mind. "Wait here."

He circled through the bunkhouse, peering out each window to ascertain the level of danger. Three more wolves paced around the clearing. Fresh paw prints crisscrossed the snow, indicating additional animals.

Jack spun the gun chamber. He had six rounds in his pistol, and more than three animals circling the home-

stead. They could wait it out in the bunkhouse until the
wolves resumed their search for food elsewhere. He cut
a glance at Elizabeth fidgeting near the door. No chance
of that. Keeping a mother separated from her baby was
out of the question. They'd have to make a dash for it.

He considered his options. The safety of three females
depended upon him. If the pack was bold enough to attack the chicken house in broad daylight, he had to assume the worst. With food scarce for the winter, the pack
was growing bolder. Gray wolves rarely attacked during the day.

He reloaded the rifle with quick efficiency while Elizabeth paced the floor, chewing a thumbnail and peering
out the windows every three paces.

"It's only been a few minutes?" Her tremulous voice
rose at the end like a question. "They should be safe,
right?"

She didn't have to say the names. "Rachel and Jo are
fine." He slid back the hammer. "If it came down to a
fight, I'd put my money on Jo against a wolf any day."

Her face blanched. Jack leaped to his feet and wrapped
his arm around her shoulder. "Don't worry, they're fine
as long as they stay inside. I haven't met a wolf yet who
can unlatch a door."

"But what if Jo decides to check on us? What if she
opens the door?"

"I've never known two females so intent on creating
trouble in their own heads."

"I'm not looking for trouble. I'm planning for the
worst."

Jack gave her shoulder a quick squeeze. "We're going
to run the distance between here and the house."

Pulling away from her, he stilled his racing thoughts,

drawing into himself, into the place where emotions and feelings weren't allowed. A place where logic ruled.

Emotions clouded judgment, and poor judgment got people killed.

He carefully let the hammer down, squared his shoulders and settled his hat on his head. "How many wolves have you counted?"

"I can't tell for sure. They weave in and out of view." Her head snapped up. "Will the rest of the farm animals be safe? Do you think they'll get into the barn?"

"Everything is locked up tight."

Relief flitted across her face. "I think maybe five or six wolves. I can't tell for sure. They all look the same."

The twenty or so yards to the main house might as well have been a mile. Jack could manage the distance without much worry, but with Elizabeth, his options were restricted. "I'm going to step onto the porch and fire off a few rounds with my pistol to scare them off, then we're going to make a run for the house. Stay behind me and don't look at anything except where you're going."

He handed her his rifle. "You've already managed the shotgun. This isn't much different. It's a Winchester Repeater. After you fire off the first shot, you've got a toggle action to load the second bullet. Ratchet back the lever arm. Make sure you hear the next round snap into place before you…"

Her eyes had glazed over and her face was blank.

"Uh." She frowned at the gun. "A toggle action what?"

"New plan." He cocked the rifle, dropped the next ball into place and returned the gun. "You've got one shot. Make it count."

She nodded, her gaze fearful but determined.

He propped the rifle against the wall and tugged on

her hands. "Take off your mittens or you won't be able
to pull the trigger."

The minute their bare hands touched, his heart skipped
over three whole beats. The barriers he had erected weakened. Taking a deep breath, he leaned his forehead on the
door. A gentle hand touched his shoulder.

"What's the matter?"

"Nothing. We're going."

Determined to fight the distraction of her gentle touch,
Jack handed her his gun. He grasped the doorknob, then
paused. He caught Elizabeth around the waist and pressed
a quick kiss to her lips. "Just follow me. You'll do fine."

She stared at him, bemused. He couldn't help himself.
He kissed her again. The soft press of her lips, the way
her body yielded, swaying into him, inflated his courage.

"For luck," he said.

Right then, he felt like he could conquer the world.

Elizabeth didn't know if her quickened pulse was from
the thought of facing down a pack of predators, or Jack's
astonishing gesture. The minute he'd released her, his
face had gone blank.

"Are you ready?" he asked.

The stock rested against her shoulder as she carefully
aimed the sights away from him. For the second time
in so many weeks, she risked shooting a Texas Ranger.

"I'm ready."

Jack cleared his throat. "Dear Lord, keep us safe."

"Amen," she murmured, wishing she had more words
of wisdom to offer.

He strode onto the porch first, firing off two shots in
rapid succession. Elizabeth winced. He gestured to the
left. "Keep an eye out that direction. I'll focus on the
right. Go!"

Together they dashed across the clearing toward the cabin. Elizabeth struggled to keep her footing on the slick snow and still hang on to the rifle. As if attuned to her speed, Jack kept pace with her.

A wolf bounded around the corner. Before she blinked, the animal lay dead from Jack's bullet.

He reached the porch first, then shouldered his way through the door and shoved her inside ahead of him. A rasping howl sounded behind them. The barn cat raced across the clearing, a mammoth gray wolf close on its heels.

Jack bounded down the stairs, firing another shot. The wolf collapsed to the ground. The barn cat reached the bunkhouse, safely clawing its way up the porch support. To Elizabeth's horror, a dark form appeared behind Jack.

Gritting her teeth, she leveled the rifle and fired. The bullet caught the wolf in the hind quarters. The animal bellowed in pain, writhing in the pinkening snow. Jack pivoted on one heel and fired another shot, stilling the animal's struggles.

"What's going on out there?" Jo shouted. "Is everyone all right?"

"Don't worry," Elizabeth called. "I'll explain everything."

Disturbed by the noise, Rachel whimpered. Elizabeth swung her gaze between Jack and the open door to the back bedroom. He loped up the stairs, brushed her aside and secured the door.

She expelled her pent-up breath. After another quick glance at Jack to ensure he wasn't injured, she rushed to retrieve Rachel. Moments later, she returned to the kitchen, bouncing the infant on her shoulder.

Jack perched on a chair, casually inspecting his weapon.

The daft man didn't even have the sense to realize he'd narrowly escaped a fatal mauling.

She paced before him. "Why on earth did you risk your life to save that silly cat! You might have been killed." Her voice caught on the last word.

He bent his head over the rifle. "I knew how upset you were over losing Myrtle. I didn't want you to lose the cat, too. You'd never keep the mice out of the feed bin."

Her anger evaporated as she realized he'd actually been thinking of her the whole time. "I suppose she did save my life."

"Myrtle?"

"No, the barn cat. Maybe it's time I actually name her."

Jack appeared confused at the rapid change of subject. "You're not still mad?"

Elizabeth pinched her lips together. "Of course I'm still angry. I'm furious. That was foolish and foolhardy. You might have been injured."

"I'm fine. See." He swept one hand down his chest. "Nothing happened. Tell me something. Why are women so bent on arguing about stuff that never happened?"

"And why are men so determined to make even the simplest task a feat of danger?"

She slammed into the bedroom with a huff. If she lived to be as old as Methuselah, she'd never understand men.

Chapter Twelve

Jack perched on a three-legged milking stool, his hands clasped before him, his knees bent almost to his nose. The barn doors had been opened to the corral, letting the farm animals enjoy a rare slice of winter sunshine through fluffy white clouds dotting the brilliant blue sky. Ely McCoy paced before Jack's view of the sunny afternoon, his arms folded over his barrel chest, a scowl darkening his heavily bearded face.

"Strange business," Ely said.

"Yep," Jack replied.

The McCoys had appeared Sunday afternoon, distraught over the numerous gunshots fired and frantic to check on the women. Upon their arrival, the realization of Jack's continued presence at the homestead hadn't sat well with Ely McCoy.

"'Spected you'd be gone by now," Ely repeated for the third time in so many minutes.

Jack sighed. "Couldn't leave the women alone."

"Yep." Ely bobbed his head. "I s'pose that'd be a problem."

The bearlike man resumed his agitated pacing. Jack was being called to task, and though he had a fairly good idea of the offense, Ely had yet to voice his exact displeasure. Jack's confusion stemmed from Ely's failure to form a coherent sentence. The neighboring farmer had paced and muttered for the better part of the last half hour. Every so often the burly man paused, opened and closed his mouth a few times as if preparing to speak, then muttered something unintelligible and set to pacing again.

Jack puffed a warm breath into his cupped palms and chafed his hands together. He cleared his throat to defend himself, only to be halted by Ely's stinging glare.

Partially visible behind their father, the McCoy children roughhoused around the corral. One of the smaller boys climbed up the sturdy corral rail, spread his arms and plunged face-first into a snowdrift.

Jack jerked to his feet. "Your son!"

Ely swung around, then shrugged. "That fence will hold."

Jack pressed one hand to his throbbing temple. "It's not the fence I'm worried about."

The youngest McCoy child, Adam or Abraham, had already scrambled back into position. His legs splayed for balance, he leaped into the air and belly flopped onto the packed snow.

"Doesn't that hurt?"

Ely shot Jack a look encompassing both incredulous shock and weary resignation. "Iffin' it hurt too much, I guess they wouldn't do it anymore, would they?"

Settling the stool back into place, Jack resumed his submissive posture with a roll of his eyes. The man had a point.

Ely set to pacing again, his fists braced beneath his biceps, highlighting beefy arms encased in a heavy wool coat. Jack blew out a long breath. If the farmer was going to pummel him, Jack sure wished he'd get on with it.

The waiting was turning out to be more torturous than the punishment.

"My wife!" Ely shouted.

Jack winced.

Noting the reaction, Ely lowered his voice to a less booming decibel. "My wife sent me over here. She's concerned with the, um, the arrangements, you see."

Jack decided it was time to change the subject. "You've got a curious lilt to your voice, Mr. McCoy. Where are you from?"

The brawny man visibly relaxed at the innocuous question. "County Cork, originally. My da came over during the blight." He scrubbed at his chin, staring into the distance, past the boisterous antics of his children.

Jack's attention remained riveted on the tableau playing out before him. The oldest boy planted his knee into his younger brother's back, then set to shoveling handfuls of snow down his collar.

"Get off me, Caleb!" the squirming boy shouted.

Aha, Jack finally had names for all three boys present. Thank heavens they'd left the toddler at home. Jack shuddered at the thought of an even younger boy in the mix.

"Make me, Abraham," Caleb shouted.

The middle child, David, ignored his brother's antics, climbed back up the railing, and plunged backward into the snow. Jack recoiled from the bone-shattering leap. The boy scrambled to his feet and scurried back up the railing, ice still crusted in his light brown hair and eyebrows.

Unable to watch the raucous horseplay any longer, Jack turned away. Even from the barn, a muffled thump sent his bones aching in sympathy. He faced the corral again. Didn't those boys feel pain?

"Pa!" the middle child shouted from his supine position in the icy snow. "Can I ride the cow?"

"No, you may not, David. Now sit up. You've landed on your brother."

Jack craned his neck. Sure enough, David rolled over to reveal a red-faced Abraham. Jack blanched at the boy's woozy rise to his feet, but Abraham appeared otherwise unharmed from his ordeal and Ely certainly didn't seem concerned.

Evidently their father hadn't been as distracted as he appeared. Jack mentally noted that interesting character trait for future reference.

"Now where were we?" Ely continued.

Jack tore his gaze from the corral. "I believe we were discussing your wife."

"Ah, yes. Don't get me wrong. Mrs. McCoy is grateful for all you've done. But things have gone on a bit too long if you get my drift."

Jack wasn't sure he got anything. The conversation kept wavering between cordial discourse and thinly veiled threats.

"Yep. Strange business," Ely repeated.

"Strange business," Jack echoed, resigned. If you couldn't beat 'em, you might as well join 'em. "Strange business."

Ely planted his hands on his hips. "The missus thinks of Mrs. Cole like her own daughter. The poor thing came out here wet behind the ears, with no one to show her the way. That Will wasn't good for anything but holding up a fence post."

Jack raised an eyebrow.

"Not to speak unkindly of the dead," Ely quickly added. "But I don't cotton to a man who leaves his woman all alone that long. This here is dangerous country. Up until a few years ago, we had Indian uprisings. No siree." He shook his head forlornly. "This land is no place for a woman alone."

Finally, someone who understood what Jack was dealing with when it came to the widow. "Can't you talk some sense into her?"

"Me?" Ely jabbed a thumb at his own chest. "I hear it enough from the missus. We've had this conversation every day in the months since Will's death." Ely's voice took on a falsetto ring. "'You go over there and get that poor girl, Ely. If something happens, it's all your fault, Ely.'" The beefy man pinned Jack with a fierce scowl. "What am I supposed to do? Throw her over my shoulder and drag her back like a sack of feed? I don't think so."

"Can't Mrs. McCoy—"

"She's tried. Believe me." Ely threw up his arms, as if petitioning the heavens. "Believe me, she's tried."

The three McCoy boys had ceased their roughhousing long enough to finish building a snowman. Caleb snatched Abraham's hat for the top, and David snatched it back. Abraham danced between the two brothers as they tossed the stocking cap over his head. The younger boy finally socked the snowman in frustration, sending its crooked coal smile exploding to the ground.

"So are you going to marry her, or what?"

Jack blinked. He'd lost the thread of conversation during the snowman's destruction. "Excuse me?"

"You heard me, Ranger. What's it going to be?"

"Well—uh—that is—I—uh," Jack stuttered.

"That's what I thought." Ely hung his head, swinging his bearded face from side to side. "Now you've gone and made things difficult for me."

Here comes the pummeling.

Jack scrambled off the stool, knocking it to the hay-strewn floor. He knew how much Elizabeth treasured the McCoy friendship, so he couldn't very well hurt the older man. Calming this not-so-gentle giant was going to task his powers of mediation. "We're both reasonable men. I can assure you, everything has been perfectly proper. Just ask Jo."

"She's not exactly fit as a fiddle. How's she supposed to know what the two of you are doing in the barn and the bunkhouse?"

Heat crept up Jack's face. One kiss was hardly improper. It wasn't even a kiss really, more of a peck. A comforting gesture from one friend to another. There was nothing improper in that, was there?

Ely squinted one eye at Jack. "Is there something you want to tell me, Ranger?"

"No, no," Jack replied briskly. Once again, the situation had spiraled out of his control. "Listen, even if I wanted to marry Elizabeth, I'd be no better husband than Will. My job is mostly in Texas. I'm always gone. I can't remember the last time I stayed in one place more than a few days."

"I can," Ely interjected. "Feels like you've been here half the winter."

This time Jack knew a telling blush had reddened his cheeks. "As soon as I have a new lead, I'll be gone."

"And we all know that could take a while. You must be one incompetent lawman. After all, you practically shot a pregnant woman."

"I did not almost shoot Mrs. Cole. There was an unfortunate misunder—"

"I guess there's always the doc." As if suddenly bored by the conversation, Ely rubbed his beard.

Jack glanced around, unsure what Doc Johnsen had to do with anything.

Ely slapped Jack on the back, nearly sending him to his knees. "You've just stumbled onto the perfect solution. If the two of us can talk Mrs. Cole into marrying the doc, it'll save us both."

Jack's stomach dipped. "Save us?"

He pictured Elizabeth and the fair, curly-haired man standing side by side. They made a striking pair, both of them blessed with blond hair and those Norwegian blue eyes. Their children would probably look like the cherubs he'd once seen decorating a church ceiling in St. Louis.

A sudden need to punch something tightened Jack's fists. Doctors made terrible husbands. Always leaving at odd hours to attend sickly patients, exposing themselves and their families to a plethora of deathly illnesses.

Ely grinned, revealing an enormous gap-toothed smile. "Well, sure. With Mrs. Cole married to the doc, the missus will stop telling me what I should and shouldn't be doing, and I don't have to bash your face in."

"Doc Johnsen seems like a nice man," Jack replied weakly. "But I think Elizabeth already turned him down."

Ely quirked one bushy eyebrow. "I see how it is."

"How what is?"

"Nothing, nothing at all, my good man. We're a team now. I'm grateful not to have to kill you."

"Me, too," Jack replied, unsure what else to say.

He felt as if he'd agreed to something, made a covenant, but he wasn't quite sure about what.

Off in the distance, the McCoy boys appeared to have formed a truce. Abraham rolled a new head onto the battered snowman. They laughed and playfully chucked handfuls of snow at each other. Once again Jack's thoughts drifted back to his own brothers. There wasn't much snow in Paris, Texas—but they'd managed plenty of mischief just the same. That curious longing for home surfaced again, rising like a tide of paralyzing emotion, threatening to drown him.

Suddenly Jack realized what he'd agreed to. He'd just agreed to find Elizabeth a husband.

Ely McCoy paced before Elizabeth, his hands crossed over his chest, his forehead scrunched into a frown. She had the uneasy feeling she was being chastised for something, but she wasn't quite sure what.

"Mr. McCoy," she began. "Why don't you have a seat and tell me what's wrong."

The bearlike man slumped onto a ladder-back chair, splaying the support legs. He thoughtfully rubbed his beard, unaware of the strain he placed on his seat. She'd never seen him so talkative before, or so agitated.

"The missus and I are worried about you."

"There's really no—"

"I won't be hearing none of that. People look out for one another around these parts, and Mrs. McCoy thinks of you as one of her own."

"That's very kind—"

"It would do us both good if you moved to town. Why there's a mercantile, and a livery and a bank. Even a doctor." Ely's cheeks bloomed a brilliant shade of red.

Elizabeth tilted her head to one side. She had no idea why mention of the town doctor would cause him embarrassment.

Mr. McCoy cleared his throat. "A doctor is good to have around when you've got young'uns."

"I'm sure you're right—"

The large man leaped to his feet. The chair sprang back into shape. "The missus is up nights pacing the floor and muttering. She's fretting about you and the baby out here all alone. And if she's fretting, I don't get any rest."

Elizabeth clasped her hands together. She'd assumed since she was self-sufficient, never asking for help or needing assistance, then she wasn't a bother to anyone. The muscles in her shoulders knotted with tension. It appeared she was wrong in her assumptions.

She'd never considered how her actions might affect her neighbors. "I didn't mean to be a burden."

Mr. McCoy waved his hands in denial. "You're not a burden, lass. But if something were to happen to you, the missus and I would never forgive ourselves."

His pleading words tugged at her conscience. She pursed her lips, avoiding his pleading gaze. No one needed to worry about her. She'd been doing just fine on her own. Even with the addition of Rachel's birth and Jo's unfortunate accident, they'd gotten along well.

Of course, their continued self-reliance had a lot to do with Jack's help. He managed the work of three men.

"Look, Mrs. Cole, if something happens to you, your young'un is all by herself. What if it was you that took that tumble off the back steps? And no one was here to help you? That baby needs a mother. A father. It's time to do the right thing."

Elizabeth sniffled, blinking back tears. She thought she was doing the right thing. She *was* taking care of her child, maintaining the farm and the animals. Didn't anyone appreciate the time and energy she'd invested in running her household? Didn't they understand how much she needed a home? This home? Certainly Jack didn't empathize. And now her staunchest supporter, her dearest friends, were asking—no *telling*—her to leave.

"Ah, no," Mr. McCoy moaned. "Now don't go and do that. You're a fine mother and we all love you. It's because we think so highly of you that Mrs. McCoy wants to see you settled. The doc has a two-story house with leaded windows and everything."

"I'm sure he has a very nice house."

Relief swept across the large man's bearded face. "See, it's all settled now. The Ranger and I both agree."

Her spine stiffened. "Agree about what?"

"That you should move to town, find yourself a nice fellow with a private cistern." Ely slumped back into the chair, clutching his drooping head with both hands.

"A what?" She wasn't so much angry any more as confused.

"A private cistern for rainwater." Mr. McCoy massaged his fists over his eyes in tight circles. "But that doesn't matter. He's a fine-looking fellow and I'm sure this land will benefit someone else. Why you've got a pump right in the kitchen. No fetching water from the well."

Dawning understanding finally cleared her muddled thinking. Elizabeth had a good idea where this conversation was headed, and she didn't want to pursue the subject any longer. "Thank you so much for your concern. I'm so grateful to you and Mrs. McCoy for all that you've done. I'll do everything in my power to ease your worry."

She stood, forcing Mr. McCoy to rise.

"Excellent," he said. "Then it's all settled." Lifting his arm, Ely tugged back his sleeve to reveal a patch of red, flaky skin. "Say, when you see the doc, could you ask him what he thinks this might be?"

"Perhaps you'd best ask him yourself." Brushing at her skirts, she glanced out the back window. "Your boys appear to be starting a small fire. You might want to check on that."

"Yes, yes. Of course." Mr. McCoy rolled his sleeve

back into place. "It'll be nice to finally get a full night's sleep."

With a great yawn, he shuffled out the rear door, avoiding her eyes. Elizabeth followed his exit, then pressed her back against the closed door. Mr. McCoy's words rang in her ears.

So Jack Elder thought she should move to town and marry a man with his own cistern? *The nerve of him.*

Her blood simmered as she crossed to the bedroom to check on Rachel. The infant rested on the bed next to Jo. Will's trunk sat in the corner. Elizabeth straightened her back and stared.

She wasn't going to put off searching the contents of that trunk any longer. She'd break the lock if she had to.

She slanted a glance at Jo, relieved to note the girl couldn't see over the edge of the mattress. Elizabeth didn't know what she was going to find, but she didn't want anyone else looking.

"Jo, how do you and your family spend Sunday?"

Elizabeth gently tested the truck lid. The latch sprung free. Bemused, she sat back on her heels.

The bed support squeaked as Jo shifted. "We don't do anything much in the winter," the girl replied. "In the summer we go into town for church. Ma spit-shines the boys and browbeats them into submission. Afterward, we usually exchange pleasantries with the other families. Sometimes there's a potluck and Ma always brings her famous chocolate cake."

Elizabeth flipped up the trunk's sturdy black lid, disappointed to find a stack of neatly folded shirts. She'd expected to discover something much more flagrantly revealing. Perhaps that was why Will hadn't bothered to lock the trunk. He'd taken all the secrets with him. "Do you ever work around the farm?" she asked.

"No, sirree. The tradition around here is pretty strong. It's a day of rest."

Elizabeth bent her head with a sigh. She'd always worked on Sunday. Always. Growing up, the girls in the orphanage had never been allowed to take a day of rest. The work had never ended. "What if you didn't know about this tradition?"

"I suppose the Lord is more concerned with what you do once you've received His calling."

Elizabeth hadn't had a lot of choice in the matter growing up. In order to set a good example for Rachel, she'd conduct her life much differently. "You're very wise, Jo."

Gingerly lifting Will's shirt from the trunk, the stench of his overpowering cologne wafted out. Nausea rose in her throat. She thrust the shirt aside. A tissue-wrapped package fell to the floor. She carefully opened the bundle, astonished to find a familiar, bright gold tassel.

The decoration appeared to be the same one used to tie back the scarlet-velvet curtains on the Pullman car she and Will had taken across the country. Elizabeth thought back to that fateful trip. She'd been fascinated by her first train ride. The rail car had been sumptuous and opulent, a far cry from the stark plaster walls of the orphanage.

She'd oohed and aahed over every minuscule detail until a sharp rebuke from Will had spoiled her fun. He'd spent the rest of the trip cajoling her into a better mood, but his weak attempts had been filled with derision. He'd jovially mocked her, rubbing his cheek against the red-velvet curtains and playfully twirling the gold-threaded tassels like ropes. Yet despite his obvious contempt, he'd kept one of the decorations. Had even stored the memento in his trunk for sentimental reasons. Or had he planned on mocking her further? Confused by Will's purpose, she rewrapped the mysterious tassel.

"Jo, what sort of traditions does your family have for celebrating the Sabbath?"

"Ma usually makes a cold supper, and mostly we sit around and read the Bible. I know I shouldn't say this, but sometimes it's real boring. Still, it's nice not to have to work so hard one day of the week."

Elizabeth supposed young people looked at it differently, but a day filled with quiet contemplation sounded absolutely heavenly. She felt around the edges of the trunk, discovering a sheaf of papers stuffed into a side pocket.

She reluctantly tugged the stack loose and leafed through the pages. The documents had an official, aged look with browned edges and scrollwork writing. She separated one of the pages out for a closer look. Emblazed across the top was the word *Homestead*.

That was it? Paperwork showing the purchase of the land and outbuildings from the previous tenants?

"You still here?" Jo called from over the side of the bed.

"I was just going through some clothes."

Elizabeth tucked the documents into their snug pocket. All this time she'd been terrified of the trunk's contents, when there'd been nothing but clothes and paperwork inside. Jack was right again. She sure spent an awful lot of time worrying for nothing.

Jo shifted on the bed. "I sure hope my brothers don't accidentally burn the place down. That Abraham is a real firebug."

"Mmm-hmm," Elizabeth murmured, her thoughts distracted.

Will might have been a gambler, but he'd also worked. She had no reason to doubt the money used to purchase the outbuildings had come from anything but his railroad pay.

"My pa sure was interested in how much time you and that Ranger spend together. Alone. He musta grilled me for twenty minutes."

"That's nice."

If she sold the property and moved, the sheriff would find someone else to bother. She certainly wouldn't be marrying the doctor with his private cistern, but she'd have a modicum of security, nonetheless.

"Anyway, I told him not to worry. Told him the two of you mostly bickered and avoided each other."

Elizabeth dug deeper, pulling out a burlap sack with the initials W.F. stamped on the coarse, twill threads. She tugged the drawstring loose to reveal a wad of bills.

Her heart plummeted. She sat back on her heels with a sigh. Just what she needed—more money. She stuffed the bills back into the bag and shoved them into the bottom of the trunk. How could she use money gotten from dishonesty? Was she guilty by association?

"You're awful quiet," Jo called.

Elizabeth stood, brushing her hands together. Perhaps she'd donate the extra cash to the local church. "I think it's about time I started some traditions of my own. We have leftover turkey from yesterday. I'll make sandwiches and we can all eat together."

Jo scooted her legs to the edge of the bed, and gingerly set her feet on the floor. She clung to one of the bedposts until she gained her balance. "I think I'm going home with Pa tonight."

"Are you sure you can make the trip?"

Jo limped her way to the dresser. "You've been real nice and all, but I need to get home and help with chores."

The thought of caring for Rachel without Jo's gruff guidance left Elizabeth frozen with doubt. "JoBeth, the world is not going to come to a standstill without you."

"You, either."

Elizabeth started at the note of censure in Jo's voice.

The younger girl caught Elizabeth's gaze, her spruce-green eyes full of determination. "I can't be worried about you and my own family all at the same time. You know how much I love working over here, but I can't keep splitting my time."

Elizabeth folded her arms over her chest. "You don't have to help out. I don't want to be a burden to anyone."

She knew she was being childish, but finding the money had rattled her. What was the right thing to do?

"It's not that at all," Jo denied. "But I've done a lot of thinking since I've been laid up. If I'm at home, I feel like I should be here helping you out, and if I'm here, I feel like I should be at home."

Regret pierced Elizabeth's heart. She sympathized with Jo's confusion, and it pained her to acknowledge the part she'd played in Jo's turmoil. There was one way to ease everyone's fears.

"Don't you worry about a thing." Elizabeth smoothed the quilt and busied herself with fluffing the pillows. "You take care of your family. We'll be just fine."

"No, you won't." Jo limped over to lean on the bed. "Don't you see? We're already behind on all the chores, even with Jack's help."

Elizabeth visualized the papers in the trunk. The wad of bills in the burlap sack. "Well, there's good news for all of us. I'll be moving to town when the weather clears."

She'd be moving to town, but not to Cimarron Springs. The memories were too raw, and her late husband's reputation too vivid. She'd been a burden on the McCoys for too long. It was time to start over.

Chapter Thirteen

"If the three of you want to start a fire," Elizabeth patiently explained to the McCoy boys, "why don't you join Mr. Elder down by the creek bed? He's burning the wolves' bodies."

"Nah." David lifted one shoulder. "We already thought of that, but he said we had to stay ten paces away from the flames. What fun is that?"

Elizabeth blew out a long breath. Only one evening had passed with her unexpected company, yet she could no longer tolerate the raucous McCoy boys. After months of living in isolation, their rowdy behavior and incessant arguing had driven nails of pain into her skull.

She braced her hands on the scarred surface of the worktable. Removing the boys from the house was proving more difficult than she'd anticipated. "It's probably better that you stay in the house with the baby. Burning those carcasses is bound to be grisly and disgusting. And the stench." She wrinkled her nose. "I bet the stench is nauseating."

Though his arms remained in a stubborn knot over his chest, Abraham's head swiveled in her direction.

Elizabeth brushed aside the flapping ends of a freshly

laundered flour sack. The boys had been "helping" her with the laundry since first light, stringing sheets and nappies from a knotted rope stretched across the parlor. The constant commotion rattled her nerves. She'd felt nothing but relief when they'd disappeared halfway through the chore. Her solitude had been short-lived. They'd sheepishly returned with a basket full of Jack's shirts.

One of their pranks had gone amuck, and they'd drenched the Ranger's tidy laundry with coffee. After much begging and cajoling, Elizabeth had agreed to wash and iron the shirts as long as the boys promised to stay out of the bunkhouse—and muck out the barn stalls as punishment. All three had eagerly agreed to her terms. No one wanted to face the Ranger's wrath.

Unfortunately, they'd finished her punishment far too quickly. There wasn't enough muck to keep them busy all afternoon.

Elizabeth noted the spark of interest in Abraham's eyes at the thought of a potentially disgusting experience. "Watching the flames devour those carcasses is bound to be quite foul," she continued. "Best you boys avoid such a disturbing task."

David sat up straighter, his face bright with anticipation. "Do you think there's gonna be blood?"

"Buckets."

The ensuing stampede of young McCoys nearly bowled her over. She watched their mad dash across the clearing toward the creek bed with weary resignation before licking her finger to test the iron's heat with a sharp sizzle. A better person might have felt remorse for hoisting the boys off on the unsuspecting Ranger, but in the quiet solitude of the still cabin, Elizabeth decided she was *not* a better person. Idle hands gave the McCoy boys far too much opportunity to think up new trouble. Keeping their fertile imaginations occupied kept them out of trouble.

Rachel cooed and smiled, kicking her tiny sock-clad feet free of her blanket.

"I'll never understand boys," Elizabeth spoke to the smiling baby. "Why would they choose to spend the day at such a repulsive task when there's a darling little sweetie to be fussed over?"

Rachel caught her hands together, exclaiming in delight at her trick. Each day brought new wonders. Elizabeth marked each milestone with awe—Rachel's annoyed grimace when the bathwater was too cold, her wide-eyed delight when Jack lifted her in the air above his head while Elizabeth fretted. She'd become so attuned to her daughter, she often woke in the wee hours of the night, straining to hear the soft flutter of Rachel's breathing.

Even mundane chores took on a new significance as Elizabeth toiled to create a perfect home. She hadn't thought she was capable of experiencing such a deep, abiding love, such depth of pride and affection. Caring for the newborn had unleashed wells of soul-aching emotion. To her dismay, with the diamond-sharp feelings came an unexpected fear, the realization that love came with the uncertainty of loss.

Elizabeth pressed her cheek against Rachel's. "Do you know what I read in the Bible last night? 'For I know the thoughts that I think toward you, saith the Lord, thoughts of peace, and not of evil, to give you an expected end.' I think that means the Lord has plans for us to prosper. What do you think?"

Rachel gurgled in reply. Elizabeth shrugged and returned to her task. In truth, she didn't mind ironing. The chore was pleasant and warm in the winter's cold, and watching the wrinkles melt away from the crisp cotton gave her a rare sense of accomplishment. She hummed a merry tune, flashing cheerful smiles at Rachel in her basket. For reasons she couldn't explain, her mood had lightened, her smile was more at the ready.

Beneath her protective gaze, the baby's face screwed up and grew a brilliant shade of red. Moments later a distinct odor drifted from the basket.

Elizabeth set the iron aside with a resigned sigh, then reached for the smiling infant. "You seem awfully proud of yourself for such a dubious accomplishment."

With practiced care Elizabeth changed the nappy, and stepped out the rear door to rinse out the soiled cotton. She returned inside, startled to smell the faint scent of something burning.

She bolted to the stove, relieved to find nothing out of place. She glanced around and gasped in horror at the source of the pungent odor. The iron had slipped from its trivet and onto Jack's laundered shirt. Heart pounding, she darted across the room and grasped the rag-wrapped handle. To her horror, a black triangle darkened Jack's shirt.

Jo limped into the room, dressed in her usual drab, oversize boy's clothes. "You burning something in here?"

"Just the usual." Elizabeth instinctively stuffed the ruined shirt into the extra laundry basket at her feet.

"It's good to see you up and about," Elizabeth said to cover her furtive movements, her voice a touch shrill.

"I'm not up to racing speed."

Though Jo still walked with a distinct limp and a permanent grimace, her wounds were healing well. Mr. McCoy had decided to delay his trip home until today in order to give his daughter plenty of time to rest before the grueling ride through heavy snow atop the McCoy's sturdy draft horse.

Jo leaned heavily on the table. "I feel like I've been run over by a stampede of buffalo. It's good to be up, though. Thought I'd go check on the boys."

"I've sent them down to help Mr. Elder."

"Now that was downright cruel. What did that man ever do to you?"

Elizabeth quirked an eyebrow.

"I guess he had it coming." Jo took a hesitant step forward, resting her weight gingerly on her injured foot. "As long as he has his gun, I'm sure he'll be fine."

Elizabeth wiped the sweat-dampened hair from her forehead with the back of her hand. "They're not bad children. Just full of energy."

"You're too soft." Jo leaned over and adjusted the eyelet-lace bonnet covering Rachel's head. "Looks like her peach fuzz is falling out. I bet she's going to be a blonde, just like you." Jo touched her own dark braid with a forlorn sigh. "Jenny at school says the boys prefer curly blond hair."

Elizabeth slanted a curious glance at the younger girl. "Any boy worth his salt is more interested in a girl's heart than the hair on her head."

"Don't matter none to me, anyway. I'm never gettin' married."

Elizabeth grinned. The heated denial was telling. "You might change your mind later."

"I doubt it." Jo straightened. "Would you ever get married again?"

Unbidden, an image of Jack flashed into Elizabeth's mind. She blinked the affectionate memory away. "We weren't talking about me. We were talking about you.

Someday you just might meet someone who makes you change your mind."

"Well, I ain't met him yet, that's for sure."

Jo wrapped her serviceable coat around her slim shoulders. "Why did you marry Will?"

Elizabeth rested the iron on the trivet, giving it a shake to ensure it was secure, then adjusted Jo's collar. "Because he was the first man to notice me. I was in love with the idea of love. I just wanted to belong someplace, to someone."

"*We* love you. You always have a family with us. And you're never alone in God's love."

Elizabeth blinked. "I didn't know that then. I do now."

She worried over the dropping temperature until the younger girl practically shouted in frustration.

"I'm fine," Jo declared. "Now stop fussing."

"I'm sorry. It's just that I feel responsible. If you'd been home with your family instead of here with me, you wouldn't have been hurt."

"If I'd have been home with the boys, they probably would have pushed me down the steps. By accident, of course."

"They'd never harm you on purpose!" Elizabeth suspected the McCoy household was a good deal more hazardous than her own. "Just promise me you'll be careful. I've had enough of accidents and disasters to last a lifetime."

"Well, don't have any more children," Jo snorted ruefully. "And especially don't have any boys."

The two of them laughed as Jo stuffed her battered slouch hat over her ears and limped out the rear door. Elizabeth leaned over the sink to track her painful progress to the barn. Smoke from Jack's fire floated in the distance, curling above the treetops into the overcast sky.

Recalling his quick kiss before they'd dashed across the clearing, she pressed her fingers to her lips.

She'd lain awake wondering what he meant by the gesture. Hours later, she'd finally decided the kiss meant nothing. She should have been relieved, but instead, she'd spent a restless night tossing and turning. Her thoughts had lingered on each of their encounters, from the first moment he'd stormed into her life, until the moment he'd risked his life to save her mangy barn cat from the wolf's sharp teeth.

Perhaps living in town wouldn't be so bad, after all.

Without Jo or the boys, and with Rachel sleeping soundly, the house felt eerily silent. Elizabeth finished up the last of the ironing and put away all the laundry. Everything except Jack's blackened shirt.

The baby woke from her nap, fed contently in the cradle of Elizabeth's arms, and promptly fell back asleep. After tidying the house, Elizabeth set about making another batch of kolaches. Jack had enjoyed the pastries earlier. She folded the blackened shirt and placed it atop the pile in the laundry basket at her feet.

Her experience with Will had taught her that men could be awfully particular about their belongings. She'd just about convinced herself that everything was going to be fine, when Jack stepped through the front door.

She whirled around, spilling a glass of milk.

"I'm hiding from the McCoy boys." He glanced furtively over one shoulder. "They had that little one tied to a chair this morning. Lord help me, but I don't know how those three are still alive and kicking."

Elizabeth sopped up the advancing spill. She'd been thinking the same thing earlier. "I believe they were playing outlaws and Texas Rangers when they tied David to the chair. Perhaps you should take that as a compliment."

"They were playing 'who can make the most noise.'"

A sudden thought had her glancing out the back window into the clear afternoon sky. "You didn't leave them tending the fire alone, did you?"

His eyes widened. "Not hardly. I had them crack through the ice in the creek and carry buckets back to douse the flames. They won't be able to start a fire in that spot unless we get ourselves a hundred years' drought. And I should be dead and buried by then."

She laughed, but the sight of his folded shirts in the basket at her feet dimmed her joy. "I've made kolaches."

"I thought I smelled something tasty."

Her attention snagged on the laundry basket.

He followed her furtive gaze. "Say, are those my shirts? You didn't have to wash them."

"Actually, I did." Her knuckles white, she laid two plates on the dining table. "The McCoy boys were in the bunkhouse pretending to be soldiers when one of them decided to dare the other two to drink coffee. Turned out the brew wasn't as appetizing as they'd supposed. One of them spit a whole mouthful over your shirts."

Jack scowled. "Well, I hope they're the ones who cleaned up the mess."

"Yes and no. I sent them to the barn to muck out all the stalls."

"I suppose that helps. But it still sticks in my craw that they made you wash up after them."

"I don't mind. Except. Well." She pulled her lower lip between her teeth. "Except there was an accident."

She lifted his ruined shirt with stiff, numb fingers.

He frowned in confusion. "What's wrong?"

"Well…" She gathered her courage and handed him the shirt.

Dawning awareness spread across his face as he unfurled the cotton to reveal the singed triangle. To her burgeoning relief, he appeared more confused than angry.

Then his face hardened, and his lips twisted into a thin, white line. "You have a scar. A triangle on your forearm. I saw it that day in the barn. Show me your arm."

Elizabeth felt the blood drain from her face. She backed away, bumping against the stove. "Wh-what?"

He advanced toward her with relentless determination. Fear warred with her disappointment. She'd thought he was different. He stepped closer. She flung up her arms to cover her face.

He grasped her arm and tugged her sleeve until he revealed the arrowhead scar on her arm. "There's no way this was an accident. I can tell by the placement. Who did this to you?"

Elizabeth reached to cover the mark, but he brushed her hand aside.

She ran the tip of her tongue over her parched lips. "None of your business."

He angled his head, forcing her to meet his gaze. "You cower away from me like a whipped dog. I've never hurt you, not once. Someone did this on purpose."

She shook her head, tears of shame welling in her eyes. "Why?"

The question felt more like an apology, and she couldn't bare the pity in his voice. "It wasn't his fault. Will was usually quite kind. He'd come home from his job tired and hurt. He'd been drinking. He wasn't the same."

"Did that happen often?"

"No, of course not."

"I'm not a fool, Elizabeth."

She twisted away. "None of this is your concern."

"Elizabeth." He rested his hand on her shoulder, the

sensation heavy and comforting. "You can't hide out here forever. You're trapped by your own fears."

The warmth of his hand steadied her. "Don't be silly. Living out here all alone is more frightening than anything I've ever done before." She bit out a humorless laugh.

"You're afraid of yourself. Afraid of getting close to people."

"Now you're being foolish."

He brushed his thumb against the bare skin of her neck. Elizabeth shivered.

"It's not just the things that happen to us that keep us awake at night," Jack said. "It's the part we played in our own mistakes. I've rescued people over the years, and you know what haunts them? They can't let go of their own infallibility. They obsess over every detail, every perceived mistake. They can't let go of the past, asking themselves why they didn't trust their instincts, retracing their actions, questioning their decisions. You have to stop blaming yourself."

Her throat tightened. "I don't blame myself."

"You're lying."

Her eyes burned, but she ruthlessly blinked away the tears. She'd traveled to Kansas full of foolish dreams and false hopes. At some point during the journey, she'd stopped living in the present and pinned all her hopes on the future. *Everything will be different when...* How many times had she repeated those words? Even now, she was trapped in her dreams of the future. *Everything will be different in the spring. Everything will be different when the snow clears. Everything will be different when...*

She tipped her head to the side, pressing her cheek against Jack's knuckles.

"Look at me," he pleaded.

Though her heart ached, she lifted her head and shrugged off his hand. This growing dependency on Jack had to stop. He was leaving. Soon. The more she came to rely on his help, the more she came to crave his touch, the harder their parting would be. To Jack, she was simply an obstacle to his case. For her, he'd come to mean a great deal more.

Busying herself at the stove, she wiped down the cast-iron surface, carefully arranging her pots and utensils for supper. "I need to check on the baby. Jo sewed the most atrocious rag doll, but Rachel just adores the horrible thing...."

She didn't resist when he pulled her into his arms. He was warm and strong, a balm to her aching heart.

"Tell me about him."

"I'd rather not," she spoke, her words muffled in the smooth leather of his black vest. "Living in the past is a dull and lonely business."

He set her back, his hands still clasping her shoulders. The distance separating them felt like an ever widening chasm.

His hand glided through her hair. "'Let us therefore cast off the works of darkness, and let us put on the armour of light.'"

She inhaled the scent of wood fire on his shirt, pungent, familiar and comforting.

He sighed. "Sometimes the only way to bury the past is to pull it out into the open first."

The baby whimpered.

Relieved to focus her attention on something else, Elizabeth turned away to pick up Rachel and hug her close. "I don't know if that's such a good idea."

"Maybe it's the best idea."

She gently bounced the baby on her shoulder. "I'll think about it."

Will was the father of her child. Her husband. She'd cared for him once. Gossiping about him to a stranger felt like a betrayal of his memory—a betrayal of her daughter.

She pressed Rachel into the hollow of her neck. The baby cooed and rooted at her cheek. The infant's trust, the unabashed joy she showed at even the simplest activities lent Elizabeth courage. Perhaps she *had* been too hard on herself.

Living in the past might be a dull and lonely business, but wallowing in the present was no better. Maybe she should take up Jack on his offer and purge herself of all the bitter memories. Maybe then she could concentrate on the good times she'd shared with her late husband. He was her past, and it was time to concentrate on the future.

Jack regretted asking her to share this glimpse into her past, even while he hungered for knowledge about her life. To his surprise, she'd offered only a token resistance before she'd started talking. Though his heart ached, he forced himself to listen. After all, he'd asked for this—begged her to tell him about her past.

He didn't dare question his need to understand what her life had been like, how she had arrived on this Kansas homestead. Even the tiniest details haunted him. He woke up each morning with her image crowding his thoughts. The way her hair curled around the temples, the way she chewed on a thumbnail when she was nervous.

Watching her care for Rachel enchanted him. Mother and daughter shared a special bond, a secret communication that intrigued him. There was even a familiarity in the way they smiled.

He'd put off taking the steel box and its curious mix

of watches and rings into town because he wanted to avoid the truth. He'd stayed one more day just to catch a glimpse of the widow smiling.

She wasn't smiling now, and he was the cause of her somber mood. She kept her back turned while she worked at the stove. "I told you before about how my father opened a bakery in New York. He had difficulty supporting us after the shop burned down. We moved several times, but the work was never steady. Then one day he didn't come home. We waited for days. He'd never done anything like that before. Some fisherman discovered his body in the river."

Jack yearned to comfort her, but she kept her back turned, scrubbing at the black cast-iron surface of the stove as if she might rub away the memories, as well.

"My mother wasn't well. She'd taken ill on the ship from England, and I don't think she ever fully recovered. The conditions on board were foul. People died every day. We considered ourselves lucky to have survived the trip at all. Anyway, after my father died, she grew worse." Elizabeth paused, he studied her profile, her bleak expression. "I tried to hide her illness from the other tenants in the building, I tried to take care of her myself, but one day the nuns from the orphanage showed up and took me away."

Her revelations gave him insight into her character. She'd fought to care for her mother alone, just as she fought to remain on the homestead, alone. She considered self-sufficiency a virtue.

"Did you ever see your mother again?"

"Once." Elizabeth swiped at her nose with a sniffle. "She was very ill. She asked me to forgive her for letting them take me to that awful place."

Bitter resentment laced her words.

"You can't blame yourself for something that happened when you were a child."

Elizabeth shook her head. "I was so angry, I refused to forgive her. She died before I could tell her I was sorry." She pressed her hands to her cheeks. "I'm an awful person and God has punished me for it."

Jack leaped out of his chair and crossed the distance in two steps. He turned her to face him and clasped her shoulders. The anguish in her pale blue eyes humbled him. Without a second thought, he cradled her in his embrace.

Watching her suffer unleashed a fierce protective instinct within him. "God loves you. The Lord doesn't punish people, Elizabeth."

She sobbed into his vest. "You're wrong. He does. He took away my mother. He took away Will."

Her late husband didn't sound like much of a loss, but Jack held his tongue. "That's not the way it works."

She strained away, not quite meeting his eyes. "Will was handsome and charming. I'd never had anyone notice me before. I was overwhelmed by the attention. And he never seemed to want for money. I liked that he bought me things. It had been so long since I'd had anything nice. He made me feel special. Like I mattered to someone."

The walls closed in around Jack. His lungs hurt from the effort to breathe. "You're loving and kind. You're a hard worker. I can see why he wanted to marry you."

She snorted softly. "It was a whirlwind courtship. I worked for a baker and he didn't like Will hanging around the shop all the time. He gave me the sack. I didn't have any place else to go. Will took me to the courthouse that morning and we were married. A few hours later we were on a Pullman car headed West. Everything happened so fast, I didn't have time to consider what I was doing, or where I was going."

Jack forced himself to think like a Ranger instead of an infatuated fool. She was vulnerable, but she was also part of his case. The more she revealed about her late husband, the more convinced he became of the man's guilt. "Why did Will risk his life the night he died? The sheriff said the creek bed had almost washed out."

"He was leaving me." Her chin tilted up a notch. "I'd told him about the baby the day before. He was angry. He didn't want the responsibility of children."

Jack seethed with impotent rage. The source of his fury was beyond justice, beyond vengeance. "Yet he married you, brought you all the way to Kansas and bought this homestead. What did he think was going to happen?"

"I think he wanted to do a lot of things, he just didn't have the courage to see them through. I was like a toy to him." Her lips twisted into a sad smile. "Will bored easily with toys. He was bored with me almost from the beginning."

"You didn't do anything wrong. The sin lies with your husband. He took a vow to stay with you, and he broke his promise to God. What happened up on that creek bed was an accident."

"It's just that every time I pray, things seem to turn out wrong. I prayed for a husband, and God sent me Will. I prayed for a child, and my husband deserted me rather than care for his growing family. I prayed for Will's return, and God sent me his body to bury." She ducked her head. "I'm afraid to pray any more. For anything."

Jack tucked his knuckles beneath Elizabeth's chin and gently forced her to look at him. Tears swam in her eyes, darkening the pale blue color. "The Lord knows what's in your heart."

"That's what I'm afraid of," she whispered. "I'm not pure of heart."

"No one is. We can't change the past, but we can make a better future. It's where you're going in your faith that counts, not where you've been."

Jack should know that better than anyone. He'd spent his entire life searching for justice, but evil still walked the earth.

She pressed closer. Voices sounded outside, indicating the return of the McCoy boys. Jack made a sound of frustration in his throat. He and the widow had unfinished business, and he was determined to settle things before he left. With the homestead overrun by McCoy boys, finding a quiet moment was going to be difficult.

At the sound of footsteps nearing the house, she pulled away from him. "Thank you, for everything. I'm all right now."

She swiped at her eyes.

"We can finish this conversation later."

"There's no need. I'm perfectly fine."

Any fool could see she was lying.

Jack was no fool.

Jack hated being right sometimes. He kicked another stump into place. The McCoys, sensing his dark mood, were giving him a wide berth. They were helping their father build a new ladder for the loft.

He touched his cheek where Elizabeth had brushed her thumb against his skin. He'd been mule-kicked all right.

Ely McCoy was correct. Elizabeth needed to be protected. She needed to marry a nice man who wanted a family. Jack recalled all the bachelors in town who had offered for her hand. No wonder she'd been reluctant to accept a proposal after her husband's death. She probably feared a repeat of her first marriage.

Doc Johnsen was a good choice for a husband. He held a respected job. He was handsome and intelligent, everything Elizabeth could ask for in a man. Yet she'd refused his offer of marriage once before. No doubt she was gunshy after her first experience. Perhaps if she moved to town and they courted properly, she'd change her mind.

Jack forced himself to imagine the two of them together, the widow and Doc Johnsen. Elizabeth deserved better than a rat like Will Cole. How much more was there? How much had she left out about her life?

At least the doc worked around Cimarron Springs. He wouldn't be traipsing all over the country, leaving her alone for weeks at time.

Jack swung the ax. The thought of Elizabeth married to another man tore at his insides. He swiped at his forehead with the back of his hand. What other choice did he have? He'd told Ely the truth. He wasn't husband material. If Jack wasn't going to care for her, Doc Johnsen was a good choice. She was too beautiful, too fragile beneath her bravado to be left all alone. And Rachel needed a father. Someone to dandle her on his knee and shoo the boys away when she grew older.

The next crack of the ax split the three-foot stump clean in half.

"You okay, Ranger?" Ely spoke from behind him.

"Swell."

Jack resumed his attack on the hapless stump.

"I can't wait to get home to the missus," Ely spoke loud enough to be heard over Jack's steady *thwack-thwack-thwack*. "I'm telling you. When I was younger, I never once thought about settling down. Then I saw

Mrs. McCoy in the mercantile. She was picking out a pair of white cotton gloves."

Jack glanced over his shoulder. "Does this story have a point?"

"Sometimes I get stuck on a goal. And when I can't achieve that goal, I start to thinking that there's no way out." Ely tugged a fragile white cotton glove from his pocket. "I look at this, and I know nothing else matters."

Jack turned his back on Ely's somber gaze.

He was doing the right thing. He always did the right thing. "There's a pile of brush over by the creek bed. If we clear it out today, the widow will have enough kindling for the rest of the winter."

"Takes more than a fire to keep a body warm some days."

"I know what I'm doing."

"I hope you do." Ely sighed. "You can't punish a dead man, and you're not going to get another chance to make this right."

Jack thought of Bud Shaw. With Will Cole dead, Elizabeth was his only chance at discovering the truth. "I ran out of chances a long time ago."

Chapter Fourteen

"Jo." Elizabeth glanced up from settling the last loaf of bread dough in a pan to rise. "Can I get your help in the bunkhouse before you leave?"

"I don't know if we're ever going to leave now," Jo replied. "Pa and Mr. Elder are down by the creek bed pulling up a stack of brush for firewood."

Elizabeth rolled her eyes. "Will started that project last spring. He piled a mountain of brush in one spot, and then lost interest. I don't ever recall seeing him work so hard."

"Musta been hard on those girly hands of his."

"JoBeth McCoy!"

The girl stuck out her tongue. "Don't you go scolding me. That man wasn't good for anything but telling tall tales and keeping the saloon in business. I'm glad he's gone."

Elizabeth pressed the heels of her hands to her ears. "Don't say that. Don't ever say that."

She didn't want permission to think ill of Rachel's father. She'd made her own peace, hadn't she? The sound of his name barely stirred feelings of regret in her chest. Yet she worried the sins of the father might rest on Rachel's tiny shoulders. The baby was innocent of Will's wrongdoing, and speaking ill of the dead wasn't going to solve anything.

Jo's smile faded. "I didn't mean to upset you, Mrs. Cole. You said we were going to the bunkhouse?"

"I'm sorry. I've been emotional ever since the baby was born. I hope I never have to cry over something real, because I've used up all my tears." Elizabeth concentrated on draping towels over the rising dough. "Mr. Elder was searching for bank robbers when he arrived here. I've read all the newspaper accounts, and I keep feeling like there's something I'm missing. He's got his clippings tacked to the bunkhouse wall. Maybe if we put our heads together, we can figure out what's bothering me."

Jo passed Elizabeth a wet rag. "I'm not sure if I can help, but it's better than keeping the boys out of mischief all afternoon."

After wiping her hands clean, Elizabeth tugged her apron strings loose. She plucked Rachel's rag doll from a shelf and handed it to the smiling baby. Chubby hands grasped the soft material and pulled it into her mouth.

Elizabeth grimaced at the odd toy. Two mismatched arms jutted from the overly round body. A pair of sausage legs strained at the seams. Offset eyes perched above a button nose and cross-stitch mouth. Elizabeth found the resulting combination of uneven stitching gruesome, but Jo had labored for days over the project, and the baby adored her new toy.

"Let's go, then," Elizabeth said, forcing determination into her voice.

She snuck a glance at the clock ticking on the mantel. They didn't have much time before the men finished their chores. An hour at most.

Together she and Jo crossed the clearing, their attention drawn to the blood-streaked snow. Elizabeth adjusted Rachel's laundry basket on her hip, careful not to disturb the warm blanket stretched over the top to keep out the cold. They paused in front of the bunkhouse door.

Jo lingered on the porch. "Feels wrong to go inside without Mr. Elder here."

Elizabeth took firm hold of the doorknob. "This is my home, and Mr. Elder is an uninvited visitor. There's nothing wrong with the two of us entering *my* property."

As she breezed into the building, anxiety at odds with her brave words tightened in her chest. Elizabeth sucked in a lungful of air. There was no reason to feel like an interloper in her own home. "See, there's no reason to feel uncomfortable."

Jo followed with a resigned shrug. Elizabeth set the basket on the nearest bunk, almost tripping over a pile of neatly stacked wood on the floor.

Jo nudged the pile with her square-toed boot. "What do you suppose this is?"

"Firewood?"

"I don't think so." Jo knelt for a closer look. "He's cut and sanded all the pieces. Looks like he's going to build something."

Elizabeth plucked a length of wood from the stack. Someone, Jack she presumed, had painstakingly carved a pattern of ivy into the sanded piece. "Why on earth is he in here whittling? It's not like he can carry something so large when he leaves."

Angling another piece of wood to one side to catch the light, Jo leaned in. "I guess maybe he's bored."

Suddenly exhausted, Elizabeth slumped on the bed next to Rachel. She wasn't the sort to keep a man's attention riveted. The pile of wood might as well be stacked to the ceiling for all the excitement she provided.

Had she made a mistake in confiding in Jack? Even

though they were destined to part, she wanted him to see her differently. She wanted him to enjoy her company.

She stuck out her lower lip and blew a breath, ruffling the hair resting on her forehead. He'd listened to her tale of life with her late husband, his expression somber and closed. She'd thought he was concerned, now she realized he was indifferent. Who wanted to spend time with a sniveling woman lamenting her life?

She didn't know what he thought about her checkered history, and she didn't want to find out. Revealing her past had been cathartic, but the truth of her own accountability had made her sick inside. No matter what happened, she was through making foolish, impulsive choices. From this moment on, she'd think before she acted. She wasn't the only one affected by her decisions.

Jo moved across the room to peer at the newspaper clippings. "These are all railroad towns." She glanced at Elizabeth while she jerked a thumb at the wall. "You think the outlaws bought tickets like regular folks? How funny is that? Maybe they just rode into town like carpetbaggers, robbed the bank, then climbed right back on the train with the money."

"Don't be silly." Elizabeth flashed a grin at the mental image of bandanna-clad men lugging tattered satchels overflowing with money onto a fancy Pullman car. "Someone would recognize them."

"I don't know." Jo rubbed her chin, lost in thought. "The best place to hide is in plain sight. I can always fool the younger boys with that one. People see what they expect to see, not what's really there."

Once again, something struck Elizabeth as familiar about one of the outlaws. "Jo, do you recognize this fellow?"

The younger girl grimaced. "They all look the same to me."

Elizabeth's shoulders slumped. They *did* all look the same. The artist hadn't given the men much detail. She traced her finger along the towns Jack had underlined. The names were all familiar, but Will had been a railroad man. Of course he'd mentioned the names of the towns. She squinted, forcing a pattern to emerge in the dates or the routes the outlaws had taken.

Jo studied one of the reports, her nose inches from the paper. The type had nearly rubbed off with repeated handling. "As far as I can tell from this account, the people who lost out most were the saloon owners. I mean, they certainly complained the loudest. Says here they were counting on all those railroad boys getting their money and spending it on liquor." She planted her hands on her hips. "I bet one of them railroad boys stole that money. They'd have known the bank was going to have extra cash for payroll."

A railroad man. Elizabeth ran her gaze along the neatly displayed clippings, taking in the sketched picture of the bank. A sickening dread pooled in her stomach. She recalled the burlap sack in the bottom of Will's trunk. The initials W.F.

The last bank robbed had been a Wells Fargo. The bank where the outlaws murdered Jack's sister-in-law.

She backed away from the truth, physically and mentally, desperate to deny the evidence. Just because Will had worked for the railroad didn't make him an outlaw. His money had come from gambling. A lot of men supplemented their income by playing cards. Will was only violent with people weaker than him. She didn't see him storming into a bank. Towns sprouting up around the rail lines were teeming with unscrupulous people desperate for money.

There was no reason to believe Will had earned his extra income any other way. "Everybody in that town knew the railroad payday. For all we know, one of the saloon owners stole the money."

Considering the motives of transient workers eased Elizabeth's tension.

"Yes, but look at this." Jo motioned to one of the yellowed clippings.

Elizabeth reluctantly leaned forward.

"See." Jo pointed to an article farther down in the paper. "The railroad was building a mighty large bridge. Says here the area swelled by almost two hundred men. And here, look at this. They were digging a tunnel straight through the mountainside. That brought almost three hundred men to town. And where this last robbery took place, the railroad was laying new line through some rough terrain. That's gotta bring in almost a hundred men."

Jo pursed her lips, her expression thoughtful. "You know what I think?"

"No," Elizabeth replied weakly.

"First off, all these robberies took place when there was a big railroad project in the works."

The idea that had been nagging Elizabeth suddenly took shape. She grasped for an innocent explanation. "So you think transient workers robbed those banks?"

"Nah." Jo shook her head. "I think it was someone looking for a bank with lots of money. See here." She pointed to the rail schedule at the bottom of the page. "Payday isn't until the fifteenth, right? But the train doesn't run until the sixteenth. Only there was a rockslide, which set the schedule back another two days. That meant the money came in late, on the eighteenth. Look at the date the bank was robbed."

"The eighteenth," Elizabeth whispered over the blood pounding in her ears.

"Whoever planned those robberies knew plenty about the railroad. They knew the schedules, they knew what projects were being built, and they knew the payroll dates. This new line here was scheduled to start on the twentieth. There's a notice about the ribbon-cutting ceremony, but the robbery took place a week before the work started."

Hope flapped its delicate butterfly wings in Elizabeth's chest. "Then the pattern doesn't work. Someone who worked for the railroad would know there was no extra money in the safe."

Jo grinned from ear to ear. "'Course the pattern still works. Says here there was a brawl the day before the robbery. According to this article, the men arrived a week before the ribbon-cutting. Whoever robbed that Wells Fargo knew the men were coming into town early. He also knew they'd be receiving a stipend for living expenses before their first paycheck."

The butterfly wings ceased flapping. "A stipend?"

"Yep. They paid my Uncle Pete a whole paycheck in advance when he moved to St. Louis. Called it stipend."

Elizabeth's stomach flipped.

"It's all right there in the type," Jo continued. "The fellow that planned these robberies was no construction worker. He was a fellow whose hands never got dirty. Sending a telegraph to the Santa Fe rail offices would give Jack a few names. It wouldn't take much to piece things together after that. Just figure out who was running those projects. Simple as pie."

Spots formed in the corners of Elizabeth's vision. She

sank weakly onto the cot next to Rachel. "He's a smart man, Mr. Elder. I'm sure he's already thought of that."

Her late husband had never dirtied his hands with anything but dollar bills. He'd never been talkative about his job, but his fingers had always been covered in ink stains. He oversaw the movements of workers, or something along those lines. Elizabeth rubbed her temples, desperate to refute the evidence. Yet everything made sense. Will's absences, his endless supply of money. The wads of bills he'd left behind.

Her husband had been a bank robber.

"I see your point." Jo tapped her forehead. "Even the Ranger's not that dumb. 'Course, they were probably looking for someone on site. A foreman or a laborer. What if it was a paper pusher? Didn't Will do something like that?"

"He scheduled trains and work crews."

"You all right, Mrs. Cole?" Jo asked. "You've gone real pale."

"I'm fine, Jo. It's nothing."

Perhaps Will's involvement had been periphery. He never even shot game, could he have shot an actual flesh-and-blood person? A sharp pain throbbed behind her eyes. Had the outlaws blackmailed Will into giving them information about the railroad schedule?

"Look here," Jo exclaimed. "A deputy even shot one of the outlaws in the leg. Sounds like those boys weren't very good at their job."

"When was that?"

"Looks like the end of May."

Elizabeth unconsciously touched the scar on her arm. The shooting had occurred just prior to Will's return from Colorado. He'd been angry and out of sorts. And hurt.

He'd been limping because he'd injured his leg.

Her husband was the fourth outlaw.

What did it matter now? Will was dead. His justice was in heaven.

Jack was searching for Bud Shaw when he should have been looking for both Will Cole *and* Bud Shaw. Why reveal her discovery at this point? Her husband was beyond revealing his secrets. She certainly didn't know where to find Bud Shaw, and Will was gone.

How had she missed the signs of Will's activities? The truth had been obvious. *I've made excuses for him all along, that's why.* The first time he'd appeared outside the bakery to accompany her to the market, he'd walked a half pace ahead of her the entire distance. Even from the beginning he'd been leaving her behind. She'd made excuses for him from the start—instead of trusting her instincts.

Jack trusted his instincts.

She chanced a glance at Rachel chewing contentedly on her rag doll. The baby studied her surroundings with wise, solemn eyes. As Will's wife, what were the consequences for Elizabeth, for her child? If the sheriff could seize her land because of Will's cheating, what would he do if he discovered Will was an outlaw?

She stumbled out the bunkhouse door into the sunlight, blinking her eyes against the bright afternoon.

Jo followed her outside. "You don't look good."

"I just needed some air. Go back inside." She needed time to collect her thoughts, to make decisions for her and Rachel's future.

Instead, Jo brushed past her and loped down the shallow stairs. "Say, are you cooking something again? There's smoke coming from the house."

Plumes of smoke billowed from the window across the way. Elizabeth's heart leaped into her throat. An acrid smell teased her senses. She gripped the porch rail. "Stay with the baby!"

Desperate to retrieve her homestead documents, she lifted the hem of her skirts and ran. If the house burned to the ground, she still had the bunkhouse and the barn. But without those papers, she had no way of proving ownership. She bolted up the stairs and jerked open the door. A wall of hot air singed her cheeks. She threw her arm over her face against the advancing black cloud and dashed through the kitchen. Fire licked at the parlor walls. Flickering orange sparks danced behind thick heat waves.

Lungs burning, she felt her way to the bedroom, then slammed the door behind her, blocking the worst of the acrid smoke. She plunged forward and smacked her hip against the dresser. Rubbing at the painful sting, she knelt before Will's trunk and tugged on the handle.

A gray cloud curled beneath the door and snaked up the walls while she searched. Her eyes and nose watered. She frantically dug through Will's clothes until she located the sheaf of papers. Clutching the precious documents to her chest, she surged to her feet. With the room enveloped in a thick haze, she blindly groped her way back to the exit.

As she touched the brass knob, fiery pain enveloped her hand.

Glass shattered to her left.

Jack slapped the rump of the sturdy work horse hitched to the enormous stump he and Ely were struggling to pry from the ditch. "We're almost there."

The winds had picked up, whipping at the branches and driving dust into his eyes.

Ely McCoy tugged on the harness, his massive biceps bulging as sweat trickled down the side of his bearded face. The horse's forelegs stumbled to find purchase at the top of the rise. The animal tipped and bucked the next ten feet, dragging the stump over the crest before jerking to a halt.

Ely collapsed onto the ground, resting his elbows on his bent knees. "I'd like to dig up that fool Will Cole and give him a piece of my mind. Then I'd bury him back down again."

Jack slapped his hat against his thigh. A cloud of dust billowed from the brim. "I'm not sure how that's going to help us clear this brush."

"Why on earth does a man go to all the trouble of piling trees at the most impassable dip in the creek bed?"

"I dunno. Maybe he was letting the wood dry. This area is protected from flood. The waterline doesn't go up the embankment this far."

"It's still an idiotic place to gather brush. Why not just drag the branches up the shallow side?" Ely pressed a hand to his knee and surged to his feet. "That man didn't have the sense God gave a dandelion."

While Jack couldn't help but agree, he kept his own council. "Either way, we've cleared out most of the brush. One or two more trips and the pile will be cleared. The extra wood should keep the widow set through spring."

"If I live that long." Ely squinted into the distance. "Say, that's awful thick smoke coming from the house."

Jack glanced up from his stooped position down the embankment from where Ely stood. Dark gray tendrils lapped at the sky before blustery wind scattered the curling plumes. "Looks like chimney smoke to me. Nothing unusual about that."

Jack grasped a bundle of branches and tugged. The pile loosened, sending him stumbling back. He flailed his arms to catch his balance. After bracing his feet against the frozen earth, he straightened, then arched, pressing his fists against a tight muscle in his back. His gaze snagged on a dark hollow revealed by the brush he'd just hauled aside.

Crouching, Jack peered into the dark entrance of what appeared to be shallow cave.

"Mr. Elder," Ely called.

Jack glanced over his shoulder. "What is it?"

"I think those boys have gone and started a bonfire." Ely muttered something Jack couldn't quite make out. A moment later he hollered, "I'll be back in a few. I'm going to tan those boys' hides."

"Take your time," Jack called back, his attention drawn to the cave. He yanked free the dried grass and twigs covering the mouth, revealing a much larger opening than he'd first suspected. With a surreptitious glance over his shoulder to ensure Ely had left to check on the boys, he knelt down and felt his way through the entrance.

Sunlight illuminated the first five feet. Pitch darkness lay beyond. Jack reconsidered. He'd most likely find a hibernating animal in there, and animals weren't too keen on being awakened. He slanted his gaze up the hill at the neat pile of brush. Someone had deliberately arranged those tree limbs in front of the cave opening. Someone who didn't want the entrance seen by passersby. That someone certainly wasn't a bear or a raccoon.

Crawling through the entrance, he winced as dampness seeped through his pants, icy cold on his knees. Undeterred, he pushed through the darkness, bumping his hand against a sharp metal corner. Wind whistled past the entrance. Humid, stagnant air settled in his lungs. Jack reached into his pocket and pulled out a match.

With a scrape on his boot, the match sizzled to life.

Flickering light exposed dangling tree roots. The shallow ceiling prevented him from standing or even sitting fully upright. The space stretched no wider than a horse stall. A pile of boxes appeared in the dancing shadows before him. As the flames touched his fingers, Jack blew out the match with a muffled curse. He lit another, and strained forward until he could make out the writing.

Wells Fargo.

He grasped the handle with his free hand as he shook out the second dying match. Unless he wanted to burn off his own fingertips, he had to drag the cases into the light.

Using his heels as leverage, he scooted backward to the mouth of the cave, towing the sturdy boxes behind him. The heavy boxes dug into the soft soil. His muscles strained at the awkward position. The pulled tendon in his back screamed in protest. An eternity later, he emerged into the sunlight, gasping. A fine layer of silt dusted his skin and clothing. Slumping onto his haunches, he took a moment to catch his breath. The scent of burning wood teased his nostrils.

A dark leaf fluttered onto his bent knee. He brushed it aside. The leaf crumbled into ash.

Jack leaped to his feat.

A haze of smoke billowed in the air above him.

His chest seized. *Elizabeth.* All thoughts of outlaws and loot fled his brain. Arms heaving, he sped up the hill. Flames licked the sky as he approached the house. Jo and the boys pumped water from the well into buckets.

Ely shattered the bedroom window with an ax. "She's in there!" The burly man threw his coat over the cut-glass edges.

Jack added a fresh burst of speed. Ely didn't need to say the name. Elizabeth was trapped in the house.

With a boost from Ely, Jack shimmied through the

window. Smoke stung his eyes. His coat snagged on a shard of glass. Wrenching the material free, he jumped to the floor. Elizabeth appeared before him.

She gasped and coughed, burying her nose in the crook of her elbow. "I tried to leave through the kitchen, but it's too hot."

"Get away from the door."

He yanked the wedding-ring quilt from the bed and threw it over the sill, adding a cushioning layer to Ely's coat. "I'll lower you down. Ely is waiting."

Cold air rushed into the room, feeding the fire. Jack swept her into his arms. She scooted her feet over the ledge, her arms still wrapped around his shoulders. Her heavy petticoats crowded the narrow space. Jack shoved them through the opening. He slid his hands down her ribcage, then carefully lowered her into Ely's waiting arms.

The trunk in the corner snagged his attention. Smoke drifted toward the ceiling, revealing clothes strewn over the floor. Elizabeth had obviously been digging through the contents. Jack knelt and lifted one of the items. Even through the growing haze he made out a man's shirt.

She'd risked her life to rifle through her late-husband's clothing? Why?

Especially when all the loot was safely hidden outside.

Chapter Fifteen

The front room was completely destroyed along with most of the kitchen. Only the pantry and the bedroom had survived serious damage, but heavy smoke saturated every surface. Most of the food stores were ruined, and the structure itself was unlivable.

Elizabeth crouched in the wagon, Rachel snug beside her, the space was lit by three warming lanterns. Both sets of barn doors had been flung open during the chaos. The McCoy boys huddled together on the far side of the corral while the three horses and the milk cow stomped and snorted in the midst of the commotion. Jo sulked on the bunkhouse porch.

Though the fire had mostly burned itself out, fiery embers still drifted into the sky. From Elizabeth's vantage point at the back of the house, the structure appeared almost normal. If she circled around to the front, the true damage was revealed. The image of the porch roof caved into the parlor had burned into her brain.

The open barn doors framed the clearing formed by the three buildings. A scattered pile of her possessions littered the space. Ely and Jack had shattered the window in the bedroom and managed to save everything they could grab, including her, before suffocating smoke had overwhelmed them.

In a desperate attempt to save the outbuildings, Ely and Jack filled buckets from the well, splashing water onto the chunks of burning debris fluttering off the main house.

The sheltering branches of bare trees stood silhouetted against the setting sun, black and scorched. She tucked the blanket tighter around Rachel's basket, then scooted off the back of the wagon.

Jack caught sight of her, dropped his bucket and crossed the clearing. "How are you holding up?"

"I'm fine."

With a somber wave of remorse, she realized she spoke the truth. Nothing touched her anymore—not the blustery cold stinging her cheeks, not the blackened remains of her home, not even the blisters on her palm smarted any longer. She was more than fine, she was numb.

Jack lifted her hand. "How is your burn? Does it still hurt?"

Elizabeth shook her head. Feeling as if she were outside her own body, she studied the charred remains of her life and felt…nothing. "I used to wonder who planted all those trees. I think Hackberry Creek might be the only place in Kansas with grown trees. When I first saw the spread, I thought the house was real fine, but I fell in love with the trees first. I'll miss them most when we move to town."

"You can always rebuild."

"We both know that will never happen."

A beam cracked and popped, tumbling into what had once been her dining space with a shower of orange sparks.

Still nothing. Not even a twinge.

Jack cleared his throat.

"I'm not lying," she defended herself. "After Jo's accident, and then the incident with the wolves, well, I realized you were right. You and Mr. McCoy and Jo. I can't stay out here alone any longer. Once spring comes, the work will be too much to manage on my own. Jo has her own family to attend. She can't keep splitting her time between here and home and school. I wouldn't feel comfortable hiring a stranger to help."

Jack shrugged out of his coat and wrapped the heavy wool around her shoulders.

Shivering, she touched the collar. The pungent scent of wood smoke wafted from the saturated wool. "I thought Texas Rangers wore long slickers."

"I bought the coat off a retired sailor earning his way toward a train ride to the desert. He said he was tired of winter, and never planned on seeing snow again. Told me this was the warmest coat he ever owned."

The heavy wool sealed out the biting cold. Her fingers tingled as warm blood pumped through her veins. "He was right. I don't think I've felt this warm since September."

Ely shouldered his way into their conversation, his lips set in a hard line. "The boys claim they had nothing to do with this fire, but I don't know if I believe them."

Elizabeth nestled deeper into the safety of Jack's residual warmth. "I'm certain the boys wouldn't lie."

"I can't say for sure either way," Mr. McCoy growled. "Usually the little one will tattle on his older brothers, but he's keeping his mouth shut this time." Ely ran a thumb and forefinger down the length of his beard. "I don't know what to think."

He swiveled around to face his daughter. Jo lounged

forlornly against the bunkhouse railing. "Did you see anything?"

She shook her head. "We were only gone about twenty minutes."

"In the barn?"

Jo flipped one heavy mahogany braid over her shoulder. "The bunkhouse," she replied with a sullen glare at Elizabeth.

If Jack noticed Elizabeth's sharp intake of breath, he didn't say anything.

Instead, he drew his dark brows together, his hazel eyes inscrutable. "Looks like the fire started in the parlor near the woodpile. Those boys are full of energy, but I don't see them doing anything this deliberately cruel. Must have been an accident."

"I just clipped the wicks this morning." Elizabeth brushed her cheek against the wool collar to brush aside a stray lock of hair. "None of the lamps were lit. I'm sure of it."

Jack's gaze skittered away. His hand crept over his pocket, as if he was unconsciously hiding something. Elizabeth's scalp tingled.

"Maybe the lamp fell over after the fire started," he replied. "There's no way to tell for sure."

"Why don't you talk to them?" Ely jerked his head to where the boys had disappeared behind the barn. "I've already got them shaking in their boots. We'll let that gun on your hip do the rest."

Jack's gloved hand slid farther down his thigh, protectively covering the weapon. "Bring the boys around."

Elizabeth studied the Ranger. This was the first time she'd seen him don his weapon. There was a new determination in the set of his jaw.

Ely stomped across the clearing, his arms swinging

resolutely. He returned moments later with the three boys trailing in his wake, their heads bent, their feet dragging in the soot-darkened snow.

"Boys," Jack spoke, his voice firm but kind. "Tell me what happened here today."

Caleb swallowed audibly. "I don't know. Honest. We went back down to the creek bed to see if we could find any wolf bones in the bonfire. David heard a wolf bone in your pocket brings good luck."

Ely guffawed and rolled his eyes. Jack shot him a quelling look.

"Maybe that other man did it," Abraham squeaked.

Jack's head snapped around to face the boy. "What man?"

The three adults and Jo closed the circle around the cowering boys.

Abraham's frightened gaze darted around the group. "There was a rider earlier."

"Why didn't you say something?" Ely demanded.

"He was just riding through. He headed toward the creek bed, so I figured you'd see him, too."

Ely swung his gaze around the clearing as if the man might still be lurking in the shadows. "We didn't see anyone."

"Did you girls see a rider?" Jack snapped.

Elizabeth and Jo exchanged a guilty look. "We were in the bunkhouse trying to piece together the bank robberies," Elizabeth began. She needed more time to gather her thoughts before she decided what to do with the information they'd discovered. "Is the bunkhouse safe? Rachel needs to be out of this cold."

Jack gave a distracted nod. "The women will stay there tonight. Ely and I will patch up the roof for the short term. The boys will sleep in the barn. We're burning daylight and it's only getting colder."

"There are more beds in the bunkhouse," Elizabeth pointed out. "It makes more sense for the boys to stay in there."

"The barn is too cold for Rachel, and Ely and I aren't exactly equipped to take care of a baby."

"Fine." Elizabeth scowled at his withering expression. "Rachel, Jo and I will stay in the *warm* bunkhouse tonight."

"Fine." Jack started toward the barn.

Elizabeth hesitated for a moment, then fell into step beside him. "Thank you for coming after me."

He swiveled on one heel, his expression thunderous. She sucked in a sharp breath.

"What's so important in that trunk that you risked your life?" he demanded.

"The homestead documents. The deed to the house."

His rigid shoulders deflated. He rubbed a weary hand across his eyes. "I didn't mean to yell at you. I just thought...nothing. Never mind."

He stomped away, leaving Elizabeth dumbfounded, and more alone than she'd ever felt in her whole life.

Jack ached to comfort Elizabeth, but with night rapidly descending, he worried they'd lose any chance of discovering more clues to the source of the fire. He didn't have time to ease the betrayal he'd seen in her eyes. The hurt caused by his harsh words. Realizing how close he'd come to losing her had unleashed a raging fury that hadn't yet dissipated.

Jack eyed the ragtag bunch of McCoys milling around the clearing. He faced Ely. "Do you have room at your place for the animals?"

"Some."

"Enough for the milk cow and the chickens?"

"Should be."

"Excellent." Jack glanced at Elizabeth to see how she was taking the news. She held Rachel, gently rocking the sleeping infant. The wind whipped at her hair, tugging blond tendrils loose from the tight bun at the nape of her neck. Her detached gaze speared him like a lance.

He envisioned the woman in Texas after the Comanche raid, setting the table for her slaughtered family, wearing the same dulled expression. His throat tightened. A body could only take so much.

"Okay, then," he continued, yanking his muddled thoughts back to the present. "We're losing daylight. I'm taking Abraham to check for prints before this wind destroys any evidence of the boys' story. The rest of you can move Mrs. Cole's belongings into the barn."

He chanced another glance at Elizabeth, but she appeared oblivious. Numb. His heart went out to her. Jack stepped forward, drawn by a force more powerful than his own good sense. He knew what he wanted: he wanted her to trust him.

Abraham jumped ahead of him, blocking his way.

"Over here," the boy pointed excitedly into the distance. "Come on."

Jack tore his gaze away from Elizabeth. He'd had his suspicions for days, but he'd done nothing. Her husband was the real outlaw, and he finally had the proof. Jack also had a suspicion someone else knew about the hidden money. If he'd faced the truth sooner, none of this would have happened.

And he still didn't know what Elizabeth was hiding. Was it her suspicions, or her involvement?

"C'mon," Abraham urged him forward.

He and the boy traced a path around the side of the house. Away from the distraction of Elizabeth and the fire, he realized his feet had turned to blocks of ice. He recalled the wistful look in her eyes as she'd nestled into his coat for comfort. He understood how she felt. He sometimes wondered if he'd ever be warm again.

After twenty minutes of fruitless searching, he and Abraham stumbled over the barest hint of animal prints in the drifting snow.

The boy shouted, jumping up and down at the proof of his innocence. The edges of the prints were ill-defined, but the tracks appeared to be from a large animal. A horse. They followed the spotty trail to the creek bed where the tracks veered left.

As if the rider had deliberately avoided Ely and Jack as they worked.

Jack circled the clearing in ever-widening arcs. The incessant wind howled through his brain, muddling his thoughts. His lips grew numb with cold. He kept picturing Elizabeth's haunted expression, the white cotton glove in Ely's pocket, the sun setting over the Texas sky. The widow had avoided the sheriff's involvement on more than one occasion. How much did she suspect? Why wasn't she willing to trust him?

He was about to declare the source of the tracks inconclusive when a divot in the snow snagged his attention. He crouched. The charred remains of a cigarette had melted into the ice. A check of the paper wrapping and a slight whiff indicated the Durham brand.

Digging into his pocket, Jack retrieved the curious item he'd discovered in the parlor. Side by side, the Durham cigarette he'd found in the house was an exact match for the one he'd just retrieved from the snow.

The animal tracks were definitely from a horse. And

the man riding that animal had mostly likely started the
fire. Jack searched the horizon. There weren't too many
places to hide along the desolate prairie. A rider might
escape detection by riding down the creek bed, away
from him and Ely. Not exactly the easiest path.

"Abraham," Jack said. "Do you know if Mrs. Cole has
a sled in the barn?"

"Yep. But one of the runners is broken."

Jack blew out a long breath. "You go back up to the
house. I have something to take care of, then I'll be right
there."

Abraham bobbed his head and bounded through the
snow. Jack set off for the creek bed. He thought better of
his action, and pivoted on his heel. Glancing up, he discovered Abraham staring at him from a few paces away.

"We didn't do it," the boy declared, his head canted
at a forlorn angle. "We didn't set that fire."

"I know."

The boy's shoulders straightened with relief. "You'll
tell that to my pa, then?"

"Of course I will."

Abraham jerked his head toward the main house.
"Let's go, then."

Jack cast another look at the creek bed. He'd like to
explore that cave once more. What else would he find in
those boxes? More money? More evidence?

Will Cole always rode a distinctive bay mustang.

That crotchety old sheriff had actually managed to
stumble onto the truth.

The same questions swirled through Jack's head. How
much did Elizabeth know? Did she know her husband had
stashed stolen loot for a gang of bank robbers? Would his
feelings for her change if she was involved?

Jack pinched the bridge of his nose. He didn't know what to think.

She'd been terrified from the moment he'd burst into her life. He'd always assumed her fear had been directed at him, but what if something more sinister had frightened her? What if she was being blackmailed?

If she'd known the money was in the cave, surely she'd have steered him and Ely away from clearing the brush. Yet when they'd mentioned the task this morning, she'd only smiled, her pale blue eyes clear and innocent. She couldn't have known about the money, or she'd have been terrified of discovery.

He glanced over the rise at the charred remains of her house. He had the uneasy feeling someone else knew of Will's involvement, and they were looking for that money.

His chest constricted. He'd found the loot and the real outlaw. Yet he had the uneasy sensation he'd just lost. And he'd lost big.

Elizabeth pulled down the galvanized tub and flipped it over onto the floor. She clambered atop the metal dome and stretched until her fingers closed around the rough wooden slats of the crate containing Will's saddlebags.

"Jack's gonna be real mad when he finds out we're in the main house," Jo called from the kitchen. "He gave mighty strict instructions about staying outside."

"I told you to wait outside," Elizabeth grumbled.

"If you don't have to listen to instructions, why should I?"

"At least be careful and stay out of the parlor. And the bedroom."

Elizabeth harrumphed as she set the box on the floor. She tore open the flap, then paused. What she didn't know, couldn't hurt her. "I want to see if we can salvage any of these canned goods."

For the next few minutes she puttered around the pantry, rubbing her towel over jars blackened with soot. All the while the saddlebags rested near her feet. When she'd discovered the Bible, something had bothered her. Will never did anything without a purpose. And he certainly wasn't a religious man. A Bible was innocuous, innocent. No one would search through the pages if the book was discovered. She certainly hadn't. If Will had left behind any clues to Bud Shaw's identity, she owed it to Jack to look.

Mustering her resolve, Elizabeth wiped her hands and knelt. She tugged on the leather flap and pulled out the Bible. A neat row of hand-written names adorned the inside cover. The Cole family tree. She ran her finger along the cascading history. One name in particular caught her attention—Bradford Shaw.

A sudden memory shocked her upright, Jack's voice, *Is he in there? Where's Bud Shaw.*

Bradford and Bud. A coincidence?

"We need to get going," Jo urged.

Elizabeth shoved the Bible into the saddlebag. "We're having a fresh chicken for dinner tonight. We might as well have one last celebration before we close up the house for good."

She stepped into the kitchen and grasped a soot-darkened pan from its neat perch on the wall.

"Thank you," Elizabeth said. "For everything. For taking such good care of Rachel and me. For lining up the pots by size."

"That was Mr. Elder. He's awfully fussy for a man."

Jo accepted the pot from Elizabeth's limp hand. "I'm going to miss having you close like this. But it'll be fine.

We'll see each other every Sunday at church when the weather is nice. And maybe after school. Next year is my last."

"Of course we'll see each other." Elizabeth folded Jo into a quick embrace. "I never thanked you properly for helping me out the night Rachel was born. I don't know anyone as brave as you."

The girl's cheeks bloomed crimson. "I didn't do anything special."

"Of course you did. Do you remember when you ordered that Ranger around?"

Jo worried the braid draped over her right shoulder. A smile kicked up the corner of her mouth. "You should have seen his face."

The two of them giggled.

Elizabeth smiled. "I imagine Mr. Elder wishes I *had* been a bank robber."

Jo's giggles erupted into outright laughter. "He probably would have preferred being shot."

"Those big strong men could never survive having babies."

"We're worth more than rubies."

"Amen," the girls spoke in unison.

Unable to find a moment alone to speak with Jack, Elizabeth spent the next day salvaging what they had retrieved from the house. She separated the items she planned on giving to the McCoys from the items she planned to auction. Kneeling on the hay-strewn floor, she emptied the remainder of Will's belongings from his trunk and replaced his clothing with Rachel's.

In order to air out the worst of the acrid smoke, they stretched her clothing on lines outside to flap in the gentle breeze. Elizabeth retrieved her wedding dress and rewrapped the satin gown in sheets of tissue paper. She'd have little use for such a fine outfit in the future, and the memories associated with the beautiful dress were best left to the prairie winds.

She tucked a note to Jo inside the lace-edged bodice and stacked the box against the stall wall. Someday, Jo would need a courting dress. Elizabeth hoped the younger girl would heed her advice and trust her own heart when choosing a husband. Turning, Elizabeth surveyed the items she'd be taking with her to town. She'd whittled her possessions down to a trunk and satchel. Her entire life in a tiny heap—just enough to start over fresh, some-place far away.

She crossed the length of the barn just as Jack draped a blanket over something in the wagon they'd moved inside for loading. He straightened at the sound of her footsteps. If she didn't know better, she'd think he looked almost guilty.

"What are you covering?" She peered over the edge.

His gaze didn't quite meet hers. "Just a couple of hay bales. You can throw a handful under the wheels if the wagon gets stuck in the snow. Hope you don't mind me packing them. With the animals over at Ely's, I don't sup-pose they'll be much use here."

"Remind me to tell Mr. McCoy that he can gather the rest of the bales if he needs them."

Jack leaped down from the wagon bed.

"Sure." He rested one hand on her trunk. "Is that all you're bringing to town?"

Elizabeth shrugged. In the chaos after the fire, she kept putting off telling Jack what she'd discovered about her late husband. This was her opportunity to blurt out the truth, to admit that nothing here truly belonged to her since she didn't know what had been purchased with stolen money.

The words stuck in her throat.

They'd been getting along so well, she didn't want to lose even one minute of their limited camaraderie. She'd confess once they arrived in town. "I'll be staying at the boarding house until Rachel and I can find a new home. I can send for the rest later."

"Seems like a baby needs more stuff. Strange how the littler they are, the more they seem to need." He paused for a moment. "I have something else you can bring."

He motioned for her to follow him to the work area. As they approached the space, the pungent odor of varnish stung her nostrils.

Jack skirted aside, revealing a gleaming wooden crib resting on a drop cloth. "I found a tin of varnish in the cupboard there. I cut up one of the trunks in the bunkhouse. I figured you'd need this more." He rubbed the back of his neck. "I don't know much about carpentry, but the joints are real solid. Should hold a baby just fine."

Tears pricked behind her eyes. The pieces she and Jo had seen in the barn had all been assembled. Carved ivory decorated the head of the crib in an arched leafy trail. Jack hadn't been bored. He'd been making Rachel a gift.

"I just thought the baby should have something besides a drawer and a laundry basket." He scuffed at the floor with his boot.

Elizabeth knelt and studied the piece.

Jack stuck out a warning hand. "You'd best not touch it. I don't think the varnish has dried yet."

Resisting the temptation to run her fingers over the wood, she rested her hand on her chest. The painstaking detail he'd carved into the piece enchanted her. "So that's what you've been doing all morning. I wondered where you disappeared to."

That same shadow of guilt crossed over his face. "Yep."

Elizabeth folded her hands together. Her whole life was slipping away. She was leaving everything behind—everything that was familiar, all the little things that had brought her so much joy over the past few months. Even the memories of Will seemed to fade into the past. They were hazy and distant, out of focus, while the good times stood out in sharper relief.

"Do you like it?" Jack asked, a heartbreaking note of doubt in his voice.

Contentment swelled in her chest. "The crib is beautiful. Thank you."

"You're welcome." He sighed, his shoulders relaxing.

"You've been such a blessing to me."

"Anyone would have done the same."

"You and Jo are too stubborn for your own good."

"I'll agree with you about Jo, but I like to think of myself as decisive, a man of action."

Elizabeth smiled at his posturing. "Not to mention modest and unassuming."

"I never was one to hide my light under a bushel."

I have fallen in love with him.

The truth struck her like a lightning bolt. The process had happened so gently, she hadn't noticed the signs. The way her heart flipped when he entered the room, the way her thoughts strayed to fond memories of his kisses, the way she had begun to think of the three of them as a family. The source of her melancholy finally made sense. She had given her heart to a dream.

Elizabeth blinked. Falling in love slowly was much

more binding and endearing than instant infatuation. "Do you think you'll ever marry?"

She regretted the question before she even finished speaking.

Head bent, he considered her question. "I'm not good husband material. My job is my life, and my job requires me to travel. I'm never in one place for too long."

"Of course."

"I suppose I could always settle down and become the sheriff of some sleepy hamlet. I could arrest the town drunk every Friday."

"And let him out of jail every Sunday for church?"

"Well, of course! As town sheriff I'd consider it my duty to rehabilitate the disorderly."

He was joking with her, to put her at ease, and she appreciated the effort. "It's getting late. If I want to make it to town before sunset, I'd best finish packing up the rest of the things we salvaged from the fire." She thought about the fire. "Say, did you find out anything about the man Abraham saw? Mr. McCoy said you discovered tracks by the creek bed, but he didn't appear concerned."

A look she couldn't quite read flitted across his face. "I didn't." He hesitated. "But I don't think you should stay here any longer than necessary. I don't like the idea of a stranger lurking around."

Elizabeth suppressed a shudder. "Me, either."

Jack moved to stand before the stall. "Do you think this horse can pull the wagon all the way into town?"

"She's stronger than she looks."

Jack patted the mare's muzzle. "Seems like all the gals on this farm are stronger than they appear."

"I believe you've just compared me to a horse. I don't know whether to be complimented or insulted."

Jack laughed good-naturedly at his own gaff. "Point

taken." His expression grew somber. "Do you have the resources to move to town?"

He hadn't said the words outright, but she knew he meant money. "Will left us set pretty well."

Her answer didn't seem to comfort him. "I'll drive with you into town."

"Of course."

"You know you can always trust me," he spoke quietly.

My husband was a bank robber.

She longed to confess what she'd discovered in the Bible. About seeing the name, Bradford Shaw. They'd all teased and tormented Jack for barging into her home all those weeks ago, but he'd been right all along. Her husband was involved. He was also dead.

A distinctive bay mustang.

Will had won the horse from Mr. Peters, the owner of the mercantile, in a card game. Once again her late husband's activities had come back to haunt him—and her. He'd covered his tracks well. In the end, his vanity had done him in. A less flashy horse might have garnered less attention.

With the weather and the heavy load, the long wagon trip to town was bound to take two hours at least. She didn't think she could stand sitting next to the Ranger with the weight of Will's betrayal hanging between them.

Jack couldn't do anything until he reached town, anyway. She'd wait until they arrived, and give him the Bible when they separated. She didn't know if Bud Shaw was guilty or innocent, but she owed it to him to let Jack find out. She had to do everything she could to ensure an innocent man didn't hang.

Suddenly chilled, she pressed the back of her hand to her forehead. Jack could wire the Santa Fe railroad line and get a copy of Will's work schedule.

She wasn't sure how deeply Will had been involved in the scheme, or how his actions would affect her. Maybe one of his relatives had been involved, and he'd been too loyal to turn in his partner. Either way, Jack needed to track Will's job schedule. Once the truth was revealed, she'd face the consequences. She was an outlaw's widow, and Jack wasn't the marrying kind.

As for her love, she had the rest of her life to mourn that loss.

Chapter Sixteen

Twenty minutes later, a somber group gathered in the center of the clearing. Jack chafed at the delay, anxious for the journey. He didn't want any distractions while he questioned Elizabeth. Instinct told him he was close to a breakthrough with her.

Mr. McCoy held the milk cow by a knotted-rope tether. "I'll miss you, lass. But we'll be up to town before you know it." He shifted in the snow. "The boys and I will come back tomorrow for the rest of the animals."

"Don't forget the barn cat." Elizabeth wrapped her arms around her body and rubbed her shoulders. "She saved me from the wolves. I'd hate to think of her out here all alone."

"I've got some salted fish. We'll lure her back to our place, all right. It'll give the boys something to do other than wrestle one another."

"Are you certain you have enough room? Won't this be too much of a burden?"

"We can always use another milk cow around the place."

"Of course."

Jo stepped forward and pumped Elizabeth's hand. "I'll see you in church."

Elizabeth nodded, but her gaze shied away. Jack's instincts flared.

Ely embraced the widow in a bone-crushing bear hug, tears shimmering in his eyes. "You take care of the little one, lass. And take care of yourself. Don't you worry about a thing. We'll keep an eye on the place while you're gone. Looks like this weather is about to break. It'll be spring before you know it. Don't forget to ask the doc about my rash."

"I will." She grinned indulgently. "Thank you, for everything."

"Get on with you. It's going to be dark soon."

Jack assisted her onto the plank-wood carriage seat. Rachel's basket rested on the floor with the baby tucked snugly inside. Tethered to the back of the wagon, Midnight snorted and balked, as if offended by the subservient position. Jack clambered up beside Elizabeth and slapped the reins to wake up her tired old mare. The horse jolted forward.

They lumbered to the end of the drive. Elizabeth touched his sleeve.

"Wait," she said. "I want to take one last look. I want to remember this."

The worst of the damage centered on the front of the house, lending the scene a neglected, forlorn appearance. The wind whipped the hair loose from beneath her bonnet. The strands snapped at her eyes.

Jack cleared his throat. "I'm sure someone will rebuild."

"Someone has been rebuilding this place for more than thirty years. Maybe it's cursed."

"There's no such thing as a curse. This is a harsh land.

Everyone who lived in this house left the prairie a better place."

"Except for me."

"You did your best. That fire wasn't your fault."

"Then whose fault was it?"

Jack shrugged.

He had an idea who had caused the damage, but he wasn't ready to confide in Elizabeth just yet. Will had probably bragged about his escapades, and someone was looking for the money. The boys had seen the man, and Jack had seen evidence of a rider. He'd started to tell her about the cave a hundred times, but the words stuck in his throat. He wanted her to trust him.

Using the evidence he'd discovered as proof of Bud Shaw's innocence, he'd telegraph the jail in Texas once they arrived in town. He still wasn't sure why Will had chosen to steal Bud Shaw's identity, but it really didn't matter anymore. He'd have the sheriff keep an eye on the homestead in case the man who started the fire returned.

The grueling miles to town passed in tense silence. Jack attempted to start up a conversation a few times, but Elizabeth mostly ignored his overtures. She stared into the distance, somber and distracted. When the town's smokestacks appeared on the horizon, Jack reined the horse to a halt. "I'll ride Midnight the rest of the way."

He swung out of the driver's seat. "You okay to handle the reins?"

He spoke to her bonnet as she bent to retrieve something from beneath the seat. Straightening, her expression pinched, she held out a book.

"I should have told you sooner." She cleared her throat. "But I didn't know how."

Realizing she held a Bible, he frowned. "Told me what?"

"This belonged to Will. I think maybe he was related to Bud Shaw. There's a family tree. A man named Bradford Shaw is Will's first cousin. It can't be a coincidence."

His heart sank. "How long have you known this?"

"Not long. The Bible was tucked away in Will's saddlebags. I never went through his things until after the fire."

"Your husband has been dead for eight months."

"I don't expect you to understand." She rubbed her temples beneath the rim of her bonnet with mittened hands. "You've got his whole family laid out in the front of that book. I'm sure you'll be able to prove Bud was involved because he and Will knew each other. They were cousins...." She paused. "There's more."

His head throbbed. *Emotions clouded judgment, and poor judgment got people killed.* "How much more?"

She scooted toward the driver's seat. "Check the Santa Fe work records for Will Cole. You'll find proof my husband was involved with his cousin. Will scheduled work crews for railroad projects near the banks robbed." She lifted the reins to spur the horse forward: "That's all I know."

Jack slammed the brake into place, preventing her from fleeing. "Why didn't you say something sooner?"

She'd known for days, maybe even weeks, and she hadn't trusted him with the truth. She didn't trust him. Despite everything he'd done for her, she'd never trusted him.

Her face averted, Elizabeth sighed. "Jo put it all together earlier this week. I know I should have told you sooner, but the fire—"

Despite her lack of faith in him, he forced himself to think like a Ranger. Since the moment he'd discovered proof of Will's involvement, he'd been wondering why the man's name hadn't surfaced during the investigation. "We checked all the railroad crew managers. Will's name never came up."

"He wasn't a foreman. He only put together the schedules. Will had access to information on payroll and large projects. He knew exactly when the banks had the most money. He knew when the trains were delayed, when the projects started, everything." She met his gaze, her clear blue eyes stricken. "And he always had money. Too much money for a working man. I lied to myself all along. I made excuses for him. Especially after I found out how much he gambled. Some of the people in town thought he cheated."

Comprehension slammed over Jack. "How could I have been so stupid? We checked foremen and managers. We never once considered a pencil pusher."

He circled to the back of the wagon and grabbed Midnight's reins.

Elizabeth twisted in her seat. "Tell the sheriff he can auction off whatever is left on the property." Her bonnet shielded her face. "He knew Will was a cheat. He's been wanting the property since Will died."

Jack winced at the stark pain in her voice. "We'll settle up with the sheriff later."

"Aren't you listening to me? You don't have to worry about hanging an innocent man anymore. Will was related to Bradford Shaw. They were first cousins. They must have been working together."

Jack knew exactly what had happened. Why Will Cole had assumed Bud Shaw's identity. All the puzzle pieces fit. Every loose end came together. The two men looked alike because they were related. The resemblance had confused the witnesses.

Jack looped the reins over the saddle horn. "There

were only three outlaws—Slim Joe, Pencil Pete and your husband."

Angry with his own stupidity, he fisted his hands. He'd been sitting on the proof for months. *A distinctive bay mustang.* He'd followed the trail of a man riding a distinctive bay mustang all the way through Texas to Colorado to Kansas. The horse had been on at least four different trains, several witnesses had attested to that, but no manifest had ever indicated the presence of the animal.

Jack had assumed the rider bribed the workers, but a railroad employee could get away without signing the manifest.

Elizabeth's husband was guilty as sin, only she refused to believe it. "You're right about one thing, Mrs. Cole. There's a man sitting in jail, set to hang in less than three weeks. But he's definitely innocent." Jack lifted his head. "Your husband was impersonating Bud Shaw."

Elizabeth frowned, her face as pale as the snow sweeping across the prairie. "Will wouldn't betray his own kin."

"It was the coward's way out. Your husband *was* Bud Shaw. He framed his own cousin."

Her breath puffed clouds into the chill afternoon. "That's absurd. They must have been partners."

"Did your husband take his horse with him when he traveled?"

"Always. Will said he didn't like the mounts the livery provided. He liked to stand out."

"I'll prove it to you. Show me something with your husband's handwriting."

"My papers are in the trunk."

Elizabeth brushed aside his proffered hand, leaped off the wagon seat and circled around the bed. Jack tugged the trunk until it rested on the edge and flipped open the lid. He stood aside, allowing Elizabeth access. While she searched, he snatched his own documents from Midnight's saddlebags.

After rummaging for a few moments, she pulled out a sheaf of papers. "There."

Jack flipped through the pages. He brushed the snow from the wagon bed and laid her documents beside the sheet he'd torn from the hotel register. "Bud Shaw signed his name on the register at the hotel in Texas. Look at that handwriting. It's the same man."

"How can you be sure?"

"The slant of the letters is the same. Look at the *W*. Will puts a flourish on the end. Even you have to see that."

"The signatures are similar," she replied. "I'm still not certain they're the same man. Why didn't Pencil Pete declare Bud's innocence? Certainly he'd know the man wasn't involved."

Jack stepped onto the back of the wagon. "This is why Pencil Pete kept quiet."

He whipped off the tarp and revealed the stash of Wells Fargo boxes. "I found these on your property."

"No!"

"I discovered them in a cave by the creek. This is why Pencil Pete was so all-fired-up arrogant. He thought your husband was coming back to bust him out. Except Will never made it back, did he? Come to think of it, I don't believe Will ever planned on busting his partner out of jail.

"See, that's what's been bothering me this whole time. Why did Will make a trip down the creek bed in a storm? I think your husband was going to take the loot and run. After Pencil Pete and his cousin were hanged, he'd have all the money. No one was looking for Will Cole."

The betrayal in her eyes stabbed him like a lance.

"Everything you say makes sense," she spoke, her

expression stricken. "I can't believe he was willing to let his own cousin hang for his crimes. But it must be true, right?"

"I'm sorry, Elizabeth. I know how much this must hurt. But all the evidence points to Will."

"Does this mean you can free Bud Shaw?"

He raked his hands through his hair. "Should be. Everything against Bud is circumstantial."

"What if I come to Texas?" she asked eagerly. "What if I testify that my husband was the third outlaw? That Will assumed Bud's identity?"

"It'd just be your word. They'd want some kind of proof."

"I suppose you're right." She climbed back onto the wagon seat, her movements stiff and weary.

For a moment she sat, hunched over the seat. Jack rubbed Midnight's haunches, unsure how to comfort her.

Then she jerked upright, snapping her fingers. "Bud Shaw was shot in the leg during a robbery in Colorado last spring. Will came home with a wound on his leg around that same time. Once you show the Rangers the stolen money and tell them where you found it, and Bud proves he doesn't have a scar on his leg, that should be enough."

"We better put you on the payroll. It's perfect. You won't even have to be involved."

There'd be no reason for her to accompany him to Texas.

His heartbeat stalled.

No reason for him to see her. Ever.

She adjusted the reins and sat forward. "We'd best get his money to town."

"You can still come to Texas," he blurted.

"There's nothing for me there," she replied, her expression bleak.

I'm there.

The carriage surged forward. Jack whipped off his hat and slapped his thigh. What did he have to offer her?

Everything.

Love, marriage, a home and a family.

He'd never thought of himself as the kind of man to marry and settle down. Until now.

He mounted Midnight. Kicking the horse into a trot, he searched the horizon. They were safe. For now. But someone else was searching for that money, and money had a way of forcing men into desperate acts. It wasn't going to take long before they discovered the loot wasn't at the homestead. None of them were safe for long.

"Are you following me, Mr. Elder?" Elizabeth demanded in a harsh whisper. She glanced around the quiet mercantile, relieved no one had noticed their heated exchange.

"Where is Rachel?" he asked.

"I left her with Mrs. Wilmont from the boarding house."

"It's not safe."

"Of course it's safe. All the stolen money is at the bank."

"You and I know that." Jack circled her upper arm and tugged her behind a display of penny candies. "But the man searching for those Wells Fargo boxes may still think you have them."

After their discussion the previous day, she hadn't thought their next meeting would be a whispered conversation in the general store.

Glancing around, he slapped his hat against his thigh. "I didn't want to alarm you until I knew for certain. Pencil Pete escaped, and he's looking for the stash. I had some suspicions after the fire. When we arrived yesterday, I telegraphed Texas. Pete broke out of jail three weeks ago. That's plenty of time to make his way to Kansas."

"Why didn't someone tell you sooner?"

Jack snorted. "They sent the notice to the sheriff in town. Only he was too drunk to care. I don't know why Pete set the fire. I think it may have been an accident. I think one of the McCoy boys spooked him and he knocked over the lantern."

Panic sucked the breath from her lungs. "It's not going to take him long to figure the money isn't there."

"He's been watching the place for at least a day. He's seen me. He'll assume I have the money."

"I'd better—"

"Mr. Elder!" a feminine voice called. "Mr. Elder, is that you?"

A pretty dark-haired woman with coffee-colored eyes rounded the corner, a bundled infant in her arms. "I can't believe it's actually you."

Jack frowned before dawning recognition spread across his face. "Helen Miller, as I live and breathe."

"I'm Helen Smith now." She and the Ranger shared an awkward embrace with the baby pressed between them.

"Mr. Elder," the woman exclaimed again as she backed away. "What are you doing in Kansas?"

"Working," Jack replied shortly.

The woman's violet calico gown enhanced her striking brown eyes, a crisp bonnet framed her creamy complexion. Helen Smith glanced curiously at Elizabeth. "Won't you introduce us?"

"I'm Elizabeth Cole." She stuck out her hand. "It's a pleasure to meet you, Mrs. Smith."

"Call me Helen. Any friend of Jack's is a friend of mine."

"And how do you two know each other?"

"That's not—" Jack began.

"It's all right." Helen interrupted with a wave of her hand. "Jack negotiated my release from the Apache when I was just a girl. They raided our settlement." The woman's expression clouded at the memory. "Without Jack's intercession, I don't know what would have happened."

Her whole body trembled. Sensing her mother's distress, the baby whimpered.

"It's my job." Jack scuffed his boot against the floor. "Everything turned out for the best. Looks like you've been busy."

The woman adjusted the baby to the opposite shoulder. Two spots of color appeared on her high cheek bones. "I'm a married lady, all right. My husband and I were visiting his sister in Wichita. We're on our way home now. Our train doesn't leave until tomorrow. Will you still be here?"

"I'm here for a few more days."

Mrs. Smith's face lit with pleasure. "Isn't that wonderful? We can catch up."

Elizabeth narrowed her eyes. Having a beautiful woman from Jack's past "catching up" with him didn't feel wonderful at all.

It wouldn't hurt to remind Jack that Mrs. Smith was a *married* lady. "How old is your baby?" she asked pointedly.

The woman's attention immediately turned to her child. "This is Mary. She's almost four months old. I can't believe how quickly she's growing."

Helen turned down the blanket and revealed a plump-cheeked, adorable infant with enormous dark eyes. Elizabeth's heart melted at her obvious affection. Of course, Mrs. Smith wasn't interested in Jack romantically. How silly of her to be jealous.

"Mrs. Cole has a baby girl, too," Jack offered. "Maybe we can all have dinner."

"How wonderful!" Helen exclaimed. "We can compare notes. I feel so ill equipped to raise an infant sometimes. My mother died in the Apache raid. I miss her more than ever."

"I know how you feel." Elizabeth responded to the warmth in her gaze. She didn't have a rival, she had a friend.

They shared a knowing look. Once again Elizabeth was ashamed of her uncharacteristic bout of jealousy. She had no right to be jealous about anything. When you loved someone, you wanted what was best for them. Even if what was best hurt like a thousand bee stings.

Helen glanced at Jack, but she directed her question to Elizabeth, "I'll be looking forward to meeting your husband."

"Mr. Cole passed away."

Helen's expression immediately sobered. "I'm so sorry, Mrs. Cole. My family is planning on staying at the boarding house. If you need anything tonight, you just give me a holler. We women have to stick together."

Elizabeth's throat tightened. "That's very kind of you."

"Don't be silly. Jack and his family were there for me when I was alone. I don't know what I would have done without them."

The women exchanged a quick hug before Helen motioned to the door. "I'd best be going. My husband worries if I'm out of his sight for too long. You know how men are." She winked at Elizabeth, then turned to Jack. "Your brothers are going to be happy to see you home again. The way they sing your praises, you'd think you hung the moon and stars. Not that I'd ever disagree."

Jack squirmed beneath the praise. After Helen disappeared around the corner, out of earshot, Elizabeth turned to Jack. "I didn't know you were a negotiator."

"That's my specialty. I negotiate the release of Indian hostages. Not a real exciting job, eh?"

Elizabeth's heart filled with pride. "I can't imagine a braver or more noble job."

Jack set his hat onto his head. "I need to talk to you. Privately. I'll call on you at four. Between now and then, stay close to the boarding house. I've spread word through town to look out for Pencil Pete. I've got men watching the train depot and the livery. But you've got to be careful."

"You be careful, too."

He blinked at the suggestion. The reaction shamed her. She'd never thought of the danger Jack faced every day, or what a solitary, and lonely, life he led. He spent his career looking out for others, putting his own needs last. That's what she'd done—she'd put Jack's needs last, as well. A man that special deserved someone just as special to love him in return. Someone without a past.

"Elizabeth, you do know I'll always protect you," he spoke earnestly.

"I know."

Everything that brought them together was destined to tear them apart. If she'd never married Will, she'd never have come West. If Will hadn't been an outlaw, Jack would never have appeared in her life. No matter what brought them together, one truth remained. An outlaw's widow made a poor prospect for a lawman's bride. Her husband had been a party to his sister-in-law's murder. How could his family ever forgive her, even if Jack somehow could?

Jack caught her gaze, his expression uncharacteristically grave. "A man gets to thinking sometimes, and he realizes his priorities have changed. Texas isn't such a bad place to settle down and raise a family. You know?"

"I know."

Her heart thumped madly in her chest. She loved him with a wild, desperate abandon. He wanted to take care of her. Just like he'd taken care of Helen, and Jo, and even little Rachel. Eventually though, he'd regret his decision.

She'd always be a reminder of Doreen's murderer. "You don't have to worry about me."

"I'm not worried." He lifted his hat and raked his free hand through his hair. "Of course I'm worried. But that's not the reason I hung around all this time." He paced the narrow aisle. "I'm sorry your late husband dragged you into this mess, but I never would have met you otherwise. And I can't be sorry about that. Once Pencil Pete is caught and Bud is cleared, none of this will matter."

Of course it mattered.

Everyone in his hometown knew about the outlaws. Even if they tried to hide her identity, there'd be no hiding her involvement from Jack's fellow Texas Rangers. People would wonder how much she knew. They'd speculate on her involvement. And Jack's family. She shuddered to think of their reaction to Will Cole's widow. She could live with scorn, but Rachel deserved better. Jack deserved better.

He stared at her expectantly. The tinkling bell over the door saved her from a reply. Half a dozen men streamed into the store, their hobnail boots drowning out any chance for further conversation.

With one hand on his front brim, the other hand on

the back, Jack straightened his hat. "We'll finish this conversation later. Promise me you'll go right back to the boarding house."

Elizabeth flashed a watery smile. "I will."

"Because I'll be watching."

"I know."

She followed his exit. He wouldn't stray far. He had shadowed her every move for the past twenty-four hours. He was too honorable for his good. When she met him tonight, he'd ask her to marry him, of that she was certain. Elizabeth glanced at her hands. Was she selfish enough to accept his offer?

Maybe Jack was right. Maybe people would forget about her past. He felt something for her, maybe not love, but certainly affection. He cared for Rachel. He wasn't a man to enter into a bargain lightly. If he thought they could forge a future together, perhaps it was possible. In time, he might even grow to love her.

She stepped forward and placed her purchases on the counter. The mercantile owner, Mr. Peters, leered at her from his perch on a three-legged stool. He wore a crisp, white apron knotted around his waist. His black hair was slicked back, the comb marks still visible. He'd refused to serve her after Will had won his horse in a poker game, but that was months ago.

One of the cowboys approached the counter, his boots click-clacking across the wood floor.

Mr. Peters pointedly turned his back on Elizabeth. "You need any help, *sir?*"

The cowboy jerked his thumb in Elizabeth's direction. "She was here first."

"I ain't gonna take her blood money, *anyway,*" Mr. Peters sneered.

Elizabeth winced from his withering stare.

"The sheriff says your husband was a murderer and a cheat. Not that any of us around here are surprised. The sheriff says you're going back to Texas to hang."

Heart thumping, Elizabeth backed away from the venom in his steady gaze. People rarely forgave, and they certainly never forgot. She was fooling herself to think she and Jack might share a future.

The cowboy blocked her exit. "You wanna have some fun before you hang, little lady?"

Mr. Peters spit on the floor at her feet. "Since they can't get at your husband, they gonna take you."

The cowboy licked his fleshy lips. "I can get you outta town without that Ranger knowing. Just say the word."

"'Course, you'll have to leave the brat behind," Mr. Peters cackled.

Elizabeth elbowed past them, their jeers cut off by the slamming door. She didn't believe their lies, but she'd just received her answer.

Jack was better off without her.

Jack paced outside the parlor door, his hat in his hands. He'd rehearsed the speech a hundred times over the past few hours. Maybe even a thousand. His solution was perfect. Inspired.

He'd been in love with her from the moment he'd caught her crying because she hadn't named Rachel yet. Even when all the evidence told him she was protecting a man who didn't deserve her, his heart had known her innocence. He loved them both. She and Rachel were the puzzle pieces missing in his life.

He rapped on the door, tipping forward when the heavy weight swung open beneath his fingers.

Elizabeth perched on the edge of a spindly chair. Sunlight shafted through the windows, highlighting the golden amber in her hair. She turned slightly, just enough for the light to silhouette her profile. She wore a familiar white shirtwaist, its crisp cotton tucked into the wide band of a calico skirt. She kept her hands clenched in her lap.

Jack cleared his throat. "I've wired the boys in Texas. The judge is willing to review the evidence."

She appeared more fragile, the circles beneath her eyes darker than when he'd seen her this afternoon.

She smoothed her skirts over her knees. "I wanted to apologize for not revealing my suspicions about Will sooner. I keep looking back, and everything is so obvious. I don't know why I didn't see it before. I guess I was fooling myself. If I didn't face the truth, I didn't have to face the consequences. Except Bud Shaw might have hanged because I didn't want people to know I was an outlaw's widow. I'm not proud of myself. I should have done the right thing straight away."

He worked the brim of his hat. "You were busy holding your family together."

"I suppose."

A sense of foreboding hung over him. He'd never seen her like this, quiet, almost cowed. "No one blames you for what Will did. It was his sin, not yours."

"I've been praying, you know." She pleated the blue calico draping her knee. "Praying for answers, praying for Rachel, praying for myself. I think that's all I've done for the past few days, pray."

"Did you pray for us to be together?"

"No."

The floor dropped out from beneath him. "You didn't?"

She faced him then, so breathtakingly beautiful he had difficulty concentrating.

"I finally understand. When you love someone, you want what's best for them. Even if what's best isn't you." She met his gaze, her expression distant. "You knew that all along though, didn't you?"

"No. I don't understand. I know you feel something for me."

"It took a lot of praying, but I know what I need to do. I always told myself that I was doing the right thing, that I was following God's path, but I wasn't. Not really. I was doing what felt right for me. I put Rachel and you, and even the McCoys, in danger because I was selfish. This time I'm going to do the right thing for everyone, not just me."

Her refusal to acknowledge his words pounded in his brain, a deafening pain that drowned out everything but his own shock and hurt.

I love you.

The words clogged in his throat. If he said them out loud, she still might reject him, and he couldn't bear her scorn.

She faced him then. "Remember that first night? The night Rachel was born? You made me a promise. Even then I knew there was something special about you. Something strong and honorable."

Jack swallowed around the emotion tightening his throat. He wasn't brave. He was a coward who couldn't admit his own feelings. "I'll take care of you, Elizabeth. I'll take care of you *and* Rachel. I'll raise her as my own."

"I know you would."

She stood then, moving away from him. Moving away from the future he'd only just begun to plan. Moving away from a life he'd only just begun to yearn. She didn't love him. His instincts had failed him. She'd rather be alone than be with him.

He pictured his future without her. He'd go back to his job, back to the endless travel, back to never putting down roots. How could it hurt so much to lose something he'd never had?

The desolate image jolted his courage. "I don't care if you don't love me. I have enough love for both of us. Marry me? We'll build a future together. You and me and Rachel."

She didn't even blink, didn't react at all to his declaration or his question. If anything, she appeared to grow colder, more distance. "No. I can't. Don't you see? Will is always going to be between us."

"Don't you feel anything for me?"

Silence answered his question.

Jack didn't know how a body could feel so much pain and still be standing. All the sorrow in his heart burned into his brain. He smashed his hat upon his head. "You lied to me. Maybe not in your words, but in your actions. You made me think you felt something for me."

Elizabeth rested one hand on the mantel, her gaze averted. "I'm sorry."

He was mad, no furious, with her for tying him up in knots. For making him love her, then turning away. He didn't want to talk to her anymore. He didn't even want to look at her.

He stomped toward the door then paused, his gaze riveted on the brass knob. "You *are* selfish, Elizabeth Cole. Selfish with your affection, selfish with your prayers and selfish with your love."

Chapter Seventeen

"All aboard!" the conductor called.

The train chugged forward with an ever-increasing *click-clack, click-clack, click-clack* over the rails. Elizabeth perched on a velvet-covered bench, Rachel snug in her lap. Helen and her husband, along with their own baby, sat across from her. Elizabeth stared out the window. The prairie stretched white all the way to the horizon.

She hadn't seen Jack since last evening. She hadn't even told him she was leaving. Not that he'd even care anymore. Her refusal had driven him away for good, leaving a gaping emptiness in her chest that would never be filled.

The train was headed for Texas, and that was as good a place as anywhere to start over. The state was big enough that she'd never fear running into Jack, yet she knew she'd feel closer to him there.

She'd left the deeds for the homestead with the town agent. Together she and Rachel would start a new life.

"Look at the brass fittings over the windows!" Helen exclaimed. "And the velvet benches. This is so much

better than my first trip across the plains. In a wagon."
She grimaced.

Her husband, a balding man with a round stomach
and kind gray eyes, smiled indulgently. "And faster, too."

"I wish Jack hadn't cancelled our dinner last evening.
I so wanted to catch up."

Her husband patted her hand. "He has his reasons."

Helen leaned forward and snagged Elizabeth's attention. "The whole town of Paris, Texas, is crawling with
Elders. Their cattle ranch must take up half the county.
It's a good thing they have so many sons running around
to help care for the place. Those Elder boys are all so
driven. *And handsome.*" Her husband rolled his eyes.
"Why the Elder family built the church, the hotel and
even the courthouse."

In a weak comparison, Elizabeth had forty dollars in
her reticule. The same forty dollars she'd brought with
her from New York. Her life savings.

She wore the original dress she'd donned to cross the
plains nearly two years ago. She'd stuffed the money Will
had left, the ominous wad of bills, into Rachel's crib and
placed the whole thing in a sturdy wooden crate in the
baggage cart. Jack had refused to take the money, saying all the stolen loot had been accounted for. His refusal
hadn't left her a lot of options on such short notice. She
definitely didn't want to face the sheriff, especially after
he'd been gossiping all over town. Carrying the money
around in her satchel wasn't an option, either. The bills
felt heavy and tainted. When she and Rachel found a new
home, she'd find a suitable charity and donate the cash.

The train lurched. Gasping, Elizabeth flung out her
arm to save Rachel's basket from sliding off the seat. The
passengers grumbled. Heads popped up over seat backs.
The train shuddered to a halt. A middle-aged woman in

a dark burgundy gown lowered the window and peered outside. Her hat feathers fluttered in the cold breeze.

"Say," one of the passengers called, "what's going on?"

A uniformed conductor entered through the rear pocket door. "There's been a slight delay," the man called.

He held up his hands to still the cacophony of protests erupting from the passengers. "There's a dead animal on the tracks. We haven't built up enough speed to push it aside with the cattle guard. If I can get eight or ten sturdy, strong men, we'll drag it off and be on our way in no time."

Helen Smith's husband rose to his feet. He dropped a kiss on his wife's forehead before sidling down the aisle, his body angled to traverse the narrow path. Elizabeth smiled at the obvious affection between the Smiths. Helen's husband obviously didn't hold his wife's past, her capture by the Apaches, against her.

Prodded by jabs in the ribs from their wives, grumbling husbands shuffled into the cold. The railcar soon drained of able-and-not-so-able-bodied men, leaving only women and children. Elizabeth glanced at Rachel.

With nervous chatter filling the car, the delay gave her unwelcome time to think. She *was* selfish. Just not the way Jack thought. She wanted more than anything to accept his proposal, but she could never face his family. Jack's sister-in-law was dead because of Will. Every time the Elders looked at her they'd be reminded of how Doreen died.

She'd convinced herself that leaving was the right thing to do. Why, then, did her decision feel so wrong? She pressed her check against Rachel's. Elizabeth's tear slid down her daughter's cheek.

She could go back and face Jack, confess her love and

her fears. Her heart wrenched. Loving Jack wasn't the easy choice, but was it the right choice? Is this how her own mother had felt when she'd been forced to send Elizabeth to an orphanage? This soul-deep pain? All these years Elizabeth had wallowed in her own misery, never considering her mother's anguish.

Jack was smart enough to know his own mind. He wasn't a man who made rash, impulsive decisions. If only Elizabeth could say the same. She'd followed a man because of an infatuation. Not even two years later she was running away from love. She was forcing her child into a life of secrets and lies and running rather than face the consequences of her late husband's actions.

What was she teaching her daughter? That it was okay to run when life became difficult?

Elizabeth shot upright. She didn't know what she was going to do once she saw Jack, but she was going back. They were only a short distance from the rail station. How long did she have before the tracks were cleared? No matter what happened, she wasn't leaving without Jack's gift. He'd carved the wood with loving hands, and she wasn't going to leave behind his treasured present.

Elizabeth grasped the seat back. She scooted into the aisle and stood beside Mrs. Smith's seat.

"I need to get my crate from the baggage cart," Elizabeth said. "Will you watch Rachel for a moment?"

Mrs. Smith bounced Mary in her arms, her expression one of earnest concern. "Of course. What a delightful child. I know you're newly widowed, but there's no finer man than Jack Elder. If you don't mind my saying so."

"He's the finest man I've ever met."

Her resolute decision faltered. He deserved someone better than Elizabeth. He deserved to find love with someone who wouldn't jeopardize the career he treasured. Someone without a past. Someone he could proudly introduce to his family.

The train lurched. Elizabeth clutched the seat back for balance.

As if sensing the tension in Elizabeth, Helen covered her hand. "I don't know what happened between the two of you. It's none of my business. But I think you should know something about Jack. He never stopped searching for me. Even when everyone said it was hopeless. For three months he searched. When he found me, it took another three months to negotiate my release. But Jack never stopped trying, even when everyone told him to stop. Even when my uncle told him a child captured by Indians wasn't worth saving, Jack never gave up. There aren't many men who hold honor above their own needs."

That was the whole problem. "He deserves someone just as honorable as he is."

"He deserves someone to love him. That's all any of us wants or needs."

"That's what I'm counting on," Elizabeth's voice sounded unconvincing, even to her own ears.

"Jack told me something once." Helen squeezed her hand. "He told me, it's not the things that happen to us that define who we are, it's what you do about it."

Elizabeth realized one thing for certain. Even if they didn't have a future together, Jack deserved to know how much she loved him.

"Thank you," Elizabeth choked out. "I'll be right back. I have to make things right."

Her vision blurred by tears, she stumbled down the aisle and slid open the pocket door.

Glancing up, she blinked at the sky.

"I forgive you, Mother," she whispered. "You did what you thought was best, even though it must have torn you apart. Just like I feel now. I'm sorry I was so bitter. I needed to be a mother to understand the sacrifices we make for our children."

Clutching the chilly rail for balance, she placed her right foot on the second metal stair.

Jack was a good man.

Her left foot sank into the snow piled near the rails.

Knowing everything about her past, he'd still declared his love. He knew her secrets, the whole unvarnished truth, and he had offered to love and protect her. He'd offered to care for her child as his own. No, he'd begged her to let him care for Rachel.

He loved the infant and he wasn't ashamed to show his affection. The gruff Texas Ranger and her tiny daughter shared a bond forged the moment she was born. He loved Elizabeth. He'd said so, and Jack never lied.

Her right foot sank to her ankle in snow.

She had been scared of loving someone again, scared of picking the wrong man again. Frightened of ending up alone again. Terrified of losing her only love.

Wind whipped at her skirts.

Elizabeth pivoted to face the train. A fresh coat of brilliant red paint glimmered in the sun. Jack was right. She had been selfish with her love. Selfish because she was scared. And she wasn't going to be scared anymore.

Her decision made, she set off for the baggage cart.

An enormous hand clamped over her mouth. Rancid breath puffed against her cheek.

"I've finally found Will's little fancy piece," a gravelly voice spoke in her ear. "You'll show me where the money is, now won't you, love?"

Jack watched as men filed off the stalled train. Like a great metal snake, the cars stretched into the distance with the depot still visible. He knelt before the enormous steer splayed across the tracks. Lifting the animal's ear, he noted a bullet hole. The hairs on the back of his neck stood on end. Something was wrong. Surging to his feet, he strode back through the crowd, jostling his way toward the passenger car, only to find himself blocked by the steady parade of bodies. He shoved them aside.

"Easy there, fellow," one of the men grumbled.

Jack slammed into the railcar, searching frantically for Elizabeth.

She was gone.

He bolted down the aisle.

"Jack," Helen called.

He whirled. "I have to find Rachel and Mrs. Cole."

"Don't worry. Rachel is right here."

Relief weakened his knees. For a moment he'd thought he lost her again. Elizabeth wouldn't leave her daughter behind. "Where is Mrs. Cole?"

Helen adjusted Rachel's eyelet-lace bonnet and grimaced at the baby's rag doll. "She was getting her trunk. I think she changed her mind about leaving."

His heart hammered in his chest. *She was coming back to me.* Once he'd discovered her gone, he'd raced to the station. He'd thought he was too late, until he saw the train chugging to a halt.

"Are you Jack Elder?"

Startled, he spun toward a lanky uniformed rail worker.

"I'm the train detective," the man said. "One of the coal boys thinks he saw that fellow you were looking for. Pencil Pete. Says he saw someone hanging out on the platform earlier this morning."

His worst fears realized, Jack drew his gun. "This train doesn't move until I say so. Not one inch. Understand?"

"Y-yes, sir."

Jack raced down the narrow aisle beneath the curious stares of the remaining passengers. Ripping open the door, he planted his feet on the metal stairs. Two pair of footprints marred the otherwise-pristine snow near the tracks.

He leaped to the ground just right of the footprints, careful to avoid marring the trail. The evidence indicated a small woman, and a much larger man.

Elizabeth had plunged right into Pencil Pete's hands.

Hushed voices sounded ahead of him. Jack flattened his back against the railcar.

"I don't have the m-m-money anymore."

Elizabeth's frightened voice tugged at Jack's heart. He tightened his grip around the gun stock. Charging into the situation with his guns drawn guaranteed certain disaster. No matter the personal cost, he had to remain detached. Sensible.

"The Ranger already found it," she continued. "He moved it all into town."

"I don't think so, missy," Pencil Pete grumbled. "I been following you, and I been following that Ranger. I seen him put the boxes in the wagon. You two were planning on double-crossing old Willy boy all along, weren't you? Did you kill him yourself, or did the Ranger shoot him so he could have Willy's bride...and the money?"

"It's not like that."

Her voice trembled so violently Jack had difficulty discerning the words. He clenched his jaw.

Pencil Pete guffawed. "I mighta believed you 'cept I also saw the sheriff in town. He was drinking over at the saloon. Drinking so much, he even talked about a pretty little widow living over by Hackberry Creek. That old sheriff jawed for hours, but he didn't say nothin' about a Ranger finding a stash of loot. So I asks myself, why didn't the Ranger turn over the money to the sheriff? Then I remembered the way that Ranger looks at you."

Jack pinched the bridge of his nose. He'd avoided telling the sheriff about his findings to prevent gossip. Looked like his plan had backfired.

He crouched. Under the railcar, he watched the scuffle of feet.

Pencil Pete shoved Elizabeth ahead of him. "Go on. I know the money is in the baggage car. I saw you loading something into a big crate."

Pencil Pete dragged Elizabeth toward the back of the train. Jack slid between the cars. He pointed his gun at the sky, his thumb positioned over the hammer. All the money was sitting in the bank vault in town. That outlaw was going to be mighty angry when he discovered a crib.

His mind racing, Jack stalked them to the baggage car. He leaned in, straining to hear their conversation.

"It's in here," Elizabeth said.

Pencil Pete tossed her into the baggage car. "Your husband always wanted the money. He sure did like his fancy things. Once Slim Joe shot that woman, though, Willy didn't want any part of the gang. Got yellow on us, he did."

Jack peered through the door. His back turned, Pencil Pete knelt before the crate containing the crib Jack had built for Rachel.

"I know you wouldn't lie to me, now would you?" The outlaw snickered. "Let's open this up and check."

Unable to wait any longer, Jack surged into the crowded space, his pistol arm outstretched. "Not another move."

"I wouldn't dream of it," Pencil Pete drawled, his left arm rising into the air. "If I moved, my hand might slip.

I wouldn't want to blow this little lady's head off, now would I?"

Jack stilled. The outlaw's right hand remained out of view. Elizabeth gave a subtle nod of her head.

Pencil Pete held a gun on her. He cautiously rose to his feet. "We've got ourselves a real live stand-off here. First thing we gotta do is make sure this box is the right one. You wouldn't double-cross me now, would you pretty lady?"

Elizabeth shook her head. "Of c-course not. I'll sh-show you. Hand me the pry bar and I'll open it up."

Pencil Pete tipped to the side and grabbed the metal bar, keeping it just out of Elizabeth's reach. "You wouldn't be thinking about hitting me with this would you? Because if you get any funny ideas, I'll blow your head off. Then I'll take care of your man."

Elizabeth blanched. "N-no."

She accepted the crowbar with shaking hands. Jack appealed to her with his eyes to defy Pencil Pete's orders, but she ignored his silent urging and knelt before the crate. Time slowed as she pried open the cover and stuck her hand through the narrow opening. Sweat beaded on Jack's forehead. A moment later she removed a large stack of bills.

"See," she said. "It's all in here."

Jack's eyes widened. If he wasn't mistaken, she'd revealed the wad of cash he'd refused to take from her earlier.

Elizabeth leveled her gaze at him. Jack winked at her clever ruse.

"Put it back." Pencil Pete licked his lips. "Now, then—"

A commotion sounded behind Jack.

"I'm the train detective," a man called. "What's going on here—"

His words choked off as Pencil Pete aimed his gun at Elizabeth's head.

"Well, looky here." The outlaw faced them, grinning as if the whole situation was some sort of lark. "We got ourselves a party. Lay your guns on the floor, boys, and kick them toward me."

Jack bit off a muffled curse. The train detective flashed him an apologetic grimace. Together the two men scooted their guns across the narrow space between piles of mail bags.

The outlaw crouched and stuffed the weapons into his pocket. "You're just what I need, detective man. You and that Ranger are going to drag this box off the train. Then you're going to board and be on your way. I'll keep the lady with me. Just in case you get any ideas."

Jack ground his teeth together. "I'll kill you before I let you hurt her."

"Ain't that romantic? Don't you worry. I'll leave her safe and sound in Cimarron." Pencil Pete leered at Elizabeth. "If he's willing to take you without the money, he might even come back for ya."

Jack didn't believe the outlaw for a second. Once he and the detective reboarded the train, Elizabeth was dead.

The outlaw swiped at his nose with his filthy sleeve. "Get moving, boys."

Jack eyed the ashen face of the train detective. "Listen to the man. Let's get this over with."

The outlaw kicked the crowbar to one side. "Wouldn't want the two of you to get any ideas."

Since the stolen money would weigh more than a crib, Jack made a show straining as he lifted the crate. The train detective frowned before reluctantly following suit.

"You're gonna let Bud Shaw hang." Jack feigned a

weighty groan. "Even though he had nothing to do with the robberies."

"I sure am." Pencil Pete cackled gleefully. "That Will Cole was smart. He had a cousin with a record of cattle rustling. Willy used his name and hid some money on the fellow's property. We counted on Bud getting caught all along. If any of us got captured, Will was free to break us out of jail. Then we'd all split the money hidden on his spread and let Bud hang. Not like he could identify any of us, since he wasn't even part of the gang."

Pencil Pete shook his head forlornly. "Except Willy didn't come back like he was supposed to. I had to break out myself. Now I'm the only one left, and all the money belongs to me."

Jack and the detective strained to the door. Pencil Pete pushed Elizabeth ahead of him. She tumbled to her knees. Impotent rage surged through Jack's blood. As the outlaw jerked her upright, she threw him a weak, encouraging smile that did nothing to alleviate his fears.

Jack jumped to the ground, then waited for the detective to join him. Together they yanked the crate over the edge into a snow drift. As he backed away, Jack sized up the situation. The outlaw kept the gun aimed at Elizabeth's head, his arm wrapped around her body. Something glinted at her side. She pointedly glanced down. Jack followed her gaze. She held the crowbar hidden in the folds of her skirts.

Pencil Pete shoved her from the baggage car. She floundered in the snow, struggling to rise to her feet and still keep the weapon hidden. The outlaw lumbered after her, his gun arm never wavering.

Jack kept his gaze locked on Elizabeth. She winked at him.

The outlaw snatched the back of her collar, hauling her

upright. Jack lunged forward. Elizabeth twisted around, the crowbar arcing through the air. The blow glanced off Pencil Pete's arm. The outlaw howled. A wild shot split the air.

"Run," Jack yelled.

Elizabeth struggled to her feet.

Pencil Pete spun, aiming his gun at Jack's advancing form. Elizabeth clutched the outlaw's arm, hindering his aim. Pencil Pete backhanded her. Her limp body crumpled onto the snow.

Jack heaved toward the outlaw. Another shot exploded. Jack slammed the man into the ground. They scuffled, rolling in the snow. Pencil Pete was strong, but he didn't have the added power of Jack's rage. He threw the man onto his back and slammed his knee into the outlaw's chest, winding him. Circling the outlaw's wrist in a fierce grip, Jack pounded Pencil Pete's hand against the crate until the weapon sprang loose.

From the corner of his eye, he watched the detective scurry for the gun. Jack rolled away to give the guard a clear shot. Still dazed from the scuffle with Pencil Pete, he crawled toward Elizabeth's sickeningly still form.

Behind him, the outlaw flailed.

"I ain't going to jail again," Pencil Pete growled.

Another gunshot exploded. A grunt of pain preceded an ominous silence. Jack didn't need to turn around to know the outlaw had just met his maker.

He cradled Elizabeth's still form in his arms and tugged her bonnet strings loose. "Wake up, Elizabeth. Please, God, be all right."

Her eyes fluttered open. "Don't you yell at me. I just saved your life."

"I know you did." Tears of relief filled his eyes. He

laughed and cried and hugged her in arms. "You risked your life to save me, fool woman."

"You saved me first. I guess we're both fools."

Jack gathered snow in his handkerchief and pressed the ball against the blood streaming from Elizabeth's forehead. "You lied to me, Elizabeth Cole. You know I don't abide liars."

She touched his cheek with her bandaged hand. "I love you, Jack Elder. That's the truth. If you're willing to marry an outlaw's widow, I'm willing to be a lawman's bride."

"Then I guess we're getting hitched."

"What about Bud Shaw?"

"We'll go back to Texas together."

"But what about your family?" Her expression dimmed. "I'll always remind them of what happened."

"You were a victim, just like Doreen. You have to give my family the credit for knowing that."

Tears streamed down her face. "If your brothers are anything like you, I won't worry."

"You gotta stop crying, or your face will freeze in this cold."

Elizabeth giggled.

Jack brushed the matted hair from her forehead, relieved to find the bleeding had slowed. "Why'd you put the money in the crib?"

"It's a long story."

"You've got the rest of your life to tell me."

Elizabeth's mouth tipped up at the corner. "You'd marry me still? Even though I hurt you so much?"

His heart pounded in his chest. "I'm awfully pigheaded not to have understood what you were saying. You thought by leaving, you were being noble and doing what was best for me. That's why you didn't pray for us to be together." Warmth flowed through his veins. "I love you. Don't you know you're the best thing for me?"

Blushing color livened her face. "I love you, too."

"I'm not like that fellow in the book, Mr. Darcy. I'm not one for fancy words or flowery speeches. But I can do some of the things he did, I can make things right for you. I can take care of you."

"You already have. I think I loved you from that first night. When you said—" she lowered her voice to a gruff impersonation of him "—Lady, you got a heap o' trouble, but I ain't part of it."

Jack grinned. "I kept wishing you were a big ugly outlaw with a pair of six shooters."

"And I kept wishing you were a tiny little midwife."

His heart thumping in his chest, Jack held her close. "I'm glad we didn't get what we wished for. Now will you marry me?"

"God gave me exactly what I prayed for. Not the way I planned, or the way I thought I wanted, but he gave me what I needed just the same. He gave me Rachel. And you. He gave me a family."

Drawn by the commotion, passengers streamed from the rail cars. The guard tossed his coat over Pencil Pete's body, shielding the gruesome sight from gawkers. Jack lifted Elizabeth into his arms.

Helen's husband rushed to meet them. "Is she all right? What happened? We heard shots. Is everything okay?"

Jack pressed a kiss to Elizabeth's lips. "Couldn't be better."

"Yep," Elizabeth replied, love shimmering in her pale blue eyes. "Couldn't be better."

Epilogue

"You look so beautiful." Jo stepped back and sighed.

Elizabeth stood in the kaleidoscope of light shining through the stained-glass church windows. "I can't believe I missed Christmas."

Jo had even worn a dress for the ceremony, albeit reluctantly. "You missed Christmas by a long shot."

Elizabeth smiled. "I've been busy this winter."

She and Jo had braided her hair and woven the thick ropes into a knot at the nape of her neck. An artfully arranged lace veil with a sprig of evergreen covered the bruise on her forehead.

Elizabeth patted her temple. "It was so nice of Mr. Peters to open up the mercantile."

"He's an a—"

"Jo," Elizabeth shook her finger in a warning. "I know he hasn't always been kind to me. But he made a special trip to the boarding house to let me know he had a dress fit for a wedding. He even found a new sack coat for Jack."

Elizabeth smoothed the satin fabric at her waist. The dress had only needed a few minor alterations. The two-piece ensemble had been ordered a year before, but never claimed. Packed away in the storeroom, the white fabric had aged to a delicate ivory. A fitted jacket nipped in at her waist, and three-quarter-length sleeves ended in a fall of lace. Additional lace edged the beaded, scoopneck collar. Kid-leather boots peeked out from beneath the sweep of her ivory skirts. A modest bustle adorned the back, trailing the barest hint of a waterfall train.

Jo held out something in her hand. "There's no hothouse in Cimarron Springs, so I made you this."

A length of blush-pink ribbon had been wrapped around the base of a posy of pink fabric roses. The fluted ends dangled a foot below the tiny bouquet.

Elizabeth accepted the lovely present. "They're absolutely beautiful."

"Go on with you," Jo ordered. "I'm sure that Ranger is getting impatient."

Ely stepped forward and offered his elbow to escort her down the aisle. He wore his best Sunday suit, a dark wool coat over neatly pressed trousers. Even his beard and mustache had been trimmed for the occasion.

He enveloped her in a rib-crushing bear hug. "We all love you, lass. Are you sure you want to move all the way to Texas?"

Elizabeth glanced up the aisle to where Jack waited before the altar, resplendent in his new charcoal-gray suit. "My family is there. According to Jack, there's going to be a new sheriff in town."

Ely wiped a tear from his eye with a loud sniffle. "You keep in touch, you hear?"

"I will."

They made their way down the aisle past a smattering of well-wishers. The Smiths had offered to hold Rachel during the ceremony. The infant wore her best pink dress and crocheted booties. A white eyelet-lace bonnet framed her cherubic face. Elizabeth paused long enough to run the back of her fingers along the baby's downy cheek.

Jo had scurried back to her seat, taking her place beside her mother. The four McCoy boys sat stiff in their seats, tallest to shortest. The youngest swung his feet and sucked on his thumb.

When they reached the altar, Ely nodded and Elizabeth placed her hand in the crook of Jack's arm. Tall and handsome, his hazel eyes twinkled with joy. His new jacket stretched across his broad shoulders and his dark hair waved back from his forehead. He was the most handsome man she'd ever seen.

Her heart swelled so large, she feared it would burst from her chest in a shower of light. "I love you, Jack Elder."

"I love you more."

She grinned. "You better."

With a roll of his eyes, the minister cleared his throat. "Shall we begin?"

The couple stifled smiles and nodded.

"We are gathered here together—"

Rachel wailed her way into the ceremony. The small gathering turned at the commotion. Sighing resolutely, Elizabeth tugged her arm free.

Jack held up his hand. "I'll handle this."

He strode down the aisle and retrieved the red-faced baby from a fretting Mrs. Smith. Cradled in the safety of Jack's arm, the wailing ceased.

The minister released his pent-up breath.

Jack returned and tucked Elizabeth against his other side. "I've got my daughter. We're ready to begin."

"Oh, Jack." Elizabeth rested her head against his

shoulder. She had everything she'd ever prayed for. Beneath the sure knowledge of God's love, her family had come together.

Their daughter slept through the whole ceremony.

* * * * *

SPECIAL EXCERPT FROM

LOVE INSPIRED
INSPIRATIONAL ROMANCE

*Temporarily in her Amish community to help with her
sick brother's business, nurse Rachel Blank can't wait
to get back to the* Englisch *world...and far away from
Arden Esh. Her brother's headstrong carpentry partner
challenges her at every turn. But when a family crisis
redefines their relationship, will Rachel realize the life
she really wants is right here...with Arden?*

Read on for a sneak preview of
The Amish Nurse's Suitor *by Carrie Lighte,*
available April 2020 from Love Inspired.

The soup scalded Arden's tongue and gave him something to
distract himself from the topsy-turvy way he was feeling. As he
chugged down half a glass of milk, Rachel remarked how tired
Ivan still seemed.

"*Jah*, he practically dozed off midsentence in his room."

"I'll have to wake him soon for his medication. And to check
for a fever. They said to watch for that. A relapse of pneumonia
can be even worse than the initial bout."

"You're going to need endurance, too."

"What?"

"You prayed I'd have endurance. You're going to need it, too,"
Arden explained. "There were a lot of nurses in the hospital, but
here you're on your own."

"Don't you think I'm qualified to take care of him by myself?"

That wasn't what he'd meant at all. Arden was surprised
by the plea for reassurance in Rachel's question. Usually, she
seemed so confident. "I can't think of anyone better qualified to

take care of him. But he's got a long road to recovery ahead, and you're going to need help so you don't wear yourself out."

"I told Hadassah I'd *wilkom* her help, but I don't think I can count on her. Joyce and Albert won't return from Canada for a couple more weeks, according to Ivan."

"In addition to Grace, there are others in the community who will be *hallich* to help."

"I don't know about that. I'm worried they'll stay away because of my presence. Maybe Ivan would have been better off without me here. Maybe my coming here was a mistake."

"*Neh*. It wasn't a mistake." Upon seeing the fragile vulnerability in Rachel's eyes, Arden's heart ballooned with compassion. "Trust me, the community will *kumme* to help."

"In that case, I'd better keep dessert and tea on hand," Rachel said, smiling once again.

"Does that mean we can't have a slice of that pie over there?"

"Of course it doesn't. And since Ivan has no appetite, you and I might as well have large pieces."

Supping with Rachel after a hard day's work, encouraging her and discussing Ivan's care as if he were…not a child, but *like* a child, felt… Well, it felt like how Arden always imagined it would feel if he had a family of his own. Which was probably why, half an hour later as he directed his horse toward home, Arden's stomach was full, but he couldn't shake the aching emptiness he felt inside.

She is going back, so I'd better not get too accustomed to her company, as pleasant as it's turning out to be.

Don't miss
The Amish Nurse's Suitor *by Carrie Lighte,*
available April 2020 wherever
Love Inspired books and ebooks are sold.

LoveInspired.com

**IF YOU ENJOYED THIS BOOK
WE THINK YOU WILL ALSO LOVE**

Believe in love. Overcome obstacles. Find happiness.

Relate to finding comfort and strength in the
support of loved ones and enjoy the journey
no matter what life throws your way.

6 NEW BOOKS AVAILABLE EVERY MONTH!

*Harrison McCord was sure he was the rightful owner
of the Dawson Family Ranch. And delivering Daisy
Dawson's baby on the side of the road was a mere
diversion. Still, when Daisy found out his intentions,
instead of pushing him away, she invited him in, figuring
he'd start to see her in a whole new light. But what if
she started seeing him that way, as well?*

*Read on for a sneak preview of the next
book in Melissa Senate's
Dawson Family Ranch miniseries,*
Wyoming Special Delivery.

Daisy went over to the bassinet and lifted out Tony,
cradling him against her. "Of course. There's lots
more video, but another time. The footage of what the
ranch looked like before Noah started rebuilding to the
day I helped put up the grand reopening banner—it's
amazing."

Harrison wasn't sure he wanted to see any of that. No,
he knew he didn't. This was all too much. "Well, I'll be
in touch about that tour."

*That's it. Keep it nice and impersonal. "Be in touch"
was a sure distance maker.*

She eyed him and lifted her chin. "Oh—I almost
forgot! I have a favor to ask, Harrison."

Gulp. How was he supposed to emotionally distance
himself by doing her a favor?

She smiled that dazzling smile. The one that drew him like nothing else could. "If you're not busy around five o'clock or so, I'd love your help in putting together the rocking cradle my brother Rex ordered for Tony. It arrived yesterday, and I tried to put it together, but it has directions a mile long that I can't make heads or tails of. Don't tell my brother Axel I said this—he's a wizard at GPS, maps and terrain—but give him instructions and he holds the paper upside down."

Ah. This was almost a relief. He'd put together the cradle alone. No chitchat. No old family movies. Just him, a set of instructions and five thousand various pieces of cradle. "I'm actually pretty handy. Sure, I can help you."

"Perfect," she said. "See you at fiveish."

A few minutes later, as he stood on the porch watching her walk back up the path, he had a feeling he was at a serious disadvantage in this deal.

Because the farther away she got, the more he wanted to chase after her and just keep talking. Which sent off serious warning bells. That Harrison might actually more than just like Daisy Dawson already—and it was only day one of the deal.

Don't miss
Wyoming Special Delivery *by Melissa Senate,*
available April 2020 wherever
Harlequin Special Edition books and ebooks are sold.

Harlequin.com

HARLEQUIN

Heartfelt or suspenseful, inspiring or passionate, Harlequin has your happily-ever-after.

With new books published
every month, you are sure to find the
satisfying escape you know you deserve.

HNEWS2020